SEEKERS
OF THE
BOOK

SEEKERS OF THE BOOK

BOOK ONE
OF THE SERIES
THE FIVE-PERCENT

DEALIA PIERATT

TATE PUBLISHING
AND ENTERPRISES, LLC

Published by Tate Publishing & Enterprises, LLC
127 E. Trade Center Terrace | Mustang, Oklahoma 73064 USA
1.888.361.9473 | www.tatepublishing.com

Tate Publishing is committed to excellence in the publishing industry. The company reflects the philosophy established by the founders, based on Psalm 68:11,
"The Lord gave the word and great was the company of those who published it."

Book design copyright © 2016 by Tate Publishing, LLC. All rights reserved.
Cover design by Chloe Ross of Salmon Idaho
Interior design by Gram Telen

Published in the United States of America

ISBN: 978-1-68333-088-2
Fiction / Religious
16.08.13

To Mary Pieratt, Derynda Davis, and Joy Turner.

These ladies are my number one support group. They have read and reread my books and keep asking for more!

Contents

1

The Hospital Room

She struggled to clear the murky gray/black gloom from her mind. In this mental dimness, it seemed that she was lying in a great cavern with mist swirling around her. Dark gloomy walls surrounded her. She opened her mouth to scream, but no sound escaped her dry cracked lips

She sought to pull together one coherent thought, so far only jumbles of words swirled around within the creepy clouds she lay in. Words like *help, scream, cold, terror,* and *pain* bounced back and forth inside the cavern walls, reminding her of the screen saver on a massive computer. The images were bizarre and disturbing. She shivered both from the cold and from fear.

When the cold became unbearable, and her animalistic instinct kicked in, she tried to pull her knees into a fetal position but was unable to move. She was stuck, spread eagle, to a hard surface. Abandoning this attempt, she went back to watching the giant screensaver until the blackness overtook the grayness. Soon there were no words, no swirling clouds, and no fear.

Passage of time meant nothing to her. It could have been mere seconds or days between complete blackness and the murky grayness. Periodically, a searing light flashed into her eyes, bringing her back to the cavern. At times the light seemed to become a great searchlight, with threats and screams interspersed with the random bouncing words.

The first conscious thought that her befuddled brain pulled together was, *What is causing this stabbing, pounding, pain in my head?* The throbbing was stalling her thought processes, almost to the point of wanting to return to complete blackness. Resisting the blackness, she tried to open her eyes; however, she could not find the strength. Resigned to the fact that she was too weak to even open her eyes, she lay listening to the sounds around her. Many assorted hums and beeps. All familiar yet unknown sounds. She knew she should know those sounds but was unable to match the right words to each one.

She tried to remember what had happened to her, but her mind was completely empty. She told herself to start from the beginning; however, she soon realized her only beginning was vague eerie dreams of strange clouds and disturbing words.

My name, she thought, *I must know my own name! Shouldn't I at least know my own name?* Panic began to flutter up inside her chest, making it hard for her to breathe. *Think, think,* she admonished herself, still nothing came. Her only clear memories, as of this moment, were the feel of smooth crisp sheets against her skin and those continuous annoying sounds—the ones she still could not identify but were so hauntingly familiar.

As she lay motionless, she began to distinguish other sounds outside the room. The low hum of far off voices, a telephone ringing then abruptly silenced, and a whoosh of an elevator door as it closed. All the noises were more than her pounding head could take. She fell back into the comforting embrace of unconsciousness.

The next time she awoke she could hear the alarm of a cardiac monitor. She could also hear an IV pump beeping, a steady beep, that told herself and anyone else with ears this noisy pump was finished infusing.

"The bag is empty! Would someone please turn off the alarm?" she wanted to scream; however, it was a futile wish. At least now she knew what the sounds were. She was hooked up to an IV pump and a cardiac monitor. *I must be in a hospital, but why?*

As she lay listening and thinking, she heard a comforting female voice softly saying, "No, Dr. Eddie, the Jane Doe in room 101 has not regained consciousness since she was transferred to the ICU." The soft voice continued. "I've never known you to leave the ER to come see a patient. What gives?"

She heard quiet footsteps coming close, felt a warm hand gently touch her wrist, and a pleasant male voice say, "Well, Molly, this woman and I bonded. For just one second down in the ER, we bonded. I suppose I just can't get her out of my mind."

There was another pause while someone straightened her covers and readjusted the pillow. Then she heard the nurse ask, "Well, what happened?"

The room was again silent, until she heard the man's voice. He spoke as if he were reliving the moment.

"We had her in the trauma room. The nurses were working frantically to stabilize her. She was as pale as a ghost, white as the sheets on that stretcher. I was sure we were going to lose her. The amount of blood she had lost was nearing the point of no return. As I continued to monitor her face, her eyes opened. I saw raw panic building. She rolled her eyes around the room, ending up looking straight into mine. Even though she spoke not a word, her eyes said, 'Help me, please, help me.' Slowly her eyes closed, and as far as I know, she has been unconscious ever since."

She wanted to open her eyes. To look again into the face of the man who had helped saved her life. However, the pain in her head had been steadily increasing. The hazy feeling was creeping over her. She was too exhausted to fight back. She let the darkness take her.

The next time she awoke the room was dim, everything was quiet in the hall. This time her head hurt less. She felt she even had the strength to open her eyes. Nevertheless, she hesitated. Something cautioned her to lie still and keep her eyes closed. Then she heard a swishing sound. The unusual sound heightened her caution to lie still. As the sound drew nearer, a faint musty smell came with it. The scent gripped her heart with sudden terror. With the fear came a flash of memory. She was in a cold dim room; someone struck her across the cheek bone. She could not see who had hit her; however, that same scent was now permeating her hospital room. The memory faded, the scent and the fear remained. The fear propelled her instincts into overdrive, keeping her very still.

She heard a heavily accented female voice ask, "*Infermiere* (nurse), has she awakened yet? Has she said anything?"

She could hear other footsteps come into the room. In a hushed voice, the voice she recognized as Molly say, "You can't be in here. Please come out, we'll talk at the nurse's station."

The accented voice resumed, "I need to talk to her, now! I have a signed document by Derwood Feildsrum, the director of the Office of Homeland Security. This document gives me permission to interrogate this woman." As the accented voice continued, it increased in intensity and turned hard as steel. "I demand the right, and the privacy, to ask this woman some very important questions. It is of the utmost importance—a matter of national security!"

Molly insistently replied, "I don't care if President Margaret Rivers herself signed your important papers. This is my patient, and I won't have her disturbed until she is completely stable!"

There were sounds of someone being pulled or pushed from the room. The voices grew fainter until again there was silence.

She wondered why the smell of the woman and her voice brought on such a terrible sense of fear. All the thinking, listening, and panic had caused her head to nearly burst from pain. She could feel the hazy feeling returning. This time it was as welcome as a friend. Sleep was what she needed. She could worry about everything else later.

It was daylight the next time she became conscious. She could feel a bright light directly on her face, too bright to comfortably open her eyes. The sounds out in the hall were louder. More people were talking and phones were ringing. She could hear clinking sounds as if meal trays were being passed around. She was slipping back to sleep when she heard that accented voice talking loudly in the hall.

A second voice, one she did not recognize, sounded confident when she said, "No, ma'am, this patient is still unconscious. However, I will be glad to call you the minute she starts to rouse. It's no trouble at all."

This was not Molly. This nurse sounded ready to jump, and ask how high, if and when this accented-voiced sister commanded— she dubbed the accented woman "The Sister"; she figured it was as good a name as any.

"Well, you're much more helpful than the other nurse," the Sister said in a haughty voice. "I will report her to her superior."

She could tell the Sister was coming closer to the bed. She could actually feel the woman's penetrating eyes staring at her. The room was filling with that awful smell again, and with it a feeling of hatred emanated from the woman.

She felt her head becoming fuzzy again; the pain was getting much worse. She fought the sleepiness. She was terrified of being left alone in the room, completely helpless, with the Sister. Thankfully the intruders said no more. She soon heard their footsteps leave the room. With the fear receding, she allowed the deep, painless sleep claim her once again.

She slept long peaceful hours of healing rest and was brought to sudden consciousness by someone talking in a clear loud voice. The words rang in her ears like the toll of the death bell.

"Yes, ma'am, you may come and try to interrogate her now!" The voice of the second nurse chirped into the phone brightly.

She cautiously opened her eyes; they felt like sandpaper had been rubbing them for days. She opened them just wide enough to peer through her lashes. She found she was looking through the observation window into the nurse's station. A woman in a putrid, pale yellow scrub suit was standing at the desk talking on the phone. The nurse was talking loud enough to wake the dead.

"Yes, ma'am, you can come over and try and talk to her. The patient has been moving her extremities some. All her vital signs have been stable for hours now, ever since she got that last unit of blood. These are signs that she might be starting to come around soon…. Okay, that will be fine. See you in thirty minutes."

Alarm and fear crept into her groggy mind. The Sister was coming. This time Molly would not be there to stop her. Her thoughts raced, *I must get out of here—now!*

By the conversations she had overheard, she believed the Sister most likely had the power to interrogate her until she extracted whatever information she wanted and, by whatever means she saw fit to use.

Through her lashes, she scanned the room. Next to the bedside table was a shelf with boxes of rubber gloves, masks, caps, and shoe covers. Quickly she felt down her left arm until she found the tape holding the IV needle. She pulled it out, careful not to bend the small plastic tube in her vein. Somehow she knew she should not stop the flow of fluid or the IV pump would start to beep. Vaguely she wondered how she knew this bit of information but quickly brushed away the thought. It was now time to move. She did not want to be there when the Sister came back. Fear was her strong driving force.

She waited until the nurse left the desk then slid sideways off the bed. Squatting, she took a deep breath, slowly letting it out. Reaching up, she pushed the pillow under the sheets, attempting the appearance of someone still resting there. Just before she moved away from the bed, she reached up to turn off the cardiac monitor at the same time she ripped off the patches sticking to her chest. Wincing with sudden pain from the tape and with tears stinging her eyes, she swiftly grabbed supplies off the shelf and moved quietly to the door.

She crawled to the elevator and pushed the down button. Moving back next to the half wall of the nurse's desk, she waited until the elevator door opened. Peering around the wall, she spotted a white lab coat on a chair next to her; grabbing it, she scurried into the elevator. Without pausing to take a breath, she reached up and pushed the button to take her to the ground floor.

As quickly as the door closed, she pulled on the lab coat, yanked the shoe covers over her bare feet, and stuffed the cap on her head, over a mass of ratty hair. She put the mask over her face, and reached into the coat pocket pulling out a stethoscope. She was putting it around her neck as the elevator reached the next floor. The door opened letting three people in.

She stepped back keeping her head down carefully inspecting her fingernails, as if that was her only care in the world. All the while her heart was pumping as fast as though she had just finished running the Boston Marathon.

After a moment, she looked up and was relieved to see that no one had noticed her. All three were looking down. One man was skimming pages on his smart phone while the other two appeared to be checking messages.

Each time the elevator stopped, she held her breath, hoping she would not see the Sister. Ten times the doors opened and closed, and each time she let out a sigh of relief.

She was all alone by the time the elevator reached the ground floor. As the door opened, she cautiously peered out. Seeing no one, she thanked her lucky stars. Luck or something like it was with her so far.

She let her eyes sweep the garage. She saw a large opening for cars straight ahead and a smaller door for pedestrians to the right. She moved as quickly and as quietly as possible to the front of the building. Stopping to catch her breath, she slowly peeked around the door. What she saw started her heart pumping faster and her head pounding again. Standing just ten feet away was a nun in a long black habit. The woman's back was to her. She could see a cigarette in one hand and a cell phone in the other. As she listened, she could clearly hear that accented voice talking loudly.

"I want her *ho trovato*, how do you say in English, found. I want her found now!"

No wonder she had the impression the Sister would be a good name; the woman was really a nun!

Turning, she ran, ducking behind the first car she came to. Her heart was pounding so hard she was sure the whole world could hear it. Not to mention the Sister walking by just three feet away. From behind the car, she had a clear view of the woman. The Sister's entire bearing was one of tension and controlled anger. She watched as the nun threw down her cigarette butt, stomped it with her foot, and stepped into the elevator.

Hidden behind the car, she continued to hold her breath until the elevator door shut. Immediately she was on her feet running toward the small door. As she rounded the open door, she saw she was headed into an alley. To the right, a street with cars and pedestrians going by, and to her left was the hospital ambulance entrance. She decided her only hope was to get lost in that crowd and fast. She started to walk quickly; however, she instinctively knew not to run.

She came to the end of the alley. Turning left, she slipped into a group of tourists—cameras and all. She kept pace with the people and kept her head down.

She was looking into shop windows as she passed them, and soon a sign caught her attrition, Third Avenue Thrift Shoppe. After reading the sign, she told herself to keep walking, knowing she needed to get as far away from the hospital as she could. Suddenly, she felt a very strong urge to go inside the thrift shop. Trying to resist the urge, she stumbled and went sailing through the door, as if a large hand had pushed her. As she was passing the doorframe, from the corner of her eye, she saw a long black car turn onto the street from the alley beside the hospital.

She quickly ducked behind a tall rack of hats and scarves and watched as the black limousine passed by. She could not see who was inside the car, but she knew it was the Sister. She could just feel it. The car turned right at the next block.

What to do, she strategized. To leave the store would put her back on the street exposed to everyone. However, to stay in the shop might trap her, with no way out.

As she stood rooted to the spot, she realized the mask was still hanging around her neck, her hands were balled up into fists in the pockets of the lab coat, and one fist was clutching something. She pulled it out and found a twenty dollar bill. "Wow, just like magic!" she whispered.

Looking around, she saw a scarf on the table next to her and shivered. She could almost feel the icy wind still blowing down the back of her open hospital gown—with only the thin lab coat for protection. Taking the scarf and money to the cash register, she asked, "How late do you stay open? Would it be okay to browse through your books until you close?"

The cashier smiled at her and said, "Sure, honey, we close in about an hour. However, someone will be in the store for a while after closing time. Feel free to look all you want."

A thought came to her: this shop could be a good resting place until closing time; when the darker streets would hide her better.

The books were near the back. Behind the book rack was a stack of folded blankets in a big wooden crate. They looked so inviting. If only I could spend the next hour resting my pounding head, I would be able to think better. With only a moment's hesitation, she climbed into the crate. Laying her head down, she pulled up the top blanket, covering herself completely. Closing her eyes, she sighed deeply.

After a moment, she could hear the cashier ringing up another customer. Then she heard the woman call back to someone. "Hey, Lacy, you need to come run the register. I've got to beat it, or I'll miss my bus."

She heard someone walk past her. After that, everything was quiet. With the pain in her head slowly deceasing and feeling weary to the bone, she was asleep in seconds.

Just before closing time, as Lacy was counting the day's deposit, the door opened, and a tall nun walked in.

Arrogantly, the nun walked up to the checkout counter and asked, "Have you seen a woman wearing a white lab coat come into the store?"

"No, I've not seen anyone like that today. Nurses do come into the store, but not today. You're welcome to look around if you like. We close in fifteen minutes."

"That won't be necessary," came the curt, heavily accented voice.

"Come back tomorrow," Lacy called out nervously. "We're having a sale on winter jackets."

The door shut with a thud; the nun was gone.

2

The Thrift Shoppe

She awoke with a vague disquieted feeling that she had been dreaming about something important. It hovered near her conscious thoughts, challenging her to remember.

As her mind cleared, she lay very still. With what was becoming her custom, she kept her eyes closed listening. She could hear none of the hospital sounds. In fact, there were no sounds at all. She carefully opened her eyes. Everything was very, very dark. *Have I gone blind from my injuries? Is that why I'm having these headaches?* Panic arose in her chest, squeezing off her breath. Through sheer willpower, she fought the panic and took a deep breath. Moving her head a little to the right, she felt something scratchy on her cheek. She put her hand up to investigate and felt the wool blanket she had earlier pulled over her head. Memories slowly began to seep into her still-groggy mind.

"I wonder how long I've been asleep," she whispered to the darkness. Cautiously she removed the blanket; raising her head, she looked around. There was a sliver of light to her right. Straight ahead she saw a faint yellowish glow shining through large windows.

She slowly sat up to take a better look. As her eyes adjusted, she could see rows and rows of clothes hanging on racks. Now she remembered the thrift shop. *I could sure use a flashlight,* she thought. As she threw her legs over the crate, she heard something hit the floor. It rolled to a stop with a tiny clinking sound. Once both feet were firmly planted on the floor, she bent down to pick up the object. Thinking it felt like a pen, she clicked it and a small light came on. *A penlight! How very nice. This is truly a magic lab coat.*

After wrapping the top wool blanket around her shoulders, she followed the row she was standing in toward the thin strip of light. Soon the outline of a door materialized. She stopped to listen for any sounds on the other side but could hear nothing. Only after she pressed her ear to the hard cold surface of the door could she hear a quiet drip, drip, drip. The sound made her think of the last time she had, had a drink of water. She was sure she had not drunk anything in the hospital. Her mouth felt uncomfortably dry. Her tongue stuck to the roof of her mouth as if it were glued.

Opening the door, she stepped through, closing it quickly. The room she stepped into was a large storage room with boxes stacked all along the back wall and a door that had a bright yellow exit sign over it. Walking over to the back door, she checked it for a possible escape route in the morning.

She then followed the sound of the drip and found a bathroom. "Water!" she exclaimed. She drank as much as she could hold then used the restroom. She washed her hands, face, arms, and feet; these simple actions refreshed her. She turned toward the mirror and noted she had to duck to see the top of her head. She saw long, auburn hair, dull and ratty from her stay in the hospital. Her thin, pale face caused the startled green eyes to stand out— golden flecks on a field of jade. These words resounded in her mind. *Someone had said that to me before.* The hair, the face, nor the eyes gave her any hint as to who she was.

A clock in the bathroom showed 2345 (quarter to twelve). She calculated she would have seven to eight hours until the store would open.

Stepping back into the storage room, she saw a notebook and pen on a table and sat down. She began to write down everything she would need for a plan of escape. Her tentative plan was to walk out of the city, staying undetected until she could figure out what had happened to her, and why the Sister was so insistent on questioning her.

First thing would be to find clothing that would disguise her identity. She considered for a moment that it would be stealing to take things from the store. However, if she kept a list of everything she took and how much everything cost, she would send money back. She rationalized that it was a life-and-death situation; normal rules did not always apply.

Taking her penlight, she slipped back into the main store looking for clothes. The store was very well organized organized; browsing would have been fun if the situation had been different.

She found the essentials, underwear, jeans, and a shirt, putting the things on as she found them. She also took an extra pair of jeans, two each of underthings and socks, a thinner shirt, and a warmer shirt.

Getting dressed made her feel more like a real person, even if she still could not remember her own name. Every time she tried to remember any of her past, her head started to hurt again. For now, she decided, she would put it all out of her mind until she was in a safe place to rest and think.

Her arms were full, and she soon realized she needed a backpack to carry her borrowed things in. She discarded many purses and bags of different descriptions. Finally she found just what she wanted: a large, very soft, well-worn leather bag with straps like a backpack hidden behind a duffel bag. Picking it up, she took everything back to the storeroom. She packed the bag with the extra things she needed.

It was not long until she felt the weariness overtaking her. Sitting down at the table, she rested as she continued to plan what she needed to do to escape from the city. Most importantly, she needed a way to disguise her build, as well as her looks. *But how would I disguise my height?* she wondered. "My height has been the bane of my existence," she spoke aloud to the mirror across from the table. "Another memory!"

Going back out into the main store, she walked up and down the aisles looking for ideas for a disguise, ducking down behind the rows periodically when she saw car lights on the city street. Once, while using her penlight, she saw a shadow pass by the store's front door. She quickly extinguished the light and held her breath until the person walked out of sight. *No more penlight*, she warned herself.

She stopped in front of some really large dresses. As she looked at one in particular, she saw herself as an old lady. She was hunched over with a cane. She wore an old sweater, maybe a hat or wig, to cover her long red hair, some glasses, and old-lady shoes and socks. With this idea in mind, she gathered everything together and went back to the storage room.

Soon she was back in the store looking for another disguise. She thought maybe she could dress as an old man. She found a pair of bibbed overalls and a large, white, button-up shirt; the kind that a country farmer might wear to church. She added an old felt hat, a red bandanna, and a pair of lace-up hiking boots that would pass as a man's footwear. Once again she carried it all back to the storage room.

In the bathroom she found a hair brush and brushed out the tangles caused by hours of lying in bed. Without even thinking about it, her hands braided her hair into a French braid down the center. She fastened the bottom of the braid with a rubber band.

"That should help hide my hair," she whispered to her reflection in the mirror. "Anyone looking for me will be looking for a tall woman with long red hair."

She fastened the leather bag on over her front, instead of her back, to make herself fatter and to keep it hidden. Over it went the big dress. Next she pulled on the gray wig and the plastic rain hat—the kind old ladies are fond of wearing, rain or shine. She finished by putting on a pair of large glasses that made her eyes look like saucers. Picking up her cane and hunching her shoulders, she walked over to the long mirror and took a look.

"Wow! I look about ninety-five years old and very believable," she spoke aloud to her reflection. The backpack helped her look like a plump, cushiony figure. With all her other clothes on and a heavy coat, even her arms would look overweight. The one thing she could think of that would help her look the part was some gloves because her hands did not look ninety-five years old.

Next she tried on the old man disguise with the felt hat. She tied the red bandanna around her neck. Turning around, she looked in the mirror. "This getup looks really good too." She wondered which would be the best outfit for the next day to escape the city. She did not think the Sister would expect her to disguise herself so quickly. Both disguises were good. She would decide in the morning.

At the table she started to write down everything that had happened, and anything that felt like a memory. Maybe writing will help me put it all together and figure out what to do next. She wrote down all her feelings and fears, and everything she remembered about the Sister—especially that musty smell and the accented voice. After writing everything down, she felt more rested and ready to finish preparing for the morning.

As she was putting everything away, she thought how strange it was that she had found just what she needed to hide herself, along with clothes to keep warm and a bag to pack everything in. It was as if someone was pointing everything out to her, to help her leave the city and be safe.

"In the hollow of his hand," she whispered out loud. "Where have I heard that before?" Somewhere in the back of her mind came a wisp of an idea, a heavenly being perhaps. She wondered what she had believed in before she lost her memory—anything, nothing. She guessed it did not really matter. Nevertheless, at the moment, it sure seemed as if someone was on her side.

She continued to speak out loud, working her vocal cords. "All of this is something to ponder when I have the time, when I feel safe and hidden from these dangerous people. It is getting late. I had best see what time it is. I need to be out of sight when the streets start filling up with people on their way to work—or even worse, with the people who are trying to find me."

The bathroom clock showed 0400 (4:00 a.m.). She would have just enough time to take one more look around before climbing back into the crate.

Out in the store she found a cloth tote to put her old man outfit in, and a large purse for her old lady outfit. In the purse she placed her dress and other things she needed to become a short, plump, stooped old lady. She also found a man's wallet, some makeup, a comb, and other things. She put everything away so she could easily change if need be. She tied the cloth tote and purse onto the backpack.

In the bathroom trash can, she found two empty glass juice bottles. After washing them, she filled them with water. She packed one of them in her purse and one in the outside pocket of the backpack. Again she drank her fill of water before using the restroom. Looking to make sure that everything was left just the way she had found it, she closed the bathroom door for the last time.

She checked the storeroom drawers and cabinets for anything she could eat. In one of the drawers, she found two candy bars and a package of peanut butter crackers. She took one of the candy bars and the package of crackers, hoping no one would notice they were missing.

Back at the table, she went over the things she had found and repacked everything. She put the wool blanket on the very top so it would be easy to get to when she needed it. She put on all the clothes she would wear under the disguise, even the heavy jacket.

After pondering both disguises, she decided on the old lady. *After all, how often did anyone see an old farmer in a thrift store in the city?* So she unpacked the dress and things from the big purse, and put on her old lady disguise. She then checked in the mirror to see if her disguise looked just right.

"Yep, ninety-five years old and not a day younger," she smiled to herself as she slipped on the soft white gloves she had found.

She could think of only one other thing that was missing as she stood in front of the long mirror, leaning on her cane. She needed three names. She decided on Lucy Pope as her old lady persona and Jeb Bodiene for the old man, but what about herself? She could think of no name to fit the redheaded woman. "Later," she said, "a name will come to me, later."

It took her a bit to climb back into the crate with all her extra clothes on. Lying down on the blankets again felt wonderful. All the searching and thinking had tired her. Her head was beginning to pound like it did back in the hospital, just before she passed out. She closed her eyes planning to only rest and then to slip out the back door as soon as the store opened.

She was suddenly awakened by someone speaking rather loudly. "Ma'am, is all the red-dot items on sale for fifty percent off today?"

She opened her eyes and waited a few moments before peering out from under the blanket. The room was full of light. *I have slept far too long!* She looked around. Seeing no one, she slowly climbed out of the crate of blankets. She peeked up the back row. The woman who had been talking must have moved on because the row was empty now. She pulled her cane out of the crate, hunching over, she started toward the back door. With all the extra weight, she had to move slowly. She reminded herself this is how an old lady walks.

As she stepped up to the storage room door, she stopped short. Standing near the back door was a tall young man and a slight young woman. Near them sat an older man looking at a book and swinging his feet in childlike abandon. The two younger people were emptying the boxes she had seen the night before. She immediately turned around and headed toward the front door.

As she slowly walked up the middle aisle, she had to control an urge to hurry. Hurrying was not even possible. The weight of the clothes and backpack kept her at a slow steady pace.

Just as she was passing the checkout counter, a voice from behind her said, "Have a nice day, ma'am." She recognized the voice of the cashier who had checked her out the day before. Her heart began to accelerate again. Will she recognize me, she wondered? Slowly, she turned, and looking up, she peered out of her thick glasses. In her best Lucy Pope voice, she said, "Why, thank you my dear. You have a nice day too."

The cashier turned back to the customer she was ringing up without another word. Miss Lucy Pope, leaning heavily on her cane, continued on her slow journey to the front door.

Once outside the store, she turned left, away from the hospital. Down the street she went with a slow stooped walk. Every few minutes she stopped to look into a store window, just as if she was out for a nice day of window shopping.

She soon realized she could see a lot of the street behind her by using the windows as mirrors. She had just stopped again and was leaning on her cane when she saw a large black car with tinted windows coming from the area of the hospital. As the car passed her, she spotted the Sister looking straight at her.

Trying to keep calm, she turned and moved slowly down the street, telling herself she was doing fine. As she walked on, she could still see the Sister's face looking right past her as if she was not even visible. At a snail's pace, the black car passed out of sight.

"Wow!" she exclaimed under her breath, "the Sister did not appeared to see me at all. Am I invisible, or have I created a really good disguise?" She was proud of herself for keeping calm; however, it was time to make tracks and really disappear.

At noon she slipped into the bathroom of a gas station and changed into Mr. Jeb Bodiene. While hidden from watchful eyes, she ate a bite of her candy bar and again drank as much water as she could.

"It seems like I cannot get enough water," she said to the empty restroom. She replenished the water she had drunk from the juice bottles and was ready to continue her escape from the city.

By sundown she was on the western outskirts of the city. Dark clouds were moving across the sky interspersed with lightning strikes. She needed to find a place to get out of the cold and rain. Scanning the area, the only thing she could see was the overhang of an interstate highway bridge. Hopefully there was enough room to crawl up into the space between the road and the dirt. Before climbing, she stripped off her disguise and removed the backpack still attached to her front. She worked as quickly as possible before any traffic came along. She rolled up the disguise, stuffing it into the cloth bag. Swiftly she climbed up under the bridge. At the top was just enough room to crawl under the overpass and curl up. She used her backpack for a pillow. Then she covered up with the wool blanket and let out a long pent-up sigh. Feeling safe and warm as a rabbit in a den, she was asleep before she could even think of how tired she was.

3

Under the Overpass

It was the sound of something rattling over her head that woke her. She lay quietly listening. In addition to the occasional sounds overhead, she also heard the rustling of leaves blowing in the breeze to her left. She opened her eyes just enough to peek through her lashes. Seeing no one, she opened them wide. Without moving a muscle, she scanned the complete circumference of her vision. To her far right she saw the road she had traveled down the night before.

Yesterday she had learned the city she had fled from was Baltimore, Maryland, and the hospital she had escaped from was St. Peter's. She had written all this in her notebook. Someday she would reread everything and maybe remember her life before the hospital.

She continued to scan the area across from where she lay checking the other side of the interstate overpass. Further to the left were woods running along the road. The area was clear of any living thing as far as she could see. Slowly she sat up. She stayed very still for a few minutes waiting for her head to stop spinning. She was still feeling a bit dizzy each time she sat up; however, the dizziness was decreasing. Her head was not pounding or aching, which she thought must be a good sign.

Her mind slipped back to the idea that someone had watched over her all yesterday and throughout her escape the day before. If she were a praying person, she would say thank you. After giving it some thought, praying did not seem to come naturally to her.

Still, what harm could it be in saying thank you? She started with, "To Whom It May Concern." Laughing at herself, she thought, "I sound like I'm writing a business letter. Oh well, so what?"

"To Whom It May Concern," she whispered to the clear morning air. "Thank you from the bottom of my lonely lost heart. I don't know who you might be. Nevertheless, I do feel your presence. Will you keep doing the same for me today as you did yesterday? Yours truly, Nameless in Baltimore."

She folded her wool blanket placing it inside her bag. Grabbing the handles of her backpack, she was just about ready to stand up when she felt something restraining her. Something said, "Be still." Taking heed of this feeling, she sat frozen to the ground trying to become invisible. Within seconds she heard tires slowly turning on the pavement overhead. As the car passed by, she slowly turned her head to look over the guardrail. What she saw made her silently say thank you to her unknown protector. Her eyes were riveted to the back of a large black limo as it moved slowly away from her. She was sure it was the same limo she had seen on the street outside of the thrift shop. She was not sure where this convection came from, but she was sure it was one and the same. She stayed totally immobilized until the car came to a stop and turn on the median to come back.

"Go now, go to those woods!" The words seemed to be as real and loud as any she had ever heard. She did not need to be told twice. She slid down the rocky embankment of the overpass, ran toward the woods, and ducked down behind heavy bushes. She lay on her side, her knees tucked up toward her chin, her backpack in front, with her face to the road. She tried to slow her breathing. She felt sure she was completely hidden, but her breathing sounded to her own ears like the roar of the ocean.

She told herself to take slow, deep breaths, in through your nose and out through your mouth. This became her mantra. Her breathing slowed, and she felt calmer; just in the nick of time. The black car was now stopping right over where she had been sleeping.

She realized if there had not been someone watching over her, telling her what to do, she would have been down on the road where anyone going by would have seen her. *Who are you? Why are you helping me?* she pondered. *Maybe it's only my own sense of danger. Whatever it is, something, just saved my life!*

She watched the limo as the front driver's side door opened. A man dressed in black with a clerical collar got out of the car. As the man got out, the back window rolled down.

A now-familiar voice said, "Look under the overpass on both sides. I know it is a long shot, but we have to cover every angle before I call my superiors. Thank you, Father Frances. You have been such a great help."

The Sister's accent was the same, but her voice was dripping with honey instead of acid like in the hospital.

She watched as Father Frances looked all around the guardrail, where she had been sitting only a few minutes ago. Just as the priest was walking across to the other side of the interstate, a cell phone rang inside the car. With the window open, the sounds carried to where she was hiding.

"Hello." The Sister's voice changed again. This time the nun did not sound very much like a Catholic sister at all, instead more like a woman talking to her boyfriend. "Yes, my charisma (dearest), I can talk freely. Father Frances is out looking under the overpasses for any signs of her. He thinks we are searching for a poor, lost, sick woman. I do not think he would approve of our plan if we told him the truth," she chuckled. "He thinks she might have slept under the overpass last night, so I told him to go ahead and look. But I think she is still hiding somewhere around the hospital."

There was a pause in the conversation, "I've missed you too. No, I'll be in Baltimore for a few more days. Not a sign of her yet." A pause, then the Sister's voice escalates into almost a scream, "Yes! I know how important it is for us to find her. Don't you think I know that? I know, I know, I am calm. I'm not losing it, just tired."

There was a longer pause, and when the nun spoke again, it was the business voice from the hospital. "Thank you. I'm sure we'll find her. We're all very worried about her here too. Sorry for the interruption. I thought Father Frances was near enough to hear me. So how is the plan going? That well! I am glad to hear it. I have been out of the loop so to speak. I have been wondering what was going on in the technical department of our plan.... So we will start in five days. Right on target! What are Einstein's estimates after the last test group went through the treatment? Ninety-five percent, wow, that is excellent! What about the other five percent? Have you found out what is keeping the treatment from working on them?"

Again there was a pause in the conversation as the Sister listened to the answer. Then the Sister sounded incredulous, "Reading? You have got to be kidding. Shakespeare, the classics, and the Bible? You mean the Bible is the best, really! I will have to remember that." The Sister snickered a sound more evil than humorous. "I stopped reading that old book years ago when I lost all my young naive faith in the church. Still, I guess if a person keeps their mind stronger, through whatever means, reading would help to prevent the treatment from getting a hold on them. For the most part though, the plan is going to work better than we thought. We will think of some other way of dealing with the five percent when the time comes."

After a still longer pause, the Sister continued. "Yes, I know, I know. If we do not find her, it could all come crumbling down around our ears, and we could be in big international trouble. But it is not going to fail. I just know it. I feel very strongly about our plan. Besides, I see no way for a woman in a hospital gown to get very far. Her doctor said she has a concussion that could cause blackout, headaches, and slow thinking. A person that sick could not think up a plan good enough to evade our team."

Again there was a pause, and then the Sister said, "I did talk to the Ghost, but he said it would be impossible to put out an APB (all-points bulletin) on a person legally considered dead. Still, he will notify his top men, men who know the plan and are in with us. He will tell them to keep a watch out for a woman of her description. What? You remember, her family and everyone else think she is dead. They held a funeral for her a few weeks ago. The same week as the funeral for that reporter we found with her. Yes, that is the same reporter who was working with her when she was snooping around looking to find our real identities."

The words stopped her from listening for a moment. *A family, I have a family! But they think I'm dead. How sad for them!* She wondered where her family lived. *International trouble—what could that mean? Were they talking about a company or something bigger? Why would someone with the power to put out an APB be involved? Who are the five percent who couldn't be affected by the treatment? More importantly, who are the ninety-five percent who could be controlled by the plan? And controlled to do what?* All these thoughts were rolling around her mind.

She could not let these thoughts overwhelm her. She must listen and try to hear everything. She needed to know what was going on and what these people were up to. However, at this moment, the Sister was not saying anything.

Suddenly the Sister said, "Oh, Father Frances is coming back. I will call you as soon as I hear anything, good-bye."

Father Frances walked up to the window and asked the Sister if she wanted him to look anywhere else.

"No, we will drive up to the next exit then turn around and go back to the city. I do not see how a sick woman could get this far. However, keep your eyes on both sides of the road just in case."

The father got back behind the wheel. The window rolled up, and the big black limo moved on down the interstate, out of sight.

She lay hidden until the coast was clear. Only then did she move. Crawling farther back into the woods, she stood up and stretched her arms and legs. She was very stiff from being so still for so long.

If they were going to keep looking for me along roads, I need to stay as far away from the roads as I can.

She decided to follow the sun toward the west as long as she could stay hidden. Following the sun would keep her going away from Baltimore and her known enemy. Of course unknown enemies would be harder to avoid.

After walking for what seemed like hours, she was deep into the woods and tiring badly. She decided to stop, rest, and write down everything she had heard earlier. If only she could remember who she was, and what this was about, maybe she could do something to stop it from happening.

It took her a while to finish writing everything down. She drank half of one of her water bottles and ate a bite of the candy bar. She wanted to eat more but did not know when she would find more food; she needed to conserve her supplies. Rested and somewhat nourished, she was ready to move on; always heading west following the afternoon sun.

After some time she began to feel greatly fatigued, as if she had walked for a month. She was afraid she might fall and not be able to get up. *Where can I sleep tonight?* she wondered. She looked around but saw nothing that would keep her hidden for the night. In fact, the trees were thinning out. She needed to move to the other side of the clearing.

Halfway across the clearing, she heard a whirling sound coming over the trees—the sound of a helicopter. Her feet took off running, as if they had a mind of their own. She ran without thinking, ran without looking, and kept running long after she could no longer hear anything but her own labored breathing.

As the sun was just beginning to set, her foot caught on something and down she went, everything fading to black. Her last conscious thoughts was, *Who is up there, did they see me, and are they looking for me?*

4

Each Day

A crisp cool breeze woke her as it blew dry leaves around her head. She listened to the sounds around her and tried to remember where she was. She could hear birds chirping to each other and the sounds of something scampering just above her. She also heard a sound like water rippling in a brook. That would be too good to be true, to have some kind of clean water close by.

"Oh, my head hurts," she groaned out loud as she touched the tender area on the outer edge of her left eyebrow.

She wondered how long she had slept. She tried to remember finding a place to sleep. She wondered why she did not have her blanket over her. Groping for the blanket, she soon figured out it was nowhere near her. Still, she realized even without a blanket she did not feel uncomfortably cold.

She lay perfectly still and thought about what had happened yesterday. She remembered the long black limousine. She also recalled the one-sided conversation she had heard between the Sister and someone she guessed to be a very important person in this plan. She remembered walking a long way then hearing a sound overhead. She remembered running, running for dear life, away from the sound.

Did I fall? Did I black out? That must have been what happened. The same questions came popping into her mind. *Who was up there, did they see me, and were they looking for me?* She did not want to be seen by anyone. That information could somehow get back to the Sister.

She realized she was wasting time. She had to figure out where she was and get herself together for another day of walking. She scanned the area where she lay. She saw she had fallen under several large evergreen trees with their big overhanging limbs touching all the way to the ground. The area under the trees made a den-like place where she felt hidden and safe.

She removed her backpack and carefully stood up. Moving aside the soft green limbs of one of the tree, she looked all around. She was in a thick forest. She could faintly feel the sun directly over her head. *I must have slept all night and half the day too. No wonder I feel so stiff and sore—I sure needed the sleep.*

Realizing her mouth was dry and parched, she wondered how much water she had remaining. She opened her purse and retrieved the two water bottles. They were empty. Pulling aside the tree limbs, she carefully stepped out of her den. Following the sounds, she took only a few steps around a large rock and found a small waterfall with a pool at the bottom. The water rippled and gurgled down a little hill and out of sight.

She took a moment to look carefully around for signs of danger. She neither saw nor heard anything that concerned her. She started forward and then stopped.

On the far side of the pool, a twig snapped. It resounded in the quiet woods. She shrank back against the rock. Her eyes riveted to the spot where the sound had originated. Holding her breath, she waited. Then she saw what had startled her. Coming down from the hill above the falls were a doe and her half-grown fawn. The doe stopped and smelled the air looking for any signs of trouble. The woman stood as still as a statue, enjoying the show. They were beautiful animals—very graceful, with dainty little hoofs.

She watched until the deer drank their fill and wandered back into the woods. Then she walked down to the pool. Reaching out her hand, she let the cold spring water run through her fingers. Stooping down, she cupped her hands and drank as much of that wonderful cool water as she could. She did not think she would ever enjoy any other kind of drink as much as that wonderful water.

After making a hasty trip to the bushes, to do what nature demanded, she again returned to the pool. Everything was quiet and very peaceful. Feeling safe, she took off her outer clothes and stepped into the pool. She washed her face, arms, legs, and feet. The water was too cold to go completely in, but it was refreshing and made her feel a lot better. The cool water was somehow easing the pain in her head. The sun shining through the trees felt warm on her back. She almost felt, for the first time since waking in the hospital, like she was a strong person. She began to believe she could do what she needed to do to learn the mystery surrounding the Sister. She could find out what the woman was really up to and stop her evil plans.

The idea was forming in her mind that she should stay at the pool, at least for the night, and continue to rest. She knew her body could use another day of rest to mend the concussion and build up her strength.

The days were warm and the nights cool, so she guessed it must be fall—hopefully early fall. She decided to look around the pool area. She might be able to find some berries or other food to keep her alive for the next few days and weeks of her journey. She had no idea where this journey would lead her or what she would find when she got there. She hoped the really cold weather was still a ways off. She did not know what she would do if she was still out walking in the open air when winter came. She shivered just thinking about it and quickly put the thought away.

Carrying her water bottles to the falls, she filled them with fresh water. She returned to her hideout and emptied her small tote bag, returning again to the pool. She walked away from the pool counting twenty-five steps, looking at everything. At the twenty-fifth step she turned and walked back the way she had come. She wished she had a book on finding food in the forest. Glancing down to the right of the path, she saw a root-looking plant sticking partly out of the dirt. As she stooped down to get a better look, she saw a flash of a page. On the page was a picture of a plant with words under the picture: "Genus: Pastinaca (wild parsnip): an edible plant found in the woods in most of the Northeastern states. The root is good for food but the leaves can cause a rash if contact occurs during the early spring and summer."

Just as fast as the picture came to her, it was gone again; however, not before she understood she could eat this plant. *Wow, just when I needed it, a picture came to my mind. It must have happened because I was hungry and thinking about food. Surely it couldn't be that someone is really helping me find food. No, that was too farfetched.* She shook her head at the strange thought. She told herself it was simply a memory that came to her mind because she was hungry. But it was pretty good timing!

She went to work and dug up every one of the roots, taking care to cover up any signs someone had been digging there. "Just covering my tracks," she whispered to the plant she held in her hand. "I'm not being paranoid, just cautious. No harm in that."

She went back to the pool, and after rinsing off the dirt, she laid the roots in the sun to dry. After a bit, she took a bite, but only a small bite. Just because she remembered a page did not mean she was ready to trust it completely. She thought she had better go slowly. She did not want to get sick and die out here. The small bite she took did not taste bad, maybe even a little sweet. Going back to the pool, she took a long drink of water and sat down with her back to a rock and her face to the sun. Closing her eyes, she let the healing rays warm her, giving her a sleepy peaceful feeling.

She was startled awake by something hitting the water. She did not move; she only barely opened her eyes. After a few minutes she heard the sound again. This time she saw the silvery flash of a fish tail and a ripple of water where the fish had been. "Now, there is an idea for something to eat," she whispered. However, she would need a hook and line to catch any fish, so fishing would need to wait. Instead she headed back into the woods.

All afternoon she searched for and dug roots laying them in the sun to dry. Each time she finished a new batch, she took one more bite of the parsnip she had started. So far she could feel no ill effects and she had not felt hungry at all. She decided she would only eat the parsnips and not any more of the candy bar. It was for emergency chocolate cravings only!

By nightfall she had a nice bundle of food stored in the den. Before it got too dark, she took a bath. The water did not feel as cold as at noon because the sun had been heating it all day, and she had become quite warm digging. This time she really washed. She wished she could wash her hair, but the night air would be too cold to go to sleep with a wet head. She used the wool blanket to dry with and put on her clean underclothes. She placed her clean pants and shirt to one side, wanting to wait until she left the woods to wear then. Rinsing out her dirty underclothes, she hung them from branches inside the den. She was careful not to leave anything lying around by the pool in case someone came by; not even a leaf from her food supply.

In the morning she awoke feeling refreshed and ready to put in a good day's walk. As she stood and stretched, she thought about everything she needed to do to get ready, mentally checking off her list. She needed to repack her backpack with all her new food supplies, fill the water bottles, and check that nothing was left behind. While she continued her mental list, she looked out of the den checking to make sure everything was safe. Finding everything just as she had left it, she again walked over to the pool and took a long drink of the purest water she could ever imagine tasting. Rinsing and refilling her water bottles, she realized how important it was to be ready to leave at a moment's notice.

She decided to take the time to wash her hair; it was driving her crazy, itching all the time. She was sure it had not been washed in days; she had brushed it out, but that was all. Somewhere she had heard that American Indians used sand to wash their bodies. She wondered if sand would work on her scalp and hair. Since she had no soap, she decided to try it. At first it felt good, but then she could not get the sand out of her hair. She moved closer to the falling water. While bending over, just a little bit too much, she toppled right into the water, fully clothed, and got completely wet again.

Sputtering as her head came out of the water, she shouted, "Man this water's cold!" She crawled out onto the sandy beach. Removing her wet clothes, she went back in the water. She soon became used to the temperature of the water, not feeling the cold at all. She swam getting all the sand out of her hair. The water felt so good. She wondered if this was how the first people of the earth felt not needing to wear clothes and not feeling even the least bit embarrassed about it.

While washing out her wet dirty clothes, her thoughts went back to who the first people on the earth were. She had heard of cave men and Adam and Eve, and the ever famous apple, but were they the first people? She did not know. She decided to write down the question in her notebook for later.

She put on clean underwear and her other pair of jeans, shirt, socks, and boots. After drying her hair with the blanket, she hung it up to dry along with her wet clothes. She realized the clothes she had washed would not dry for a while. She decided that continuing her trip today was out of the question. She could not carry wet clothes in her backpack or everything would get moldy and disgusting. Instead she would scout around again. There was nothing so pressing she could not stay one more night. She would use the time to look for more food.

The day was a quiet, pleasant one. She found berries, which some birds were eating. She figured if the birds could eat them so could she. There was a handful left after she had eaten her fill, so she carried them in a big leaf, back to her den to put them away for supper. Wild parsnip, fresh pure water, and juicy berries for dessert—not a bad dinner, not bad at all.

She went to sleep early that night, still becoming tired easily. After her swim in cold water and the walk in the warm sunshine, her bed underneath the tree felt wonderful. The dried pine needles were pushed up for a mattress and the wool blanket smelled of sunshine. She thought she would sleep like a baby. She wondered if she had ever had a baby. However, she did not have long to ponder the thought because she was asleep in a matter of seconds.

The next morning her clothes were dry, her food was packed, and all she needed to get started on her way was to eat, drink, and load up. On her way back from the little girl's room—in the bushes—she noticed something shining in a branch above my head. She stopped to investigate and could see a fish hook and line tangled in the tree branches. *Wow!* she thought, *This is just what I needed to catch a fish.* She worked for a few minutes to untangle the line then found a small stick to wind the line onto. She had just finished winding, and had begun her walk back to the open area around the pool, when she became conscious of a sound overhead. A sound she now realized she had been hearing for a while but had been so engrossed in untangling the fishing line she had not noticed the ominous sound, until that moment.

She stopped walking and stepped back deeper into the trees. She crouched by a heavy thicket of bushes, waiting until the plane flew over. When the sound grew fainter, she went to the pool and looked all around for any signs someone above might have seen. Everything was just as if she had never been there. She took a long drink and headed back to her den to think.

She wondered if she should try to walk out of there right then or wait until dark. Before she finished the thought, she could hear the plane returning. She decided this could be a search plane; her safest plan was to stay right where she was. Even if someone walked close by the den, no one would see her or even see that there was an open area underneath the trees. She would wait them out and leave when it was dark.

Last night she had seen the moon was full. A harvest moon, so there should be enough light to walk. She hoped no one would be flying at night, but if they were, maybe they would not see her.

Sometime later she was getting restless. She had not heard any planes for a while. Maybe it would be safe to start early. Then she heard a low hum overhead becoming louder and louder. *Okay, no starting early. I need to learn patience.* She looked around for something else to do. Spying her notebook, she decided to reread everything she had written so far. Maybe if she had any new thoughts she could write them down too.

She began at the beginning. When she came to the part where the Sister said, "So we will start in five days. Right on target! What are Einstein's estimates after the last test group went through the treatment?" she thought about how many days it had been since she slept underneath the overpass. She counted how many mornings she had awakened in the den. The first morning after the fall was one, the second morning when she took the unplanned swim in the pool was two, and today when the planes came again was three.

She reread the part about Einstein—whoever that was—and came to the conclusion that somehow those people were going to try to brainwash most of the world's population. And they would start in only a few days. The words *international trouble* warned her they were planning something big. The question was how could anyone brainwash the minds of the world? She would need to keep her eyes open for any signs of people acting strange and keep track for others acting the same way. She went on to read about the five percent of people who could not be brainwashed because they had kept their minds strong by reading—and the best book to read was the Bible. *Maybe I could pick up a Bible somewhere, along my travels, and begin to strengthen my mind so I will not come under the control of those people.*

She had gone through her whole notebook and now her eyes were becoming tired. It would be good if she could get some sleep before nightfall. After repacking everything, she lay down with her head on the backpack and went right off to sleep.

5

The Moonlit Walk

She awoke to quiet night sounds. In her sleep, it seemed she had heard planes continuously. However, she did not know if she had been dreaming or if someone was really flying over her all afternoon. She could not see much inside her den, but there was some light from the moon outside. "Time to go," she whispered to her temporary refuge.

She picked up her backpack, taking the penlight she checked one more time to make sure she had left nothing lying around; everything looked good.

She headed out to the pool and took one last drink of that wonderful water. She wished she could take the waterfalls and pool with her—she placed her courage in the fact that whoever this unseen friend was, he or she would lead her to an abundance of good water when she needed it.

Before starting out, she stopped and sent a plea out into the cosmos. Her own voice startled her in the darkness as she asked for protection in her travels and to be able to find whatever else she might need. "And thank you for everything so far, whoever you are."

Shouldering the pack, she started in the direction the sun had been setting the night before. She had to go slow at first until her night vision became clearer. It was not long before she was moving at a steady pace.

The moon was very bright, just as she had hoped it would be. Before long she came to an old road. The road appeared to have been neglected for some time, but it was easy to see that this had once been well traveled. The road appeared to be going west, so she thought she would give it a try. Walking along the road was easier, and she covered the miles with ease.

As she walked, she thought about the past few days. She realized she had needed these days to build up her strength and rest until her injuries healed. She remembered overhearing the Sister say she had a concussion that could cause blackouts, headaches, and slow thinking. Now she felt much stronger; her mind was certainly clearer than it had been when she had tripped and fell into the den three days ago.

She realized she had almost been seen by those in the plane this morning. If it had not been for the fishing hook and her desire to catch a fish, she would have been out in the open when the plane first went over. She continued to ponder this mysterious friend. *If I had not fallen in the water and gotten my clothes wet, would I have postponed my trip for a day? What if I had left earlier? I would not have had a nice den to slip into and be safe from searching eyes.* She thought all of this was very reassuring. *Someone is still looking out for me!*

As she walked along, her thoughts turned again to who she was before the hospital stay, and what she had done before losing her memory. Feeling a headache coming on, she abandoned her thoughts on her past life.

After walking along for a time, she remembered she still needed a name for herself. She thought of many names, but they all left her feeling flat and empty. Like none of the names had any real meaning to her. She was looking up at the moon, taking in the beauty of the golden orb, when a name came to her all at once: Valentine.

"Valentine," she exclaimed to the night air. "I am Valentine." She said the name out loud several times to get used to the feel on her tongue. However, even though she continued to rack her brain, she could not think of a last name. "It will come," she said aloud. Walking a few more paces, she exclaimed, "I feel as if I have just been reborn!"

Suddenly, without any warning, her old road teed up into a newer paved road. Off to the left, some distance away, she could just make out the lights of a small town. She did not want to go down into the town at night; however, she did want to go there and investigate. She wondered if she would find anything strange or different about the people she came in contact with.

She made her way back to the woods and found a place with a thicker stand of trees. Taking off her backpack, she removed the blanket. She ate a little parsnip, drank some water, and lay down. Using the backpack as a pillow and her blanket, she soon felt snug and warm. Before she went to sleep, she whispered, "Thank you, friend, and good night."

6

The Town's People

When Valentine awoke, she was in a cold dark room. A single naked bulb burned in the corner, giving off faint light. She immediately recognized the room as where she had been hit across the face. Looking down she saw her hands and ankles were tied to a chair; the chair was bolted to the floor. Her heart began to race. "How did I get back here? I was sleeping in the woods," she whispered to the cold room.

There was a damp numbing feel of stone under her bare feet; a shiver ran down her spine. Looking around, she saw a cot on the other side of the room. The wall behind the cot was made of very old gray stones. She could smell that heavy fearful smell, as if the Sister was somewhere nearby. To the left of her, she began to hear the creaking sound of an old door slowly opening.

She tried to turn her head toward the door. As she did, a bright searchlight blinded her; she could see nothing. Quickly she closed her eyes, turning her head away from that blinding light. After the hot light burned her eyes, the pain in her head intensified unbearably. Nevertheless, she desperately wanted to see who was coming into the room. She closed her eyes tighter, waiting a few moments, then she tried opening them again.

This time, when she opened her eyes, she saw no dark walls or even the bright search light. What she saw was a cloud passing over the sun. Without the bright light, she was able to see again. Her eyes took in the tall evergreen trees, dark against the blue sky. She knew with a great relief that she was still in the forest, next to a country road, and not in that dreadful room at all. It had been only a dream. Nonetheless, she knew she had been in that room before. It was a real memory, not just a scary dream—not something her overactive mind and the stress of the past few days had conjured up.

She snuggled back into her warm wool blanket and closed her eyes again. She made herself remember every detail she had seen in that room. The cot was just a small wooden cot, one that might be seen in an old WWI movie. On the cot she could see a crumpled, soiled sheet. From where she had been sitting, the sheet looked blood-stained—but was it blood? If so, was it hers or someone else's? She could remember nothing else that stood out about the room, except the smell of course. That smell seemed to stay with her, and the only name she could put to it was fear.

Sitting up, she dug into her backpack and got out her notebook. She wrote down every single detail about that dream, no matter how small.

As she wrote, she felt the sun beginning to warm her back and knew it was time to start the day. She wanted to spend some time in that town, to watch and see if there was anything unusual about the people there. She remembered today could be the ominous fifth day. The plan, whatever it was, might be starting this very day!

Looking around she saw, in the darkness of the night, she had picked a spot more out in the open than she felt safe in. So, taking her backpack, she went deeper into the woods. Then she began turning herself into a down-on-his-luck, overweight, sixty-five-ish old man. She again put the backpack on in front. She fastened her jacket over it to soften the look and to make herself look like a potbellied man. Then she pulled on the white shirt and the overalls. She took the coins out of her purse and shoved them down into her overall's pocket. As she shoved them deeper into her pocket, she felt something hard and smooth. Pulling it out, she discovered a knife, with a pair of little scissors, a screwdriver, and two blades.

"You will come in handy," she spoke aloud to the shiny object in the palm of her hand. "I sure could have used you to dig parsnips. My hands are a mess. But they do look more like a man's this way. I guess dirt under my nails won't hurt." She continued to speak aloud working her vocal cords and trying out the old man's voice.

Valentine put the gray wig on her head and pinned it securely with bobby pins. She surely did not want the wig to slip at the wrong time. Since the wig was short and rather ragged-looking, she could use it for either Jeb Bodiene or Lucy Pope. She put on the felt hat and started to tie the red bandanna around her neck. However, it really did not go with the white button-up shirt, so she folded it and put it away in her back pocket. She used the eyeliner to darken her eyebrows and make them bushier. She looked into the compact mirror for a final check and liked what she saw.

She took some parsnips out of her backpack, placed her Lucy purse in the bottom of the cloth tote, and piled the parsnips on top, to hide the purse. It would be hard to explain why a man had a woman's purse in his possession. She placed one of her water bottles on top. Putting the tote over her shoulder, she picked up her walking stick and was ready for whatever the day held.

As she left the woods, she felt a little sad. The forest had been her home. It had been her safe haven in a storm; a storm not of bad weather but of danger. She felt that somehow her unknown friend had led her there and, if need be, would lead her to another safe haven.

Coming up to the paved road, she saw a road sign: Leaving Patapsco Valley State Park. She had wondered why there was a forest right outside of Baltimore; now she knew. She had been hiding in a park.

As Valentine was walking down the road toward the town, she thought of things to look for while in town. She should watch and see what the townspeople were doing, and any possible similarity that ran through each of them. The things she wanted to watch for was if anyone looked hypnotized, dazed, or just different. As soon as possible she would write down anything and everything she saw and heard. One of these days something would click. When that happens, she hoped she would be able to put it all together.

As she was nearing the town's outer edges, she saw a sign that read Sykesville, Maryland. She had noted scattered houses along the way. She realized she did not have a story for this disguise. She had better think up one quickly.

She decided Jeb Bodiene's story was, "My name is Jeb Bodiene, from Virginia." She spoke the story aloud, continuing to perfect a man's voice. "I just lost my wife, June, to cancer. I had to sell our home to pay the hospital bills. I sold everything in my apartment to pay for the funeral. Now I'm broke. Not wanting to trouble my son for money—I know my son has little enough to take care of his young wife and the new baby—so I decided to walk partway to my son's house in Kansas. Walking will be good for me and will help me grieve in private over my dear June. I'll say I am catching the bus in the next town. That story should keep most people from wondering how a sixty-five-year-old man could walk to Kansas." *A good story*, she thought, *for being off the top of my head. Maybe I'm a writer in my former life.*

Before long she came to a sidewalk and a street lined with old oak trees. The houses were old-fashioned and the street looked like a picture from a Norman Rockwell book. She walked along for three blocks before finding the main street of Sykesville. Turning west, she came to a café in the first block of buildings. The café's front windows had booths in them—a good place for reconnaissance.

As she walked through the front door, she seemed to have stepped back in time. *If I didn't know better, I would have thought I was a time traveler.* There was a counter running the length of the right wall. In front of the counter were rounded stools, bolted to the floor. The stools were covered in faded red vinyl. There was also an old-fashioned soda fountain behind the counter. While she was looking around, the booth to the left of the door was taken by an older couple. So she sat down in the booth to the right.

Valentine took off her felt hat, smoothing her gray wig, as she smiled at the waitress who was walking up to her booth. The waitress was young, with short pink-and-black hair. She wore a ring on each finger and a small diamond in her nose. The look was interesting, and Valentine liked the girl instantly. The name tag on her short, red gingham uniform was, Tess.

The waitress said, "Hey, what do you want to drink, mister?"

"Could you speak up, please? I don't hear well."

The waitress laughed and spoke louder, "What. Would. You. Like. To. Drink?"

"Oh, drink, you asked what to drink. Water, please, just water, thank you."

After Valentine ordered a boiled egg and two pieces of whole-wheat toast, she walked to the bathroom in the back of the café.

After using the toilet, she washed her hands but left her face alone. "A little bit of dirt smeared on my chin looked somewhat like a day's growth of whiskers, hopefully helping me look more like a man," she spoke to the unrecognizable face in the mirror.

Valentine looked long and hard in the mirror to see if any scrap of memory came, but it only made her feel like a headache was coming on. She quickly checked to see if everything looked in order with her disguise and headed back out to eat her breakfast. As she slowly ate her egg and toast, she watched people on the street going by.

Most people were in cars, but some were walking. She watched all of them carefully, while trying not to seem as if she was too interested. Everyone she saw so far appeared to be normal. She really did not know what she was looking for but felt she would know *it* when she saw it. From quick observation, they appeared just like big city people. All of them had cell phones or some kind of electronic gadget they were playing with. She saw a mother and teenage daughter go slowly by in their SUV. Both were talking away, but not to each other, on their cell phones—they were not even looking at each other.

Valentine thought, *How sad that families have broken down so far. No one talks to each other anymore.* She slowly shook her head.

A few moments later, a nicely dressed lady walked by, wearing business clothes. Behind the lady, trailing by a few feet, was a pretty little girl. The girl looked to be about five or six; she was looking at everything and not keeping up.

As the little girl walked past the window, she looked up and smiled at Valentine. She had the sweetest smile, with sad puppy-dog eyes. Valentine smiled back—a spontaneous smile she could not have stopped, even if she had wanted to. Then the mother turned around and said something to the little girl. She turned away from the window and ran to catch up with her mother, who was again speaking rapidly on her cell phone. The picture of the mother and young daughter stayed with Valentine. She thought about all the precious time that mother was losing, never to get back. Valentine wondered if she had a daughter herself, and if so, she hoped she had been different with her. Valentine thought back about what the Sister had said, about having a family. *When this is all over,* she thought, *I will go find them—and that is a promise I will not break.*

Valentine had finished eating and was just starting to get up, when a car going by caught her attention. Slowly on the other side of the street, an officer was driving a sheriff's patrol car. The man had the window down and was carefully searching each side of the street. From where she sat behind the curtain, she could see him well; she hoped he could not see her. His face had no emotions showing at all. The man's entire being was directed to the search he was conducting. He looked more like a store mannequin than a human being. He had the coldest eyes she had ever seen.

Valentine shrank even further behind the curtain. Whomever he was searching for, herself or someone else, she did not want him to see her. The patrol car was just across the street from the door of the café when a customer, just exiting the café, stepped out and hailed the officer. The patrolman slowly blinked his eyes twice then the strangest thing happened. His face changed, as if someone had flipped a switch. He stopped the car, looked up, and talked in a very friendly fashion to the farmer who had hailed him.

Valentine could not hear what was being said, but the difference in the officer was night and day—like the devil showing his friendly human face.

After the two finished talking, the officer drove away out of Valentine's sight. The farmer turned and walked in front of the window where she was sitting, shaking his head. *Had he seen what I was*, Valentine wondered? Was he confused about the officer's strange behavior as well? Valentine got up and walked to the cash register to pay for her meal. Tess took the money as she popped her bubblegum and said, "You forgot your fedora, mister."

Looking back at the booth, Valentine saw her old battered hat lying on the bench seat. "Thank you so much, young lady. I'd be missing that when my head gets cold. By the way, I like your name, Tess. I've never heard it before."

Tess smiled and said, "I was named for my grandmother. She became my best friend." A sadness came over her face as she continued to speak. "She died last year." Slowly, her face changed into a radiant smile to take the place of the sadness as she said, "I will see her again!"

Valentine wanted to ask her what she meant, however, a costumer was calling out for more coffee, and Tess quickly grabbed the coffee pot. Valentine turned away, out the door, and back out on the street going west again.

That morning Valentine walked in and out of stores, talking to people when she had to, but mostly she watched them. She watched for any signs in the townspeople of what she had seen in the man driving the sheriff's patrol car. Valentine saw the officer drive by two more times, but each time she was indoors.

At the farthest end of town was a used bookstore. Valentine had been thinking of getting something to read, something that would strengthen her mind. *Maybe in here I could find something inexpensive,* she thought. As she opened the door, quiet music floated out mixed with the fragrant smell of warm cookies. The inside of the store was pleasantly arranged. An overstuffed chair and love seat were in front of a wood stove that was emitting warmth and bidding her to come closer.

From the back of the store, a female voice said, "I'll be right with you. Please feel free to look around."

Valentine started in the novels. Most of the books in the classics were too expensive for her, but she kept an eye out for bargains.

She had just opened a book on poems when the gentle voice said, "Can I offer you some cookies and milk?"

Valentine looked around. Standing at the counter was a middle aged woman. She was slender and of medium height. Her straight white hair hung around her face like a soft curtain. Her smile was contagious.

Smiling back and trying hard to sound like a man, she answered, "I would love some cookies and milk, thank you."

The cookies were on a counter close to the stove. She took the cookies along with the book in her hand and sat on the couch. As she read, she nibbled on the best homemade cookies she had ever tasted. *Of course, I do not remember any other cookies.* Nevertheless, they are very good, and the milk sure does hit the spot. Valentine got up and, after throwing away the trash, asked the storekeeper if she had a sale table.

"Yes, sir, it's in the back on the right. Feel free to wash up in our restroom. It is also in the back."

"Thank you, ma'am, thank you very much. I'll take you up on your kind offer, before I start browsing again. Those were wonderful cookies, ma'am."

After Valentine came out of the bathroom, she started browsing through the sales table. She found a paperback book of Shakespeare's work for only a quarter. She was just turning away from the table when her eye caught sight of a corner of a small black book beneath the other books. It looked like an expensive book, bound in real leather. She pulled out the book. As she read the title, a shiver ran down her spine. The name of the book was, *The Gospel of John*.

Opening the cover, the first words leaped out at her:

To my beautiful daughter, Valentine,
On her birthday,
January 18, 1941 Love, Mother

Valentine wanted this book very much but wondered what the cost would be. She knew she only had seventeen dollars and some change, so she had to be careful with her money. She had no idea when she would be able to work again. She still needed to send money back to the nurse she had borrowed the lab coat from, as well as to the thrift store.

Valentine looked the little black book over carefully but found no price tag. She carried both books up front to the counter and waited her turn. Soon she was the only customer in the store. As she smiled at the lady, Valentine wondered if she could be the bookstore owner. The place had a touch of love in everything she saw.

"I would like to buy this book on Shakespeare, and could you tell me the price on this other book?"

The shopkeeper took the books and opened the black one. "The Gospel of John," she spoke the name with reverence. "I used to read this every spring, and I used to read my Bible every day. I wonder what happened to that," she spoke as if to herself.

The storekeeper gave her head a little shake and smiled. Handing Valentine back the book, she said, "Sorry, this little book just took me back to when I was a young mother. As you can see, that was a long time ago. Tell you what. I'll sell you both books for seventy-five cents. No one reads these kinds of books anymore. Even though the book might be worth more, I don't think I will sell it any time soon. Times are getting harder and people are not spending money on books."

"Thank you, that's very fair of you. Thank you so much," Valentine croaked, still trying to talk like a man and feeling touched by what the woman had said about being a young mother. "I guess people are buying more video games for themselves and their children. It would do the world good if they would put down their cell phones, turn off their TVs, and read something good like this book here." Valentine held up the black book. "I heard somewhere that reading books like these will keep your mind stronger, and since I'm not getting any younger, I thought I'd try it for myself."

As the storekeeper was putting Valentine's books into a plastic bag, she said, "Maybe I'll leave the TV off tonight and look for my old Bible, the one Mother gave me. It won't do me any harm to strengthen my mind either. By the way, my name is Mary, Mary Vanderhorn. My sister Martha and I own this store. She's home sick with a cold today, but I think I'll see if she will read with me tonight. I find it so cozy to read out loud when there is someone to listen."

"Well, thank you again for the cookies and milk, and a pleasant place to read. If I lived around here, I would come back, but I'm traveling to Kansas to live with my son."

Valentine held out her hand to shake Mary's and said, "I hope you do read more. I know you will enjoy reading a good book, much more than spending every night in front of the television."

She was putting her books inside the cloth tote and turning to the door to go out when Mary said, "Here, won't you take the rest of these cookies for your trip?"

Mary held out a bag of the cookies as she turned to answer the phone. The exchange lasted only a few seconds; however, it kept Valentine away from the front door and off the street, just long enough. By the time she was on her way again, she saw the back of the sheriff's car driving away from her, back toward town.

"It has happened again. Someone is watching out for me," she whispered to the empty street. She took the time to say a silent quick thank-you as she turned the corner to a side street, away from danger.

After a few blocks, Valentine turned onto a road heading west out of town. She did not know her destination, but her feelings of being cared for were reinforced. She knew someone was walking with her every step of the way. Even if she did not know who this being was, she knew her safety and comfort were taken care of. She just needed to do the work she had been sent to do. Valentine thought about that work as she walked along. She saw now that it was a twofold work. Not only was she to try to find out who was behind this plan and stop them, also as she traveled along, she would talk to people about reading and strengthening their minds. She knew she could not tell anyone why they needed to do this—people would just think she was crazy, but if she could put the idea into their heads, that might be enough to start.

Valentine was walking along in the open country now. She was trying to stay close to the tree line when there was one. She felt like she needed to reach the next town before it got too late in the evening. Not long after leaving the city limits of Sykesville she had seen a sign that read, "Gaither Seven Miles." She had decided she would continue on this road till she neared Gaither. Then she would find somewhere safe to sleep during the night. She would travel on into Gaither when it was light, when people would be out and about.

Just as the sun was becoming a big red ball in her eyes, she saw a thick stand of woods in a pasture not far from the road. Valentine crossed the road and headed toward it. Her back was killing her after walking with this backpack on her front all day. She had removed it only twice. Now she felt like she might fall down if she did not sit down soon.

Valentine checked to see if any cars were in sight. Seeing the coast was clear, she climbed the fence. She knew she would look funny if anyone was watching a portly old farmer climbing a fence. She hoped she did not fall over backward. "I'd look like a turtle on its back," she chuckled to herself. *It's good to see the funny side of life*, she thought. *I've not seen very many funny things in my short life of five or six days.*

The woods were about a hundred feet from the fence. It took her only a short time to cover the space and enter the trees. The coolness of the woods felt good. She had gotten rather warm walking along in the late afternoon sun. It was time for a rest. Standing behind a tree, Valentine checked the road again to see if it was still empty. Far off down the road toward Gaither she saw a vehicle slowly moving in her direction. She felt it would be a good idea to stand still until the car was past her. It took a few moments until an old Ford truck was close enough to identify. She waited, wanting it to be far past her before moving deeper into the woods.

Valentine's mind was thinking about everything she would do before she slept, and not paying attention to the road in front of her. Suddenly she realized the old truck was stopping. She could see two men in the cab of the truck, one older and one younger. The younger man was driving. She wondered why they had stopped. Surely they hadn't seen me, she thought, they had been too far away.

Then she saw that while she had been watching the truck and thinking about the tasks she needed to do, another vehicle had been slowly driving toward her from the other direction. It was a sheriff's patrol car. As it drew near, she could see the same man driving whom she had seen earlier. The patrol car slowed to a stop next to the truck.

Valentine could hear one of the men in the truck say, "Hey, Sheriff Joe, you're going mighty slow. You looking for someone?"

"Well, not anyone dangerous, just an old guy I need to talk to. He was seen in and out of stores today, and no one knows who he is. I just like to keep tabs on any newcomer, that's all."

Valentine heard the younger man in the truck ask, "What does he look like? We'll give you a call if we see him." She heard Sheriff Joe describe the man. It was Jeb Bodiene to a tee. Valentine felt like the wind had been knocked out of her. She knew the sheriff did not just want to talk to the old man. He wanted to find and apprehend Jeb Bodiene, in other words the woman from the hospital. *He wants to stop me*, Valentine's mind exploded in worry. Sheriff Joe is one of the people the Sister had described as being in the ninety-five percenters!

Valentine listened to the men talk until they drove off—nothing more was said about the old man. When she felt it was safe to move, she continued to watch the road as she stepped back a few paces; then she walked deeper into the woods.

She walked until she found a small spring that someone had put a pipe in. The pipe ran along the ground and then out through the trees; she guessed to a pasture. Around the pipe, a small stream flowed and made a puddle. "I could fill my bottles up and drink my fill before I leave in the morning," she said, smiling at the sight. She looked around the spring, finding it too open and wet; she moved back where the trees were closer together and the ground was drier.

Valentine took off her disguise and removed all the contents from the cloth tote bag. She placed her disguise in the bag and covered it with parsnips. She realized she could not be seen as Jeb Bodiene for a long while. She stretched her arms and back, feeling the great difference in not having a large weight hanging out in front. "I'll need to remember not to eat too many parsnips and get a big belly. It would be terrible on my back," she exclaimed!

She laughed at the thought of how many parsnips it would take to get that fat of a belly.

Before she had put the overalls away, she had removed the knife, wallet, and bandanna. She placed the coins and knife in her jeans' pocket then took the red bandanna and went back to the spring to wash her hands and face. She sat on a rock and removed her boots and socks. She soaked her feet in the puddle of water under the pipe from the spring. The water was cold and felt good on her tired, aching feet. Valentine could tell she was not much of a hiker because her feet were killing her after being on them for only one day.

Back at her campsite, she got out the parsnip she had washed earlier in the day and sliced off a few slices. With her fresh water and a cookie, she had a nice simple supper. She thought of Mary, the shop owner, who had given her the cookies. She hoped Mary and her sister would turn off the TV and read the Bible, to strengthen their mind for the coming trouble. She wondered how the world would change if those people got control. What did they intend to do, and how far would people succumb to their control? Judging by Sheriff Joe, the treatment worked, very well! If she let her mind go, she could imagine all kinds of fearful things. However, she reminded herself, she needed to keep on track for her own work, not get a numbing fear of what her enemies were doing.

After her meal, she got out her notebook and wrote everything she had seen and heard during the day—everything that would help her in her quest for the truth about this awful plan. She wrote carefully about Sheriff Joe and the change in him when he blinked his eyes.

"Was it just my imagination that the change happened when he blinked?" she asked herself. "No, I think the man from the café saw the change too." She decided to watch for this change in others.

It was getting dark by the time Valentine had written everything she could remember. If she continued, she would need her penlight. She reminded herself she needed to take care and not use it much because she did not know when she might really get in a bind and need a little light.

After trying to get to sleep and failing, she decided to read from one of her new books for just a few moments. She got out the Shakespeare copy to try first. Finding she could not concentrate on what she was reading, she picked up the Gospel of John and opened the first page. She reread the note to Valentine from her mother. She felt again that it was a message to herself, from someone who cared about her, just as this mother cared about Valentine back in 1941. It did not bother Valentine that she did not know who this being was, who was taking care of her. Whoever her guardian was, Valentine knew she would be safe for tonight. That was all she needed, a reminder that she was being cared for. Now she was ready to sleep.

Valentine had already made sure everything was packed and ready to go in the morning, so she laid her head on the backpack, covered herself with the blanket, and closed her eyes. She said quietly to the night air, "Thank you, friend, for my safety today, and good night."

7

The Games

Throughout the night, Valentine slept poorly. She could not get comfortable. No matter how she lay, there was always a rock poking her. She felt the cold, more deeply than at any time since leaving the hospital. When she finally did sleep, she kept dreaming of the cold damp room. She awoke with the thought of Sheriff Joe and the conversation she had overheard concerning the old man.

To get her mind off her fears and the cold, she began to plan how to change her appearance for the next day. She could not look like an old fat man that was for sure. She thought about being Lucy Pope. However, she would have to creep along too slowly. Valentine felt an increasingly strong urge to get out of the area. She needed to get some miles between herself and the sheriff, not to mention the Sister. *I must keep my red hair concealed,* she thought. *Maybe when I am farther away from Baltimore I can be myself, but for now, I must not be a redhead.*

She would re-braid her hair and pin it flat to her head. She would put the red bandanna on, low over her forehead, and tie it in the back gypsy-style. She would keep her eyebrows dark with the eyebrow pencil. Over the plaid-flannel shirt, she could wear the reversible jacket, turned to the brown leather side. She would wear the backpack and carry the cloth tote over her arm. She hoped she would appear, to most onlookers, like a middle-aged, down-on-his-luck traveler. She needed to tell people she was going south. Maybe that would throw off the people who were hunting her. She realized she should not have told anyone she was going to Kansas. She tried to think of how many people she had told and could think of only one: Mary Vanderhorn. Valentine hoped Mary would not talk about the old man she had spent time visiting with.

By the time Valentine had finished planning what she would wear in the morning, her eyelids were drooping. No matter how hard she tried to get comfortable and go to sleep, she could not. She felt very antsy. The feeling that she was not safe became stronger with each passing moment. She felt fear in the dark woods even though she had not felt any while in the park. Looking around in the shadows, she imagined she could see the sheriff's cold, hard, unblinking eyes staring at her. Valentine turned over and squeezed her eyes tightly shut trying to regain the peaceful feeling she had, had in the park.

Before long she could hear Sheriff Joe's voice in her ear giving out Jeb Bodiene's description again. Just hearing the sheriff talking about Jeb Bodiene this afternoon was enough to give Valentine the creeps, but hearing his voice in the dark was uncanny.

After Valentine had tossed and turned for what seemed like hours, she started to see the night sky changing color. She could just make out a very light gray-pink tint to the sky in the east. Yesterday morning she had waited until people were up and about, but today, she felt compelled to get up while it was still dark and get out of those woods.

Valentine washed up and drank cold water from the spring. Working as fast as possible, she dressed as she had previously planned. When she finished, she took her penlight and checked her face in her compact mirror. Satisfied with her face, she then noticed some red hair was showing out around the sides. She redid her bandana to cover the sides and back of her head. Retrieving the old man's fedora, Valentine placed it low over her face. Rechecking in the mirror, she saw this made her look manlier.

Valentine checked her sleeping area for any signs that she had been there. She then walked to the spring and checked there also for signs. She smoothed out a few footprints and threw dry leaves over the area. Only then did she feel ready to move out of the woods and head west to Gaither.

At the edge of the woods, she checked for any oncoming vehicles' lights. Seeing all was dark and the road empty, she headed for the fence. She was over it and starting down the road in a flash. She walked fast along the road. To be able to stand up straight felt so much better, and she was able to cover the miles quickly. She passed farmhouses with lights just beginning to come on. She would hear a dog bark now and then, but none came to the road. When the sun was still not visible but the sky lighter, she came to the edge of town. She realized not many people would be out and about for her to compare to the sheriff but decided to continue on. She did not have a good feeling at all about lingering in that small town.

She passed through the main part of Gaither, staying in the shadows as much as possible. Soon she came to the end of the town's main street. She had not met anyone, and all the stores were still closed. Valentine stood at the corner of the last building of the street, waiting and watching before stepping out in the open. She was watching for any signs of traffic—especially the sheriff's patrol car. She had looked both ways and had taken one step away from the dark wall, when out of the corner of her eye she saw a flash of light. She hopped back in the shadows and slowly peered around the corner of the building.

Coming toward her from the east was a car that looked very much like it had lights on top. Not stopping to think, she ran to the back of the building as fast as she could go. Finding some trees and thick bushes, she dodged behind the protective screen. She had just enough time to calm her rapid breathing before the car turned into the lane beside the building.

Valentine began to panic and prepared to run with everything she had. In that moment a voice, as soft as velvet, whispered to her heart.

"Peace, be still."

Immediately Valentine felt a calm spread throughout her whole being. She felt she had been tossing on a rough sea, and now she was floating serenely; no fear was left. Valentine felt as if she were hidden so well no one could ever find her. She watched the car come around the end of the building and stop. The car door opened and the inside lights illuminated the vehicle's interior. She could see the driver well; it was not Sheriff Joe. This man was younger and did not have that funny, glazed look in his eyes. In fact, this man had a pleasant face. However, at that moment, he was looking straight at Valentine.

She then heard a static-filled noise coming over the radio. It was a voice she remembered from the day before. "Did you find anyone?" Sheriff Joe asked.

The young man answered over his shoulder radio. "No, Sheriff Joe, I don't see any signs of anyone passing this way. In fact, there is still dew on the ground, and I see no footprints at all. The movement I saw must have been just the sun, shimmering off the store window."

Valentine looked out of the bushes and could clearly see her own footprints in the dew on the grass leading toward where she stood. *What is wrong with that man's eyes?* she wondered. *Why can't he see my footprints?* She again thought of the peaceful feeling she felt when the quiet voice spoke to her, the feeling that she was hidden. She knew the feeling was real. Somehow she was hidden, and even her footprints were hidden.

Valentine heard the sheriff say to the younger man, "Well, I'll have a team go over the woods between Sykesville and Gaither. A person was seen walking on that road last evening. This woman may still be hiding in the woods. If so, we'll have her incarcerated by day's end. By the way, boy, what do you think of that new video game the guys and I gave you on your birthday?"

The young man answered, "Well, ah, Sheriff, I really have not had the time to, ah, get into it yet. You know we're expecting our first baby, and I have been spending all my spare time working on the nursery."

"But you must do something for fun!" the sheriff protested loudly.

"Well, yes, my wife and I like to read, actually."

"Read!" Valentine could hear the sheriff's voice getting louder. "What kind of fun is that? Well, do as you like, but I know if you try this game you will be hooked. Everyone says it's the best game they have ever played!" The radio went silent when the sheriff signed off suddenly.

The young man muttered to himself, "How can I get them all to understand? Reading is our fun. I don't see why he's so adamant about me playing some old video game. You'd think it was life or death the way he keeps at me about it."

Valentine heard no more because by then he had shut the door to the patrol car. Still, he kept shaking his head and muttering as he drove off. The whole conversation struck her as really strange. Why did that sheriff switch the subject from finding me to playing a video game? It is as if the video game was as important as finding the Sister's escapee. It's a mystery, she thought, it is all a mystery!

When she could no longer see the car, she moved further back into the woods. The woods were thicker there and it was harder to get through.

After a bit, Valentine came upon a very thin trail. It was hardly wide enough to put both feet side by side, but it was easier to walk on it than to fight through the bushes and trees. She followed it south and soon came to a railroad track. Looking left, she saw the sun peeping over the tops of the trees, so she turned right to continue west. She walked for an hour before she heard a train coming from behind her. Valentine found a large tree at the edge of the tracks to sit behind until the train went by. She decided to read while she waited and got out the black book. She reread the inscription on the front page again. Each time she read it she felt the message was for herself as well as for the Valentine that lived fifty-something years ago.

She opened to the first chapter and began to read: In the beginning was the Word. She continued to read until the train had come and was long gone. She was deep into the little book when she looked up and realized she had been sitting there for quite a while, caught up in the unusual way of writing and the wording of the book.

Valentine thought of the words, "He came to his own and His own received Him not." *I don't really understand who "He" is,* she thought, *but I understand the loneliness of the words. I don't know who my own are, but if I ever find them and they do not want me, how very sad I would be.* Valentine thought she understood just a little of how the person in this book must have felt. She wanted to read more. However, it was time to continue on down the railroad tracks and out of this area.

Valentine continued west on the tracks for the rest of the morning. She came to a crossroad leading north or south with a sign pointing north to a town. She had drunk most of her water, still had plenty of parsnips, but she needed to eat something more than parsnips. So she turned away from the tracks and headed to town to find a restaurant. She again found herself walking down tree-lined streets like the ones in Sykesville.

As Valentine walked toward the center of town, she saw ahead a church with a tall steeple rising above the other houses. She could see the church looked old, and as she drew closer, she could read the sign out front, The First Baptist Church.

Valentine was on the same side of the street as the church and had almost passed by when she saw the side door open and two men walk out. She turned and stared because one of the men was dressed all in black with a white collar around his neck. The other man was very tall with a full beard. The men were talking quietly together and paying no attention to their surroundings, much less the homeless man walking past. From Valentine's quick glance, she could tell they were concerned about something. She had a feeling something was not right. There was an alley running along the side of the church with a row of thick bushes. Without really thinking why, Valentine turned and entered the alley. Walking as silently as she could, she went closer until she could hear the men talking.

"Pastor Johnson, we would be very grateful if you would watch out for this woman. We know she is dangerous to our mutual cause and she must be apprehended as soon as possible." The man's accent reminded Valentine of the Sister.

Then she heard a second voice ask, "What does this woman look like?"

The first man said, "She is tall, close to six feet. She was in the hospital with a concussion only last week and will likely look pale and sickly. That's all I know for now. Oh, wait—she has long, red hair."

Valentine could hardly stop her trembling. She stood as quietly as she could and listened as the men continued to talk about more of the details of her escape. She could not believe this. She had never seen either of these men before. Nevertheless, far away from the hospital in Baltimore were two more men trying to capture her as earnestly as the Sister was.

The subject changed to a video game. Valentine heard the priest ask the pastor, "Have you started passing out the new games to the church youth yet?"

Valentine stood straining to hear the response but soon realized the voices had become muffled and she could no longer understand what they were saying. Valentine crept back to the opening of the alley and peered around the bushes. The two men were walking down the street away from town. When they were almost out of sight, she continued on her way.

At a busy intersection, she turned west again and began to look for a café where she could rest and eat a little something.

Valentine was at the outskirts of town when she saw a building with many large trucks parked around it. Through a plate glass window she could see people eating at tables. *Oh good,* she thought, *a truck stop is a good place to get lost in a crowd.*

Valentine went to the bathroom and took care of business. She wondered if she should change into her Lucy Pope outfit but decided against it. She felt she looked more like a trucker and would fit in just fine here. Her red hair was still hidden under the bandanna and hat, and the rest of her appearance did not look like a sick woman. As she was walking out of the bathroom, she saw a sign that said, "Showers $2." The thought of a hot shower sounded so good she decided to spend the money.

Valentine took a long reviving shower and washed her hair with real soap. The water felt heavenly on her aching body, helping to clear her mind. As she stood in the shower, she decided to take time over her lunch to listen and watch everything. She was still very upset about what she had overheard between the Catholic priest and the Baptist pastor. By the sound of it, the two men both knew about the plan and the consequences of not finding her. Still, it sounded to Valentine like they had no idea that she could not remember anything. Nothing about their plan, or, for that matter, her own name or her past. Valentine only knew what she had overheard so far. That was not enough for her to be able to take this information to the authorities and stop them from taking control of the world.

While she finished drying her hair and getting dressed, she continued to think about everything until she felt a headache coming on. Valentine had not had a headache for a few days, and she definitely did not want one now. She would try to put everything out of her mind for a time and go eat a nice meal with some of the money she had left.

While she was in the bathroom, she washed a few of her underthings out in the sink and dried them with the hand air dryer. She repacked everything in her pack and tucked a cookie in her coat pocket—dessert for later. She had braided her hair again and covered it with her bandanna and the felt hat. She darkened her eyebrows again but this time just enough to keep her from looking like a redhead. She looked in the mirror and decided she still needed something, so she got out her Lucy Pope glasses; the ones that made her eyes look like saucers.

Valentine used a quarter to stash her backpack in a locker—she did not want to look like she had all her earthly belongings on her back. That would make her look more like a tramp than a trucker. "Now I am ready," she said to her reflection in the mirror. Valentine took the smaller white tote bag and her cane, and headed into the dining room. She found a seat in the back next to a window.

When the waitress came over, she ordered a hot coffee and water. Valentine said she needed to look over the menu for a moment. Through a mirror on the wall, she saw four men, in business suits, walk in, taking the back booth not far from where she sat.

She overheard one man say, "Shush, the waitress is coming."

Valentine wondered what the secrecy was all about. When the waitress brought her drinks and asked for her order, she decided to again pretend to have a hearing problem.

"What did you say, miss? I'm a bit hard of hearing," Valentine said in a loud mannish voice. After the waitress repeated herself, Valentine ordered a short stack of pancakes and some scrambled eggs.

Valentine looked out the window as if she did not know there was anyone behind her. Eavesdropping was not nice, but she had learned a lot by being in the right place at the right time.

One of the men said, "Okay, I think it is safe to talk now. The person in that booth over there is nearly stone-deaf. Did you hear the trouble the waitress was having?"

Another man said, "So have you heard from Father Irving since he left to go to Africa, to the mission fields?"

"Only a card sent to the church, the first week after he left, and that has been several months ago," the first man answered.

"That seems mighty odd," a third man commented. "Father Irving has been working in this community for twenty years, and we had plans to go to the community men's retreat this fall. I just don't understand what would make a sixty-five-year-old man want to go off to a foreign country and not even talk to any of his church people about it. Now with this Ebola scare, he needs to come home."

All the men were quiet for a while, then the last man spoke up again and said, "What do you think of the new priest, Father Mancini?"

"He's very friendly," answered another man. "The kids love him. He got them into these new Christian video games. All the teenagers love them. If you ask me, I think they're addicted to them. I can't get my son to do anything else. Father Mancini has been giving them out to everyone. He says even the adults will like them and get a lot out of them."

The men at the table were silent for a few minutes after the waitress brought their food. While the men ate and everything was quiet, Valentine pondered what all of it meant. She remembered the young sheriff's deputy talking to the sheriff about some kind of video game. The game was so important to Sheriff Joe he sounded almost mad that young man had not been playing the game. The second time today she had heard of video games was at the Baptist church only an hour ago. This makes three times in one morning that video games have come up in very important conversations. *I must not pass it off as a coincidence. I need to write it all down as soon as I can and keep my ears open for any other talk on the matter.*

Soon the talk at the men's table resumed and someone asked, "Have any of you heard from Pastor George, the Baptist minister? He left three weeks ago to go on that trip to China. I talked to his daughter yesterday, and she said she is very worried. She said the only correspondence she has gotten from him was one letter, a week after he left. He told his daughter he would be gone for a year and that the new youth pastor would be taking over for him until he came back."

Then Valentine heard someone ask, "Wasn't that trip very quickly arranged too—one that no one knew he was taking until a few days before he left?"

"Yes, his daughter said she tried to talk him out of the trip. She said his health wasn't good, but he would not listen to her at all. She said he wasn't acting like himself, and that even though it sounded paranoid, ever to her own ears, she felt like he acted afraid of something. She didn't realize it was fear that motivated him until he was gone, but she knew he wasn't himself. He said something very strange to her right before he left to go to the airport. The daughter quoted him, 'If I don't get back, and something should happen to me, please promise me that you will keep the faith, Mary. Please keep your faith in Jesus strong, and we will see each other in heaven.' Then she said he hugged her and the kids, and walked out the door. She hasn't seen him since. She also said he would not let her drive him to the airport. He explained he had a ride with someone else in the group, who was also going to China."

In the reflection of the mirror, Valentine could see the men shaking their heads. All was quiet for a while. By this time she had finished her pancakes and eggs. After drinking almost two cups of coffee and all her water, she needed to go to the restroom, but she could not leave yet. The waitress returned and asked if she needed anything. Valentine asked if it was okay to sit and finish her coffee.

"Sure, honey, we're kind of slow just now. Take your time."

The four men did not linger long. Valentine heard them agree to keep their ears open and to report anything strange at their next Bible study on Friday.

Valentine went to the bathroom as soon as the men were out of sight. As soon as possible, she got her things together from the locker, after checking her appearance in the mirror, started out the locker room door. She glanced both ways to check everything out. The coast was clear to her left, but to the right, out by the checkout counter, was a man dressed in black.

At first she thought he was the Catholic priest; he was about the same height. But as he turned a little, she saw he was clean shaven then she saw a bulge under his jacket. She stepped back into the locker room just as he started to turn toward her. She leaned on the wall and listened to footsteps walking toward the locker room. The steps continued past and on into the men's restroom.

She waited to the count of five and then peered around the door into the hall. The coast was clear. As quickly as she could, she walked out of the bathroom area, out the side door of the truck stop, and down between the parked trucks. Valentine walked at a steady pace without running. She was soon out of the parking lot and onto the main road, heading west again.

She soon realized how dark it had become while she was in the restaurant. The clouds were black and ominous, becoming more threatening by the minute. The sky looked like the storm was heading straight toward her. She needed to find a place to get out of the elements and soon. However, she saw nowhere close where she could seek shelter.

As Valentine walked, she put a plea skyward to her guardian speaking aloud, "Could you help me find a safe place to get out of this storm?"

Valentine continued to walk without a glimpse of a place to stay dry. In no time at all, she felt the first cold, wet raindrops run off her hat and down the back of her neck. She had just turned her coat collar up when an old white truck, with more rust than paint, pulled up beside her.

A woman rolled down the window and asked, "Would you like a ride?"

Valentine glanced into the truck and saw a man, woman, and small boy in the front seat and two older boys in the backseat. The rain was getting worse.

With no thought at all, Valentine said, "I would love a ride, but you look full up to me."

The man said, "We have room in the back, if that's okay with you." The truck had an old topper over the bed.

"Oh, the back would be lovely. Thank you very much for your kindness. Where are you headed?"

The man said, "We are headed west on I-70 toward Kansas."

"Oh, that will be great!" Valentine exclaimed. "I'm going west also. I will be glad for a ride for as long as you can take me."

The man got out of the truck and pulled up the topper window, opening the tailgate. Valentine quickly removed her backpack and handed it to him. She then tossed her white cloth tote up onto a bed of blankets, which were placed on the floor. She climbed right in after it. The man handed her the backpack, closing the back of the truck again.

Valentine looked out the side window of the topper. She saw the sky had just opened up, and the rain was coming down in torrents. The thought hit her that the timing could not have been better for the truck to come by. Had they come any earlier, she might not have been out of the restaurant yet, and if they had come later, they might not have seen her at all—in the terrible rain. She also realized, had the sky not been just about to dump rain on her, she might not have been willing to get into the truck. Valentine wondered at her willingness to go with these people without a second thought. And they are even going west. *Could I have been any luckier?*

Valentine's thoughts turned to the family in the truck. They appeared to be Hispanic. The man spoke perfect English. However, even though the woman spoke English well, she had a pronounced Spanish accent. Valentine was sure they were not undercover agents for her enemies, trying to obtain whatever information she knew. That was just too farfetched. For this moment, I'm just glad to be out of this torrent.

There was still enough light coming through the windows to write in her notebook. Valentine decided to write everything she could remember about the day. Starting with the young sheriff's deputy, continuing to the two men talking at the Baptist church, and then the four men and all they had said about the missing clergy. She finished her writing as she described the man in black who had begun to remind her of a CIA agent.

By now the light was going and her eyes were getting very tired. She remembered her sleep had been very restless the night before—the bed felt very soft and warm. She put her writing away in her backpack and pulled a quilt over herself. She lay her head down and fell asleep watching the rain hit the window.

Valentine awoke only one time in the night. There was no light coming into the windows at all. The rain was still coming down, but now it was only a steady rain, not a torrent as before. The truck was still moving along, so she lay her head back down without fear or worries. Soon she fell into a very deep sleep.

8

Someone to Watch over Me

The sun was shining in Valentine's eyes when she woke again. She looked around trying to remember where she was. She realized each time she woke she had to readjust her mind. She wondered if that was partly due to having a concussion or just a normal phenomenon of always waking somewhere new. Looking around her, she saw boxes and what appeared to be camping equipment. She turned her eyes upward and saw she was in a truck with a topper over it. She heard a sound to her left. Standing at the window of the topper was a boy, about six years old. The boy had a smile as bright as the sun.

Shyly, he said, "Mama wants to know if you would like to share breakfast with us."

Now she remembered where she was. She remembered the rain storm, the old rusty truck that had stopped to pick her up, and the complete weariness that had caused her to sleep like a baby all night.

The boy was saying something else. Valentine replied, "I'm sorry. What did you say?"

The young boy replied, "I said, Mama says we'll wait for you if you need to go wash up."

"That's the best offer I have had all week," Valentine said as she smiled at the boy.

He opened the tailgate and helped her out. He then pointed to the bathrooms of an interstate rest stop. She lifted her backpack and headed in the direction the boy had pointed.

In the bathroom she washed her face and cleaned off the dark coloring from her eyebrows. She brushed her hair and braided it in two long braids, and tied the bandanna around her head like a headband. She changed her flannel shirt into a lighter blouse—helping her feel more feminine.

When Valentine came out of the bathroom, she felt like a new woman. She walked to the picnic table where the family was sitting waiting for her. Smiling at everyone she said, "Hello. Thank you for inviting me to eat with you. I'm so hungry I think I could eat a hippopotamus!"

The little boy laughed and said, "I thought it was a horse."

The mother said, "That's enough, Manny. It's not polite to contradict your elders."

The man spoke, "We're glad to share our simple fare with you. My name is Manuel Sanchez. This is my lovely wife, Maria, and our three sons: Samuel, Juan, and this little guy is Manny, short for Manuel. Please have a seat."

She smiled at each one at the table saying, "My name is Valentine."

She sat down and pulled out the bag of cookies she had left over asking, "I have some homemade cookies. Can I contribute some cookies to the breakfast?"

Little Manny's eyes became very big, "Oh yes, we love cookies!" Everyone laughed.

Manuel said, "We always read a verse or two before we eat, if that's okay with you, Valentine?"

"Well, sure, please go right ahead. That sounds very nice."

They were nice people—a little different, but nice, Valentine thought as she settled down to listen.

Manuel brought out a very old black book and turned to a place already marked. He began to read.

"The Lord is my shepherd; I shall not want. He maketh me to lie down in green pastures. He leadeth me beside the still waters."

Valentine listened carefully as he read. A thought went through her mind. *If I didn't know better, I would think he was reading about my life over the past few days.*

"He restoreth my soul. He leadeth me in the paths of righteousness for His name's sake. Yea though I walk through the valley of the shadow of death, I will fear no evil: for Thou art with me."

That's just how Valentine felt; she felt hidden with no fear when the sheriff's deputy was looking for her.

"Thy rod and Thy staff they comfort me. Thou preparest a table before me in the presence of mine enemies. Thou anointest my head with oil; my cup runneth over. Surely goodness and mercy shall follow me all the days of my life, and I will dwell in the house of the Lord forever."

What a beautiful reading, Valentine thought as she watched the family members bowed their heads and closed their eyes. Manuel began to speak again.

"Thank you, Father, for our safe trip through the night and the storm. Thank you also for this food you're sharing with us. Guide us to a resting place tonight, and last but not least, thank you for our new friend, Valentine, Amen."

Manny piped up and added, "Thank you for our cookies! Amen!" Manuel and Maria smiled indulgently at their youngest son.

Maria looked at Valentine and said, "Yes, thank you."

"You're most welcome. I was glad I could share."

Valentine turned her head to Manuel and said, "That was a beautiful reading. Was it from a book of poems? I've never heard it before."

Manuel looked down at the black book and then up at Valentine, "Well, the part I just read is a like a poem, but this is not a book of poems. This is the Holy Bible. Have you never read from the Bible before?"

Valentine pondered the question, "Well, I'm not sure. To tell the truth, I have had some memory troubles lately. But I don't remember hearing anything like that. I have heard the Bible spoken of not long ago. It is thought to be very good reading to help strengthen your mind. Do you feel it helps your mind, Manuel?"

Manuel smiled and said, "I've never thought of it that way. I guess it is good for your mind, but the reason I read it is to become better acquainted with the author of the book. Do you know who wrote this book, Valentine?"

"I am sorry," she answered. "I have no idea."

Maria had been cutting slices of bread and cheese and fruit for breakfast. She looked up at that moment and said, "We believe that God our Father wrote this book. We believe He guides us just like the poem, as you called it, says. We also believe that He led the man in the poem."

Valentine thought for a minute and said, "As I listened to you read, I thought of the past few days. Some of the things you read were just like some things that happened to me. You will probably think I am crazy, but I have had the feeling, over the past few days, that someone or something has been helping me find my way..." Valentine paused, realizing some things she could not speak of. Picking her words carefully she said, "I thought at first I was going crazy, because every time I needed something I would find just what I needed. Have you ever heard of something like that?"

The family looked at each other and smiled. Manuel said, "We believe God, whom we have spoken of, is the One who helps people in need. It seems to me it's very possible He is helping you too. Maybe we could talk more about these things as we travel west."

While everyone ate, Valentine thought about the invitation. When she finished, she said, "I need to tell you that someone is after me. I have done nothing wrong, that I know of, but there is someone who wants to stop me. Even though that sounds paranoid, even to me, I don't want to get any of you into my troubles. I was going to tell you right after breakfast that I was thankful for the ride last night, but I should leave you now. I'm not sure why I'm telling you any of this, though, because I have not told anyone what has happened to me. But I feel safe in telling you. Still, I'm fearful for your safety if I continue on with you."

Valentine finished her brief, halting speech. After a slight pause, she added, "Excuse me while I go wash up. Maria, can I wash your dishes for you?"

Maria smiled and handed her the dishes. As Valentine washed the dishes, she wondered why she had said so much to strangers. She did not even know them, and yet they had been so kind to her, and now she might have caused them trouble. She decided she must go her own way, not telling them any more of her situation.

Valentine carried the cleaned and dry dishes back to the table then started to speak but was interrupted by Manuel.

"Valentine, we believe that God has led us to help you. We would like to continue to take you as far as we can, if you well let us."

Valentine's eyes misted over and she could not speak for a minute. Then she said, "Thank you. I really don't know what to say."

Manuel said, "Good, then it's all settled. Valentine, let me show you something we have used in the past, if someone riding with us doesn't want to be found."

Valentine raised her eyebrows and asked, "You travel with people like me often?"

Manuel laughed as he walked with her to the truck, saying, "Well, sometimes we help people get back to Mexico. We don't help people get into the United States from Mexico. We believe a person should do things in a legal way. On the other hand, if someone wants to go home, we'll help them when we can."

Manuel showed Valentine something that pulled down over where she had been sleeping and then moved a box or two over it; when he finished, it looked just like a stack of boxes.

"That's neat," Valentine said, "but I do hope I won't have to use it."

Manuel said, "We would ask you to ride up front with us, but you had better ride back here to be safe. Valentine, will you be okay under these boxes? One of the boys will open the window between the truck cab and topper, and he will move the boxes to give it this look."

"I think that will be just fine. I could catch up on some sleep. I feel I could sleep for three days and still be tired. Do you think I should sleep with this box thing down, just in case?"

Manuel thought a minute and asked, "What do you think? Will someone like the police be pulling people over looking for you?"

"It is possible. I know the sheriff of the county where you picked me up has been looking for me—and so has a nun."

"A nun, did you say a nun?" Manuel asked in surprise.

"Yes, a nun, at least she's dressed as a nun. Does that offend you? Are you Catholic? Will you want to turn me in now?" Valentine started to panic and to look for someplace to run, but Manuel placed a comforting hand on her arm.

"Take it easy. We will not turn you in. We feel God led us to you and you to us. God's ways are far above man's ways. We'll always follow God before man."

"Oh, I'm sorry," Valentine said with relief in her voice. "I got a little scared there for a second. I have had a few days of running from everyone, and I'm feeling a bit strange about trusting anyone. I do trust you and your family. I felt very safe when I got into your truck yesterday. I went off to sleep without a care in the world!" She smiled at her new friend and said, "Are we ready to go then?"

"Yes," Manuel said. "Let's hit the road. As they say in my hometown, we're burning daylight."

They traveled though some pretty fall colors, through farming areas and small towns. Valentine got out her notebook and wrote some things down she had thought of, to check on later. It was not long until she began to feel very sleepy. With the warm sun streaming through the windows and a feeling that she was safe and among friends, she decided to get more rest. She never knew when she might need to walk again, or even run.

Valentine pulled the hiding box down around herself, making sure all her things were hidden under the box then went fast to sleep.

Valentine woke to the truck slowing down. Earlier Manuel had shown Valentine a handle that pulled a small panel open to see what was going on. Now she opened the panel and could see a gas station and a few cars parked outside. She could not see anything that should cause concern.

Little Manny said, "It's okay for you to come out. We're getting gas and going to the bathroom. If you need to go, now is the time."

She slowly moved the box and sat up. Manny opened the back for her and she climbed out and stretched.

"Wow, I slept like a baby," she said as she ruffled Manny's hair. "Let's go in, shall we?"

They were soon back on the road and driving south of Morgantown, West Virginia, on I-79. Valentine sat close to the back window of the truck and talked to Manny and his brothers.

"What a beautiful day. It sure does beat yesterday."

She asked them questions about where they were going and what they would do when they got there. She learned from Samuel that he was a senior in high school, in the small Texas town where they made their home in the winter. Samuel told her he liked math and science best in school. Juan said in the summer they went from farm to farm helping with the harvest; he liked working outside better than going to school.

Maria said, "Yes, but Juan gets very good grades even if he does like being outside best."

"Well, Juan," Valentine said, "perhaps, you could go to school to work in agriculture or forestry. Those areas would keep you outside a lot."

The talk went on to different things about daily life and national and world news. Valentine learned the Sanchez family made this trip every year, but this year things were different. People were less friendly, even almost hostile and suspicious toward them. They had noticed that even people they had visited with on the trip up north this year were acting peculiar.

Valentine asked, "This will sound strange, but have you seen anyone with an eye twitch or blink that seemed unusual to you?"

Samuel answered, "I have, yesterday, before it started to rain. I was talking to a boy my age. He was sitting outside of the gas station where we were gassing up. I asked him about the video game he was playing. I noticed he had a funny look in his eye as he played, kind of glassy like, and he would not talk to me. He acted like I wanted to steal it or something. Then a woman, his mom I guess, called out to him and he blinked his eyes several times. Then he looked up at me and said, 'Oh hi! Did you say something?' Then he showed me his video game. I had to leave right after that and couldn't look at the game he was playing, but it seemed to me he was like two different people."

Samuel turned to Valentine and asked, "Am I crazy or what?"

"No, Samuel, you're not crazy," she answered, "because I saw the very same thing happen to a sheriff. He was very intent while searching the streets. His face was like a stone, no human expressions or kindness at all. Then someone called out his name and he blinked two times—just like the boy you were talking to, Samuel—and he turned into a human being and smiled. He talked with the man who had called his name, and then as he was driving off, I was sure I saw his face change again, but he turned before I got the chance to be positive."

Maria spoke up just then and said, "I've noticed a lot more people don't look up from their tablets and cell phones. They don't talk to anyone at all. They just talk on these gadgets. I won't have one in our home. Manuel considered getting a cell phone once, but we really didn't have the money and I just don't like them. We have done just fine with a home phone for years now, and I don't see any reason to change."

Manuel smiled at Maria and said, "Well, dear, I think you were right. We have done just fine without all those gadgets. If we get into a bind, I can use the oldest cell phone in the world and get help just like that!" He snapped his fingers.

Manny asked, "Hey, Papa, I didn't know we had the oldest cell phone in the world!"

Manuel laughed. "Why, I pray to my Heavenly Father and He sends all the help I would ever need!" Everyone laughed at what Manuel said, except for Valentine. She was not sure what he meant. She sat quietly for a minute and puzzled what the others were laughing at. Then a thought came to her and she said, "You know, when I was in need, I would just ask. I didn't know what else to do. I would ask for something and it always seemed I would get what I needed—not always the way I thought help would come, but I have been safe and not gone hungry. I've kept dry, thanks to you guys, and found places to sleep that have been soft, warm, and pleasant. Is that what you meant, Manuel? Maybe it is good I didn't have a cell phone. Whoever helped me, God or someone else, has surely been faithful and helped me beyond my wildest dreams."

Manuel interrupted speaking urgently. "Valentine, sorry to interrupt, you need to go into the hiding place. Something is going on up ahead. Boys, help Valentine."

There was a fast and efficient scramble. Soon Valentine was in her hiding place. The boys turned around with the window closed between the truck cab and topper; their school books were open and their heads bent over them in study.

Valentine lay still. She listened for any sounds that would tell her what was going on outside the truck. She decided to open the sliding panel just enough to see—she wanted to stay informed on what was happening. *It might not be anything concerning me at all.*

She could see the side of the road and could tell that the truck was slowing down; soon they were at a complete stop. She wished she could see more. However, she needed to stay calm and trust the Sanchezes. *They will protect me if need be.* The truck moved forward again, slowly stopping and starting as they went along. Finally Valentine could see something moving ahead beside the road. It was the back of a black car, a big fancy black car. The car looked just like the car she remembered from Baltimore. She slid the panel shut quickly and quietly. She could feel herself shaking and her breathing quickening. If anyone opened the back window of the topper, they would hear me for sure.

She tried to calm herself then she started remembering the feelings she had when she was in that dark room. Valentine remembered the force of her head striking the chair she had been tied to. The more she remembered, the more she could feel panic rise up inside of her like a tidal wave about to crash over the shore. *I must calm down or I will give myself away and get the Sanchez's in deep trouble.*

The memory of what the Sister had said about the reporter came back to her. "You remember her family and everyone else thinks she is dead. They held a funeral for her last week, the same time they had the funeral for that reporter we found with her— the reporter who we helped have a tragic accident. We found him when they were snooping around together, looking to find our real identities."

Valentine knew they had killed the reporter, and they could hurt or kill these good people if they found her with them. *Oh, why did I not go my own way back at the rest stop?* She was really becoming frightened. She realized she must get a grip on herself—she must calm down. She closed her eyes and tried to think of peaceful things, but nothing was working. *I must get out of this truck and at least save the Sanchez family.*

Suddenly, without warning, Valentine heard the quiet voice of Manuel.

"The Lord is my shepherd; I shall not want..." She began to say those beautiful and calming words over and over to herself. Finally she fell into a peaceful sleep. Valentine dreamed of a green field with a brook running through it. She saw beside the brook an enormous male lion. The lion's mane was a beautiful golden color. His eyes were full of wisdom and intelligence; they were looking intently into her eyes. Resting beside the huge lion was a baby lamb. In the dream, Valentine wondered what it could mean. Everyone knows a lion will kill and eat a lamb in two seconds flat; with no trouble at all. In her dream she felt the peace of the scene flow over her. She had no worries or cares. As the dream faded, she went into a deeper dreamless sleep.

9

The Park

When Valentine woke, the dream was still fresh in her mind. She felt peaceful. In her mind's eye she could still see the lion and the lamb resting together; the brook running beside them. Slowly her mind began to remember why she was inside the hiding box. She remembered seeing a big black car that looked very much like the Sister's. She realized she was not scared now or feeling any kind of panic at all. She listened and could tell the truck was moving at a normal speed—only the sound of the tires on the pavement could be heard. No angry shouts or ugly words she would have heard if the Sister had found her. *We are all safe and moving away from danger,* she thought as she breathed a sigh of relief.

Valentine opened the sliding panel and looked out. She could see the sun was on her side of the truck. Since they were heading south, it must be afternoon. She had slept for several hours even with the threat of the Sister all around her. She remembered the words she had been repeating before she fell into that peaceful, much needed sleep. The poem that she had heard Manuel reading: "The Lord is my shepherd; I shall not want. He maketh me to lie down in green pastures. He leadeth me besides the still waters."

Then her thoughts returned to the dream about the lion and the lamb. It had been a beautiful dream, almost like the reading from breakfast. Valentine wondered about the things Manuel had said about praying to his Heavenly Father. She wondered if his Heavenly Father and her guardian could be one and the same.

But she did not have long to ponder because just then the truck began slowing to a stop. She heard the window being opened and the boxes being pulled off her hiding place.

Samuel quietly said, "You can come out now—if you're awake, that is."

Valentine slowly lifted the box covering her, sat up, and stretched her arms over her head. "I can't believe it," Valentine said through the open window. "I fell asleep. I got so scared that I might get you guys in trouble I was thinking of getting out the back and making a run for it. Then I heard Manuel's voice repeating those words that he read this morning. I don't know how, but I heard them as clearly as when he read them earlier. When he finished saying them, I started saying them to myself, and the next thing I knew I was waking up to the sound of the wheels on the pavement. Thank you for reading that, Manuel. It really helped me. How did you know I was getting so scared?"

Manuel looked over his shoulder at Valentine, with a quizzical smile on his face, "I didn't read anything to you after you got into the hiding box. I didn't know you were scared, but I know who did know."

"Are you saying that your God said those words to me, to help me be calm? I wish I knew how to believe that. I don't know what to believe. However, I do know that whoever or whatever helped me, the words worked because I was just about to bolt. By the way, what was that all about back there? I never did see anything except a black car parked on the side of the road."

Manuel answered, "If you can wait for just a little while, we're about to stop for the night, and we can talk better around a campfire. Is that okay with you?"

Valentine nodded. "I think that's a wonderful idea. Are we really going to camp with a campfire and everything?"

Manny asked, "Do you like roasting marshmallows over the campfire? That's my favorite thing to do!"

Valentine smiled, "I'm not sure, but I would love to try. Maybe you will show me how?"

They pulled into a state park a couple of hours before dark. They choose their campsite near a nice-size creek. Manuel and the two older boys set up the tent while Maria got food out to cook. Manny and Valentine looked for sticks to start the fire. Manny told her it was his job to find small dry sticks to get the fire going nicely. The big boys would get the larger supply of wood that would keep the fire burning until they all went to bed. Valentine was impressed with how the family worked so well together. Manuel, Samuel, and Juan laughed and joked while they worked. Now and then Manuel would point out things in nature. There was a peaceful atmosphere all around the camp that helped Valentine relax and forget, for a while, the fears and worries she had been carrying for the past week.

All the beds were made up before supper. Manuel, Maria, and Manny slept in the tent while the big boys always slept in the truck.

When Samuel and Juan wanted to give up their beds to Valentine, she said, "Thank you, guys. That's very thoughtful, but I really love sleeping out in the open. I love the night air all around me, the cool breeze on my face, listening to the night sounds."

So the boys got together and made her a small tent out of a tarp with the front open and the other three sides enclosed. They shared their extra blankets with her, cutting small evergreen boughs to place under the blankets. They were very proud of their handiwork. When Valentine saw what they had done for her, she was very impressed.

"Samuel, Juan, this is so thoughtful of you. I feel like a queen. Thank you so much!" she told them as she gave them each a quick hug.

After the tent was up, beds made, and the wood gathered, all the guys went to the creek with fishing poles to try their luck at fish for supper. Valentine found her bags and brought out several parsnips. She carried them over to Maria and asked if they could be used for supper. Maria turned from the fire. Spying the parsnip, she let out a squeal of delight.

"Oh, Valentine, how wonderful. We love fresh parsnips. Thank you. Wherever did you get them?"

Valentine explained about finding them in the woods when she was hungry. She told Maria, "Just when I was wishing for a book on edible foods in the wilds, I got a flash of a page in a book that had a picture of these plants. I dug them up and let them dry in the sun. I have been eating them ever since."

Maria took them, peeled them, and cut them up along with an onion. She said, "I'll just set these aside until we're ready to cook them—until we see if we'll be having fish as well."

The two ladies could hear the guys down at the creek laughing, then all would be quiet for a while. After a time there was an outburst of, "You got a bite, Dad, reel him in!" and, "Boy, he's a beauty!"

Maria smiled and said, "I think we'll be having fish and parsnips for supper. I'll make some cornbread too." Valentine wondered how to bake cornbread out here in the woods. However, she kept quiet and watched, and helped when she could. Valentine continued to watch as Maria cooked the cornbread like hotcakes and placed them in a warming pan beside the fire. It was not long until Manuel and the boys returned with enough fish for supper and breakfast.

The camp was filled with the wonderful smells of sizzling fried fish, parsnips, and onions cooking. Valentine did not think she had ever smelled anything as good as that supper prepared right in the woods. She thought of how she found this wonderful family. She thanked her lucky stars, or whomever, for bringing her here to be a part of this beautiful scene.

After supper, everyone helped to clean the dishes. When all was cleaned and put away, they sat by the fire. Manuel began to read from the Bible.

"Unto thee, Oh Lord, do I lift up my soul. O my God, I trust in thee: let me not be ashamed. Let not mine enemies triumph over me, Psalms 25:1."

Then Manuel quietly, but with surety, spoke again to the one they called Father God. He thanked his Father for safety, good food, and a wonderful place to spend the Sabbath. He spoke of the scare they all had that day at the roadblock and thanked Him for the guardian angels He had sent to keep them safe. He thanked God for keeping Valentine hidden in the palm of His hand while all around her there was an enemy looking to find her. While Manuel spoke, Valentine listened with an open mind and heart. She realized that whatever this prayer thing was, it sure helped her feel peaceful.

When Manuel finished the prayer, the family sang a song about the day dying in the west and something about heaven touching the earth with rest. The song was so beautiful and the family harmonized so well Valentine could have listened all night. For a time, after they had finished singing, no one spoke. Everyone sat quietly for a few minutes. The only interruptions being the night sounds and the crackle of the fire.

After a bit, Manny got out marshmallows for everyone, along with the sticks he had gathered before supper. For the next few minutes, each camper carefully cooked his or her own marshmallow. As they were cooking their little sweet treats, talk around the fire resumed. Soon it turned to the afternoon and what had happened after Valentine went into hiding. Manuel told how he had seen something that at first looked like a wreck, but soon he saw it was a traffic stop with both state police and a sheriff's vehicle pulled to the side of the road. That was when he had advised her to climb into the hiding box until they saw what was going on.

Each of the family took turns telling what each had seen. Maria told about seeing the big black car pulled over behind the state trooper's car. She thought whoever was in that car was in trouble, but then she saw a priest get out of the car. Every so often the sheriff would go over and talk to the priest, who in turn would talk to someone inside the car. The windows were tinted very dark and she did not see who was inside the car; whoever it was, they had the appearance of being someone important. Manny told how he had done just what his dad told him to do; he sat and read his favorite Dr. Seuss book so he would not cause any trouble. He said he didn't want Valentine to have to go away.

He looked up shyly at her, smiling his big beautiful smile. She looked down at the little boy. For just a second she wondered if she had a little boy or girl somewhere who was missing her. Then she told herself to stop thinking like that. Time would tell about her own family. At the moment there was a sweet boy who wanted to be her friend. She needed to be content with what she had.

Valentine took Manny's hand and said, "Thank you, Manny. You were a very big help, and very brave."

There was a pause in the talk for a little while until Samuel spoke up, "I think the person in the car was a woman. I saw the very top of a head when the window came down farther. It was quickly rolled back up. Still it was down long enough to see her eyes and a nun's headwear. The eyes were very hard and blue."

When Samuel finished talking, Juan spoke in his quiet voice.

"I thought the state trooper was nice, but I didn't like the sheriff's face. It was very hard and mean-looking. He looked mean enough to shoot his own mother if he had to."

Manuel listened to his boys and then spoke again.

"It took a long time for them to get to our truck. I watched as they checked each vehicle carefully. When we finally got to the front of the line, the state trooper came to my window asking a lot of questions—where we were going and what we were doing, things like that. While he was talking with me, the sheriff walked around looking into each window. I heard the state trooper call the sheriff by the name of Joe. He seemed to be the head of the search, under the person in the car that is. Then I was asked to get out and open the topper and tailgate. But when I got there and started to unlock the topper window, the state trooper said, 'Don't bother to unlock the window. I can see there is no sick woman in the back.' I asked the trooper who they were looking for. He said some woman escaped from the state psychiatric hospital. There was a large multi-statewide manhunt for this woman. He said they wanted to find her before she hurt herself or someone else. He then gave me a quick description of the missing woman. I'll have to say, Valentine, you're the spitting image of her."

No one spoke for a few seconds. Then Manuel smiled and said, "You're the sanest-looking crazy person I have ever seen!"

Everyone looked at each other, the tension was broken, they all burst out laughing until tears came rolling out of their eyes and down their cheeks. No one could talk for a while.

When things calmed down a bit, Valentine said, "The person they are looking for is me. You know that, don't you, Manuel? I want to tell you everything, but I need to think about this, make sure I don't say something that could later get you in trouble for helping me. Sometimes the less you know the safer you are."

A quiet came over everyone. They all sat and looked at the dying embers of the fire until Maria said, "I think someone is falling asleep."

Sitting beside Valentine, with his head resting on her arm, was little Manny. His eyes closed with a sweet smile on his face, as if he was dreaming of a big marshmallow.

Manuel turned to Valentine as he got up saying, "We won't be traveling tomorrow, so if you would like to sleep in, feel free." Then he stooped, picked up the little boy, and headed toward the tent, with Juan going to help open the zippered door. After that, everyone quietly said good night, going to their places to sleep.

The night was peaceful. As Valentine lay on her comfortable and sweet-smelling bed, she thought of everything that had been said. She figured she would never get to sleep with all the fearful thoughts of the Sister going through her head. Then she realized she didn't feel any fear for the future. Someone—she was still not sure who—but someone was taking care of her. *And I have a job to do, to help people wherever I go to stay free from these evil ones who want to take control of everyone's minds.* She tried to remember what she had overheard so far about the plan and how it worked, but the more she tried to think the sleepier she became. Soon Valentine's eyes closed for the last time that night—the sweet sounds of the forest lulled her into a deep sleep.

The next morning showed signs of being a beautiful Indian summer day. At breakfast, Manuel told Valentine they stopped here every trip because the park was their family's favorite camping place. They liked it because of the creek and the nice hiking trails.

Valentine asked, "Is that why you won't be traveling today? You want to hike?"

Maria answered her question, "No, today is the day the Bible asks us to rest and spend time with our Heavenly Father and with our families. We believe when God created the world He rested on the final day of creation, so on the seventh day of each week, we stop what we're doing and honor our Father, our Creator, and also to commemorate the life of Jesus. I wish we had a Bible to give you, but maybe you will find one soon."

Valentine thought of the little black book she had bought. "I bought a book the day before you picked me up and it reminds me of your Bible. Let me get it and show you. Maybe you can tell me what you think of it."

Valentine got up and went to her little tent to get her book out of the backpack. She brought it back to the table and gave it to Maria.

As soon as Maria saw the name, she smiled and handed it to Manuel. She said, "Valentine, you've bought a book that is a small part of the Bible. Your book is found in what we call the New Testament."

"Wow," Valentine said. "How strange is that? I bought two books that day but couldn't get into reading Shakespeare's works, so I left it at a truck stop. I didn't need any more weight to carry and thought maybe someone else would like it."

Samuel spoke up just then, "I'm glad you got rid of it. I sure don't want to have to listen to that old stuff again. We had to read Shakespeare last year in school!"

Manuel chuckled and turned to Samuel. "You did very well in that class. As I recall, something about studying with a pretty girl helped."

Manuel handed the book back to Maria, saying, "This is a very good book to start on. Maybe you don't need anything else, for now. Read the inscription in the front, Maria, it's very beautiful."

Maria opened the front page and read aloud, "To my beautiful daughter, Valentine, on her birthday, January 18, 1941, Love, Mother."

Tears came to Maria's eyes as she said, "I can't believe you just bought this book and it has your name in it written many years ago. That's amazing!"

Valentine said, "That's exactly how I feel each time I read it, like someone was trying to tell me I am loved. Sounds very crazy, I know."

The boys were getting antsy about hiking, so all talk was stopped as the camp was cleaned and all food items were put away in the very back of the truck. Manuel explained to Valentine that they had been robbed before, so now they took precautions.

"You've been robbed! Who would do a thing like that way out here in the woods?"

The whole family spoke in unison, "Raccoons!"

They had a wonderful day hiking and looking at all the fall colors. Valentine found some wild parsnips and showed the family. No one really wanted to dig parsnips or mar the beauty of the area, so they just looked and went on. They had a picnic lunch at a waterfall. The falls was near the headwaters of the creek they were camping alongside.

When they returned to the camp, it was late in the afternoon; the sun would be setting soon. Each of the family had a job to do, so they started as soon as they got into camp. Valentine decided to stick with Manny. The two of them picked up as many dry sticks as they could find and carried them to Manuel, who was starting the fire for supper. Soon the two older boys came into camp with armloads of bigger wood they started chopping into fire-size pieces for the night. Maria began preparing for supper but didn't start cooking yet.

When all had finished their jobs, they found seats at the fire and Manuel started the singing again. This time they sang several songs, songs Valentine did not know. However, they were as beautiful as the one they sang the night before. The words of one song kept going through her head, about someone named Jesus. She wondered who Jesus was. The words of the song were beautiful and haunting.

> O soul, are you weary and troubled?
> No light in the darkness you see?
> Turn your eyes upon Jesus.

Something, something, something, she couldn't remember all the first part, but the last part had really stuck in her mind:

> Look full in His wonderful face
> And the things of earth will grow strangely dim
> In the light of His glory and grace.

When the song was over, Manuel opened his Bible and began to read. This time Valentine could not concentrate. She kept hearing those words, "O soul are you weary and troubled, something, something, something, turn your eyes upon Jesus."

When reading and prayer time were over, the sun had set. Maria called for all hands to help with cooking. They had fish again, but this time they had somehow attached the fish to a stick—one for each of them—so they got to cook their own supper. There was lots of fun and laughter throughout the making and eating of supper; afterward came the marshmallows to cook. Valentine told them she could not eat another bite, so Manny was happy to help her by eating all of her marshmallows for her.

They talked and told stories around the fire. Manuel told of his family, growing up on a Texas ranch, stories of good times and bad. He talked about his grandfather, his mama's father, of how he was half Indian. Manuel told how he had sat around a fire just like this and heard stories of great Indian warriors. "The way Granddad weaved his stories," Manuel said, "I could almost see the herds of buffalo and the strong Indian hunters, quietly sneaking up on them for their winter food and warm buffalo hides."

Juan asked Valentine about her own childhood. She replied hesitantly, "Well, Juan, that's part of my problem. I can't remember my childhood."

There was an uneasy silence for a moment, then Maria spoke in her quiet and soothing voice.

"That's all right, Valentine, we understand. You need say nothing more. Juan didn't mean to pry."

Valentine looked around the campfire at all of them, "Juan, you were not prying at all. Please don't worry. It's not anything like that. You've all been so good to me, and I would like to tell you my story, but not tonight. I am going to miss you when we part."

"But, Valentine," little Manny said, "you can come live with us. We would love you always."

There were tears in his eyes when he finished. Valentine reached over and pulled the little boy closer to her, to give him a big hug.

"Manny, I would like nothing better than to travel with you to Texas. However, I must keep heading west. I don't know why. Nevertheless, I have felt very strongly there is a reason for me to go west. But don't be sad, Manny. I will be with you awhile yet. Now, Maria, I have a very important question that has been puzzling me since I met all of you. Why is it that all of you have Spanish names except Samuel? Samuel is not a Spanish name, is it?

Maria smiled and looked lovingly at Samuel as she spoke, "When Manuel and I married, we wanted ten children, but we knew that was too many for our economic times. So we settled for at least four. After we'd been married five years, I still had not been able to get pregnant. We went to one doctor after another with no luck. Then Manuel and I started studying the Bible with a young couple in our neighborhood. We learned to love God—not to just go to church each week—to really love Him. When we started to study the Bible, we learned so much that our church had not taught. Now we're in a church we love. More importantly, we're with a God we love. When we learned we could talk to God about anything, we started to pray about having a baby. One day, as I was reading in the Bible, the Old Testament, I read the story about a woman named Hannah who had been praying for a baby, just as I had. After years of not having any children, she went to the temple praying and crying. A priest named Eli spoke to her and said God had heard her prayer. Then Hannah had a son. She named him Samuel, meaning, 'because I have asked him of the Lord.' So I prayed the prayer that Hannah prayed. And when we had a son, I named him Samuel, just as Hannah did. That's not the end of Hannah's story or mine, but it's late, and I have only time to say that my story has three beautiful sons. God was wonderfully faithful to us."

Maria smiled at her three young sons, adding, "Let's sing one song before we go to sleep. Valentine, do you have a favorite song?"

She thought about it, answering, "The only songs I know are the ones I have heard you guys sing. The song that has been going through my mind is the one about turning your eyes. How did that one go?"

Through the quiet of the night, the words of the song floated out:

O soul, are you weary and troubled?
No light in the darkness you see?
There's light for a look at the Savior, and life more
abundant and free.
Turn your eyes upon Jesus,
Look full in His wonderful face,
And the things of earth will grow strangely dim
In the light of His glory and grace.

They watched in quiet peacefulness until the fire was almost out then everyone said good night. Tomorrow they needed to be up early to break camp and get back on the road.

As Valentine was drifting off to sleep, she thought about how beautiful that song was. But then she realized she still needed to ask, who is Jesus?

10

The Phone Call

On the other side of the world from where Valentine slept peacefully in the woods, in a well-furnished office, deep within the walls of the Vatican, a phone rang. The cardinal who answered the call was one of the pope's closest advisers. He had ties to the Jesuits, an old and much respected order of the Catholic Church. He was also very handsome. Women often said that even with his priestly robes and collar on, he was an extremely attractive, even sexy man. Men in high places around the world respected and listened to him when he gave them his advice.

The man answered the call on the first ring, knowing ahead of time who the caller was. The man had made arrangements months before for this call, on this day, for one purpose only. It was time. Time to start "The Plan."

"Hello, Sonny. Yes, this is the Father. Remember, before we continue, code names only. The walls and even the phones have ears. This phone cannot be tapped. However, one never knows what to expect these days. Caution is our first line of defense."

"Good day to you, my friend," said the voice on the other end of the line. A voice with an accent most people would have had a hard time placing. The accent spoke of a well-educated man; in the West most likely, but with an underlying Middle-Eastern flair. "Yes, I most firmly agree. All care should be taken at this late date, to lose none of the element of surprise. Also, all areas of this plan should be guarded with our lives. Well, my friend, it has been a long time since we were able to talk. How goes everything in your life?"

The man in the Vatican—code name, the Father—cleared his throat, "I am assuming you are talking about my second-in-command? She is fine. I just finished talking to her an hour ago. She has been keeping me up-to-date over these past few days on our situation in Baltimore. You are aware, are you not, of the problems we were having with that reporter and an emergency room nurse?"

"Yes," Sonny stated, "my contacts in Baltimore have been sending me daily reports. I understand the reporter is no longer a problem. Plus the nurse has been injured and weakened, hiding someplace in the city."

"That is correct," replied the Father. "The reporter had a very bad auto accident. They were also able to make it look like the nurse died in the crash. We kept the nurse alive for more than a month. We were encouraging her to remember what she knows about us and our plan. She has been a very hard nut to crack. We know the reporter did not know very much. However, the nurse was very well informed. We have yet to find out what she knew and who else, if anyone had the same information. There has been some kind of a resistance for about a year now, but we have been unable get to the bottom of it. We will, though, mark my words. We will!"

The Father then asked, "How is your family? Are your wife and children well?"

"Yes, yes, all is well. Thank you for asking. I'll be glad when everything is completed, and we can all step out into our new roles. I'll be able to tell my beloved wife what all the secrecy has been about. She is very wise and understanding. She knows that when the time is right, I will tell her everything."

There was a pause in the conversation, then the Father spoke.

"This has been a long journey we have traveled together. Do you remember the little café where we first met in Greece?"

"Yes, as I recall, the date was September the eleventh, 2001. The reason the three of us were there in the first place was that our airplanes were all grounded because of the terrorist attacks in the United States. None of us knew quite what to do with ourselves."

The Father replied, "That day, when the Twin Towers went crashing down in smoke and dust was a major turning point of my life. So you do realize if it had not been for that horrendous day in 2001, none of this plan could have had a chance?"

"Yes, I know," Sonny replied. "It is almost as if we were guided there to meet. I know my plans called for me to be on the other side of the world from that little café in Greece. However, someone changed the meeting place at the last moment, for no reason that I could ever learn. I found myself wandering the streets looking for a café, to get a good cup of espresso. I have been thinking a lot about that experience, for the past few months. Why were the three of us there? Was there someone else guiding us? I'm not talking about a human being because I know no other human could have gotten us to that place in that time—not only the actual place, but a place where our minds were ready to accept each other's ideas and help. That could not have happened even a few months before the attacks of September the eleventh, for me anyway. I presume not for you either. I do believe in Allah, even though I know you continue to tell me you have lost all belief in the God of your Catholic Church. I feel sometimes as if we were being led by someone, although I'm not sure who."

The Father interrupted, "We were being led all right. Nevertheless, I have to disagree on the source. We were being led by our own selves, the three of us—our own minds, ambitions, and desires to see a change in the control of the world, and to step into our rightful places to govern the masses."

"Only your part of the world, remember," Sonny interrupted in turn. "My people will be the reigning rule in the Muslim world, and we will rid all our lands of the infidels, present company not included of course. You know I don't hold with all the ideals of my leaders either. Still, I will rule my people just as you will rule yours, my friend."

The conversation then turned to the Ghost, the third and last of their godhead, as the Father jokingly called the trio.

"So, what have you heard from the Ghost?" asked Sonny. "You know, I have to keep contact with him to a minimum."

The Father answered, "I have not heard from him in a few weeks. However, I am expecting his call soon. He has assured me his teams are ready and standing by for the start of 'The Plan' in his country. He also told me Einstein has the last test group's results, with incredibly encouraging findings. Ninety-five percent of the treated people can be completely controlled. The remaining five percent are completely the opposite matter. We will have to come up with a plan on how to deal with those five percent, when the time comes."

"But ninety-five percent is great news!" Sonny exclaimed. "The last I had heard the results were only sixty percent, tops. What has changed?"

"I cannot tell you the details over the phone. However, you will be getting a complete report in a few days. I sent your copy by the usual method. So be watching for a courier with the weather report. We will not start the second phase until a month after the plan is showing signs of working well on the first group. Then we will start on the masses.

"Right now we are working on the clergy of all churches. As you know we already have our people replacing the clergy who were considered uncontrollable. We have tagged them, 'Five Percenters.' We are sending most of these people to the mission fields. We can do more testing with the treatment on them, without their families or churches getting in the way. Some of the most hardheaded we are sending to the Ebola-stricken areas of Africa," the Father chuckled a most disturbing sound, sending a chill down Sonny's spine.

"But how are you getting them to go peacefully," Sonny asked?

"We just help them to see that it would be better on their families if they cooperated with us. This method works every time! Most of them are old, and they have read their Bibles so much that nothing can gain control of their minds. We have also started to treat some top people, in places of authority, like the police and sheriffs' departments so they can help the clergy when they need it. We are trying out the videos on some youth. We have stayed away from using the plan on children and teens because we did not know what the plan would do to them. We did not want upset parents trying to find out why their little Johnny's or Jane's brains are fried. Too much investigation at the wrong times could be disastrous. You remember the first few people we tried the plan on? Those indigents in Baltimore whom no one would miss. Oh my! That was a disaster. But they did help us get the kinks out. Now the plan is working without a hitch! Einstein is proposing complete control by this time next year. That is when the presidential election, in the United States, is to be held. We will plan our own takeovers at the same time. Do you foresee any problems in that time frame, Sonny?"

Sonny thought for a minute, "No, no foreseeable problems anyway."

The Father's tone became very serious. "On a final note, I need you to put together a small team to work with my men to re-apprehend Father Patrick. We have one reliable lead. Your men will be briefed when they get here. Can you have a team ready in five days?"

Sonny answered promptly, "I have a team ready now."

"Very good, have them rendezvous with my team, at the café, in five day, at twenty-one hours."

"Well, that is all I have to discuss, unless you have more. Let us set up a time for our next phone call."

With the arrangements made and a promise to report any new problems to each other, the two said farewell.

11

Two Stories

Valentine awoke to the sound of a fire crackling and the smell of smoke floating in the early morning breeze. She felt safe and warm in her small makeshift tent. She heard a twig snap near her. When she looked, there was the smiling face of Manny peering in at her. Her face broke into a huge smile. How could she not respond to a smile like Manny's?

"Good morning, Valentine. I didn't wake you, did I? Mama said not to wake you if you were sleeping."

"No, my sweet young man, you didn't wake me. The smells of cooking and the sounds of the fire woke me. However, that was a really nice way to wake up. Was there something your mama needed me to do?"

"Well, not really, it's just that we'll be leaving right after breakfast. You'll need to be packed, that's all."

"If you're sure your mama doesn't need me, I'll get right up and start packing."

"Can I help you, Valentine?"

"That would be wonderful, then I can help you with any chores you have. Is that a deal, Manny?" Valentine watched his eager face as he nodded his head. "Just let me go take a trip to the restroom and I'll be right back."

By the time she got back, Manny had folded all the blankets and was starting to untie the ropes holding the tarp tent. They worked together smoothly. Soon they had everything ready to be stowed away in the truck.

The group started breakfast with a prayer and a reading. This time Manuel asked if one of the boys would like to pray.

It was Juan who quietly said, "I would like to pray, Papa." Juan prayed a beautiful prayer of thankfulness for the blessings that God had bestowed on his family, for food and a Sabbath's day rest, and most of all for a family who loves each other. He thanked God for a beautiful Sunday to be traveling and asked for a safe journey. "And thank you, God, for our new friend, Valentine. Please keep her safe for the journey she must make and send your guardian angels to guide her and protect her, Amen."

"Thank you, Juan. It's funny I have been calling 'the someone' who has been taking care of me 'my guardian,' and you've asked your God to send His guardian angels to protect me. I guess it's just a coincidence."

The others at the table smiled but did not say anything; they just kept on eating. However, Valentine could tell they did not think it was a coincidence at all.

The camp was checked twice to make sure nothing was left, and that the fire was completely out, before they all climbed into the truck and drove away.

It was decided, that even though they would like Valentine to sit up front in the cab, it would be safer for her to ride in the back, where she could quickly get into the hiding box if there were any signs of trouble.

They were heading west on I-64. Lexington Kentucky was the next big city they would be passing through. After looking out the window for a while, Valentine decided to read from her little black book. She got it out of the backpack, opening it again at the beginning. She soon laid the book aside. Looking out the window, she thought about all the things she had learned from the Sanchezes. She wrote questions in her notebook that she would like to ask—the first one being, who was Jesus?

While Valentine had her notebook out, she decided it was time to get back to her mission. She realized she had, had a wonderful, restful pause in her journey, but now it was time to get to work. She needed to put together some of the facts she had learned. She began by rereading the entire notebook. She then turned back to the phone call she had overheard. The call had been between the Sister and someone of authority. She carefully looked for new ideas she might have missed before. Then she went back through and underlined anything that was a clue or needed an answer to.

When she had finished reading her notes all the way through, she realized again how important her self-imposed mission was. Even if Valentine could not stop the people with this plan, she could warn others; the ones who would listen anyway. She could tell them to read more, to strengthen their minds, to withstand the treatment. Then she reread the part about what the four men at the truck stop had said. Valentine again underlined the important parts that seemed to have a bearing on her mission. It might help to make an outline that would pull the clues together, she thought.

1. There were two main people in the plan: the Sister and whomever she had been talking to on the phone.

2. Other people were somehow involved: a person named Einstein, Sheriff Joe with the changing face, Father Mancini, and the Baptist pastor.

3. There was something strange going on with the video games.

Valentine's hand was getting tired, and her mind was swirling with all the facts that did not fit. She put down her pen and closed her eyes. However, her brain would not stop going at full speed. The thought of churches being involved was crazy. Wouldn't church people be the very ones protected from the plan, she wondered? People who went to church would be the ones who read the Bible the most, right? Manuel and Maria believed that reading their Bible brought them closer to God. Could that be why people who read their Bibles could withstand the plan, because God kept them safe?

That was a totally new idea to Valentine. Not only could a brain be stronger from just reading, because even people that read only the classics were somewhat protected from the plan, but people that read the Bible could not be controlled at all. Maybe there was something more to the Bible than just words.

Just as she was drifting off to sleep, she heard the window open.

Samuel said, "We're about to stop at a rest stop. You can get out and stretch or whatever else you might need to do."

Valentine sat up, "Thank you, Samuel. That sounds good."

She put her boots back on and smoothed her hair. She could feel the truck slowing down as it headed up the off ramp. Everyone got out. Grabbing her bag, Valentine walked into the bathroom with Maria. They were both washing their hands when Manny called quietly through the door to his mom. Maria went to the door and came back quickly.

"Valentine, two state police cars and one sheriff's car have just pulled into the parking lot. They are parked right next to the truck. You had better not come out yet."

Valentine thought for a minute, "Marie, go tell Manuel that I'll be out in ten minutes, then come back in and walk out with me."

Maria started to protest, but Valentine smiled and said, "Trust me."

While Maria went out to talk to Manuel, Valentine went into the biggest stall and took out the Lucy Pope outfit. "It is time for a change," she whispered to the empty restroom.

When Maria returned, she called out, "Valentine, are you ready?" However, she could not find Valentine anywhere. There was only one stall in use—a mother with a small child. The only other person in the restroom was an old woman, standing at the sink, washing her hands. Maria glanced at the old woman. She was about to go look for Valentine outside, when the old lady turned and looked at her through thick glasses.

"Honey, could you walk me back to the truck? I'm feeling a little weak."

Maria took another longer look at the woman, just as Valentine slipped her glasses down on her nose and winked. Maria smiled and winked back as she shook her head slightly in wonder. Maria said, "Well, yes, I can help you. Please take my arm. I would love to help you walk to the truck, Granny."

"Oh, thank you, dear, you're the sweetest granddaughter."

They took their time walking out to the truck. Leisurely walking right in front of the three police cars. Valentine trembled a little as she walked past them.

Maria smiled at Valentine and gave her arm a little squeeze. In a loud voice she said, "It is okay, Granny, we're almost to the truck, then you can rest."

"Thank you, dearie, you're such a great comfort in my old age." She gave Maria's arm a squeeze back. By this time they were approaching the truck.

Maria said, "Here is Granny, all ready to finish the trip. Shall we go?"

Manuel started to protest, but Maria stopped him with a look. The kind of look married people have that says, I'll tell you later.

Maria continued aloud, "Let's get in, boys. Make room for me in the backseat. Granny is feeling a little queasy from riding too much in the back. Everyone climbed in, without saying another word, they did as Maria asked them.

Manuel backed up the truck and started to pull away. When he looked in his rearview mirror, he saw a long black car coming off the interstate, pulling into the very parking place they had just vacated. A priest got out. He opened the back door for a woman dressed in an ankle-length black habit. Manuel felt a chill run down his back. As he took his last glance back, he saw the police and the sheriff gathering around her like she had some kind of strange control over them. Something in this picture isn't right, Manuel thought. Then the truck rounded a curve, heading onto the interstate.

Manuel turned to the old lady in the front seat saying, "My name is Manuel. It's nice to meet you, ma'am."

He then glanced at his wife and asked, "Okay, what's going on? Where is Valentine? Are we picking her up down the road somewhere?"

The old lady chuckled and then pulled her glasses down away from her eyes and said, "I'm right here. Hi boys, hi Manuel."

All four of the guys' mouths fell open. They just stared at her. They could not comprehend Valentine's voice coming out of the old lady's mouth. Everyone in the truck started talking at once. For a few minutes there was nothing but chaos in the truck. Finally Manuel whistled loudly bring on a complete silence.

"Okay, Valentine, you go first, but let me ask you one question. Where did you get that terrific disguise?"

Valentine took a deep breath, slowly let it out. "Well,'" she explained, "I used this outfit one time before to hide from the people following me." She smiled at Manuel, "Works very well, doesn't it?"

"I'll say. You had me completely fooled!" Manuel exclaimed.

Valentine had a very serious look on her face when she continued, "Tonight, when we camp, I will tell you my whole life story—or as much as I can remember. If you can wait until after supper, I will answer any and all questions you have. Meanwhile, I have some questions for you guys. My first question is, who is Jesus?"

Manny was the first to answer. "Jesus is my best friend!"

Samuel spoke and said, "Jesus is the Son of God."

Juan said, "Jesus is our brother and confidant, so we can tell Him everything, and he always listens."

Maria said, "Jesus died for me so I can live."

There was a pause while Valentine tried to take in what everyone had said then Manuel spoke.

"Valentine, let me tell you a story. It may take a little while to tell, but bear with me. I think it will answer your question.

"Once upon a time, long, long ago, in a place far away, there were three magnificent beings. They thought alike. In fact, they even knew each other's thoughts. Now that might be a bad thing here on this sinful world, but these three were so close that it worked very well. They were God, the Triad. There was Father, Michael, and Spirit. Michael was someone like we would think of as a son. Spirit was like the different aspects of the wind. He has no form. Nevertheless, you would know He was near by the results of His actions.

"These three have been together forever and ever. In fact, you can say forever one million times and still not go back far enough. Our minds don't compute that far. It's hard to think with such large numbers, without getting all bogged down in 'the forever.' So let's just say the three of them have always been.

"There came a time when God the Triad decided they would like some friends, but there was no one. They started to make plans to create friends. The Triad had minds that could comprehend everything and could see things in the future. They are more complicated than this simple description, but for our story, we'll leave it at that. The Triad decided if they made beings to be their friends, to love and be loved by them, that these beings must be able to decide for themselves. The new friends must be free to choose if they wanted to love and obey the Triad. They must also choose to love each other, or not. They must have 'free will.' The Triad understood that to have friends who only loved them because they were programmed to do so would not be real love.

"Throughout the process, they knew there would be problems. However, they wanted friends to love and be loved by so much that they made plans to work out any problems. The Triad thought about what to do to make the problems right. They knew that with a group of beings, with free will, they must have guidelines to go by. These guidelines were binding only if everyone, the Triad included, would abide by them. When all this was ready, the Triad created a world for their new friends to live on.

"In this world, they first built a beautiful gathering place, an outdoors cathedral. The gathering place would be for singing, spending time with each other, talking and communing with each other and with the their three Creators. This place would be a wonderful place where all would desire to come. In the middle of the gathering place was a beautiful wall, made of one perfect diamond. The shape of a tree was etched into the wall. The branches of the tree stood two hundred and fifty feet tall. On the trunk of the great tree, the guidelines were carved so deep that eons and eons of time would not change the words or dim their beauty. All must choose to abide by these rules or things would not go smoothly, and their beautiful world would slowly start to fall apart. The Triad also wrote what would need to happen if the guidelines were broken, for the world to be made right again. The last line on the diamond were these words, printed in bold letters: If anyone breaks the guidelines, someone will have to die. Dying means to stop living, smiling, laughing, singing, or breathing. One would die for all. Then everything would be right and beautiful again.

"After the gathering place was finished, the three Creators started to decorate the rest of the world. They made lakes, forests, and glades with beautiful flowers of every color imaginable. They created waterfalls. As the water cascaded down, it changed into multicolored rainbows. Shimmering fish swam in the seas. Beautiful long creatures, with transparent wings, flew in formations to make a light show—as if they were dancing in the sky.

"As the three worked together, they named each of their friends who were soon to be created. They talked about how much everyone would love to live on this beautiful planet. They talked and laughed at the thoughts of how excited their friends would be when they saw this beautiful world the creators had made for them."

Manuel turned to Manny, "It would be just like making a very special Christmas present. Then wrapping it in beautiful paper, with bows and ribbons on the gift, then bubbling over with excitement until you could give your gift to your friend. But you must wait until Christmas. The Triad felt like that, but much, much more. They couldn't wait to present their gifts to their new friends."

Manny interrupted excitedly, "Oh, Papa, I know just what you mean! Remember the work apron I made you for Christmas last year? I was so excited that I almost told you!"

"Yes, Manny, that's exactly what the Triad felt. Only they were getting ready to give the gift of life. Not to mention a beautiful world for their friends to live. They could hardly wait!"

Maria asked, "Could we stop at the next rest stop, Manuel? I need a bathroom break." Manuel decided they also needed gas, and this was a good time in the story to pause. He pulled off the interstate; everyone got out stretching their stiff limbs.

Manuel got gas and filled their jugs with cold water for everyone. They could not spend extra money on other kind of drinks like Pepsi, Sprite, or even juice, so the children had all learned to like water from an early age.

Maria helped walk Valentine to the bathroom. They laughed all the way at Valentine's ability to become an old, old lady.

As the two ladies came out of the bathroom, the boys caught up to them, and Manny asked, "Granny, would you like a cookie? We want to buy you one."

"Thank you, boys, your old granny would love that."

She winked at the boys as she continued to slowly shuffle back to the truck.

Valentine was by herself and using the cane now because Maria was looking in the store for something she needed. Valentine reached the truck and was waiting for everyone, when she heard a loud roaring sound from behind her. Rolling to a stop, on the other side of the gas pump, was a young man riding a motorcycle. As he turned off the motor, Valentine could hear him answering a call on his cell phone. "Hello? Joshua here." As he spoke, he looked her way. Valentine thought, *Wow, he seemed to be looking right through me as if I'm here.*

She heard him say, "Yes sir, I will look around, but right now all I see is a family of Hispanics. Yes, I'm keeping a sharp eye out for a woman with red hair and an old man in overalls and a felt hat. I understand, yes, I'll call you or Sheriff Joe if I hear or see anything. I have the rest of the club out looking as well. What? Yes, the plan has worked very well on all of them, except for one. We'll continue to expose him when we can. No, don't worry. There is no one around to hear me."

Valentine smiled to herself thinking, *I am standing right in front of him, in plain sight but he cannot seen me at all!*

"I am very careful," the young man continued to say. "As you can hear, I'm talking very quietly. Where are we meeting tonight? … Okay, that will be fine. I'll be there. This is a meeting only for the Elite, those of us in on the plan, right? Okay, I'll send the rest of the guys to our bar to wait for me. Yes sir, good-bye."

The young biker walked right past Valentine nearly bumping into her.

When Juan walked up, Valentine quickly asked him if he could get her notebook out of the back from the sleeping mat where she had left it. As soon as Juan brought her the book, she wrote down what she had just heard. She added the name, the Elite, describing those who were a part of the plan, and the name Joshua as a member of this group. Valentine described him as a clean-cut young man with an expensive, sleek, shiny black bike.

Valentine thought as she wrote, *I wondered who the one biker is, who couldn't be controlled by the plan. Does he read the Bible, or is he a reader of the classics?* She had just finished writing when everyone else came back to the truck.

Manuel asked, "Everyone ready? Granny, can I help you to get into the truck?"

"Yes, thank you, son, I could use a little help."

Everyone climbed in and Manuel headed the truck back out onto the interstate.

Valentine tried to clear her mind of what she had heard. However, her mind was buzzing with thoughts of the plan and everything it represented. She knew Manuel would continue with his story, and she really wanted to focus on this amazing story.

The family was talking around Valentine about things they had seen at the store. Samuel was interested in the motorcycle parked next to the truck. Manuel, Juan, and Samuel talked bikes, weighing the pros and cons of each. Maria and Manny talked about cookies; Manny wanted to know if it was okay to eat one. Valentine thought it was nice to sit and listen to the family. The talk calmed her nerves and helped her put aside all her jumbled thoughts.

Soon Manuel asked, "Is everyone ready for the rest of the story?"

Everyone spoke as one voice, "Yes, we are!"

Manny added, "Yes, Papa. This is a neat story!"

"So where were we?" Manuel pondered, "Oh yes, I remember. The Triad were just finishing the last touches on the homes for their new friends. The Triad knew all things, even the future as well as the past, and so they already knew each and every one of them, even before they created them. Before they started creating the beings, they looked over the whole planet and saw that it was good and that everything was ready. Father named the friends 'Beings of the Light' because they would always live near Him. His light would radiate around them and through them, causing them to always shine. The first beings were to be leaders. Those leaders would instruct and help teach the others, one by one, so each would know how very special the Triad felt about them.

"First to be brought forth was Lucifer, meaning the morning star. He was extremely handsome with an exquisite mind. He could sing so beautifully that the birds quieted just to listen to him. The Triad loved Lucifer with a love unfathomable so deep no time could ever dim their love. Lucifer returned their love. However, he had a special place in his heart for Father. He loved that Father was so very powerful and yet He taught him so lovingly. Lucifer loved Michael and Spirit also, but always his heart would thrill to the way he felt about Father.

"Soon a second friend was brought forth. His name was Gabriel, which meant 'God is my might.' Lucifer and Gabriel became brothers and friends at first sight. Michael and Spirit were their daily teachers. They walked through the woods and sang as they walked. Everything was new to them. They were filled with love for each other and love for the Triad.

"Time passed and one day Father, Michael, and Spirit brought Lucifer and Gabriel to the Gathering Place. They had not been there before and both were in awe at the sight. They could see beautiful jewels, hanging like stars over the entire expanse, shimmering with light from the Triad. The floor of the Gathering Place was made of pure transparent gold, clear as glass. The center was like a great amphitheater, and at the very center of the amphitheater was the wall. The beautiful wall that had been made of one perfect diamond. The two Beings of Light saw the shape of the tree etched into the wall. They saw the beautiful words on the trunk of the great tree. Lucifer and Gabriel had been carefully taught by the Triad why these words were written there and how important the meanings of those words were. They fell down on their knees before the Triad giving them all honor, glory, and praise.

"The Triad had two more gifts to give to the Beings of Light. On each bowed head, they placed a golden crown with each of their names etched with precious stones. Lucifer's name was etched in rubies and Gabriel's name was with emeralds. Then the Triad touched each of their shoulders and two shimmering white wings appeared. The wings were made of soft white feathers. As they began to move their wings, the feathers made beautiful sounds like that of violins. As the relationship dawned on Lucifer, he began to sing praises to his creators with the accompaniment of his wings. Soon Gabriel joined in. As they moved their wings and sang, they rose from the golden floor and flew up, circling the Gathering Place as they sang. When the song was finished, they again lighted in front of the Triad and bowed touching their crowns to the ground. At that moment, there was nothing the Beings of the Light would not have done for the Triad.

"Now it was Lucifer and Gabriel's turn to teach the new created beings. Each one was brought to them for guidance. They helped each new friend to learn of the Triad's love for them and showed them the beautiful place they lived in. They taught them the guidelines to live by. The guidelines were placed in their minds when created, but now they would be placed in their hearts as well.

"When the God Triad brought them to the Gathering Place, each new Being of Light spontaneously fell on their knees and thanked the Triad for their lives and the beautiful place created for them. Each was given golden crowns with their names inscribed with jewels and wings with different musical instruments.

"The Triad worked with the new ones just as they had worked with Lucifer and Gabriel, spending time with them every day. The Beings of Light treasured this time with Father, Michael, and Spirit. Their love grew daily. They would rather not eat than to miss this personal time with their creators.

"Every seventh day, everyone would celebrate. Father called these rest days the Holy Sabbaths. These Sabbaths were not only for rest, but also to remind the created beings of the Triad's love for them and of the Triad's creative power. These Holy Sabbath days were the happiest because the beings were able to spend the entire day with their creators, the God Triad.

"Time passed and more and more of the Beings of Light were created. The forests and riversides rang with songs the being wrote, songs to show the Triad how much they loved them. All was peaceful, all was happy. Michael created new lesser creatures to play and frolic around each of the Beings of Light.

"When all the Beings of Light were created, Father announced a new special Sabbath to celebrate the finished work. All came together to the amphitheater, and as if one being, they fell to their knees and placed their golden crowns at the feet of their creators. Everyone then stood as one to sing a new magnificent song. Lucifer had been preparing and teaching the Beings of Light this song for this very special Sabbath Day. Some flew in unison as they sang, and their wings played the breathtaking song.

"Father spoke to all the Beings of Light that day. He told them that from now on His son, Michael, would be creating new worlds and creating new beings to live on these worlds. The Beings of Light would work under Lucifer and Gabriel, who in turn would work for Michael to teach everyone in the new worlds all the things the Triad had taught them. After Father finished speaking, there went up a great shout from the Beings of Light. A shout of praise and love for the Triad, their Creators.

"World after world was created, and the new beings on these worlds came each week to celebrate the Sabbath and praise Father, Michael, and Spirit. When each new world was finished, they would celebrate with a special New Sabbath.

"Throughout the eons and eons of time, Lucifer, without realizing what he was doing, let one thought begin to disturb his peace. He began to wish he could be like Michael. Lucifer wanted to stand near Father; helping Him create a new world and sharing in the praise as Michael did. *Am I not just as good as Michael is?* he asked himself. *Am I not the first created Being of Light?*

"At first, when these thoughts came to Lucifer, he felt Spirit speaking to his heart. Lucifer would chide himself and told himself that this could never be. Michael was one of the God Triad, a creator, and he, Lucifer, was the created. Spirit continued to speak to his heart. Lucifer thought about going to Father and telling Him how he felt, to ask for His help, but he hesitated. What would Father think of me? He decided to fight these feelings himself, but with each new world that was created, these feelings grew stronger. Finally he stopped telling himself how wrong these thoughts were. He stopped hearing Spirit speaking to his heart. He let the evil fester inside of him.

"Everyone loved Lucifer. He was the first created being. Lucifer was beautiful. He was also the head of the choir. Everyone looked up to Lucifer with awe and delight. But Gabriel, his best friend, saw a change in Lucifer. He didn't understand what he saw. When he tried to talk to Lucifer, Lucifer would only put his arm around his best friend and say, 'What could be different about me? You, my friend, have been swimming in the oceans with that big fish of yours too much. Your brain is water logged!'

"Gabriel would laugh and say, 'Luc ole buddy, you might be right.' They would go off together, arm in arm, singing the newest song Lucifer had prepared for the choir to try out.

"The Triad, being all-knowing, knew what was going on, so Spirit went again to Lucifer and tried to talk to him. 'What is in your heart that is keeping you from happiness?' Spirit asked. Still, Lucifer wouldn't talk of it. At these times he would feel bad about his rebellious thoughts, but he wouldn't confide in Spirit or go to Michael. Lucifer told Spirit he would go to Father and talk to Him. After Spirit left Lucifer to think, he again talked himself out of going to Father. For now, he would again try to fix himself. Lucifer told himself he'd wait a few more Sabbaths, but he kept feeling worse. The turmoil in him was taking possession of him. One day, when he was standing in front of the guidelines, he realized they were not as beautiful as he once had thought.

"Not long after that day, he told one of his closest friends, Beryl, that he questioned the guidelines. He wondered if they were really necessary. After all, the word *guidelines* meant suggestions, not concrete rules. Beryl replied earnestly, 'The guidelines are for our happiness. The Triad did say someone would have to die if the guidelines are broken. They love us so much. The Triad wants us only to be happy. Don't you think so, Lucifer?' Lucifer turned on his beautiful charm and smiled at Beryl, 'Of course the God Triad only wants us to be happy. Don't think another thing about what I've said, Beryl.'

"One day everyone was called to come to the Gathering Place. Lucifer learned that Father and Michael were making great plans for one last beautiful world. When he heard this, Lucifer turned and left the amphitheater before Father had finished speaking. Gabriel, realizing how strange Lucifer was acting, followed him. When Gabriel found Lucifer, he was feeling the worst he had ever felt. He blurted out all his feelings to his best friend.

"Gabriel was shocked and overwhelmed with the hate that was coming from his friend. He didn't know what to say or do. When Lucifer finally finished his speech, wearing himself out with the emotions of it all, Gabriel tried to comfort him. He pleaded with Lucifer to go and talk to Father. Gabriel had never been confronted with anything like this before; he felt lost. He suggested they must go together and talk to Michael. 'Michael will know what to do.'

"Hearing that name, Michael, the name Lucifer had come to hate, he lost his temper with Gabriel and stomped off into the forest. As Gabriel watched Lucifer walk away, he noticed for the first time that there was no light shining around Lucifer. Lucifer held his head arrogantly high. However, his wings hung down dejectedly. The very forest looked gray and dark where Lucifer walked.

"Gabriel felt his life would never be the same again. As he sat trying to think of what to do with the sensations of such strange feelings inside of him, he heard a soft footstep. Looking up, he saw Michael. Gabriel threw himself into the arms of his Creator and friend, and, for the first time in his life, felt the wet tears of sorrow flowing down his face. Michael told Gabriel that from the very first second that Lucifer had begun to think like this, Father, Himself, and Spirit had known about it. Spirit had gone, that instant, to speak with Lucifer. However, he would not ask for help. No created being can fight these feeling alone.

"'You do not have the power. That is the great problem, Gabriel, only the God Triad has the power. We knew this would happen before we created any of the Beings of Light, but we have such love in our hearts to give to others that we devised a plan.' As Michael talked to Gabriel, they began to walk. As they were walking, Michael explained the plan of salvation to Gabriel. Very soon they were standing before the great beautiful wall, with the guidelines carved into the diamond. The words began to dawn on Gabriel. Someone would lose their life. Someone would need to die, to be put to death, stop living, and stop smiling or laughing, stop singing or breathing. If they broke the guidelines, this would need to happen to make everything right and beautiful again. Bowing low before Michael, Gabriel said, 'I will die for my friend.' Michael spoke with tenderness, 'It is all up to Father. However, your willingness to stop living for your friend is noted in the great Book of Life.'

"Time continued and Lucifer started talking to more and more of his friends, saying it wasn't fair that Father made them follow the guidelines. Some of the Beings of Light listened to him, though most didn't. Michael tried to talk to his friend, Lucifer, but Lucifer hardened his heart to what anybody said— even Father. Finally things got so bad Michael told Lucifer he needed to leave. There was a meeting called for everyone to come to the Gathering Place. Father told everyone they must choose, the Triad's way or Lucifer's way.

"Suddenly, there was war in the beautiful world. Michael and the Beings of Light fought Lucifer and his followers. Michael's side won, but there was no joy in the winning. Lucifer and all of his followers were made to leave, to fall from Father's presence. They would be called ever-after, fallen angels.

"There was no more singing for a long time. Gabriel's heart was broken because he missed his friend Lucifer. Morning and evening he went to sit at Michael's feet, to draw strength from him, to carry on."

Everyone in the truck was stunned and quiet. Manuel's voice had started to break as he spoke the last few words. Up to that point, the story was so beautiful, but the fall of Lucifer was a hard thing to tell, and to hear.

Maria said in a hushed voice, "I think we should take a break for now."

It had started to rain, and the sound of rain hitting the truck sounded so sad to Valentine, like the tears of the Beings of Light or angels, as Manuel had explained they are called in the Bible. She did not know if she had ever heard any of this before, but she would never forget it now.

Manuel stopped at the next gas station and everyone ran for the restrooms, except Valentine. Since she was still posing as an old woman, she needed to go slow. Samuel turned as he started to go into the store and saw her. He ran back to grab a really big umbrella for the two of them then helped Valentine into the store.

Valentine turned to Samuel and said, "You're a very nice young man. Thank you."

Samuel turned a little red and answered, "You're welcome, Granny. It was my pleasure."

Valentine was just coming out of the restrooms in the back of the store when a young man pushed passed her from behind, almost knocking her down. Leaning against the wall she managed to steady herself. The young man paid no attention; he was looking down at the video game in his hands. He was bobbing his head to some music he alone could hear. Valentine watched him until he was almost out of the store. He stopped by the door as if waiting for someone. Valentine started to the door herself, moving slowly. When she came near to the young man, she stopped one aisle over. She was about to step up to the door when it opened from the outside. A man dressed in black came in. This man was not a priest. He resembled the same man she saw back in the truck stop, talking to the cashier. Valentine stopped and started looking at the hair brushes, trying to appear totally engrossed. The man in black looked around and, seeing the young man standing by the door, nodded his head at him. It was a very slight nod. Still, Valentine saw it, and she saw the responding acknowledgment from the young man. Both men looked around the store, except for Valentine; there was only a man stocking cold drinks far in the back. They both looked right through her, not appearing to see her at all.

A shiver went through Valentine. Without a second thought, she said, "Thank you, guardians."

The man in black spoke first. Nodding toward the toy in the young man's hand, he asked, "New game?"

"Yeah, it's really cool. I just got it from my scout leader. He gave them to everyone."

Then the conversation took a whole different turn. The young man said, "I've been watching this store all morning. There has been no tall, redheaded woman or old man in a felt hat and overalls. I've been talking to the other guys and they say the same from the other stores and gas stations in this area."

The man in black took off his dark sunglasses and gave the young man a strange look.

Then the young man blinked twice, "Excuse me, sir," as if he had never seen the man in black before then walked out the door. The man in black bought water then he too left the store.

Soon after this, Samuel came back in and said, "Sorry, Granny, I was helping Papa a minute. Are you ready to go?"

"Oh yes, Samuel, I am very ready to go!"

Samuel held the umbrella for Valentine and they walked slowly to the truck. After helping her get comfortable, he climbed in the backseat, and Manuel started the truck.

Because of the rain, they did not get as far as they had planned. Manuel had to drive much slower because his tires were wearing thin and it was not safe. The rain had stopped by the time they reached a park where they could stay for the night. There was only about an hour of daylight left. Everyone got started right away to set up camp and get supper ready. They used some of Valentine's parsnips, and Maria fried some chicken they had bought at the store. Maybe it was the rain or maybe the story, but everyone was quieter than the other evenings.

Manuel saved the Bible reading for after supper, starting in Genesis, chapter 1: In the beginning God…. They ended by singing Valentine's favorite song, "Turn Your Eyes upon Jesus."

Then Manuel continued the story. "I stopped the story where there was war, and Lucifer and his angels had to leave. Michael and Gabriel went to all the other worlds and talked to the other created beings. They told them about the war. The Bible does not tell us if Satan was allowed to tempt the other worlds. However, we know the other planets did stay true to Father, Michael, and Spirit.

"Lucifer's fallen angels were not happy. Some of them went to Lucifer and started to complain that he had taken them out of their homes and away from their friends. Now they had nowhere to go. Lucifer calmed their fears, saying, 'We have one last place to try. When Michael makes the new world he and Father have been drawing up plans for, this new and special world, we'll take over it.'

"Some of the fallen angels silently wished they had not listened to Lucifer. They were too scared and embarrassed. Possibly they just had too much pride to go to Father and say they were sorry. Lucifer told them they couldn't go back now.

It was too late for them. 'Father is not going to put anyone to death,' he told them. Everyone was glad to hear that and most of them stopped complaining. However, nothing would ever be the same in the Triad's home. Father, Michael, and Spirit knew the salvation plan must be put into place. They knew the new world would be a battleground. Still, plans for creating the new world went forward. Michael had designed this place to be different. The beings there would be created in the image of the Triad, in the image of God.

"Everything was ready, and Michael went to the place where the new world would be. Michael, the Creator, spoke the words, 'Let there be light.' Michael made the new world with deep thought. Every detail was carefully designed. There would be many new little creatures, with funny habits, for the enjoyment of the new created beings. In six days He made the world and everything to sustain life, everything to make life happy. On the sixth day he made man in His own image. He called him Adam. Adam shone with the light from Spirit and needed no clothing. He wore a robe of light, a robe of righteousness."

Manuel stopped the story to explain. "I'm quoting the Bible at times now."

Manuel continued, "Michael had the animals walk in front of Adam, two by two, and Adam named them as they went by. When all the animals had passed by, Adam turned to Michael, 'Where is my mate?' So the Creators put Adam to sleep and removed a rib from Adam to make woman—a helpmate and friend. When Adam woke, Father and Michael presented to Adam his wife, Eve. The two were to live in a beautiful garden on the planet. Michael placed two trees in the center of the garden, one they could eat from any time they wanted. However, the other one He told them they were never to go near or eat fruit from this second tree.

"Michael explained it was a test. He told them about Lucifer, now named Satan, that he would try to get them to listen to him and not the Triad, but they must not talk to him because Satan was very persuasive and convincing. But no matter what, he was not right because Satan wasn't the Creator. He was presenting things from only his side, not for the good of everyone.

"Every day Beings of Light came and instructed the young couple. They also taught them to sing and explained everything about Father, Michael, and Spirit. Every evening Michael came to spend time with Adam and Eve. He taught and explained the guidelines. Michael told them he was their brother, and Spirit was there to help them and guide them. 'Spirit lives inside of you.' Michael explained that Father was High King of the vast universe.

"Adam and Eve were very happy, and their happiness helped the Beings of Light and the Triad to heal from some of the wounds of losing Lucifer and the other fallen angels.

"One evening, when Michael came to the garden, he didn't see Adam and Eve running to meet him, as was their usual habit. He called their names. He knew where they were and what had happened that day, but he wanted to hear from them.

"Finally Adam said, 'Here we are.' Out of the bushes came Adam and Eve. They had taken leaves and tried to cover themselves because they now felt their nakedness. They had lost Spirit.

"Adam said, 'Eve brought me some of the fruit we were not to eat, and I ate it.'

"Michael turned his sad eyes on Eve and asked her what happened.

"Eve said, 'I was walking by myself when somebody called to me. It was a beautiful flying serpent. The serpent told me to come and eat. He said he'd been eating the fruit and nothing bad had happened. So I took the fruit he offered me, and I ate.'

"That terrible fateful day, Lucifer pulled two more down with him. Michael explained to Adam and Eve they couldn't talk to Him face-to-face anymore, and they would have to leave their home in the garden. Michael took them out of the garden. Out in the meadow was a flock of sheep, two white, fuzzy lambs bounding around their legs as they walked. One rubbed its fuzzy head on Eve's knee, and she reached down and scratched behind the little lamb's ears, smiling at the little fellow's antic in spite of her deep sadness.

"Michael built an altar of stone. He then picked up the little lamb. He handed the spotless little body to Adam to hold. Before Adam knew what was happening, the lamb's neck was cut. Red fluid ran from the lamb's opening onto Adam's hands. The lamb's eyes lost its light and sparkle. The body went limp. Michael explained, 'This is death. This is an example of the sacrifice that must be made to pay for breaking the guidelines. You have sinned.' He did the same for Eve. Eve had to hold the little lamb that had just been playing near her feet. The red life's fluid ran over her hands. Adam and Eve had never seen death of any kind. The lifeless bodies of the little lambs were terrible. Michael made clothes for them out of the lambs' skins. He then explained that one day a man child would be born of a woman, of a virgin. He told them this child would grow to manhood. One day he would die, just like their lambs had, for their sins. 'Someday,' he continued, 'you will once again be able to talk to Father face-to-face and live in your beautiful garden.' Michael told them many things to help them live in this world marred with sin. He told them that life would be harder. From now on they would have to work in the dirt for the food they ate.

"Michael, the Creator, walked back to the gate of their garden home. He summoned two angels with bright gleaming swords. They were stationed in front of the gates of the garden. The angels were there to protect Adam and Eve from eating from the Tree of Life and living forever in their sinful bodies. The last thing Michael said to them was, 'I will come again.'

"Adam and Eve had babies, and their babies had babies, for thousands of years. Until one day a Being of Light, an angel, came to a young virgin named Mary. This Being of Light told her she would have a baby. This baby would be the son of Father God, as well as her child, and she was to call his name Jesus. The baby would save the world from its sins.

"Mary was to be married to Joseph. But when Joseph found out that Mary was with child, pregnant, he was upset and afraid. He was afraid she would be stoned because she was going to have a baby before marriage. The baby was not his child. But that night an angel came to Joseph and said, 'Don't be afraid to make Mary your wife. She is carrying the Son of God.' Joseph got up the next day and went to Mary. He told her what the angel had said. They were soon married. When the time was right, the baby was born. Satan tried to kill Jesus when he was a baby, but God the Father had his Son in the palm of his hand, protecting Him. Many of Jesus's friends, heavenly angels, were sent to protect him from harm.

"Thirty years went by. During this time, Jesus worked with his earthly father and mother. Jesus also spent time alone with his Heavenly Father by reading from the Torah, the Old Testament or the first part of the Bible and he spent time in nature where God's love showed in everything He made. He also spent time talking to His Father, or praying as we call it now. When it was time for the salvation plan to start, Jesus gathered twelve people to work with him and taught them of his Father's love for them. Jesus went around the land healing people of sickness from the body, the mind, and the soul. These twelve people were called disciples. At first they thought Jesus had come to fight the Romans for them, to make the soldiers leave their country. However, Jesus told them he had not come to fight the Romans but to fight sin and death—to fight Satan. He tried to explain to them that when the time was right He would be killed for the sins of the world, but they couldn't comprehend that. Their minds were so set on their own way they were sure he was setting up an earthly kingdom. They didn't understand he was setting up a kingdom in heaven, a beautiful place where there would be no more sin, sadness, or tears.

"Jesus wanted them to understand that he was reuniting the fallen sons of Adam with their Father. One day, after three years of talking to people and showing everyone his Father's love, one of his disciples betrayed him. Authorities preformed a mock trial. They had the soldiers beat him with a whip. They nailed his hands and feet to a big wooden cross, standing it up for all to see the Son of God. Just before Jesus died, Father surrounded the cross in a dark cloud to hide His Son Michael, Jesus Christ, from the jeering people who were laughing at him and calling him names. Jesus in turn asked God to forgive them because they didn't know what they were doing. Jesus's last words to a dying world and the entire universe were 'It is finished.' Then just as the first little lambs died, to point the way to Jesus, Jesus died for me and you."

Valentine sat by the fire, stunned. She remembered that someone would have to die, *But not Michael, Jesus, the son of Father, the Creator. He died for me! How can this be!*

Valentine shook her head and held her breath as she continued to listen to Manuel finished the story. "The entire universe was stunned. The son, part of the Triad, the creator of the world, was dead. Satan was overjoyed. He and his minions were celebrating. His evil plan had worked. The world was his forever, or so he thought. Satan did not understand the depth of the Father's love.

"Jesus's friends on earth were brokenhearted. They had lost a wonderful friend. When He died, some of His friends took him down from the cross. They readied his body for burial, as best they could, before night came. They placed the body in a tomb carved out of a rock. The rulers had a large stone rolled in front of the tomb. That was Friday evening, the beginning of the Sabbath, and they wouldn't work on the Sabbath, so that's all that was done for Jesus.

"All Jesus's followers were stunned. They didn't know what was going to happen. Satan was happy. He and his evil angels thought they had won. With Michael dead, the one Satan hated, they were kings of the planet. They would be able to do anything they wanted now, with no one to stop them.

"Before the sun rose on the third day, early in the morning, some of Jesus's friends went to His tomb. They found the stone rolled back; the tomb was empty. Jesus had risen from the dead! Never would He be brought low again. He had conquered Satan and death. Now all people of the earth could come to His Father, through Spirit, whenever they needed to. Jesus talked with His friends on earth and told them what to do and what to expect in the coming years. He would come again, when the time was right. After He had taught his friends all he could teach them, Jesus asked them to go and tell the world. Jesus took them up a hill. While still talking to them, he started to rise up into the sky. Soon he was out of sight.

"One day, not long after Jesus had left, in a meeting of His friends, while they were praying, a sound was heard throughout the room, like a great roaring wind. What looked like tongues of fire settled on each of their heads, filling them with the Holy Spirit. They began to preach boldly about how Jesus had died for them, for every fallen son of Adam's. This was the Holy Spirit. He has been with us ever since. All anyone needs to do is call, in the name of Jesus. He will come to them.

"Satan is still here, and we're still waiting for Jesus to come back, but we feel the time is very near. The Bible has given us clues to help us to know when the time is close. The story isn't over yet, and Valentine, from what you've told us, Jesus has sent you an angel, a Being of Light, to help you get away from whomever in hunting you."

Silence filled the darkened woods when Manuel finished the story.

Valentine could hardly speak. With the lump in her throat, with tears stinging her eyes, she whispered, "Thank you for the story, Manuel. It's truly a beautiful story, and I believe it."

Valentine sat staring into the dying embers of the fire for a minute then quietly spoke, "Now I must tell you my story. I am doing this with fear and trembling because I don't want to cause you trouble—but that may be too late now anyway. Eight or nine days ago, I woke up in a hospital bed with no memory of where I was, why I was there, or even who I was. I have had a flash or two of memory, but for all practical purposes, I am eight or nine days old." Valentine told them her whole story, right up to the man in black and the kid in the last store where they stopped. She told them about her notebook and offered to let Manuel read it if he thought it would help them.

"I am convinced that something ominous is happening. Someone is trying to get control of the minds of the people of the entire world," Valentine finished.

Manuel said, "Valentine, this seems impossible. Your story is very serious. Who would have the power to do this?"

Everyone thought and for a while; only the sounds of the campfire could be heard.

"How do you think it's done, Papa?" Samuel asked. Manuel just shook his head in bewilderment.

Juan said, "Valentine, you talked about video games. What about all electronic devices? Everyone has them. What if someone could get some kind of a signal into any of them? If a person is listening to music or playing a video game, or even talking on their cell phones, they would get some kind of signal to the brain? You could go on and on with devices that could be used if someone had the technical knowledge."

Little Manny said, "And didn't you say, Valentine, that the Bible was the best way to keep it from getting into your mind? We're okay, aren't we, Papa? Because we don't have any devices and we read the Bible every day."

"Well, son, I'd say we're better than most families, but we must not stop there. We need to be reading more, to be safer. Not only so our minds will be strong, we must spend time in our Bibles to become closer to our Heavenly Father, Jesus, and the Holy Spirit. I know God is taking care of us. However, I'm worried about those who don't know."

Manny said, "I could tell all my friends, couldn't I, Papa?"

"Son, we'll need to be careful. We can teach people, but we must not get caught by the same people chasing Valentine. We must not let on that we know anything. That will be the trouble. If we want to help, we must go carefully. This is mind-boggling. If this is really true, I'm going to have to think how to help our family, friends, and anyone else we can. I'm just going to have to think about this. Boys, for now, talk to only your mother and I or Valentine about any of this. We'll figure out what to do. God will help us and guide us. We must pray about this until we're shown what to do."

Maria said, "It's getting late, and we have a lot on our minds. We may never get to sleep. Let's sing Valentine's song, go to bed, and pray about this. Then stop thinking about it until morning."

So as the fire softly crackled, they started to sing. "Turn your eyes upon Jesus, look full in his wonderful face. The things of earth will grow strangely dim in the light of His glory and grace."

Valentine felt a peace she didn't completely understand. She knew she was very glad she could share this burden with the Sanchezes. She also felt like she was sharing this burden with their Father God too and with Jesus and Spirit.

As Valentine laid her head down to sleep, while soft sounds of nature were all about her, she started her very first prayer:

"Thank you for helping me to believe in you, Jesus. I give my life to you tonight. Thank you for dying on the cross for my sins. Make me a new person, and please send Spirit to live in my life tonight and forever, good night."

12

West Always West

It was a beautiful fall morning when Valentine and the Sanchezes awoke. Everything had changed in the telling of the two stories. Valentine felt very different. She woke with Jesus on her mind and a song in her heart. No matter how many songs Valentine might learn in her life, she thought this one song, "Turn Your Eyes upon Jesus," would always be most precious to her. Thinking back over the day before, she realized that the memory of Manuel's voice, telling God's story, would stay with her always. This morning Valentine started her day with a real prayer to a real person, Jesus Christ, Michael, Son of the High King of heaven, Father God.

"Good morning, Jesus, thank you for this beautiful day—for my life, thank you for these beautiful friends to share it with. Thank you for loving me even before I knew your name. Help me to do what you want me to do today. Take care of my new friends, keep them safe. Protect them with this secret. Help them to save others from this evil that is taking over the world."

Valentine let her mind go empty, enjoying her quiet time. She felt as if Jesus was sitting near her enjoying this time together. Valentine ended her prayer by saying, "In my heart, I don't want to say good-bye, Jesus, just thank you for being with me today."

She opened her eyes to see the most beautiful sunrise peeping over the horizon. "I wonder if I ever noticed the small blessings in life before I lost my memory. Before all this happened to me," she whispered to herself and the sunrise. She got *The Gospel of John* out of her bag and reread the first verse: In the beginning was the Word. Now she knew what those words meant. The Word is Jesus. The way Manuel had told the story she could hear Jesus speaking the words that brought this world to life. Yes, it was a beautiful morning.

It was not long until everyone was up and sitting around the fire. Valentine looked around at each face. She realized that the story she had told was still on the minds of her friends this morning. Smiling at Manuel, she asked, "Is everything okay? You look worried."

Manuel looked at Valentine and said, "I woke with the secret you shared with us going around and around in my mind. It is a solemn reminder that Satan is still at work in the world. I realized I am now part of a bigger campaign to stop his takeover of people's minds and souls. Satan knows even better than I do what God had told in the Bible about taking care to be ready for Jesus's return. Maybe we cannot stop Satan completely, but we could save as many people as will listen. I began to wonder how we do this without bringing the wrath of Satan and his minions, not to mention this nun, down on my family. I began to worry that I would be caught before I could help people. I know I must put everything in God's hands. I know I need to pray and wait for Him to show the way. Prayer has been my answer to everything. So I opened my heart to my Heavenly Father. When I finished, my heart was at peace. My worries were in the hands of God." Manuel smiled into Maria's eyes. "I tried to get up quietly so as not to wake you, dear, but I'm sure you were already praying before I got the fire rekindled and put water on for coffee. Am I right?"

"Yes, dear," Maria said. "I knew when you left the tent even if you did try to be quiet." She smiled back at her husband. "Manuel could never be quiet enough to keep from waking me," she laughed. "After all those years of waking when the boys made a sound, I am now a very light sleeper." Maria's face changed to a more somber thoughtful look. "I too started to think about our fireside talk of last night. I felt a chill go through me as I thought of the secret you told us, Valentine, and how it will change our lives. I really wasn't sure if I was ready for those changes. I wanted a few more years of being simply a mother and watching my sons grow to be men of God. However, I knew they were certainly boys of God. I prayed over Samuel when he was born, just as Hannah had in the Bible. I prayed over Juan and Manny as well. I knew they would take this mission as far as God asked them to, each one of them. I just don't know if I am ready to let them go yet. I also began to pray. I asked God, Jesus, and the Holy Spirit to please help me to really give my family and myself to God's purpose and mission. I have to say I shed a few tears. However, I also felt the peace of Jesus flow through me."

Manuel looked around at his family and said, "Today starts a new life for us—a new mission, or a different path to the same mission."

"Yes, Manuel," Maria said. "I have been praying for God to help me be ready to give up my family for His cause if need be. It's not easy for me. I want to keep my boys young and innocent for a little while yet. Nevertheless, I have given everything to God, and He will take care of us. I believe our sons will be wonderful soldiers for God and His tasks for each of them. I am honored to be given a chance to be part of this mission that has been given into our care." She looked directly at each of her sons as she finished speaking.

Valentine watched as Maria's eyes lingered on Samuel.

Samuel smiled at his mom and dad. "I think I was next to wake. I saw you guys by the fire and decided to give you a moment. My mind started right in on things I could do to tell people about the coming trouble. My mind was buzzing with ideas. Then I stopped. I realized I must stay close to Jesus and ask for the Holy Spirit to come help me more and more. The Holy Spirit is the one who Jesus had sent back to us to help me and all mankind when He left to go home to His Father's world. Dad, the story you told yesterday, I had never heard the story of the Bible told like that before. It had really opened my eyes to many things I had wondered about. You also brought the whole story together somehow. I saw Jesus in a whole new light and understood just a bit better what it must have been like for Him to leave His Father to come down to this world to save the human race. So many humans didn't love Him back then. In the end, it killed him because they hated what they didn't understand or could not control."

Samuel stopped speaking, and Valentine could see he was fighting for control of his emotions. She guessed Juan saw this also because he cleared his throat, began to tell what was on his mind.

"I heard Samuel getting up and could also hear the fire crackling, but I was still sleepy and turned over for just a few more minutes of sleep. The only problem was my mind wouldn't let me go back to sleep. I started going over everything that you told us, Valentine. It seemed to me that this whole thing is like a spy movie. It didn't seem real somehow. I remembered I had read of an experiment in mind control, in an article one of my teachers had lent me. The article was ten years old when I read it. Still, the work done, for mental illnesses through mind control, was very impressive. I wonder could this be the same technique that is being used on people now." Juan looked around the fire at his family, ending his gaze on Valentine's face.

He was very quiet for a moment then he began to speak again. "I feel so strange about all of this. One side of me wants to keep things as they are and the other part wants to start right in to tell the world what was going on. I love you guys, and I guess I am afraid for all of us. I realize I must not worry because God will be with His people. God can stop this thing if He wants to. I got to thinking maybe God is letting this happen. This is His plan to bring people to Him, during times of trials, just before

His second coming. The idea hit me like a bomb exploding in my head, causing all kinds of ideas to bounce around. I wondered how I can keep from getting lost in the coming trouble. Like you said, Valentine, I must read my Bible every day. You know, I have always meant to read more of the Bible, but most days I let our family reading be it. Not anymore. Now, even more than ever, I need to stay close to God," Juan finished with a determined voice. "I cannot rely on Papa anymore. I must be ready for whatever comes through my own prayer and Bible study."

Little Manny sat very quietly for his young self. He was listening to the others tell how they felt. He took a deep breath then let his words spew out. "I didn't sleep well in the night. I couldn't stop thinking about what you said, Valentine, about those bad people who were trying to hurt you. What would happen if they came after Mama and wanted to hurt her? I would stop them somehow. I know I'm just a little kid and couldn't do anything by myself—I thought of Jesus and my guardian angel. I just knew Jesus would help me whenever I call. I thought about what you said, that someone was helping you—and how you didn't remember having ever even heard of Jesus. Jesus had sent His angels to help you before you knew to ask. Isn't that really neat? Jesus is always ready to help a person before that person even knows they are in trouble. I closed my eyes tight and prayed, Dear Jesus, please help me to be strong and brave. Show me what you want me to do for you. Forgive me if I do it wrong and show me again so I can help you and the people who need you as a friend. Bye for now, your friend, Manny." When he finished speaking, he jumped up and ran to his mama. He gave her a big hug and said, "I love you, Mama."

Breakfast was a quiet affair. As Valentine watched each person sitting around the fire, she saw they had different thoughts and worries turning and churning in their heads. She also realized they all understood that most likely today would be their last day together. The Sanchezes would be turning south soon to pick up Maria's brother on a farm in Kansas, while Valentine must continue west.

Manuel picked up his Bible and turned to Valentine. "I'm going to read what's in your little black book—*The Gospel of John.* Would you like to get your book and read along?"

"Thank you, Manuel. Hold on and I'll get it," she answered. She was back in a jiffy with her small book; Manuel showed her where to turn, to John 3:16.

"For God so loved the world that He gave His only begotten Son, that whosoever believeth in Him should not perish, but have everlasting life."

When it was time for prayer, everyone held hands, and each person took a turn to pray. Valentine felt very close to this family, whom she had met only three days ago; somehow it seemed like a lifetime. She would be sad to see them go their own way.

They broke camp and the boys helped Valentine roll her bed up like a real hiker. They had given her the tarp and rope, and had helped her learn to make the small tent. They had each given her an extra blanket, beautiful blankets from Mexico. Now she would be better equipped to take care of herself out in the open. She repacked everything and had her disguises ready if need be, but today she planned to be simply a hiker. Manuel gave her a poncho with a hood she could pull over her head to keep out the cold or to be safe from detection. Maria had given her an old coffee pot and a lighter so she could heat up food and water. She also gave Valentine some dried foods they had—beef jerky, dried fruit, and other things that would be light to carry. Little Manny pulled out his Swiss army knife he had gotten for Christmas. He wanted to give it to Valentine, but she told him she had found one in her overalls; she pulled it out to show him.

"I know, Valentine," he exclaimed! "Let's swap. I'll give you mine and you give me yours, and when we see each other again, we can swap back."

Valentine said, "Manny, I would love to swap with you. Each time I use your knife I'll think of you. I will remember, that one day, we'll swap back."

Soon everyone was ready to hit the road. Because Valentine wasn't in disguise, she would stay in the back for now.

In the truck she started reading her book again. She had already read to chapter twelve. Nevertheless, she started over, for it brought to mind the story Manuel had told. Valentine read slowly, wanting to understand everything but still having questions.

Maybe, she thought to herself, *questions are a part of it all. The more questions you get answered, the more you have. That way you're always searching for Father God and always finding out more about Him. Maybe this is the way to become closer to him.*

The hum of the tires and the warm sunshine streaming into the windows made her sleepy, so she closed her eyes. She woke when she felt the truck tires hit rougher ground. Valentine sat up and looked around. While she had slept, the truck had gone through city traffic and into Kansas. Now Manuel was pulling off to the side of the road. Samuel stuck his head through the window, asking, "Hey, Valentine, are you ready to ride up front with the big kids now?"

"Ha-ha, very funny, wise guy," she laughed. "Yes, I am ready to be good and ride up front."

Everyone was laughing when Valentine climbed up into the backseat. Juan was drawing on a piece of paper and told her he was making her a map of the old road. Manuel explained that some other people they knew took back roads to keep out of sight. He also told how this was a road that his grandfather had taken him on when he was twelve. They had spent a summer just camping, hiking, and learning about living in the open and about nature.

"This road will keep you going west," he told Valentine.

Before they reached the road where they were turning south, Manuel turned right on a dirt road and drove for a few miles. He told her this road would be safer and she could live off the land as she hiked. About an hour later, Manuel pulled the truck over and everyone got out. Valentine got her things out of the back and checked to make sure she had everything. She picked up the cane she still carried from the thrift shop. It was so hard to say good-bye. She had such mixed feelings. Part of her wanted to go with them, but something told Valentine it would be safer, for everyone, to go their separate ways.

Before they separated, they ate a light lunch Maria had put together. Valentine looked at each face, sealing them in her memory. *They are my family now*, she thought. At the end of the meal, she gave each a hug and kiss on the cheek. Manuel gave her their address and a twenty dollar bill. When Valentine tried to protest, they all urged her to take the money, saying it was a gift from each of them.

"We want to know you will be able to eat if you get hungry," Manuel said. "We know God is watching out for you. However, we'll feel better knowing you have a little more cash."

Juan handed Valentine the map and told her he had written ideas in places to help her, if need be. He showed her to look at the number on the map and then check the back of the page for the ideas. Samuel told her he would be doing everything, with God's help, to tell people about what was happening. They all told her they would be careful and that as a family they would come up with a plan to spread the news.

Little Manny had tears running down his cheeks and he didn't even care. "I'm going to miss you, Valentine, but I know God will bring us back together!"

Then Manuel said, "Let's put all of this in God's hands." Standing in a circle, they took each other's hands. They closed their eyes, and Manuel prayed for God's will to be done in each of their lives; everyone said amen.

Manuel turned to Valentine. "That's the prayer that will always work. God's will be done, because if you truly want God's will to be done, He will do anything for your good. Let me tell you, Valentine, it might not always feel right to you, but follow God's leading. That's all you have to do."

The Sanchezes got back in the truck. Manuel turned it around and slowly drove away. The family waved out the windows until they couldn't see Valentine anymore. She watched until she couldn't see them anymore then she turned and started west.

She looked her map over carefully and saw she was at the very top of Kansas. The road Juan had marked ran mostly parallel with the state lines of Kansas and Nebraska. It was a simple map, with little drawings of things she guessed she might see as she went along. The terrain was mostly open and rolling from what Valentine could see.

She had not been hiking much since riding with the Sanchezes, so she would take it easy for the first day and watch for a good camping site out of view. She started slowly, giving her muscles time to warm up, but soon she was making pretty good time.

Valentine noticed on her map an X with a number one marked near it. Turning the paper over, she read, "Dear Valentine, this spot is a favorite camping place for our family. The site is not too far for the first day of walking, and we think you will like it. Besides, we want to think of you camping in one of our favorite spots tonight so we'll know you're safe, Love, the S family."

Valentine followed the careful instructions to an opening in a fence with a cattle guard. She followed the path through a thicket of heavier bushes; on the other side she found a clear pond. Dipping her hand in the water, she found it to be very cold. She guessed it must be spring fed. There was the remains of an old home with the fireplace still intact. It was a very snug and safe place to stay for the night.

First she made her tent out of the tarp and rope she had been given and made her bed inside. Then she looked for wood to start a fire. One of the boys had told her very dry wood made little smoke, so she looked for only really dry pieces. She had been helping Maria start the fires, so it was not long before a small bright fire was burning. She soon had her coffee pot next to the fire heating water. She had ground coffee Maria had given her plus herbal tea. She decided on the tea for supper and coffee for when she would be cold and need the kick to get going. She had drunk all her water while walking, so she refilled the bottles while waiting for the water to heat.

Valentine got out her "Gospel of John" and began reading about the man named John while drinking her tea. She thought John sounded like a cool guy to stand up to the law and to speak plainly that he wasn't the important one. Valentine found it interesting that John had said he wasn't even good enough to untie the important one's sandals. She realized after reading the chapter over twice that John was talking about her own new friend, Jesus; he was the important one! She really liked the part where Spirit came to be with Jesus and help him.

Valentine did not understand how Jesus could be born of a virgin woman. She wondered how Mary felt, being so young and not being married. How would it feel to be asked of God to carry His own son and raise him? Wow, what a responsibility. Valentine guessed Mary must have talked to God a lot so she could be a good mother.

Then her thoughts went again to her own family and who they might be and if she had any children of her own. *Was I a good mother?* she wondered. *Are they missing me?*

Valentine closed her eyes, as she had seen the Sanchez family do while talking to God, then prayed. She asked God to help her family in this time of coming trouble. Since she could not be there to tell them of what she had learned, she prayed someone would. She asked God to show them Jesus as He had shown her.

Valentine marveled again at how God had helped her get away from the Sister that first day at the hospital. She remembered the feeling of being pushed into the thrift shop. "I can still almost feel the hands on my back," she whispered to the evening air. She realized Jesus had sent her guardian angel to help her. It was a good feeling to know who that someone was and helping her to not feel alone.

Valentine finished her reading on the number *32* in the first chapter, about the Spirit coming to be with Jesus. The way the book was written, she realized she could find any line she wanted by noting the number beside it and the chapter. She could not remember ever seeing a book written this way, but she could see it would come in handy.

By this time she could hardly see the words on the page, so she carefully put the book away in the plastic bag where she kept it and stirred the fire a bit. She enjoyed sitting in front of the fire and watching the flames. Tongues of fire—that's what Manuel said came and sat upon the heads of Jesus's disciples when Spirit came to live with them and help them. That would have been a scary sight if you didn't know what was happening—and maybe even if you did.

Valentine had so many new thoughts running around her head she thought she would never get to sleep, but soon her eyes began feeling heavy. She banked the fire as she had seen Maria do. Her bed felt good after the long day. She said good night to Spirit, Jesus, and Father God.

A cool breeze touched her face as she snuggled warm in her bed. She soon was fast asleep.

13

The Gift

Ghost was sitting in his Washington, DC, office thinking about all he had left to do. He needed to make a four-way call to Father and Sonny, but he needed an uninterrupted hour to complete the transfer of information—and he was waiting for the call from Einstein to complete the four-way. They didn't call often. It was understood that the less calls between the four the better. He kept all the information of the Plan in his head because he didn't want any paper trail. They had enough trouble with that blasted nurse. She and that reporter had been getting too close— and all because someone had found an overview written by an individual who was no longer in the Plan or in the land of the living for that matter. At least it had taught everyone not to make the mistake of creating a paper trail.

There was still that eyewitness who had heard the whole plan. Ghost thought about that. What were the odds that one person was in the right place, at just the wrong time, to hear a conversation, that started the whole resistance? They had been fighting the resistance for more than a year now. How had the resistance gotten so big so fast? They would never know until they got their hands on that interfering nurse again. He didn't understand how she had gotten away from them. *Well, this is a mystery that would need to wait for now.*

Just then Ghost's thoughts were interrupted by the ringing of his cell phone. They all owned a second cell phone for the Plan business only. These phones were hot off the experimental phase of the CIA's new phone research. They could not be bugged by anyone. He was lucky to have gotten his hands on the five phones he had.

He answered the phone on the third ring, as they always did, and said, "Ghost here."

"Einstein here," began the voice on the other end. "Are Father and Sonny on yet?"

"No," Ghost said. "Hold on, I'm calling them now."

There was the sound of ringing and then the voice of Father came on, saying, "This is Father, and I have Sonny here on my line. Are we ready?"

Both men said, "Yes, go ahead."

Father began, "Give me an update on the situation of that nurse."

Ghost started off, "We have been tracking a person who we think is the nurse. She is wearing some kind of disguise as an old man. She was seen walking out of the town of Sykesville, Maryland. Plus one of my guys was given a description of her dressed as a younger man in a truck stop in the next town of Gaither. However, after that, no one has seen her again. I'll tell you, Father, we have covered that area with my guys in the CIA. The local sheriff's department has been very helpful as well, but no one has seen her after the truck stop. It is as if some large hand has swept her off the face of the earth."

There was a pause then Father asked, "What's happening with the resistance in your area?"

"Things in the states are fairly quiet. I'm not sure why, but I don't believe the nurse has told anyone except the reporter. So nothing new to report. I believe we clamped a lid on it just in time.

"Well, keep me informed of any change, no matter how small."

Father addressed Einstein then and asked how the plan was going so far.

Einstein replied, "We couldn't be more pleased with the way the two techniques are working together. This new chemical we're calling a sugar substitute is great. When we put it in the drinks of those people using our special devices, we get the results of ninety-five percent under our control. The really good thing about this is everyone drinks some kind of bottled drink, carbonated drinks, juice, even processed teas and coffee. If there is any color to the liquid and it can be processed, we can put the additive in without anyone's knowledge. There is no taste at all. However, it does change the color of un-bottled water red. We're not sure why this is, but hardly no one drinks un-bottled water these days anyway. Even people of third world countries drink bottled drinks of some kind because their water is contaminated. Who would have thought that contaminated water could help our cause?"

Father said, "Good, very good. We are working at getting our contacts, the people in high places like the FDA in your country, Ghost, and other like agencies in all the countries, to give permission to start ordering our sugar substitute. We have contacts in most of these agencies who have already been given the treatment and who are in our control. That's one of the things I needed to inform you of. We also must be very careful and use caution when communicating with each other from now on until we're in complete control. We must warn our troops already planted in the churches and government agencies. We start the plan worldwide tonight at midnight, US Eastern Standard Time. Our people know not to expose themselves to any of it wherever possible. The troops have been warned to stop drinking any processed drinks just to be on the safe side."

"Einstein, what will happen if we're exposed to any of the drink?" Sonny asked.

"We're continuing our testing on that area, but even our people who have been vaccinated need to stay away from both the devices and drinks with our sugar-sub in it until we know more."

"By the way," said Ghost, "where I had that vaccination, on my left hand, it made a mark."

"So did mine," said Father. "What's up with that, Einstein?"

"We're not sure, but so far everyone has started showing signs of a black mark within a few weeks of the vaccination. I can't think it will cause any trouble. It's just a side effect. If I could get the vaccination to work anywhere else beside the forehead or the hand, I would start giving it out of sight. But all our testing has shown it will only work in those two places. I'm sure you don't want me to start giving them on foreheads. After all, it's only a small mark, and maybe it will fade in time."

There was a pause in the conversation while each man thought of what else should be covered. Ghost was the first to interrupt the pause by asking Sonny how everything was going in the Middle East.

"Are the test people in your area responding the same?"

Sonny replied, "Yes, we're getting good results, but you must remember that my country is different from yours. Our people are already in our control. For the most part, people do what they are told. They also have far fewer electronic devices. We are concentrating on the leaders who were not approachable. Still, we believe we will have everyone under our control when the time comes to take over."

"Ghost, will you be able to step into power when we are ready?" Father asked.

"Oh yes, elections are next November, a year and a month from now. We are going to be in position for the party to nominate me at the last minute. That is our plan for now, anyway. We can change our plans if we need to. We are working on the groundwork for this contingency right now. This country will not know what hit it until it is too late."

Father said, "I think that just about wraps things up for now. If there is anything else before next month, send it encoded through the weather report. We will all get the message together. Does anyone else have more to add?" No one did, all disconnected.

Each man thought of the coming year and the big changes that were about to be brought upon the world. Father thought about the other two. He knew they thought they would be in control of their parts of the world, but he had been having a change of heart about that. He wanted control over the whole world. He would not stop until he gained that. When he first started thinking about the idea, he felt a twinge of guilt because he had become friends with the other two. But he didn't want to stop at just Europe. He wanted the world. He rationalized it would be better if there was one leader and not three. Three could end up fighting. It was his responsibility to make sure that did not happen.

Ghost was having his own thoughts of grandeur. Ghost was brilliant. As a young man, he had wanted to go into politics to help his country. However, because he was handicapped, he was not thought to be a good candidate to run for any higher office. When Ghost was a young boy, he had gotten sick; the disease had left him slightly deformed. Party leaders told him the people of his state were mostly country folk who would look past that, but it was different in Washington. He was fine to do their work for them but not good enough to be a leader. He would get back at all the party puppets that had followed President Rivers. Those who had not voted for him and left him to the wolves, he would show them. They would not see it coming until it was too late. He would make sure they were wide awake and understood what was happening to them. They would see he had tricked them and there was nothing they could do about it. His day was coming. He laughed to himself. It never entered his mind that Father was thinking of betraying him. His mind was not going in that direction at all; he was only thinking of sweet revenge.

Einstein thought about the money he would get and all the things that money could buy. He didn't want to be a leader of anything; he just wanted the money. He would buy himself an island someplace warm. He would do anything he wanted and life will be great. *I just have to keep doing what these guys want for a little while longer, then I will have access to my Swiss bank account that is already set up in an alias name.*

Sonny's mind was not following in the path of any of the other men. He was having some second thoughts. He believed in his God, Allah, father of Abraham of old. He was not sure this plan to control people's minds was what Allah wanted. When this had first started, it had all sounded so good. He would get control of the Middle East in order to rid the area of infidels. However, the plan had changed over time, and so had he. Now he had uncomfortable feelings that he was being led, not by Allah, but by some other thing like pride, ambition, and power. Or was it something even more evil than that? He was not sure what to do—he needed time to think. For the time being, he was going to keep the new sugar-sub out of his people's drinks. That way, his people would not be completely under control of the Plan. He could not control what people listened to. Most of the richer people in his country had cell phones and Internet access, but if they did not ingest the new sugar, they would be somewhat protected.

He wished for the hundredth time he could talk to his wife, Asilah, about all of this. Never in their twenty years of marriage had he ever kept anything from her. It was causing some strife between them. The name Asilah meant "noble origin and pure," and that was his wife completely. He had always liked her name. She was always noble and pure. She was not upset about his non-communication. However, he felt the strain of not confiding in her. They had a marriage unlike most of his fellow countrymen. He valued his wife's opinion and had always listened to her. He had not always followed her advice; however, trust and openness had always been a part of their marriage.

His wife, unlike other local wives, was a Christian and often told him of her faith. He could not leave the faith of his family; however, he often found what she told him to be very believable.

Something drew him to listen to her stories of Jesus. He did not know if he could ever believe Jesus was Allah's son, but he liked what he heard about him. The stories she told him about Jesus were so human, and at the same time, he could feel the complete love Jesus had for each person that he came in contact with. His wife had only become a Christian in the past year while he was away traveling. She had learned the story of Jesus from the children's live-in teacher, Daliyah. Asilah could not resist Jesus's call to her heart. Sonny decided he would pray to Allah every day until he could make a decision on what to do.

With this thought, he felt somewhat better and went in search of Asilah to ask her to pray to Allah for him. He knew she would pray even without knowing why.

Asilah had changed since she had become a Christian—not that there was anything wrong with her before—but she had become even more noble and gracious. She now had such a sweet spirit. The children were changing also since the young Christian teacher had come to take over their schooling. He did not know if he could believe like they did, but he sure liked his family's new attitudes. His thoughts about his family stopped when he came into the hall leading to the wing of the house where the children's rooms were. The loveliest music was coming from their schoolroom. Daliyah was playing a CD of some children singing.

When the song ended, he heard his youngest child, Shari, say, "Can we sing another song, Miss Daliyah, please?" Sonny was surprised; he never would have imagined his children could sing that beautifully. He was struck by the words of the song they had sung: "Just As I am… I Come." The melody was so haunting, and the words kept ringing in his mind: "Just come to Jesus."

Was this an answer to his prayer to Allah? Surely it was just a coincidence he had come down the hall looking for his wife at that very moment. Did Allah work like that? Sonny didn't know. He decided to keep his mind open to what Allah was saying to him. He would spend more time with his wife and children. Maybe, for a while, he would turn more of the operation of the group's plan over to his second-in-command, Fakah. That would give him some time to think and pray.

14

A Stumble in the Dark

Valentine woke slowly with the realization that she was alone again. The Sanchez family was on their way south, Valentine was on her way west. Still she thought of them as her new family and God's family. She realized they had a link, a chain of angels, to help them do what was needed. In her heart she did not feel alone at all. Valentine felt like she had an army behind her. She peeked out the tent in time to see a beautiful sunrise with the promise of a beautiful day.

When Valentine moved her covers, she felt a shot of cold air she was not ready for. Steeling herself for the cold, she hopped quickly out of her covers to stir her fire to life before she did anything else. To her delight, the coals under the ashes were still warm. Valentine put some dry leaves on top and blew gently to get the fire going. She knew it was kind of silly to start the fire this way when she now had a lighter, but it was fun to do it the way Maria had always done it each morning. She started water heating for her coffee and then went to wash up.

While her coffee was perking, she opened the little black book and started reading. She read about Jesus and his friends going to a wedding. She thought about the Creator of the entire universe going to a wedding and helping the wedding party by creating a special drink for them. They called it a miracle in the book and said He did it to please his mom. He must have loved her a lot. Valentine wondered how Mary could live every day with her own Creator and yet treat Him simply like a little boy.

She liked the part where Jesus said, "Mom, what am I going to do with you?"

She had learned from Maria the book was written in old English and, by putting the Bible verses into her own words, helped to make the story more real to her.

Valentine stopped reading when the wedding story finished; it was time to get on her way. She bowed her head, closed her eyes, and let her imagination go a bit. She thought of the world where God, Jesus, and the Spirit lived. She started to talk to them as she had heard Manuel do, as if they were right there sitting by her fire. When she closed her eyes, she felt she could see them clearly. Valentine guessed this was the reason why the Sanchez family closed their eyes. Since she had known them, they had always done this, and she had wondered about the reason for this practice; now she knew.

The fire had warmed her up nicely. Her breakfast consisted of a bite of the beef jerky and some slices of parsnip with her coffee. "That should do for now," she spoke to a small rabbit sitting close eating a bite of parsnip she had tossed to it. She let the fire die down while she got ready to travel on. She refilled her water bottles and cut up more parsnips to eat while she walked. She then put out the fire completely. She checked for any signs of her staying there. Except for the ashes in the old fireplace, everything looked as it did when she arrived. Picking up her backpack, she turned her back on the sun and started west. She had looked over the map Juan had made for her, and she felt she knew what to watch for to keep on the trail.

Valentine walked all day. That night she followed her map to camp off the road in a clump of heavy tall grasses. She had no trees to make a tent for her bedroll, but she rolled herself into the tarp and blankets like a hot dog in a bun and kept very warm and snug all night. She didn't make a fire because she could see lights ahead. The lights looked like a town, and she didn't want someone coming out here to find out why there was a fire in the prairie.

The sky was big and stars were everywhere—millions and millions of them. What a beautiful picture it was. Looking up at the stars made her feel as if she was part of the bigger picture. She felt like one of those stars except she was on earth and not floating in the galaxy somewhere. "I am one of God's stars, and there is nothing that can make me feel safer than that." As Valentine watched the stars twinkling, her eyes grew heavy, and soon she was asleep.

The next day she decided to go check out the little town, so she changed into her Lucy Pope disguise. She had not camped far out of town, so it only took her about half an hour to get to the outskirts and to begin seeing buildings. One of the first buildings Valentine came to was a small café with a sign reading, Sara's Diner. The bell rang cheerily as Valentine opened the door.

A voice from somewhere in the back said, "Sit wherever you like. I'll be right out." Valentine moved to a table near the front of the room and sat down. She noticed a round table in the back with a few men sitting at it drinking coffee. Soon a woman came out of the back bringing a cup and the coffee pot.

"Hello, ma'am, my name is Sara. Would you like a cup of coffee?"

Valentine cupped her hand around her ear, saying, "Could you speak up, dear? I'm a bit hard of hearing."

The woman pointed to the coffee pot and nearly yelled.

"Would you like a cup of coffee?"

"Oh, yes, thank you, dear. I would love a hot cuppa, as my old dad used to say."

Valentine realized it was kind of fun pretending to be someone else—when she was not scared half out of her wits. After she ordered a small breakfast, she sat back with her hot drink to see if she could get a feel of what was happening in the area. Not long into her meal, two more people joined the men in the back—a man and a woman.

She heard the woman say, "What's been happening? You guys hear anything new?"

The man with her said, "Keep your voice down, dear."

"Don't mind that old lady," Sara told them. "She's very hard of hearing—sweet old thing, though."

After that, the people talked in normal voices. Valentine could hear everything they said. The lady began, "I don't know about you folks, but my kids are acting really weird. One minute they are nice kids, they do as they are told, and are part of the family. The next thing I know they are disrespectful and won't quit playing that new video game the community center gave out. You know that nice young youth minister, what's his name? Bruce, I think his name is Bruce Priest. He's been working closely with Father John. Father John turned the old Hamilton building into a community center for kids to come and get together without getting into trouble. Bruce has been helping him over the past six months with the kids. I really liked the way he got some kids involved that don't have dads at home. Still, ever since my kids have gotten into those games, well, I just hardly know them anymore. Have any of you seen a change in your kids?" The men at the table began to agree with what the woman had said.

One of the men said, "I have always liked the way this town is far enough away from any big city that our children can grow up safe. But are these videos really changing our children? Has anyone watched or played the videos yourself?"

The woman spoke up again. "I started to play one, but just as I was getting into it, the phone rang, and I never finished it. However, I didn't see anything that would lead me to stop my children from playing them."

Another man said, "Have any of you thought more of what Sister Patricia said before she left, about sending someone to take Father John's place?"

"When did Sister Patricia say she was coming back? She sure left in a hurry. Where did she say she was going?"

"To Baltimore, I think. She called and talked to Pastor Bruce last night. My oldest son said Pastor Bruce told them Sister Patricia would be back in a week. He also said he'd like them all to be there to welcome her back."

Valentine jumped involuntarily at the word *sister. Could this possibly be the Sister?* she wondered. If it was the same person, she must travel all over getting people caught up in her scheme and obtaining their confidence. Valentine was glad she had stopped in at this café, because she had been thinking of staying a few days and checking things out. But now she must try to help these people and then leave quickly. She sure didn't want to be in the clutches of the Sister again. But her mind was wandering, and she needed to be listening.

One of the men was saying, "Not to change the subject, but did you guys hear we'll be getting our cell phone tower now? Everyone can sign up for a free cell phone."

"What happened?" Sara asked. "The last thing I had heard was we were too far out and it would cost too much money to build."

"The company called yesterday and said we were approved. Said someone was sponsoring our town. You can't beat that!"

Just then the bell over the door rang out. A police officer walked in and sat down at the counter. He turned and spoke to everyone at the back table in a friendly voice, "Morning, everyone, nice weather for the October fest this weekend."

Everyone agreed, and talk around the back table turned to general things like crop prices, farming, and the up-and-coming October fest.

By the time Valentine finished her breakfast, the diner had emptied and she was alone. She decided to get her little book out and read for a few minutes with a second cup of coffee. Valentine had just turned to the third chapter when Sara came over with the coffee pot for a refill and stayed to chat for a minute.

"What are you reading, honey?" Sara asked. Valentine showed her the Gospel of John and read the verse Manuel had read to her.

"John 3:16: For God so loved the world, that He gave His only begotten Son, that whosoever believeth in Him should not perish, but have everlasting life. Can I ask you something, dear? Do you read your Bible every day?"

"Well, I go to Mass on Sundays and I sometimes read to the kids out of our church's papers."

"I have found," Valentine explained, "that when I read from the Bible every day, even for a short time, I feel better."

"I get busy here at the diner," Sara answered. "By the time I get home, I'm so tired, and the kids need me to help them with schoolwork."

"Maybe you could read to your children before they go to bed. That could help all of you. I hear these days that kids are always playing games and no one spends any time together anymore. You could try reading to them tonight, dear, and see if they like it."

Sara got a thoughtful look in her eye and said, "Maybe I will. Maybe that will get their minds away from other influences. You know, I have a book of Bible stories that the kids used to love for me to read to them each night. It's been years since I opened that book. They had a favorite story. I can't remember what it was. I'll have to think about that. Thank you, honey, you've given me a wonderful way to get them away from those games. I'll have to say, my kids have been behaving strangely. Just like my friend was saying, her kids are acting strangely when they play this new game they got from the community center. My kids say all the kids love the game. My kids just started to play it this week. Some of the other kids have been playing it longer, but our machine was broken. You know what I'm going to do? I'm going to call all my friends and the ladies from my church group and get them to read to their kids tonight and see if it makes a difference. If it's okay with you, I think I'll just have my second cup of coffee with you while things are quiet."

Valentine said, "I would enjoy the company." Sara went and got a cup for herself and refilled Valentine's cup as well. Valentine said, "I never did tell you my name. I'm Lucy Pope. I'm just passing through, and you've a nice place here, Sara."

"Thank you, I'm so glad to meet you, Lucy."

Soon the conversation got around to the young youth pastor who was doing so much for the kids in the area. Sara said they had lost their priest about two months ago; it was a very sad accident, a hit-and-run that had killed him instantly. No one ever found the driver. The city police had tried, but they hit a stone wall when they asked for help from the county sheriff's department.

"I heard Charlie, the policeman who was in here earlier, telling someone he just didn't understand what was going on. He said he'd never had any trouble before when he asked for help. The sheriff had always been helpful. But he said the sheriff has been acting kind of strange ever since he went to that statewide seminar at the capital about a year ago. But I guess I'm talking too much. You don't want to hear all of our troubles."

"Oh, no, dear," Valentine said. "I'm always glad to lend a good listening ear when someone needs to talk. That's so sad about your priest. Who is saying the mass for church now?"

"Well, that nice new youth pastor has been helping out at the youth center, but no one has come to replace Father John. Sister Patricia has said several times she will bring us a priest from over in Italy—our church is split over it."

Just then the phone rang and Sara went to answer it. Valentine took the opportunity to visit the bathroom before she headed out again. When Valentine came back, Sara asked, "Miss Lucy, could you use a lunch for your travels?

Sara handed Valentine a paper bag. She was surprised and thankful. Sara said, "For your kindness and taking the time to listen. You know people just don't take the time to listen or help out others anymore. I can remember my grandmother used to talk of the old ways. She said people worked together so well and when someone needed something the town helped out. If someone was sick, they took food and helped in any way they could. We need to do more of that. Maybe I can get something started here in my own town. You know, Lucy, you've really got me to thinking."

Valentine gave Sara a quick hug. "I will be praying for you and your town that God will help you with your children."

Valentine turned and walked out the door and down the road heading east. When she turned to look back, Sara was standing at the window; each raised a hand to wave to the other.

At the next corner, Valentine turned and headed out of town. When she was out of sight, she turned west again. She smiled to herself because she felt like she had done what she was sent there to do. *God is leading me to where I could be the most help, and I must remember to pray for help and guidance for the mission I am on.*

When Valentine reached the end of the street, she stopped to look at her map to get back on track. She found a place to change out of her Lucy outfit and started walking at a fairly fast pace. She wanted to put as many miles between herself and the Sister as she could. She did not know if Sister Patricia was the same sister who was after her, but she did not want to take any chances.

Valentine traveled on like this for three days, each night getting colder. The skies stayed clear until the fourth day when Valentine started to see dark low clouds to the north. Soon she could not see any of the sun at all. She figured it was sometime past noon when the first snowflake fell. A nagging thought began to form. *I have no way to keep warm if it really began to snow hard.*

With each step she took, the snow got thicker.

Valentine climbed to the top of a hill and stopped. She searched the area below to see if there was any place to get out of the snowstorm. She did not know much about snow. However, this thing was beginning to look like a blizzard. As she scanned the valley before her, she thought she saw a light far down in the valley a little to her right. Valentine headed for the light, hoping she could find an outbuilding or barn to stay in until the storm blew over. She was getting very weary with each step as the snow got deeper. Valentine felt like she had walked forever. She could no longer see any light. She just kept going in the direction she thought she had seen the light last. The snow was very thick; now it swirled around her. She felt like she was in a world of cotton balls.

Valentine wondered if she should stop and try to get warm with her tarp and blankets, but the air was so cold now she did not think she could survive for long. Her only hope was to get out of the storm.

Where is my guardian now that I need someone? she wondered. She was getting scared and beginning to feel a little bit sorry for herself.

"Am I going to die out here in this storm all alone? Where are you, Jesus? Help me, please. Help me," she shouted to the raging storm.

Valentine felt calmer and decided to move five more steps forward. If she did not find anything, she would turn slightly more to the right. Remembering up on the hilltop, she had thought the lights were more to the right of her. Valentine took the five steps but could see nothing except empty, dark space. She stopped and tried to judge how far to turn to the right. Just as she started to turn, her foot caught on something and stumbled. Moving her hand out in front of her, she could feel a hard, solid surface. *Could it be a wall?* She moved her hands to the right and there was nothing but space. Then she moved her hands to the left and felt more of the wall.

Valentine had almost missed the building altogether; her stumble had thrown her onto the corner of the building.

She continued to move to the left and soon felt a change in the wall. It felt like an opening for a door or a window. She moved her hands slowly over the whole area until she found what she had hoped to find—a doorknob. *Please open for me,* she prayed. *What if I opened the door to people who were not friendly?*

she wondered. *Or, even worse, an enemy!* All kinds of thoughts were running through her mind as she turned the knob.

The knob turned smoothly and the door opened into a dark room. Valentine started forward but stubbed her toe on something. She soon realized it was only a doorstop. She quickly stepped over it and closed the door. Compared to outside, the room was almost warm. She could still not see but started forward using her hands to be her guide.

Suddenly she thought she heard something move deeper in the room. What was that? Cautiously she moved forward. Her left hand then touched something soft and warm. She jerked back but heard only a soft breathing sound. Carefully she reached out her hand again. This time she heard a low mooing and then a foot stomp on the floor. "I hope you're a friendly cow and will not start making a lot of noise," she whispered to the warm body. "I sure don't need you to bring someone to investigate." She moved on until her hand touched a pole standing straight up in the air. Investigating further, she found the pole to be a ladder to a loft. She hoped it would have dry hay. *Wouldn't that be a wonderful place to spend the night out of the storm—a soft and warm place to lie down is all I want just now.*

She carefully climbed the ladder and found just what she had hoped for. She moved deeper into the hayloft, took her backpack off, and pulled some hay together. Next she got out her blankets and tarp. Rolling herself up, she laid her head on the softness. Before Valentine fell asleep, she said a tired but happy thank-you to God for her guardian. She knew that her angel had helped her stumble in just the right way to find this shelter in a storm. She fell asleep to the quiet sounds of a friendly barn.

15

A Storm Is Coming

Valentine snuggled deeper into her blankets. In the hazy moments just before truly waking, she heard children laughing. She heard one say, "Push me higher, Darcy, push me higher." Valentine tried to get a glimpse of the girls, but the bushes were too thick. She could only hear their little childish voices and their laughter. She looked around and saw the bushes were really a hedge, tall and well groomed. There was a path through the middle of the hedge. Looking around, she saw she was standing in the side yard of an old gray two-story home with a large bay window. She turned toward the hedge. She wanted, more than anything, to go through the hedge and see the little girls. However, even though she continued to walk, she could get no closer to the path.

All too soon she woke with the dream still clearly in her mind. She could smell the fresh hay and the sound of a cow mooing. She kept her eyes closed and tried to bring back the dream. *Could those girls be my daughters?* she wondered. *Or was it a memory from a movie I once saw?* The sound of the sweet voices haunted her, along with the one name she had heard, Darcy. The name brought a feeling of family and of coming home.

Valentine wanted nothing more than to savor the sounds then she heard childish voices again. The new voices were a little different but still two voices—one older and one younger.

One said, "Should we wake her?"

The other one said, "I don't know, Rose. She looks asleep. Mama said to just see if she's awake."

Hearing a giggle, Valentine couldn't help herself. She slowly opened her eyes. There before her were two girls about seven and ten. They were sitting cross-legged by the ladder. Both had overalls on. Both girls had beautiful auburn hair. Their hair was braided in long braids hanging down on both sides of their faces, like picture frames. They had freckles covering the bridges of their noses, still prominent from the summer tans.

When they saw Valentine's eyes open, they started to jump up, but she said, "Please don't go. Stay and talk to me. What are your names? My name is Valentine, and one of you is Rose. Is that right?"

The older of the two said, "Yes, this is Rose, and I am Whitney. Where did you come from, and why are you sleeping in our barn?"

Valentine said, "I was lost in the storm last night, and I thought I was going to stay lost, maybe freeze to death. Then I asked God to help me and He showed me your barn. The cow downstairs said I could stay as long as I didn't snore."

"Did you snore?" asked Rose.

"I don't know. I guess we'll have to ask your cow. Does *he* have a name?"

Whitney laughed and said, "He is a she. Her name is Dolly. She gives us really good milk to drink. Valentine, would you like to come eat breakfast with us? The storm has stopped for now."

"Are you sure your mama wants me to?"

"Oh yes," said Rose. "Mama told us to ask you if you were awake."

The girls helped Valentine fold up her blankets, and Whitney carried her backpack down the ladder.

Stepping out of the barn, Valentine saw the back of a nice older farmhouse. By the looks of things, someone had been doing repair work on the place. Inside of the back door was a mud room where everyone hung their coats and took off their muddy boots. Valentine placed her backpack near the door. She sat down on the bench where Whitney and Rose were sitting and took off her boots. The girls showed Valentine where the bathroom was. They waited for her to wash up and they all went into the kitchen together.

Valentine thought the aromas sailing around the kitchen were heavenly. She could smell fresh perked coffee and bacon frying on an old black wood cook stove. The woman standing at the stove was petite and slim, wearing faded jeans and a flannel shirt. Her hair was the same color as the girls and she was wearing it in one long braid down her back. As she heard them come in, she turned and held out her hand to Valentine.

"Hi, I'm Esther. I guess you met the girls?" She smiled at the girls and added, "Did you girls find any eggs in the barn? Remember, that was the other reason you were sent out there."

The girls looked down at their empty egg basket, and Whitney, laughing, said, "Oh, Mama, we forgot. We'll be right back." They turned and ran out the kitchen door to the mud room.

Esther said, "Won't you please sit down? Would you like to have a hot cup of coffee?"

"The coffee sounds great, thanks. I'm sorry for not asking first before I slept in your barn."

Esther replied, "Don't say another word about it. We're just happy you're safe."

Soon the girls came trooping in with their basket. Rose said, "We could only find eight eggs this morning."

"Just enough for our breakfast," Esther told them. "We'll eat when Daddy comes in from feeding the animals."

Valentine asked if there was anything she could do to help. The girls said she could help them set the table. However, Esther intervened, "You girls can set the table. Let Valentine drink her coffee and warm up."

Just as they finished, they heard the back door slam.

A voice from the mud room hollered, "Where are my boot girls?"

Both girls squealed and ran for the back room. They tried to beat the other girl to be first to help their daddy off with his boots. There was happy laughter and talking coming from the mud room before a nice-looking man walked into the kitchen. Going to the stove first, he gave Esther a kiss on the cheek then he asked if breakfast was ready yet.

Esther blushed and said, "We have company, Caleb."

Caleb turned around and saw Valentine standing in the doorway between the dining room and the kitchen holding her cup of coffee.

"Good morning," he greeted her, "sleep well?"

"Yes, thank you," Valentine answered with a smile.

Soon they were all sitting at the dining room table. Rose asked if she could say the blessing. After the blessing was said and everyone had filled their plates, Caleb turned to Valentine and asked, "How is it you came to be sleeping in the barn? Not that we mind at all. We were just curious. Last evening, after I finished milking, I saw that the snow was getting thicker. Believe it or not, I thought anyone caught in the storm could be in danger. I prayed right then and there, asking for safety from the storm. We're kind of new to praying, but I just felt like someone was saying to me, 'You need to pray.' Do you believe in this kind of thing, Valentine?"

Valentine looked at him with a small smile on her face, a bit teary-eyed even.

"Well, Caleb, you most likely saved my life. And, yes, I do believe in that kind of thing. I too am new at believing and praying. I had seen your lights from up on that tall hill, and because the snow was getting thicker, I decided I would head for the lights to see if I could find a place to ride out the storm. I was trudging through the snow and it was getting harder and harder to walk. I was getting worried, and I had forgotten to ask

God for help. I couldn't see anything beyond my own hand. As I said before, I have not known how to pray, but for a few days, I guess I forgot in my distress. All of a sudden I wondered where my guardian angels were now that I needed them. I was getting scared and was beginning to feel sorry for myself. I thought I was going to die out there in the storm all alone.

"Finally I called out, 'Where are you, Jesus? Help me, please, help me.' Then I decided to move five more steps forward. If I didn't find anything, I would turn slightly to the right. I felt like the lights I had seen were more to the right of me. I took the five steps but could feel nothing except empty, dark space. Just as I started to turn and go more to the right, I caught my foot on something and stumbled and fell. But I didn't fall down. I fell onto the corner of your barn. You see, Caleb, if you had not prayed for anyone out in the storm, I might never have remembered to ask for help for myself."

"Wow!" said the little girls in unison.

Esther said, "That was a wonderful story, Valentine. Maybe later you could tell us more about how you learned to pray. Right now it's time to get the girls changed into their school clothes because the bus will be here soon."

There was a mad rush as the girls hurried upstairs to change and then back downstairs to get their lunches. They put on their coats for the walk down the driveway to wait for the bus.

Just before the two girls went out the door, Rose asked, "Are you going to be here when we get home from school, Valentine?"

"I will try to be, but I'm not sure."

Esther said, "Run girls! I'll try to keep Valentine here until you come home."

Quickly the girls were out the door and running down the drive, waving as they went.

"Valentine," said Esther, "I'm not sure about you, but if I slept in a barn last night, I would just have to have a bath. How does that sound?"

Valentine realized she had not had a bath since the shower at the truck stop. She had washed up at camp, but to soak in a hot bath sounded heavenly.

"Thank you, Esther. Are you sure I won't be putting you out any?"

"You won't be putting me out at all. And if you could stay at least until after the girls come home from school, you would make their day. They have taken quite a liking to you."

So it was settled. Valentine went up and had the first hot bath she could remember. She washed her hair two times and then put cream rinse in it to get all the tangles out. When she came out of the bath, there was a clean but worn bathrobe on the bed.

A note lay on the bed. "I'm washing your clothes. Come on down and have a second cup of coffee with me, Esther."

There were tears in Valentine's eyes as she thought to herself, God has led me to another family who needs me—and I sure needed them last night in that storm.

Sitting down on the bed, she closed her eyes and prayed a short prayer, "Thank you, Father God. Help me to be a blessing to this family, amen."

She took her Gospel of John out of her backpack and went down for that second cup of coffee.

Esther had just finished cleaning the breakfast dishes when Valentine entered. She said, "Why don't we sit here in the kitchen where the stove keeps us cozy?"

They talked of general things until Esther asked what the book was in Valentine's hand.

"This is *The Gospel of John*, and I've just really begun to read it. I found it in a bookstore. I was looking for a certain kind of book, but I have a tight budget. When I saw it was a nice leather-bound book, I was sure I couldn't afford it. Then when I opened the front cover and read the inscription, I just knew I had to buy it somehow."

Valentine opened her book to the front page and handed it to Esther.

After reading the inscription, she looked up surprised.

"This wasn't your book before, but here is your name. That's really curious, very cool, but curious."

Valentine explained she got the book before she knew about God and how He helps people.

"I'll have to say it gave me goose bumps when I first read it—and every time I reread it."

"I would love to hear more of your story, but I know the girls and Caleb will want to hear it also. So you won't have to tell it twice, I'll not ask any more questions, okay? When you find your place you show me where you are in the book? I'll get my new Bible and we can read together."

Soon they were reading together the third chapter of John, about Nicodemus and the questions he asked Jesus. When they got to verses fourteen through eighteen, they read them twice. Neither of them knew what was meant by Moses lifting up a serpent. However, the part about God loving the world so much that He sent His son to save it; this they understood.

Valentine said, "You know these verses make it so simple to believe in Jesus, that He is the Son of God and that we'll live with him forever. A friend of mine told me, someday, we would live with God where He lives. I like to think of living forever with someone who loves me that much."

"Wow, I have never read this part of the Bible before," Esther exclaimed. "We're studying with Caleb's Uncle Billy and Aunt Emma, but we're still in the Old Testament."

They read a bit more and then Esther said she needed to get some work done.

"Give me a minute and I'll go put on my second set of clothes and help you," Valentine said.

When she returned to the kitchen in her jeans and flannel shirt, Esther said, "I've got some small potatoes I want to put into jars and can. I also need to put the last of the larger potatoes on shelves in the root cellar to keep good all winter."

Esther and Valentine worked well together and the jobs were done in no time.

"Wow, those jobs would have taken me most of the day by myself. Thank you so much, Valentine."

They walked out to the barn to feed the chickens and look for any eggs the girls might have missed in their hurry to get back to their visitor. Caleb was still in town and would not be back for a few more hours, so they ate a simple lunch. The ladies were just cleaning up the kitchen when they heard the truck pull into the yard. Soon they could hear the voices of the girls as well as Caleb in the mud room.

"I wonder why the girls are home so soon," Esther asked as she went to the back door. "Are you girls playing hooky today?"

"No," shouted the girls in unison.

"School was let out early because a really bad storm is coming—even worse than last night. They said it would be better for everyone to get home before it hit," explained Whitney.

"Daddy picked us up at the end of the driveway," this from the happy voice of Rose.

They all trouped into the kitchen to warm up.

Esther said, "This is a perfect time for hot chocolate. You girls go change out of your school clothes. And Rose, remember to hang up yours. I had to do it for you last night."

"Yes, ma'am," they said together and ran from the room, making all kinds of racket going up the stairs.

The grownups looked at each other laughing and shaking their heads.

"To be young again with all that energy and sweet innocence," Caleb commented.

While Caleb washed up, the ladies started hot chocolate and coffee. Soon everyone was back at the kitchen table, talking and enjoying their hot drinks. The girls both tried to tell about the visitor they had that morning at school.

Rose said, "She had a funny long dress on, and it was all black and she wore a funny black hat."

Valentine had been listening and enjoying the sounds of the family and her hot chocolate, but when Rose said that, the color drained from her face.

Esther saw Valentine's face and said, "Are you all right, Valentine? You look like you just saw a ghost."

Valentine tried to talk, but she nearly choked on her drink.

Then she said, "What did you say about a woman in a black dress?"

Whitney said, "She means Sister Julia. She comes every year from the Catholic school in the next county and tells us stories. Rose has never seen her before because she just started school this year."

Valentine tried to calm her heart; slowly the color came back into her face.

"So what kind of stories did she tell today?" Valentine asked, trying to make her voice sound as normal as she could.

"Oh, she didn't tell us any stories today," complained Rose. "She just talked about another woman, sister, that's coming next week. She said the other sister is bringing us all a new video game to play at home or school. She said the game would help us in our studies. She said they would tell us some stories when they came next week. I've just never seen a lady dress so funny, and it kind of scared me at first, but Whitney was holding my hand and smiling, so I guessed it was okay."

Valentine was quiet for a minute and then asked the girls when they were going back to school.

Esther answered for them, saying, "If this storm is as bad as they say, they won't be going for a few days."

Caleb said, "I was listening to the weather report on the way home, and we're in for a big snow. This storm will make last night's look like a walk in the park. Valentine, please tell us what has made you so worried. If it's about the storm, don't be, because you must stay here until it's safe to move on."

"Caleb, Esther, there is something important I need to tell you, but it can wait until after supper." She looked at the girls and then looked at Esther, as if to say this was not for them to hear.

"Okay," Caleb said, "you've got me curious. I can wait until later. Girls, let's go feed the animals and get them settled before the storm comes."

With the idea of going with their daddy out to the barn, they forgot about what Valentine had to say and went out the door, both talking a mile a minute.

There was plenty to do to get a farm ready for a big storm. Caleb brought a heavy rope out and strung it on poles all along the path to the barn. The girls checked on the chickens and found them already roosting in their chicken house ready for night.

"I wonder why they are already going to bed," asked Rose.

"I don't know. We'll ask Daddy when we're all back in the house," replied Whitney.

They checked the chickens' food and water, and to see if there were any more eggs before starting back to the house.

Caleb finished checking the barn. He closed the door firmly before he headed for the house.

When Caleb was sitting at the kitchen table, he explained to Valentine they would be warm and safe even if the electricity went off because they had a good supply of wood, both for the cook stove and the wood heater in the basement. Plus they had the fireplace in the living room they could use.

"The wood stove was all the heat we had the first winter we were here, remember, dear?"

Valentine asked how they would know if the storm was coming because they didn't have a television or a computer.

Esther answered her, "We use the radio if we need it. We kind of like the peace and quiet of the farm. After living in

New York City, when we first married, I will never get tired of just hearing the sounds of the farm life. Caleb grew up on this farm and was very happy to exchange the sights and sounds of the city for his beloved farm. He only moved away for love. You see, Valentine, Caleb and I met in college. He was offered such a great job right out of college that he couldn't turn it down, and I, being a city girl, couldn't think of moving to the country. Boy was I wrong."

Supper was a pleasant time. Valentine almost forgot she had an important message to tell Caleb and Esther when the girls went to bed. She believed the little girls might be mature enough to hear the story, but that was for their parents to decide.

After Whitney was reminded to put her book down and turn out her light, and Rose had her second drink of water, all was finally quiet upstairs. Valentine started her story.

Valentine started with a short prayer to God then began at the beginning. She did not know how they would accept it, but there was nowhere else to start except the beginning, let the chips fall where they may. When she finished telling her story, the room was very quiet. Caleb and Esther just looked at each other. After a moment of complete silence, they heard a small sound coming from the hallway. Turning, they saw Whitney standing in the doorway.

Whitney said, "You don't think that bad nun was our Sister Julia, do you, Mama?"

Esther said, using that voice that mothers use when they mean business, "Whitney, please come into the living room, now!"

Whitney came in, hanging her head. She was trying not to cry but not quite making it. A small tear was already running down her cheek.

Caleb said, "Whitney, do you know why we didn't want you to hear this story tonight?"

"Yes, Daddy, because it would scare me. I'm sorry I didn't obey because now I'm scared and I don't want to go to bed by myself."

"That's right," Esther said. "But now that you've heard, you need to stay and let us finish talking about it. We'll try to understand more about what all this means to us."

Valentine said, "I'm so sorry. I didn't want the girls to hear this until you thought it was okay, but I do think Whitney is old enough to understand."

"Valentine," Caleb said, "I really don't know what to say. I've never heard of such a thing, and this is blowing my mind. How could this happen in the United States, maybe other countries, but not here. I would like to have my Uncle Billy hear your story, get his take on it. Would you tell your story to Uncle Billy?"

"First off," Valentine said, "I would not have told you until we got to know each other better, but this thing with the video game is worrying me. I don't want your girls to get hurt by what's coming. I would be glad to talk with your Uncle Billy. I want to tell anyone whom God leads me to tell. At first I thought I could stop this thing, but I am beginning to think that will never be. However, I will tell as many people as I can to stay away from the game and to read their Bibles daily. That might be the only way to stop it."

"It's getting late," said Esther. "I think it will do us good to think on all of this and pray about it. We can talk more in the morning."

Everyone agreed. It was decided Whitney would sleep on the floor in her parent's room. This plan made her happy and ready for bed. Valentine was to sleep in the guest room where she had taken her bath that morning. It wasn't long until all was quiet in the old house.

Valentine climbed into bed thinking about what the girls had said.

I could be in big trouble if Caleb and Esther don't believe me and they tell the authorities about me, she thought. *But if I let myself, I can come up with all kinds of unpleasant things to worry about. I need to turn my eyes upon Jesus.*

With that thought, she started to softly sing her favorite song.

"O soul are you weary and troubled? No light in the darkness you see? There's light for a look at the Savior, and life more abundant and free! Turn your eyes upon Jesus. Look full in his wonderful face, and the things of earth will grow strangely dim in the light of His glory and grace."

The words meant so much to Valentine. They calmed her down so that by the time she had finished with the song, she was ready to give the entire problem to God and go to sleep.

Her prayer was short, "Please, Father God, lead me and these families in the way that you would have us go. Thank you for your watch over me last night, good night, amen."

The wind started to blow around midnight and the temperature dropped to the negative numbers, but the snow didn't come as expected. School was held off for one more day because the weather forecasters were sure the storm would still be hitting. Everyone wanted to make sure the blizzard didn't start while the children were in school. Esther and Caleb spoke with Valentine, and it was agreed Caleb would go over to Uncle Billy's house and invite him and Aunt Emma to supper. Valentine would tell her story again to them.

Valentine went with the girls to collect eggs—if there were any. With cold weather, the chickens' egg production decreased quickly. The three had a good time, and having Valentine with them made the time special for the girls.

All day Valentine could tell that Esther was worried. She told Valentine later she had finally decided to put all these strange happenings into God's hands and not worry. With this burden put aside, Esther joined the girls in the barn where there was other work to do.

They threw hay down to Dolly, the cow. Caleb had already milked her earlier, and the milk was sitting in the mud room on the table ready to be put into jars.

Valentine was surprised at all the things that needed doing each and every day. She thought she would like to live on a farm someday. This kind of life appealed to her.

By the time everything was finished, they were really feeling the cold. Everyone was ready to go in and warm up by the cook stove. Esther said she would make everyone hot chocolate again; plus she got out some homemade cookies. It was beginning to feel like a holiday with no school, hot chocolate, and cookies. Esther told the girls this snack would hold them until dinner, because they were going to eat early so Uncle Billy and Aunt Emma could get home before it was dark.

Whitney and Rose were jumping with joy when they heard their favorite great aunt and uncle were coming for a visit. Whitney was told the reason for the visit and was asked to keep Rose busy while Valentine told her story. They did not want Rose to be scared like Whitney had been.

The afternoon sped by with the big meal to prepare and some light cleaning chores for the girls. Valentine helped where she could, however, was reminded she was not naturally good at cooking; although she was willing to learn.

Soon the house was filling with the smells of a roast cooking in the oven and the yeasty smell of bread rising on the table. Valentine was fascinated watching the bread rise. She thought, *If I ever saw such a thing before I'm not aware of it.* It seemed to her the dough was alive as it grew in the bowl.

Valentine asked Esther if there was anything else she could do. She was given the job of washing potatoes to bake, in their own skins, while the bread baked. As she washed the potatoes, she prayed, "Dear God, please help me to tell my story so my new friends will believe me and will be safe from the coming spiritual storm." She thought about the idea of a spiritual storm. There was more than an early snowstorm coming. There was a storm blowing evil everywhere. *Just as I was caught in the snowstorm and couldn't see, people could be caught and lost, and wouldn't even know because they couldn't see. Their minds would be as if they were turned off.*

Valentine was deep in thought and prayer when her reverie was broken by the sounds of happy voices in the front of the house. The sounds were moving toward the direction of the kitchen. She made a hasty last plea to her Father and Spirit and to Jesus to be with her and to guide her words.

Uncle Billy and Aunt Emma appeared to be lovely people. Aunt Emma was very gracious with a lovely soft spoken southern drawl, while Uncle Billy was just an ole sweetheart. Valentine could tell they loved this young family very much.

Dinner was a happy affair with Uncle Billy telling a funny story. It was all about when he was a boy and a mama cow had chased him for teasing her baby. Valentine could tell the girls had heard the story many times. Still, they obviously loved the ending when he fell in a mud puddle, and the mama cow stopped and seemed to laugh at him. It was a very funny story, and Valentine found she was laughing as well as beginning to relax.

After everyone had finished the apple pie Aunt Emma had brought, the grownups went into the living room to talk. Whitney took Rose upstairs to play a game. Whitney felt she was too old to play the game. But to keep Rose happy and occupied, she could play it just one more time.

Downstairs in the living room, all eyes were on Valentine. She smiled at each person and said, "Let us ask God to send His Spirit to help me tell my story."

She asked Uncle Billy to pray for her as she told her story and for them as they listened to hear only what God wanted them to hear and believe. Uncle Billy prayed just like Manuel had as if God was his friend and right there in the room. The prayer helped her as much as it did the others.

Valentine began her story at the beginning, in the hospital room, not even remembering her own name. Esther was sitting beside Valentine as she told her story. When she came to the part where Manuel told the store of Jesus, how he had died for her so she could live with God, Jesus, and the Spirit forever in their beautiful world, Valentine got a lump in her throat so big she could hardly speak. Esther took her hand squeezing it, smiling through her own tears.

When Valentine finished her story, all was quiet in the room. The proverbial pin could have dropped and it would have sounded like a cannon going off

After a few moments, they all began to hear the sounds outside that they had not noticed while Valentine talked. The wind was chasing around the corner of the porch. They all got up as one and went to the front door. Opening it, they all were taken by surprise at the snow coming down in thick, swirling, blinding flakes. They had not worried about the storm because the weather forecaster had said it would not arrive until well past midnight. It was only 7:00 p.m., and the world outside was a white wall.

"Well," said Uncle Billy, "it's a good thing you have a big house because you have two more to spend the night. And unless I miss my guess, we might be staying a few days. Can you stand us, Esther, all crowded into your house for a few days?"

Esther laughed and said, "It will be just like Christmas, Uncle Billy."

As Caleb closed the door, he said, "I had better go build a fire in the other guest room or you two old Santa Clauses will freeze to death."

Laughing, both Uncle Billy and Caleb went to the back porch to get wood for the fire. While they were at it, they decided to build a small fire in the living room to make the evening a little cozier. The ladies made a second pot of coffee and Esther made the girls some hot chocolate. She took it upstairs for them to drink while they played their game.

When Esther got to Whitney's room, she found them happy as clams with the new game Whitney was teaching Rose.

Rose looked up and said, "Look, Mommy! I'm playing Monopoly. I'm big enough now to learn it. Isn't that great?"

Esther smiled at her youngest then turned and mouthed the words "thank you" to Whitney.

"You girls have everything you need now? We're still talking about stuff you wouldn't want to listen to—old people stuff."

"Yes, Mama," said Whitney. "We're fine. You guys go on with your old-people stuff. We're having fun."

Whitney winked and went back to playing.

As she started down the stairs, Esther heard Rose say, "I passed GO! I get one hundred dollars, right, Whitney?"

Downstairs the adults regrouped in front of the fire in the living room.

Uncle Billy started by saying, "You know, Valentine, the Bible tells us about trouble in the end times and how we must be ready for that trouble by keeping close to Jesus. We do that by reading about Him in the Holy Bible and by praying. Now you have brought this story that tells us about reading our Bibles to strengthen our minds, to keep us safe from this mind-altering treatment."

There was a pause as everyone thought about what this might mean and how it applied to what Valentine had said. She was not sure by Uncle Billy's tone if he believed her story or not; she was a little concerned.

After a minute of silence, Uncle Billy continued, "Caleb and Esther have been studying with us and learning to believe and pray. However, we have not studied the parts of the Bible talking about the end-times. The prophecies give us a time line and tell us what to look for. I think it would be good for all of us to think about this story, this evil plan, and test it by biblical standards. We need to see where it stands in the biblical prophecies."

Uncle Billy looked around at each one in the room. Caleb and Esther were nodding their heads.

Caleb said, "That makes sense to me."

They all turned to Valentine to see what she would say.

She started by saying, "Thank you, Aunt Emma and Uncle Billy, for listening to my story. I very much like the idea of studying more of the Bible with someone who understands it better than I. I would be honored to study with you," Valentine finished as she smiled at each of them.

"Well, there's no time like the present to get started, as my mama used to say," said Aunt Emma. "Let's get our Bibles out and go to the dining room table to see what we can find.

There was a scramble to get their Bibles out. Because Valentine had only her Gospel of John, she was given Whitney's Bible to study. It was a nice one with study notes to guide her. She thought she might get one like this as soon as she could afford to buy one.

Uncle Billy started by directing them to the book of Daniel found in the Old Testament. They stopped reading at the end of chapter two and talked about what they had read. They decided that as a group they should write down questions and then study to find answers. Valentine said she wanted to write everything down in her notebook. She ran upstairs to her backpack to get it and returned to the dining room. She showed her notebook to the others and told them they were free to read it to help them understand the story she had told them.

However, by this time it was getting late, so they decided it was time to call it a night. The men went to the basement to restock the wood furnace and check the doors and the outside temperature. When they saw the temperature had dropped to zero degrees, Caleb turned on the water in the sink of the mud room to keep the pipes from freezing. After everything was taken care of, they all headed to their rooms.

Whitney asked if Rose could sleep in her room with her.

"Please, Mama, can I? Please?" Rose asked.

"Yes, if you both want to. But don't spend all night talking. I don't want you waking up grouchy as bears in the morning."

"We won't! We won't!" they shouted as they ran to Rose's room to get her pillow and her favorite doll, May.

Soon all was quiet except for the storms brewing both outside with the snowstorm and inside in the minds of the adults who were trying to sort through everything they had learned. Even though Valentine had just met them, she felt sure each said a prayer for help with their studies and guidance with their lives before they went to sleep.

16

Looking at the Stars

The morning dawned gray with snow still coming down and no signs of letting up. Inside the old house on the farm, all was quiet when Valentine awoke. Standing beside the window looking out, she felt as if she were in a cocoon—in a safe place brought by God. *Not only for me*, she thought, *but also to bring safety to my new friends.*

Valentine remembered what Manuel had read about the shepherd. She wondered if she could find that verse in Whitney's Bible. The night before, Esther had shown Valentine how to find things by going to the back of the Bible and looking for a prominent word in the verse you wanted to find.

Valentine left the window to retrieve her borrowed Bible from the bedside table. Coming back, she sat down in an overstuffed chair in a small sitting area Esther had prepared for her visitors so they could enjoy the view. Valentine enjoyed using the little nook to study her Bible. She opened the Bible to the back and thought of a word to help her find Manuel's verse. *Shepherd* seemed like a good place to start.

Turning to the word *shepherd*, she saw more than one suggestion. The first was Genesis 46:34, abomination to Egyptians. That didn't sound right. But the next suggestion was Psalm 23:1, "The Lord is my shepherd." "That sounded right," she exclaimed! She turned to the front of the Bible to find the *Ps*. Finding a book named Psalms, she turned to page 604 and found the first chapter.

Valentine turned the pages until she came to chapter 23 verse 1 and began to read. "The Lord is my shepherd; I shall not want." This was it! She could not believe it was that easy to find something in that great big book. She began to read the rest of the chapter. Just reading it brought back memories of her time with the Sanchezes and reminded her of the way God had kept her safe and brought her to a beautiful loving relationship with Him. The memory brought tears to her eyes. *The God of the universe wanted me to know Him and believe in His Son. Who could believe such a thing? But I believed, and that belief has changed my life forever.*

Valentine read on into chapter 24: "The earth is the Lord's and the fullness thereof." She liked the way the Psalms read and wondered who had written it. Looking at the top of the page, she saw the words "David's confidence in God's grace." Who was David? Did David write the part about being a shepherd? *When I have more time, I will look into this David and find out his story,* she promised herself.

By now Valentine was hearing sounds coming from around the house and smelled coffee perking. She decided it was time to help Esther get breakfast for the hungry crowd. But first she bowed her head and talked to God, Jesus, and the Spirit about the day and the studying that she and her new friends would be doing.

"Dear Father, help us to find the answers you have for us, and thank You for saving me and Jesus for dying for me. Help me to follow you today—your way and not mine. Thank You for spending time with me this morning. Bye for now, good friends."

The atmosphere at breakfast was like a holiday with Uncle Billy and Aunt Emma having spent the night.

As Rose set the table, she said, "I'm just happy to be alive!"

At breakfast the men talked about Uncle Billy's animals; if they would be safe until the storm died down. Uncle Billy explained, "The dogs and the one milk cow and calf are safely locked in the barn with food to last them a few days and water enough to last a week. The cattle out on the range would find a place to ride out the storm and most of them should be all right. We need to pray about it and let God take care of the rest."

After breakfast the men went to the barn using the rope to guide them; they fed and watered the animals. They were laughing when they came in presenting Esther with twelve eggs. They said the chickens were warm as toast and happy as clams and laying like it was spring. With all the animals in the barn, their body heat was helping to keep the barn warm. The snow around the outside of the barn was acting as insulation.

The women had cleaned up the breakfast dishes and planned meals for the rest of the day. Valentine told Whitney about using the Bible concordance to find a verse she had wanted to read. "It was so easy I couldn't believe it."

"What did you look up, Valentine?" Rose asked as she dried the last dish from breakfast and put it in the cupboard.

"The Lord is my Shepherd," Valentine started to recite.

The girls shouted out together, "Psalm 23!"

"Why, yes it is," Valentine exclaimed. "How did you know?"

Rose said, "That was one of the first verses Uncle Billy taught us when we started to study the Bible. He said it was his favorite in the Bible. Isn't that right, Mama?"

Esther smiled at the girls and said, "You're exactly right."

Talk in the kitchen turned to studying the Bible, which they would be doing later. Whitney and Rose asked if they could study with the adults. The answer was yes, of course. Soon everyone was sitting at the dining room table with paper, pencils, and Bibles ready. They were to hunt for clues in Daniel to learn what God had written, for them, to help them understand the future. They were trying to figure out how Valentine's story might fit with the Bible's teaching.

Uncle Billy said, "We should always ask God to help when studying the Bible so He can lead us to the right clues."

After he prayed he said chapter three was a good story about Nebuchadnezzar building a large statue of gold, but it didn't talk about the future or have any clues for them so let us start with chapter four. They ended the study in Daniel with an overview from Uncle Billy. He said Jesus would fill the earth with His goodness and banishing the evil power that had been on Earth since Adam and Eve had sinned. Everyone was quiet for a few minutes pondering what the world would be like if Jesus was in total control.

Aunt Emma broke the silence to say, "I think it's time for a lunch break. What do y'all think of that?"

After lunch everyone was ready to keep looking for clues to the puzzle about the end of the world. Everyone at the table looked at Uncle Billy who smiled at each of them.

He said, "We'll be studying Revelation right after Daniel. I do hope we all will still be together that long. How about it, Valentine? Can you stay awhile and study these two books of the Bible?"

Valentine took a deep breath, "I sure hope I can, but I must say I'm not the one deciding when or where I go. I feel God is taking me somewhere, and when I leave and where I go is up to God."

After the study had been proceeding for a while, Rose said, "I have found a clue. Mama helped me find it. Will you help me read, Mama?"

"Sure, dear, you start."

Rose started to slowly sound out the words but decided she was hungry and it would take too long. So she just told them what she understood about her clue.

"It says God has told us His mystery—that's like a clue, right? In my verse it says God would use His mysteries when the times are right, and God says He will bring all heaven and earth together, and Jesus will be over all of us. So we'll have no more unhappiness, right, Daddy? Isn't that what we read earlier?"

"You hit the nail on the head, honey. When Jesus reigns over the world, no one will be unhappy anymore. I can't think of a nicer place to pause in our studies and go eat. Whatever is cooking in the kitchen smells so good. How about it, anyone hungry?"

Everyone was ready to eat. While the men and younger girls went to the barn to feed the animals, the women put supper on the table.

The old house was full of happy sounds when everyone met again at the dining room table. If those at the table had given it a thought, they might have felt the old place was snuggling them in for the night; if houses could do such a thing. Maybe it was God's angels who were giving them comfort for the evening and strength for the coming trouble soon to plague all who live on this earth. But tonight would be peaceful while they enjoyed family, friends, and the gift of their Heavenly Father—the gift of the knowledge that they had a friend in His son, Jesus.

If only everyone on earth were looking for Him, the world would be ready for the end of this current epoch. All would be waiting excitingly for the beginning of a new life in a beautiful world with the Father who loves them, their Friend Jesus who died for them, and Spirit who fills them with their Father's love. Sadly, too many did not know any of this and would not know because they had ignored God's voice when he had called to them throughout their lives and used their minds for everything but learning of God's love and His plan for them.

In how many homes was the television turned off and the Bible read instead? In how many homes is the computer turned off and parents talked to their children to get to know them better and understand what is going on in their lives?

The old house woke to blue skies but lots and lots of snow. It would take all morning to dig Uncle Billy's car out of the snow. Once that was done, Caleb used the tractor to plow a lane to the county road. Good-byes were said to Uncle Billy and Aunt Emma, and promises made to get together soon to continue their studies. They hated to leave. However, they needed to check on their farm and the animals.

As they all stood on the front porch waving to the old couple, Esther said, "Well, back to school for you girls tomorrow."

The girls complained some, but they were really kind of glad to get back to school. Even though it had been a nice break and they had learned a lot, they would enjoy seeing their friends again.

Whitney turned to Valentine as everyone walked into the house, "Will you stay, Valentine, please?" Rose nodded her agreement.

Valentine smiled at the girls. Looking out at the snow, she said, "I'm walking, so I guess I have to stay for a while. I sure can't walk easily in all this stuff."

Esther said, "For myself, I would like for you to stay all winter. It gets pretty lonely out here. When the snow is like this, it's too hard to get to town to visit anyone."

"I'll stay until Father God tells me it's time to travel on," Valentine said. "How is that for an answer?"

The next morning was business as usual, with the girls off to school and Caleb out in the barn working on winter things that still must be done on a farm. Esther and Valentine worked together in the house and talked about all they had learned the day before.

Later in the day, as the ladies were making up the beds with clean sheets, Esther said, "Valentine, I just want you to know that I believe you, and the story about this plan to control the world. Yesterday, while we were studying, I felt a calm come over me. I feel God was talking to my heart to give me peace, and to tell you that He is with you. I will give you what little courage I have. You're very brave to be doing all of this. I would never be able to go out into the world alone."

Valentine smiled at Esther. Through teary eyes, she said, "Thank you, Esther. Your trust means a lot to me. However, since I have met God, Jesus, and the Spirit, I don't feel alone anymore. This might seem strange, but I never did feel alone from the very beginning. I have felt that some friendly someone has been with me, and was protecting me, wherever I went. At first my head was so fuzzy and in pain that I didn't question what was happening. However, soon I began to feel this presence with me. I guess I could also say, because I have no memory of my life before this, I don't worry about friends or family. I have been praying to Father God to watch over my family because I heard the Sister say I do have a family but they think I'm dead."

Esther came around the bed they were making and gave Valentine a big hug.

"I'm sure God will help you find your family. I know He is keeping watch over them. I'll pray for them from now on, even when you travel on. Valentine, do you have any memory or maybe just a feeling that you have children? I know if I didn't know where my girls were I'd be crazy."

"It's funny you mention that," Valentine said. "Just this morning, before I got up, I was thinking about the dream I had in your barn, the first morning I got here."

Esther stopped her and said, "Why don't you tell me about it over a hot cup of coffee?"

Valentine smiled saying, "Lead on. I'm ready for a cuppa. That's what my dad used to say."

"Your dad!" exclaimed Esther.

"Yes, I had a fleeting flash of memory in a coffee shop last week. I was quite happy when I realized it must be a memory—at least I'm claiming it as a memory."

They were just sitting down with a cup when Caleb came in from the barn, rubbing his hands from the cold.

"I was just thinking how nice it would be if I could find a hot drink when I got in the house, and here you were reading my mind."

Esther got up, kissed Caleb on the cheek. "You're cold as ice. Sit down and I will get you just the thing to warm you up.

Valentine was just about to tell me about a dream she had in the barn the morning we found her."

Esther set a cup of hot coffee in front of her husband and went to the back room for a minute. She returned with an old hot-water bottle, filled it with hot water, and put it behind Caleb's back.

"There now, how does that feel, dear?"

"Ah, this is heaven. Thank you, honey. You're the best."

Valentine smiled as she watched the two young people. They were perfect for each other. She was sure God had a lot to do with it. Esther refilled their cups, sat down, and looked expectantly at Valentine.

"Any time now—I love a good story," she said.

Valentine took a deep breath and said, "Well! I was sleeping in your barn in that nice hay, and boy, I must say it was a haven in that storm. I really was getting scared out in that blizzard."

She smiled at the two and continued.

"I first heard giggles and laughing. In my dream I thought I knew them, these little girls. I heard one say, 'Push me higher, Darcy, push me higher.' I tried to see them, but the bushes were too thick. I could only hear their little voices and their laughter. I looked around and saw the bushes were really a hedge, tall and well-groomed. There was a path through the middle. I wanted to go through the hedge and see those little girls. Even though I continued to walk and walk, I couldn't get any closer to the path. All too soon I woke, with the dream still clearly in my mind and the wonder of hearing what I think could have been my two little girls. But I don't feel like I have had any baby the past few years. These girls sounded young, four and six maybe. Anyway, I'm guessing about all of this, but I felt I knew them at one time in my life."

The room was quiet for a minute; each of them took a sip of coffee and pondered. Caleb was thinking, *If Valentine is faking, she is either a very, very good liar—or she really believes what she is saying. Yet I am inclined to believe her story.*

"A penny for your thoughts," Caleb said to his wife.

Esther broke out of her reverie by shaking her head and said, "I have been thinking about my little girls, how I will give each girl a really big hug when they get home from school."

Esther turned to Valentine and asked the same thing Caleb asked her, "Penny for your thoughts, Valentine."

"I was remembering and savoring the little voices still ringing in my head. I was thinking of the name Darcy and wondered what the other little girl's name was."

Esther spoke again, "You know, Valentine, this story of yours is really kind of exciting. While we were studying yesterday, I thought this could mean that Jesus is coming soon. What do you think, Caleb?"

When Caleb responded, he was looking straight at Valentine and not his wife. "I must say, I had that very same thought. What if this means that Jesus is coming for His people? Am I ready? I lay awake for a long time last night thinking about my relationship with my Savior, Jesus. I finally got up to come downstairs to check on the furnace and the storm. When I opened the back door, I was stunned at what I saw. The storm had blown over. The sky was overflowing with stars so bright I felt as if I could reach my hand up and pick one right out of the sky.

"As I was standing there on the back porch looking up, I started to pray. For the first time in my life, I talk to Jesus as I would to my most trusted friend—not someone so far away I couldn't feel Him. I felt like He was standing right there on the back porch with me looking up at His stars. I told him I loved Him and I really believe in Him. I don't think I ever asked Him to be my Savior before. I joined our church when I was a kid, but I didn't understand what all of it meant then. I was a kid. I didn't know of suffering and sadness or feeling the need for a Savior.

"Last night I asked Him to be my Savior. I spoke the words right out loud. I heard His voice. He said, 'Look at these stars. I made them just for you because I love you. I want to spend eternity with you.' I know the words were just in my head. Nevertheless, they were as real as mine are right now. I felt the worries go right out of me, and a peace flow in that I had never felt before. I knew then that your story, Valentine, was very real. I believe you. I will stand with you no matter what."

When Caleb looked up at Esther and Valentine, he saw tears running freely down both their faces, with smiles as big and bright as they could be.

Valentine said, "I feel as if I've just been to heaven and seen Jesus face-to-face, Caleb. That was a beautiful story. Thank you so much for sharing with us."

Caleb smiled and said, "I didn't know I was going to do that. Those words just came falling out. I don't think I could have stopped if I wanted to."

Esther got up and went around the table to where Caleb was sitting. Sitting down beside him, she gave him a big hug.

"You've relieved my mind. I knew you were restless last night. I was worried you couldn't believe Valentine's story. That you didn't know what to do about it. I was just telling Valentine, yesterday I felt that same kind of peace in my heart about her story. I too thought God was telling me it was all true and to believe in her."

Not long after the talk at the table was finished, the front door opened and two sets of feet came running in. Two voices were laughing and talking about their day at school. Soon Rose and Whitney came into the kitchen and gave hugs and kisses all around the table.

"Wow, I'm hungry," said Rose. "May I have a snack before supper?"

Esther said, "Just as soon as you go change into play clothes, you may. Leave your book bags here at the table so we can go over your homework later."

The girls headed up the stairs, calling out to each other, "I bet I can beat you in changing!"

When the girls came down to their snack, Esther told them to get right at their homework because Uncle Billy and Aunt Emma were coming for supper again. They were going to have another Bible study afterward. Whitney asked if they could stay up to study too.

"We'll see how late it is when we get started. But if you don't get your homework done before supper, you'll have to finish it while we study with Uncle Billy."

"Okay, Mama," said Rose.

Whitney said, "I'll try. I have a lot more homework than Rose does."

After supper was finished, the dishes washed and put away, they all gathered at the dining room table and opened their Bibles to Daniel, chapter seven, to the very last verse. Caleb prayed for God's help in their studies and started the reading for the night.

He said, "I want to reread verse twenty-eight because it reminds me of how I felt last night. Daniel says he was troubled about his dream but he kept it to himself. Last night I had the same feelings, and someday, when we have more time, I'd like to tell you of my troubling night."

"Daddy," Whitney said, "I want to show everyone something I found in my Bible. After we finished studying last night, I found this really cool thing in my Bible. I just now remembered it. In verse twenty-five of this chapter I saw a little letter *a* after the verse. At the bottom of the page, there was another little letter *a* with these words written after it, '...For a year, two years and half a year...' We were looking for the meaning of times, and in my Bible it says a year is the same as a time. What do you think of that? Do you think it's safe to believe what's written here, Daddy?"

Caleb looked at his oldest daughter and then he looked at Uncle Billy for help.

Uncle Billy said, "I've been waiting for someone to find the footnotes. I know I could have shown them to you, but I find it means more when you discover these things for yourselves. Good going, Whitney. See, it's just like looking for clues in a mystery."

"So," said Esther, "time and year is the same thing, and we can write that in our notebooks? I do like finding these clues, and yes, Uncle Billy, it does mean more to us when we discover these clues ourselves. I bet Whitney will never forget where she found this clue."

Smiling at Whitney, everyone turned to chapter eight to begin studying a new vision that Daniel was describing. Caleb read through verse twelve then they stopped and talked about what they had just heard.

After a while, the head of the youngest person was slowly bending to lie on the table. Rose's eyes closed and she was out for the night. It took a few minutes for Caleb and Esther to get Rose to bed and come back to the table.

Esther asked, "Whitney, are you getting sleepy yet?"

"No, I feel fine. I really want to stay a little while longer."

Everyone listened intently as Valentine again started reading verse thirteen. She stopped at the end of verse fourteen and said, "Those are two full-packed verses. I know you aren't going to say anything, Uncle Billy, but what do the rest of you think?"

Esther said, "Well, to start with, we have another time clue. This time we're working with days. My first thought is a day can't mean a twenty-four-hour day because the angel told Daniel these visions were for the time of the end."

"Where did you see that?" asked Caleb.

"Um, let me see."

Esther looked at the verses they had been reading.

Whitney said, "Mom, did you see it in verse seventeen, the one we have not read yet?"

Esther looked at verse seventeen and then smiled sheepishly.

"I guess I was reading ahead last night when I couldn't sleep. I read my Bible and prayed for Caleb to find peace."

Caleb turned to his wife giving her a quick kiss.

"Thank you for your prayers. They must have worked."

"Well, then," Valentine said, "Let's look at this 'time' verse!"

Whitney was writing on her notebook.

She looked up and said, "Mama, you must be right because 2,300 days is only six years and forty-six days—by my math anyway."

Aunt Emma asked if there was anything that would show us where in history those things happened.

Valentine said, "I also have read ahead in the next part of chapter eight. The angel tells Daniel the goat is the king of Greece and the large horn between his eyes is the first king of Greece. Does anyone here know who the first king of Greece was?"

Everyone at the table shook their heads except for Whitney. She was smiling as she raised her hand.

"I do!" she exclaimed. "It's Alexander the Great. We just had a test in world history last week and he was one of the test questions. I know something the grownups don't!"

Caleb turned to Whitney and said, "Good job, honey! Here, high five!"

They slapped their hands high in the air.

Then it was Aunt Emma's turn to read.

She said, "Why don't we read this next part and see what else the angel told Daniel. I believe the angel's name is Gabriel."

When Aunt Emma had finished reading chapter eight, everyone wanted to talk at the same time. Esther whistled loudly—the same kind of whistle she used to call Caleb in from out in the field. That did the trick.

"I have an idea," she said. "Because it's getting late and Uncle Billy and Aunt Emma still have to drive home, let's write down one question for each of us. Then we can work on finding everything we can about those questions, each taking one. When we get back together, we'll tell each other what we found."

"Sounds like a study group I was once in," Valentine said.

As soon as she said this, she said, "That was a memory! I had a real memory! I remember studying in college!"

Everyone around the table looked at Valentine with astonished looks on their faces. No one said anything for a minute until Esther smiled and gave her a hug.

"How many flashes like that have you had, Valentine?" Esther asked.

She thought for a while and replied, "Well, I don't know the number, but I have written them all down in my book. Someday I hope to put them together and remember who I am."

Soon they settled back to studying, and as was suggested by Esther, everyone asked a question and wrote them down in each of their own notebooks. Esther was first.

"This is not a question, but we need to learn the time of the end. My question is this. Because we already know who the first three beasts are, what is the fourth kingdom that's represented by the legs of iron in King Nebuchadnezzar's dream and in Daniel's first dream? He describes it as having iron teeth. It was very different from the others. He also said ten horns come from it. In his second dream he calls it a stern-faced king, a master of intrigue. I'm reading from the NIV Bible again."

Valentine spoke next, "I think it's interesting that Daniel never puts the name of an animal to this beast he sees. I just thought that was strange. That's my question."

Caleb was next. He said, "I want to find out who gives this king his power. In verse twenty-four it says he will become very strong but not by his own power. I also am reading from the NIV."

Uncle Billy asked, "What do think of the newer Bibles, Caleb?"

"Well, Uncle Billy, I really enjoy both the King James version and this NIV. A lot of times I read the same verse in both to get a better feel for what the writer is trying to say to us."

"Good idea, I think I'll try that too. I believe we have an NIV at home. I just never opened it before. See, you've taught this old dog a new trick!" He laughed.

Whitney spoke up next. "My question is from verse twenty-five, in the last part of the verse. It says he will destroy many and take his stand against the Prince of princes. Is Jesus the Prince of princes?"

"I'm not sure this is a question. It's more of an observation," Valentine explained, "the line right after Whitney's says he will be destroyed but not by human power. I would take that to mean only God, who created all things, can destroy this kingdom. I guess I'll treat it like a question and study up on the verse."

Uncle Billy said, "Let's pray before we break up this study that God will help us all find the answers we need to find." Everyone around the table said a prayer to help them through their studies.

Caleb walked Uncle Billy and Aunt Emma out to their car to make sure it would start. "Call us when you get home, just for safety's sake," he told them.

After Uncle Billy called, the house became quiet. Each person sleeping felt safe in their loving Father's care. Their guardian angels watched over them and kept them safe, "Your enemy, the devil, prowls around like a roaring lion looking for someone to devour" (1 Pet. 5:8, NIV).

17

I'm Not Alone

The next day dawned unseasonably warm with a southerly wind blowing. By noon most of the snow had melted—all except the piles pushed up by the snowplow. The day started with a short Bible reading and a prayer. Esther said she wanted to start doing that every day to help each of them during the day.

Everyone seemed to enjoy the verse that was selected: Jeremiah 29:11, "For I know the plans for you, to prosper and not to harm you…" It seemed like God was letting them know he was going with them wherever each of them went. He would keep them safe because He had always known the plans he had for each them.

After the girls were off to school and the house straightened up, Esther and Valentine went for a walk to check on the cattle. Caleb had hoped to check on them, but he had to go to town for a part for the furnace.

The ladies were glad to get out of the house and get some fresh air. Esther tried to loan Valentine a pair of her mud boots, but her feet were much larger then Esther's. So she settled for an old pair of Caleb's boots. They were a bit big; however, with two pairs of thick socks, they would work.

As they walked along, they talked about the Bible study. At times they stopped to look at something in nature. Even in late fall the woods, with no leaves on the trees, were pretty to look at. They meandered along so by the time they got to the cattle the sun was directly overhead. Esther explained she needed to check on the amount of hay in the covered feed lot, and also to count the cattle. As they stood on a rise above the cattle, Valentine asked if she could help. They each started from a different end of the herd. When they finished counting and added the total, Esther said, "We were lucky not to lose any. We plan to sell some of the yearlings in the spring to pay off the last of the debt still owed on the farm."

When the ladies got back to house, it was almost time for the bus to bring the girls from school. Esther got snacks out for the girls. She had just finished putting two glasses of milk on the table when the sound of the girls' voices could be heard in the hallway.

"Hey, Mama. Hi, Valentine," Whitney said as she sat down to eat her snack.

"Oh no you don't," Esther said. "Go upstairs and change into your play clothes." Esther wasn't looking at Whitney, but Valentine was and saw the strangest look on Whitney's face. She wasn't sure what it was. However, she thought she had an idea. Valentine followed Whitney upstairs and knocked on the door of her room.

A hard voice from inside said, "Yeah, what do you want?" The voice did not sound like the Whitney Valentine was getting to know.

Valentine said, "I just wanted to come in and talk for a while. Is it okay for me to come in?"

There was a pause and then she heard a little sob.

Whitney's real voice said, "Please come in, Valentine. I need to talk to someone."

Valentine opened the door and found a sobbing Whitney sitting on her bed still in her school clothes.

"What's wrong, Whitney? Why are you crying?"

Whitney looked up at her. "I acted so mean just now. I don't know what came over me. I didn't want to be mean, but it was like I couldn't stop myself. What's happening to me?"

Valentine said, "I need to ask you a question before I can answer you. Did you play with a video game at school today?"

"Well, not at school, but on the way home, my friend let me play her new Bible video game. I thought it was so cool to have a Bible game. I thought I could learn something new. I'd tell everyone at supper tonight everything I had learned. Maybe Mama and Daddy would get me one for my birthday next month."

"Okay, Whitney, one more question. How did you feel while you played the video game?"

Whitney thought about it, replying, "Well, at first it was fun, but then I began to feel mad at everyone. I remember thinking that when I got home I was going to tell Mama that I didn't need to change into my play clothes because that's for babies. Even while I was thinking those thoughts, I was wondering what was wrong with me."

Valentine was thoughtful for a few minutes. "Whitney, do you remember that story I was telling your Mama and Daddy when you were supposed to be in bed?"

"Yes, Valentine, and I'm really sorry I eavesdropped on your story, because it has made me worry ever since."

"Whitney, I'm glad you heard because you need to know to protect yourself. I'm sure that video game you played was one of the games designed to take control of young people's minds. If you play that game, it will make you feel like this every time. And I'm sure each time you play the game it will have more control over you. Do you understand?"

Whitney had a solemn look on her face. Her eyes were determined when she said, "I will never play that game again. I will sit with Rose on the bus from now on. I should have been sitting with her today, but my friend said I didn't have to always be the babysitter for my kid sister. I saw the hurt look on Rose's face, but I wanted to sit with my friend and play her video game. I guess I wasn't being nice even before I played the game. Still I couldn't believe the thoughts that were going through my head while I was playing it. Valentine, how did you know that I had been playing that hateful game?"

"I saw a look on your face when your mama told you to go upstairs and change your clothes."

"What did my face look like?"

"I can tell you in two words: pure hate."

Whitney put her face in her hands and started to cry again just as Esther opened the door to tell Whitney her milk was getting warm. What Esther saw broke her heart.

"What's wrong, honey? Why are you crying like this?" She turned to Valentine and asked, "Do you know what's wrong, Valentine?"

"Yes, I do. What I've been afraid of is happening here in your little town. Whitney is fine now. If you could wait until Caleb comes in, I need to tell you both. Whitney will help me. Won't you, Whitney?"

The little girl looked up at her mama as she threw herself into her mother's arms saying, "I'm so sorry I didn't sit with Rose on the bus on our way home."

Esther was puzzled but held Whitney until she stopped crying.

Whitney looked up. "I have to go talk to Rose and tell her I'm sorry. I know I hurt her feelings and I can't wait another moment." She was out the door and in Rose's room before the two ladies knew what happened.

As Esther and Valentine walked downstairs, Valentine said, "I'm so glad I was here and saw what I saw because we could have lost Whitney to the enemy!"

Supper was a quiet meal until Caleb said, "What's wrong with all of you? You look like you lost your last friend."

A tear ran down Whitney's face, "I think I almost did."

"Okay now, really what's up?" Caleb looked at each one at the table. "Is someone going to tell me, or am I going to have to resort to tickle torture?"

That line always got a giggle or a smile from his girls, but they didn't say anything.

"Now I'm really worried."

Esther turned to Rose and asked, "Would you go get the salt from the kitchen, dear?"

When she was out of hearing, Valentine told Caleb, "We have to talk, but Rose should not hear this just yet."

Rose came back in and said, "I can't find the salt, Mama. Are you sure it's not on the table already? I'm sure I brought it in with the pepper."

Esther exclaimed, "Oh my, the salt is right here in front of me. I'm sorry, dear, but thank you for doing what I asked."

Rose looked at everyone at the table and asked, "Is this about Valentine's story and that funny video game everyone was playing at school during recess?"

Valentine recovered from shock first. Pulling Rose into a hug, she said, "You're too smart for us. Yes, this is about my story and about a video game. Whitney, will you tell everyone what happened today?"

With a few tears and a slow start, Whitney finally told her story. She told her mama and daddy how sorry she was that she didn't sit with Rose on the bus. But even more, she was sorry she hurt her sister's feelings.

"I asked God to forgive me, and I asked Rose to forgive me. Now I just wonder how that video game could do that to me. Why would anyone try to hurt children with a game?"

Valentine told how she had seen a strange look on Whitney's face when Esther asked her to go change.

"I know God was looking out for Whitney. He gave me the thought about the video game and encouraged me to wonder if she had been playing it. I'll tell you something. The look I saw and what Whitney has told me scares me to death."

Long after the girls had gone to bed and gone to sleep, the adults sat up talking about what to do.

"At least today is Friday and the girls don't have to go to school for two days," Esther remarked.

They talked for a while. However, they did not come up with a plan. They went to bed to pray about it—with the agreement that they needed to talk with Uncle Billy and Aunt Emma. Caleb said he would call them first thing in the morning. They prayed together before going to bed. All three said they felt better after they talked to their Father in heaven.

To Caleb's surprise, when he came downstairs in the morning, Aunt Emma and Uncle Billy were sitting at the kitchen table. Uncle Billy said he'd go out to the barn with Caleb to feed the animals while Aunt Emma started breakfast.

Once in the barn, Uncle Billy asked Caleb if anyone had come to the house yesterday.

"No, not that I know of. Why do you ask?"

"Well," Uncle Billy said, "I had an unusual visitor last evening just as I was walking to the house from the barn. A man said he was looking for his wife and was worried she might have been lost in the storm."

He paused and Caleb said, "What's so unusual about that?"

"I guess the way he was dressed started me wondering who he really was, but then I began to wonder more when he described his wife to me. He said he didn't have a picture of her—he lost it or something—but he said she was tall and thin with long red hair. That ring any bells?"

"Why, that could be Valentine!" exclaimed Caleb. "He could be her husband and she would not even know it."

Uncle Billy said, "I thought of that and was thinking of giving the man a call after I talked to Valentine, but then he said something that knocked that thought right out of my head. He said, 'If you see her, please call. It's important.' Not that he was worried about her, not that he missed her but that it was important. It sounded to me like something an official would say. I took his number and said I'd sure call if I saw anyone fitting that description. I thought about coming right over last night, but something told me to wait until morning. That's why we're having an early breakfast at your house today."

"Well, I wondered why you both were up so early this morning. I tried to call you at five thirty this morning but could get no answer."

"Your auntie thinks I've gone bonkers, but like the good trooper she has always been, she got ready, and we left before daylight. I told her I'd tell her everything after I talked to you. She is a good woman, and I have to say I've not always deserved her. Back when I was young, I was bad to drink and too many nights I came home stumbling."

"You Uncle Billy! I never knew," Caleb responded.

"That's because she never told anyone—not her family and not mine—she just prayed for me every night. Finally those prayers caught up with me. My life flashed before my eyes and I didn't like what I saw. I was coming home late one night—I had been drinking as usual. That night there came a downpour the like I'd never seen before or after. I came within an inch of running over the ravine and down a hundred-foot drop to the river below. It gives me the shivers just to think about it now, and it has been fifty years ago. Caleb, someone turned the steering wheel of my car just before I went over. Something stopped my car right there in the middle of the road."

Caleb was standing spellbound with his mouth open in awe. "Well, what happened then, Uncle Billy? Don't leave me hanging here. What happened then?"

Uncle Billy had tears in his eyes when he looked up at Caleb. He pulled out his red handkerchief from his back pocket, blew his nose, and wiped his eyes before he could continue. In a hushed voice he said, "It stopped raining, as if someone had turned the faucet off. The sky turned clear as a bell. The stars were brilliant. To this very day, I can still see them. Your aunt would not believe me at first. She kept asking, 'Why are your clothes all wet, Bill?' I finally got my voice back enough to tell her. I said, 'Honey, I got out of my car in the pouring rain and gave my life to the God of heaven. I know you've been praying for me all these many years. Tonight your prayers have been answered.' Emma and I stood there in the kitchen, me dripping water all over her floor, and cried in each other's arms. I told her everything. I got out in the rain in the middle of the road, in a downpour, and I turned everything over to Him. To Him who loved me so much that he sent an angel to save me from my own selfish ways. No one but Emma and I know that story, and when Valentine told her story, it reminded me of how God brought me to Him. I think I believed her from the first. I just had to have a little more convincing from my Father."

The coffee had just finished perking when the men came into the kitchen where Esther, Emma, and Valentine were just setting breakfast on the table. Caleb had his arm over the older man's shoulder, and there was something changed in each of the men's faces.

Esther asked, "What is it, guys? Your faces look like you've seen an angel."

"You're not far off, my dear," her husband said as he gave her a hug. "Maybe Uncle Billy will tell you someday, but right now we adults need to talk before the girls wake up."

The look on Caleb's face had changed to a somber one. They all sat down at the kitchen table and Uncle Billy again told his story about his visitor the night before. The coffee was all but forgotten when he finished.

Turning to Valentine, Uncle Billy said, "You have to leave here, this morning, as soon as possible, because I think this man and maybe more like him will be going house to house and farm to farm. They are looking for you, Valentine. I've been thinking about it all night, and I have a plan.

"Every week on Saturday, Emma and I go to town. Sometimes it's here in Atwood, our closest town, and sometimes we go to the next county over to St. Francis, next to the Kansas-Colorado border. We go to get Emma's medicine at the pharmacy there. This is the week we'll be going to get her medicine. I think if you dress up like Emma and make yourself look kind of old, we could take you there."

At that point, Valentine smiled a little and said, "Not to interrupt, but I have just the thing."

Caleb said at the same time, "But don't you have to go right through our town to get there?"

Valentine shook her head and said, "It won't be a problem. Just wait and see."

"Okay," said Esther. "That's taken care of, but what will we say to the girls? If they know how you left, Valentine, it could put us all into danger. However, if Valentine doesn't say good-bye, they will be heartbroken."

Valentine asked, "Do you have to go home first, Uncle Billy? Because I think I have a plan. What if I say good-bye and leave walking just as I came here? I could hide in the trees until Uncle Billy and Aunt Emma leave. I could climb into their truck and go with them. That way the girls would only see me walking away. I believe, though, that we need to tell them the reason I'm going. I think they are mature enough to understand, and I think we need to trust in our Heavenly Father to keep us all safe."

Everyone agreed on the plan. When the girls came down to breakfast, they were delighted to see who had come to eat with them.

After breakfast Valentine headed upstairs to gather her things. She brought them down to the kitchen and told the girls she needed to leave. They cried some and hugged a lot as Valentine told them why she must leave and why she needed to leave quickly. She explained to the girls in simple ways about the people who were trying to stop her.

"Remember the Bible verse your mama read yesterday. 'For I know the plans for you to prosper you and not to harm you...'

Girls, our God is stronger than all the bad people in the world, and He will take care of me and you. These people want to stop me from talking about God, Jesus, and Spirit to others. I believe God sent me here to save you from the traps these people are setting. Read your Bibles and pray every day and stay close to your family. I know we'll meet again."

Valentine hugged each one then left by the back door. She headed toward the barn and out into the field. She turned when she got to the edge of the barn, right where she had stumbled in the storm only a few nights ago. Now it felt like a lifetime. She waved to the family as they stood outside the back door. Tears running freely down all of their faces, they watched until they could no longer see Valentine walking away.

Esther and Caleb were the first to go into the house. Soon Uncle Billy and Aunt Emma followed, but the girls stayed outside. They talked and watched the place where they last saw their friend.

"Do you really think we'll see her again, Whitney? Do you?" Rose asked.

"Yes, we will because our God is taking care of her, and He is taking care of you and me and Mama and Daddy."

"What about Uncle Billy and Aunt Emma?" Rose asked.

"Yes, you silly goose. You know He is taking care of them too. Now I'll race you to the mailbox. Get ready, get set, go!" And they were off to the mailbox. Back to being little girls, for a while yet anyway.

As Valentine walked away from the safety and friendship of the old home, she tried not to be sad. *But how will I study Daniel and all the questions we've been searching for?* she wondered. Then she remembered that God was with her now and forever, and He had a plan. She felt humbled and proud at the same time to be a part of His plan to help the people He brought her to.

"They are all my family," she said out loud. "And even if I don't see my real family until Jesus comes back, I have a family wherever I go. And my family is growing in leaps and bounds." With these words resonating in the air around her, she dried her tears and took off in the direction she was shown to meet up with Uncle Billy and Aunt Emma.

Uncle Billy and Aunt Emma left not long after Valentine had. They stopped to tell Whitney and Rose good-bye as the girls were walking back from the mailbox. They told them they were headed to town to get Aunt Emma's medicine and would not be home until late that night.

"We'll see you tomorrow evening at supper. We'll have a Bible study, so you had better go look up your questions and have some answers for everyone tomorrow," Uncle Billy told them.

Then Aunt Emma said, "Girls, there has been a report of a strange man seen in the area, hanging around the past few days, asking questions. So remember what y'all have been taught."

With that, the girls helped her finish the sentence.

"Never, never talk to strangers!"

When the girls got back to the house, Esther and Caleb sat down with them. They talked about all that had been happening and a plan was set up in case anyone came asking about a woman with red hair. The girls felt important to be included in the plans to protect their new friend, Valentine. The rest of the morning they cleaned house to make sure no signs were left that Valentine had ever been there. But in their hearts, they would always keep her near and safely hidden.

Uncle Billy turned the truck toward Atwood on Highway 36, but not far down the road he turned onto a small dirt road. He drove north about a mile and stopped the truck at a big boulder. Valentine walked out from behind the boulder dressed like Lucy Pope. The old couple had to look twice to be sure it was her.

She walked up to the truck window, smiling, and said in her best old lady voice, "Sir, my name is Lucy Pope. Can you give an old lady a ride?"

Aunt Emma just sat shaking her head. "You are the picture of a crippled old lady! I would not have known you on the street, Valentine."

"I'm sorry," Valentine said. "My name is Lucy. You must have confused me with someone else." Valentine was laughing as she said it. She then said, "I think it would be best if you don't tell anyone how I'm dressed. I didn't even tell Esther about this disguise."

They all agreed that was for the best. Billy helped Valentine into the extended cab of the truck and covered her up with an old blanket they kept there for when Emma's knees got cold.

"When I say heads up, you cover your head, Miss Lucy. When we get out of town a ways, you can sit up front with Emma and me."

Billy then turned the truck around and headed to town. As they drove along, they talked about everything that had been happening.

Valentine handed a notebook to Emma and said, "I've been copying my notebook for you to keep so you can remember what I've seen and heard. I seem to have a photogenic memory. At least I seem to recall things I've heard word for word, so most all of the conversations are written down just as I heard them. I think it will help to keep you safe."

Aunt Emma asked, "Do have any idea where you're from, Valentine?"

"Well, I've not had a lot of time to think about it, but I'm guessing Baltimore. That's where I started, and if I'm not from Baltimore, why was I there? I just don't know. Where are you from?

Emma said, "I haven't been home in years. I was born and raised in Fayetteville, Tennessee. My dad had a store on Main Street, and I loved to go in after school and stand behind the counter. I felt like I was helping him run the place. I'm sure I was more trouble than help, but he always was glad to see me. When

I was in high school, I helped him with the bookkeeping and office work.

"There was a big military base during the war, just outside of Fayetteville. I worked there when I was nineteen years old. I thought I had become very sophisticated. I worked in one of the offices as a secretary.

"One day a very handsome young soldier came in with a sealed message for my boss. He smiled at me and my knees went weak. It was a good thing I was sitting down because I would have died right there in my tracks if this young man knew he'd just knocked my socks off. He tried to flirt with me, but I would not give him the time of day—on the outside anyway. On the inside I'd melt whenever he came in with a message."

"Was that handsome young man Uncle Billy?" Valentine asked.

Valentine could hear the smile in Aunt Emma's voice when she said, "Yes, that handsome young man was William Caleb Farris, and he thought he was every woman's dream."

Uncle Billy chuckled and said, "Now, Emma, I don't think I was quite that bad, was I?"

"You, dear Bill, had the bluest eyes I had ever seen and wavy dark hair. You looked so nice in your army uniform."

Valentine could tell by Emma's voice she was taking a trip down memory lane, seeing her husband as she had first seen him.

"My father didn't want me to marry him. He said, 'You don't know anything about him or his family.' But I loved him with all my heart, and one day I packed a few things and the quilt I had made and ran away with him to the next county seat. We got married by the Justice of the Peace. I think I hurt my father very badly. I left a note saying I just had to marry Bill and I'd be home in three days. By that time I was twenty-one and could sign for myself."

"When we got home and I saw the hurt in my dad's eyes, it nearly killed me. Nevertheless, he welcomed Bill into our home. We lived there for several years."

Uncle Billy broke into the story just then, "Your dad was the first man I'd ever known that was a true Christian. He made a profound impact on me. It took me years to understand how he helped me to grow up and be a man."

"I'm sorry to say that not long after we were married I had to go overseas. That young, carefree boy came home a different man. I had learned to drink and smoke in the war, and I learned to be very selfish—even more selfish than I had been before going overseas. It took a good Christian woman and years of praying before God took over my life, and He did it in a way that left no confusion. It was God's way or the devil's way, and if I chose the devil, it soon would have been death for me."

There was a long pause and then Uncle Billy said, "I want to tell you my story of how the God of the universe, my Heavenly Father, stopped me one night and showed me where my life was going if I continued in the path I was taking."

They were almost to town by the time Billy finished his story, with Aunt Emma telling parts of it.

Valentine said, "Thank you for telling me, Uncle Billy. Everywhere I look I see a loving Father who wants His children to not only be with Him and Jesus and Spirit in heaven, but also spend time with us each day here on earth. I don't know what I believed before I lost my memory, but I'm so glad that now I know I have a Father God who loves me!"

As they came into Atwood, Uncle Billy said, "Heads up." Valentine lay down on the seat and pulled the blanket up over her head, trying to be as small as she could.

Uncle Billy said, "The town is full. I guess everyone wants to get to town and do their shopping before the next big storm hits."

They came to a red light; Valentine could feel the truck stop.

Aunt Emma asked, "Valentine, what did you say the car looked like that the Sister rode in?"

"Big, black, with tinted windows. Why, do you see something like that?"

"Yes, stopped right beside our truck. I can't see the driver's face very well, but I can see he is wearing something white around his neck," Aunt Emma replied. "I'm trying to look without turning my head too much."

At the next light, Uncle Billy and Aunt Emma both let out a long sigh. The car had turned down a side street.

"Honey, isn't the Catholic Church on that street?"

"Yes, dear," Aunt Emma answered. "I can see it from here. The black car just turned into the parking lot."

"Uncle Billy, would you feel safe in going to the next corner then going around the block so you can drive by the church and get a better look?" Valentine asked.

Uncle Billy said, "I was just thinking the same thing. Always good to know what your enemy is doing."

So at the next corner he turned right and then right again until he came to the street of the church. As he turned onto the street, he said, "Watch for anything you think is different, Emma, and I will do the same thing."

Valentine said, "If you guys could, would you describe what you see?"

Aunt Emma said, "There are a lot of extra cars parked on my side of the street, right across from the church."

Uncle Billy said, "I see four motorcycles in the parking lot. The black car is there, parked next to the back door. Wait! The driver-side door is opening and a priest is getting out. He's opening the back door on the same side. Now I see a nun getting out. She's wearing a long habit. I don't think she's from here because the nuns in our area wear the modern-day shorter habits. I don't see anyone else around. They must all be inside."

"Wait a minute, another car is pulling into the parking lot."

"Dear, isn't that the new pastor for the Baptist church, the one who came this summer after the older pastor retired?"

"Yes, I can see him clearly. He's getting out and going in the back door."

Uncle Billy said. "Wow! Do you think the new pastor could be in on this too? Could it be that he was replaced to get that church under control?"

As the truck came to a stop at the corner, Uncle Billy spoke again, "Valentine, you know that man I described, who was out at our place last night? Well, he is coming out of the front door of the church and walking to the same car I saw him in last night. This time someone else is in the driver's seat and they are both dressed in black, just alike. Those men are some kind of government agents—CIA or FBI or something. I'd bet my hat on it! And they don't look any too friendly. I can tell you that. I'm ready to get out of town and on to the next county. Hopefully St. Francis is a safer town than this town."

No one spoke for a while. Each one was thinking about what had just been seen.

Valentine finally said, "I guess I'm glad you saw what I'm talking about so you will be on your guard and alert to keep safe. I think I must have known something before I lost my memory, and they want to either shut me up or find out what I know, or both. They sure are not giving up. I'm so glad I know I have friends in high places who will protect me and will lead me where God needs me to go."

After driving for about thirty minutes west on Highway 36, Uncle Billy turned onto an old road. He drove far enough to not be seen from the main road and stopped the truck; they all got out. Uncle Billy thought it would be safe for Valentine to ride up front now. *One thing was for sure: no one will think Valentine, dressed as Lucy Pope, is the woman those men were looking for,* he chuckled to himself.

It was close to two in the afternoon when they reached St. Francis. Keeping with their routine, Uncle Billy stopped first at the pharmacy. Then they went to a little country restaurant for some dinner. Breakfast had been a long time earlier and all three were ready for something good to eat.

After they had been seated and were looking at the menu, a waitress asked, "Do you folks want to try these new drinks called Netters? They're on the house."

She went on to say that all the drink companies were putting out their own brand of the drink with different names, but with the same new sugar substitute and vitamin in them.

"It's a new craze that has hit the stores and restaurants over the past week. Everyone who has tried them just can't stop talking about them or stop drinking them. Look at me! I keep one open all the time. They give me energy. They're supposed to be good for you, got vitamins and everything. Did I tell you that?"

She looked at them intently, ready to write down their orders.

"Thank you," Billy said. "But I think we all just want coffee and a glass of water." He smiled up at the waitress.

She looked down at them with a bit of disdain and said, "Old people can never try anything new. So what do you want to eat?"

After they had ordered and the irate waitress had walked away, Aunt Emma asked, "What was that all about?" Neither Valentine nor Uncle Billy had an answer.

Valentine noticed a young man walk in and sit at the counter across from them in a seat where she could see his face well. She saw he had one of the new Netter drinks in one hand and was playing some kind of game with the other hand.

The waitress went up to him asking, "What are you going to eat today, Bryan?" The young man didn't seem to hear her, so she asked again. This time she tapped him on the arm and called his name out louder.

"Bryan, are you going to order?" After a few seconds, he looked up and blinked his eyes three times. To Valentine it looked like he had a hard time focusing his eyes, but finally he seemed to recognize the woman.

"Oh, hi, Mom, I didn't see you."

The woman said, "You get too far into those games you play. Which game is it this time? I told your father to stop buying them for you because I can't get you to do anything else when you're playing them."

"Ah, Mom, leave me and Dad alone. He just wants to make me happy. That's why he buys me stuff—and these new games are really cool. This one is a cop story. I get to be the cop and I can arrest anyone I want. Cool, huh?"

The woman changed the subject and said, "So, Bryan, what do you think of this new drink, Netters?"

"This is my third one this morning. I can't stop drinking them, and it seems to help me concentrate on my game. I got the best score yet after drinking the first one. Crazy, huh?"

"Well, I'm glad you like them because they're good for you— better than that other stuff you've been drinking." Valentine couldn't help but listen because their voices rang out loud and clear.

When their food came, they sat silently and ate. Uncle Billy paid the bill. He would not take Valentine's money to help pay. He said it was their treat and she needed to keep her money for her trip.

Outside on the sidewalk Uncle Billy said, "I've been thinking about it, and I know where we can take you so you can spend the night safely and get started on your trip in the morning. Let's get back in the truck and I'll show you." Uncle Billy headed the truck out of town going west. While they rode along, Valentine talked about the funny feeling she had about the new drink. "I can't get this disquieting feeling out of my mind. Did you hear what that waitress was saying to her son at the counter?"

Aunt Emma said she had not heard them, but she did have trouble hearing sometimes in loud places.

However, Uncle Billy said, "Yes, I did. It was very strange the way he didn't even see his mom at first."

"Did you see his eyes?" Valentine asked. "The way he blinked them three times and then and only then did he see his mom."

"Now that you mention it, I do remember his funny unfocused eyes—only for a few seconds," Aunt Emma exclaimed!

"I saw the very same thing happen in Maryland, outside of Baltimore, to Sheriff Joe. It gave me the willies then and it still gives me the willies. Like something has them under control and they have to blink to get back to the real world. Now that you've seen what I'm talking about, you can watch for it in others. I'm not sure why, but I'd be afraid to drink those new drinks. I guess your best bet would be to stay with good old water and milk from your own cow. There's no telling what other drinks this new vitamin has been put into. It seems to become very addictive very fast."

They continued for about twenty-five miles going out of town until Uncle Billy slowed the truck and turned into an old road that looked like it was rarely used. It was getting pretty dark outside and he had to drive slowly because the road had some ruts in it. After what seemed like a long time to Valentine, they pulled into an old farmyard with a dark old house showing in the truck lights.

Uncle Billy said, "This was my grandparents' place on my mom's side. I came here a lot when I was young, before they died. Then again each summer while my parents were alive to help cut the hay fields. We come back a couple of times a year to check on things. Sometimes we stay a few days to fix anything that needs fixing. There are a lot of good memories here. Let me just go in and light a lamp and then you ladies can come on in."

The house was really big and smelled of a recent cleaning. Valentine liked it as soon as the soft yellow glow of the lamp shown through the front window. The old home seemed to have a story to tell about the people who had lived in it.

Uncle Billy said, "I think we should stay the night and then leave early in the morning. It's getting late, and I'm not that good at driving in the dark anymore."

Uncle Billy soon had a fire built in the kitchen wood stove and brought in the food Esther had put together for Valentine. Emma showed Valentine a bedroom where she would sleep and could change out of the Lucy Pope outfit. Then they walked to the outhouse carrying a kerosene lantern.

Back in the kitchen they all sat around the table talking and looked over the notebook Valentine had given them.

Valentine said, "I have a favor to ask of you. I need a package sent to the hospital in Baltimore. When I was trying to get away from the hospital, I took a nurse's lab coat from the ICU floor and I have wanted to get it back to whomever it belongs to. Except I don't want it to be sent from the town where you live. That way the postmark can't be traced back to you. I have it ready to go and have written the address on the package. There's a note to give it back to the nurse it came from. I placed the twenty dollars in the coat pocket. Do you feel okay doing this for me?"

Uncle Billy thought for a minute.

"Yes, I would be glad to. However, I think I should wait until the next time we come to Saint Francis. For one thing, tomorrow is Sunday and the post office is not open. Also, just in case it does cause a stir in the hospital, you will be long gone by the time the package reaches the ICU desk. Does that sound good to you, Valentine?"

"That sounds like a wise idea."

Aunt Emma said, "Now I think I'm just about beat. Shall we hit the hay? We all have a long day tomorrow."

Uncle Billy brought out a Bible from an old desk drawer and they had a short Bible reading. He prayed for Valentine's safekeeping and for the work she was being led to do.

They all climbed upstairs. Valentine thought she was too worked up to sleep. Nevertheless, her head had hardly hit the pillow before she was sound asleep.

During the night, it started to rain, and by morning it had blown into a real storm. When Valentine looked out her bedroom window, she could see the trees bending nearly double and rain was slashing her bedroom windows.

"Valentine," Uncle Billy said at breakfast, "this farm is just inside the Colorado border. I believe it will be safe for you to stay here as long as you need to. At least until this storm blows over. Why don't you stay for at least one more night? This rain should be out of here by morning and then you can start your trip without getting soaked to the skin."

"I like that idea just fine. This is a neat old home, and I feel very safe here," Valentine replied.

Valentine gave her package to Uncle Billy for safekeeping and good-byes were said.

"Be careful not to tell anyone where you brought me. The less Caleb and Esther know, the better for them. Don't you think so?"

"I had not thought about it, but I think you're right. I had not thought of this place until we were on our way, and there wasn't much time to really talk about where we were taking you before we left. You're always thinking about safety, Valentine. I guess it starts to come naturally when someone is chasing you."

"Yes, it does. I have been covering my tracks for a while now. I just put myself in their place and think where I might look for clues to find a missing person. I'm sure God is helping me in this effort as He has helped me all along."

As they were getting into the truck, Uncle Billy said, "This place is always here for you if you need a safe place to stay. I know you have to move on now, but if you're ever back this way, please don't hesitate to stay here."

"Thank you, you both have been so good to me. I'll never forget you."

Valentine watched as the truck pull out of the yard and down the old driveway. Then she went into the house and closed the door tight against the storm.

Valentine put a few more pieces of wood on the fire and spoke aloud to the old home place, "I'm on my own again. Even so, I'm not alone, never alone."

18

On the Trail of Jane Doe

Valentine listened to a gentle rain hitting the windows as dawn brightened the sky. She realized she would not be leaving today. With this thought, she rolled over and went back to sleep for a few more hours. By the time she woke again, she needed to make a trip outside to the outhouse very badly—she could not wait for the rain to stop. Valentine found an old umbrella by the back door and headed out.

The path had been created to keep feet dry, being as it was a few inches above the yard. The people who made this path surely thought about how to make things right. That was back when they had to use their minds, she thought. She realized in this time period too many people didn't use their minds for anything but computers—most people have lost all skills to survive.

Back in the kitchen, Valentine stirred up the stove as she coaxed one red coal to life. Her camping with Maria had paid off. The night before, she had remembered to bank her fire and shut down the stove. Now she had a nice fire ready to start some coffee. While she waited for the coffee to perk, she thought about what they had seen and heard at the restaurant. She decided she needed to write all of this down. She hoped Aunt Emma would think about writing down everything in the copied notebook Valentine had given her. Valentine also hoped Aunt Emma thought to hide that notebook away. *Those people who are looking for me will stop at nothing. They seemed to think of everything. At least they seemed to stay on my trail pretty closely. It could be they really do not know where I am and they are simply being very thorough in their search.*

Valentine started by writing down what was seen at the church and then about the new vitamin drink, Netters. When she finished, she got out the Bible that Uncle Billy had read. She looked for the verse Esther had read a few mornings ago. It had been somewhere in the book of Jeremiah.

After a few minutes she found the verse she was looking for: Jeremiah 29:11.

Valentine read aloud, "For I know the thoughts I think toward you, saith the Lord: thoughts of peace, and not of evil." She stopped there and looked back in her notebook to where she had written, "For I know the plans I have for you, plans to prosper you and not to harm you, plans to give you hope and a future." She liked both readings of the different Bibles. However, she understood the NIV better than the King James.

"God has given me hope, that's for sure," Valentine spoke aloud to the empty kitchen. "I have a nice warm fire and I have friends, as well as guardians from Father God who will always be with me."

She bowed her head and prayed to God to thank Him for all the things He had done for her so far. She thought of how far she had come. Uncle Billy had said they were in Colorado. "I started clear out on the East Coast in Baltimore. Now I'm in Colorado! I've had some scares, but I've been safe. What an amazing trip."

Valentine continued to turn pages in the Bible until she came to Matthew 6:9. Here her eyes caught the words, Our Father. She read a beautiful prayer that Jesus gave to His disciples to use as an example to pray. She liked these words, so she wrote them down in her notebook.

When she finished her Bible reading and prayers, she went to see what she could find to eat. Esther had also put some things together for her and sent them by way of Aunt Emma. In addition, Aunt Emma had told her there was a pantry with some canned food that was kept there for when the old couple came or work on the place. Valentine went investigating and found everything she needed for a good breakfast.

The rest of the morning, Valentine spent exploring the house and looking at books in the front room. In the afternoon she built a small fire in the fireplace in that room and settled down to look through two books that had piqued her interest. The books where old and tied together with a ribbon. By the looks of them, they had been well read, though long forgotten. The same author wrote both books. Looking over the chapters names, she noted the book must be a book on the life of Jesus. Turning the pages, she saw many places had been marked by the shaky hand of someone, so long ago the ink had faded to a very light blue. However, the words written on the edges of the page were still legible. She turned to the front of the book and read the inscription:

> This book belongs to Joy Elizabeth,
> From her girlhood friend Joy Faith.
> Friends for life and beyond,
> Sharing names and a hope of heaven.

Valentine thumbed through the second book until she came to a chapter she could not pass by, named "The Time of Trouble." The ominous words sounded like what she had been going through the past few weeks. She started to read right in the middle of the book. The first line of the chapter kept her attention. "At that time shall Michael stand up, the great Prince who standeth for the children of thy people: and there shall be a time of trouble, such as never was since there was a nation." Valentine looked again at the front of the book to read the title, *The Great Controversy*, written by Ellen G. White. When she had first looked at the book, she had thought it to be a novel about some war. However, she had not imagined it would be about the very thing they had been studying in Daniel.

She decided to start at the beginning and see just what the book was about. She went and got the Bible from the desk drawer. She wanted to follow along in the Bible verses she found written in the book. As Valentine read, she saw that everything written there seemed to go along with the Bible. She became so engrossed in the book that sometime later she realized she needed more wood for her fire. She also needed a second kerosene lamp to read by.

The rain continued all afternoon and long into the night. Valentine read until her eyes were straining and tired. After a light supper, she took the book to bed.

In the morning the rain was a steady downpour. So Valentine made coffee, and she sat down at the kitchen table to continue reading the unusual book. It took her two more days to finish reading it. Valentine was spellbound when she came to the very end of the story—God's plan for the world. The last line of the book said, "All things, animate and inanimate, in their un-shadowed beauty and perfect joy (joy being underlined) declare that God is love." Then, in the same handwriting as the inscription:

> You and I, Joy Elizabeth, also declare that God is love. I'll see you there!

Valentine let out a long sigh and looked around her as if to bring herself back to earth. She wondered if Uncle Billy or Aunt Emma had ever read it. After giving it some thought, she realized she had found the book shoved to the back of the bookshelf, and there had been a lot of dust on top of it. Valentine was sure it had been lost and forgotten for some time. She could tell the writing in the pages throughout the book was different from that of the inscription and even different in places as if the writer was getting older and her hand was getting more and more shaky.

It was as if Valentine had turned back the pages of time and had a glimpse of those two friends, their love for God and for each other. She decided she would leave both books out on the end table with a note to Uncle Billy to tell him how much she had enjoyed the one book:

> Dear Uncle Billy, I have enjoyed this book so much.
> When I get back this way, I would like to read *The Desire of Ages* also.
> Is Joy Elizabeth your grandmother?
> I will get your answer the next time I see you.
> Your friend in Jesus, V.

While Valentine was finishing the last few chapters of the book, the rain had stopped and the sun came out from behind a cloud. She finished the book just in time to view a beautiful sunset. She made plans to get started walking west in the morning.

Valentine stirred the fire in the wood stove and made herself some soup. She wanted to use up every jar of food she had opened and have everything cleaned before she left the next morning. The soup was good, and there was enough for breakfast.

With sudden inspiration, Valentine went to the desk. In the pages of the old family Bible, she found the names of Uncle Billy's family, with an entry of "Joy Elizabeth, born 1875 died 1967." No wonder her handwriting had been getting shaky; she lived to be ninety-two years old. Joy Elizabeth must have been Uncle Billy's grandmother. She put the Bible back into the desk drawer and, after banking the fire, went to bed.

The next day dawned a beautiful fall day. After eating breakfast and cleaning everything up spic-n-span, she picked up her backpack and the cane. Valentine locked the back door and placed the key, as Uncle Billy had shown her, under the rock by the outhouse.

Valentine started again, on her trip west, where God seemed to be leading her. She followed the old road Uncle Billy had told her to look for, not far from the back of the house. He had said they kept it cleared so they could use it when they needed to. He also said it would lead to a county road so she would not need to walk on the highway.

Soon Valentine came to the county road, she continuing on for about a mile then turned west. "So far, so good," she said aloud. The sun was warm on her head as she walked. After a while, she came to a small stream. Here she stopped to drink and eat half the sandwich she had made that morning, wanting to conserve her supplies.

Before moving on, she refilled her water bottles and placed them in the tote bag.

Late in the afternoon, she came to a state highway going north and south. Waiting until she was sure there was no one coming, she quickly crossed ducking down behind a clump of willows just as a Colorado State patrolman drove by.

Before it got too dark to see, Valentine spied a small shed off the road. The building looked like no one had been around it for years. She opened the door and found a fairly clean and a dry place to sleep.

She got her bed ready with the tarp and blankets. She felt warm and snug when at last she climbed into her makeshift bed. *God is still watching over me and leading me to safety. I can certainly see that my guardian angels are beside me and who could get past them?* She was soon asleep without a worry in the world.

Valentine's package was received at the ICU of St. Peter's Hospital in Baltimore around the middle of November. Valentine's first nurse, Molly, was handed the package. It was well after midnight before Molly had time to open the package. It took only a second, after seeing the contents of the package, to realize what she was holding in her hands. "Charlotte's lab coat!" she blurted out loud. Shutting her lips with a snap, she thought, *Where did you come from?* Molly sat down hard in her chair, staring at the package contents. What will Charlotte do when she see this? Seeing an illegibility postmark, Molly thoroughly looked over the package but could not find any trace of where it might have come from. When she looked into each pocket, she found a penlight, twenty dollars, and the stethoscope. Molly knew instinctively that Charlotte would call that nun, Sister Patricia, as soon as she saw her lab coat. She also knew the sister would be up here in a heartbeat, interrogating everyone. She wondered if the nun could figure out where this package had come from and go hunt down that woman. The more Molly thought about it, the more she did not want that nun getting her hands on the wrapping paper. *I wonder if Dr. Eddie is down in the ER tonight. I think, on my lunch break, I'll run down there and just see.*

Molly knew at once, when she entered the ER doors, that Dr. Eddie was indeed in the ER; she could always tell by his laughter. Dr. Eddie's laugh was infectious; most people could not be in a room with him and not start laughing themselves. The other thing that told her that Dr. Eddie was working was the music. He enjoyed most music; however, he loved the Blues the best. Molly could hear B. B. King floating over the airways as she entered the ER.

Dr. Eddie had been talking with one of the nurses, when Molly saw him. She waited until he was alone before she approached him with her problem. Molly walked up to the desk and asked "Hey, Doc, can I have a moment of your time?"

The doctor looked up. Putting on a big smile, he said, "Molly, I haven't seen you since I made that quick visit to the ICU. What is up?" Molly came over and sat down next to the doctor telling him what had happened that night. His smile faded a bit, saying, "Yes, we still have not heard anything about her, have we?" He looked over the packaging trying to read the postmark, but could only make out smudged printing with the naked eye. He soon got an excited look in his eye, saying, "Come with me." He led her to a supply room. Here he opened a cabinet, pulling out a strange-looking gadget that fit on his head, with an eye piece that pulled over his eye. Turning on the gadget's light, he took another look at the postmark. Soon he took off the light. Turning to Molly, he said, "I can see where it came from."

However, before he could say anything more, Molly put up her hand. "Don't tell me. If the nun asked, I don't want to know any more than I already do."

When they were back at the desk, Molly asks, "What do you think I should do with this package, Dr. Eddie?"

"Well," he answered, "if I can see the postmark, then the nun will be able to also. Why don't you throw it in the trash? When anyone asks, you can truthfully say the last time you saw the package it was in the trash."

Molly nodded her head, saying, "I think that is best." With that decided, she wadded up the paper, tossing it in the trash, next to where the doctor was sitting. Turning around, she headed to the door, waving a hand to the doctor, "See you around, Doc."

19

Birth and Rebirth

Valentine continued to travel westward. She was careful with how much she ate, so her food supplies lasted about a week. She also foraged along the way. It seemed to Valentine she kept finding late berries and fruit in old orchards when she least expected them. She thanked her Heavenly Father for the blessings.

Each morning she read from her Gospel of John before starting out; it was food for her mind and her heart. She read about Nicodemus, who came to Jesus only at night, and learned he must be born again. She realized she had been born again. First in the hospital then in her heart after she had accepted Jesus, that night in the park. Valentine often thought, as she walked along, how Jesus had searched for her and then brought her to Him. She thought of His care and safeguarding when she had not known anything about Jesus, His Father, or the Holy Spirit. Her heart overflowed with so much love for her friends that often she would start singing some of the songs she had learned from the Sanchezes. Her favorite was still "Turn Your Eyes upon Jesus," and she found herself humming or singing it throughout the day.

One morning, during her readings, she read about a woman who Jesus invited to drink from the Living Water. It was water He would give her so she could live forever. Valentine loved this story because she could identify with this woman. The woman of the well had a need and did not even know it, just like herself. Valentine had been in need and did not know it. Possibly,

Valentine would never have known about this living water if God had not taken away everything so she could see her need in Jesus. The more she read about Jesus, the more she saw His love for every lost and lonely person He came to. He wanted to give them His saving grace so they too could believe in His Father God and live forever.

One night Valentine was left with nothing but half a parsnip. As she slowly ate her last bite, she knew the next day she would need to put on her Lucy Pope disguise and go into the next town she came to.

It was near noon before Valentine came close to a town. On the outskirts of this small town, Valentine found an empty barn where she could change. She would leave her backpack and bedroll there in the barn, and stay the night when she got back.

Valentine soon started out with her cane and the Lucy purse, placing the empty tote inside of it in case she found more food than she could carry.

Walking into town, she saw a sign that said, "Hoyt, Colorado." As she passed a house with a picket fence, she heard two young voices talking. She could not see anyone; however, she did see the bushes in the corner of the yard moving just a little.

She heard one voice say, "Do you think we could capture her, Chief Red Fox?"

Another voice said, "Me not know, Little Gray Squirrel. That squaw looks like a giant."

Valentine stopped and pretended to be looking at something in the tree above her head. "I think I'm going crazy." Valentine spoke loudly, "I keep hearing voices, but I can't see anyone. Oh dear, maybe I should go to the hospital just in case I am going crazy."

She did not move or stop looking in the tree overhead until she heard a voice say, "Lady, I don't think you're going crazy. You just heard Little Gray Squirrel and me, Chief Red Fox, talking. You don't need to go to the hospital. Okay, lady?"

Valentine looked down at two little boys who had emerged from the bushes. They looked so much alike she would have thought she was seeing double had she not known better.

"Well, now, are you real Indians—like in the movies?" Valentine asked.

"Not really," said one boy. "We just like to play Indians and cowboys sometimes."

Just as he finished speaking, the front door opened. A young woman came out onto the porch and slowly down the steps, moving toward the gate.

When she got close to the gate, she said, "I hope the boys were not bothering you, ma'am. They are good boys, but they like to ask a lot of questions."

"They were not bothering me in the least. We were just talking about Indians and cowboys," Valentine replied.

The young mother smiled. "Oh dear, where are my manners?" She held out her hand and said, "My name is Mary Faith, but most people call me Faith. You look a little warm. Would you like to sit on the porch and have a drink of water or something? Have you been walking long, or perhaps you on your way to the market?"

Valentine did not really want to reply as to why she was out walking, so instead she avoided the question altogether. Instead, she said, "I'd be glad to sit down for just a while. I am getting a bit tired."

When Faith opened the gate, Valentine realized the young woman was very pregnant.

As Faith slowly lowered herself to the rocking chair, she asked one of the boys to run inside and tell Bailey to bring out five glasses of cold tea.

"Tell her we have company," she said as the front door screen closed with a bang. "Such nice weather we're having for this time of year, don't you think, ma'am?"

"Well, yes, it has been very pleasant to go on walks. I've not been in this area long, so I'm not sure what the weather should be this time of year. When does it get really cold?"

They talked about the weather for a few minutes until the door opened again, and a pretty young teenage girl came out carrying a tray with glasses of tea. She handed one to everyone before she sat down to sip on her own.

Faith said, "Ma'am, this is my daughter, Bailey, and this is… I'm sorry, I didn't catch your name, ma'am."

"Oh, excuse me," Valentine said. "My name is Lucy Pope. How do you do, Bailey? And what are these two Indian warriors' names?"

Bailey smiled a shy, sweet smile, saying, "It's a pleasure to meet you, ma'am. These are my brothers, Timmy and Tommy."

Valentine felt like she had dropped into a different time period; what nice manners they all have.

She took a sip of her tea and was delightfully surprised. "What kind of tea is this? It's delicious!"

Faith said, "You're drinking peppermint tea made with honey. You can have honey, can't you? I should have asked you. You're not allergic to honey, are you, ma'am?"

"No, no," Valentine exclaimed. "I have never tasted anything so good. Where do you get it?"

Timmy spoke up and said, "We go down to the banks of the creek in the summer. We pick and dry the leaves, don't we, Mama?"

Faith said, "We ran out of regular tea. The kids and I like this so much we made some just for us. Joey, I mean my husband, Joseph, hasn't…"

She stopped speaking. A sad expression came over her face. "Never mind, I just mean we like this better." Faith looked away and tried to hide a tear that was slipping down her face.

One of the boys got up to give his mama a hug. With his little finger, he wiped the tear away.

"Don't cry, Mama. Daddy will be home soon. He told me so."

"Yes, I know dear. I'm fine. You boys take your glasses into the sink and go play. Bailey, you had better go get your homework done. I'm fine. I'm just a little tired."

The boys finished their drinks and took the glasses inside, just as their mom had asked them to do, followed by Bailey.

Faith tried to smile but could not quite pull it off. Then the words poured out as though a dam had broken, and she had been desperate for someone to talk to.

"My husband has been working, every evening, down at the church. We belong to the Seventh Day Adventist church in town. Our new pastor has been doing a lot in the community, to get the other churches involved with the youth of our town. Our pastor and the new Catholic priest have managed to open a youth community center. It takes a lot of work. My husband and some of the other elders and deacons of our church have been working long hours to get the center open. At first it was just an extra night each week. Now he has been working there every night after he finishes at his regular job. Sometimes he leaves work early to go help at the church or youth center. Money is getting pretty tight, but I don't see him enough to be able to tell him. And when he does come home, it's very late—he says we'll talk in the morning. Lately he is even gone before I get up in the morning. I tried to walk down there one evening and talk to him, but he got upset with me. He told me he'd be home as soon as he could."

By now the tears were really coming down Faith's cheeks. "I'm sorry. I shouldn't be burdening you with my troubles, but I couldn't seem to stop once I started. Please forgive me."

Before Valentine could say anything in reply, Bailey came back out on the porch with a tray of little sandwiches.

She said, "It didn't seem like a tea party without little sandwiches." Faith quickly wiped her eyes, smiled up at her daughter, and said, "Thank you, sweetie."

Turning to Valentine, she asked, "Would you like to stay for a tea party, Miss Lucy?"

"Why, I'd be delighted," Valentine replied.

By the time they finished eating the little sandwiches and had drunk more tea, Faith seemed to be feeling better.

"Thank you so much, this has been the finest tea party I have ever been to," Valentine said. "It was lovely of you to include me."

Bailey picked up all the dishes and took them into the house.

"Faith, have you prayed about this problem you're having? I know God wants to help. Would you let me pray with you?"

Faith said, "I think that's the best idea I've heard in a long time."

She called to the boys and Bailey, asking them to come to the porch. Right then and there they all bowed their heads and prayed. Valentine asked God to help Faith and the children and to bring Joseph home to his family.

Timmy looked up at her and said, "Miss Lucy, that was really nice. I've never heard anyone talk to God as if He was right here with us. Do you think He is right here with us, Miss Lucy?"

Valentine thought for a minute then smiled at Timmy, "I believe a part of God is here with us. He lives in our hearts, his name is Spirit. Before Jesus went back to heaven, He told his earthly friends, or disciples as they are called in the Bible, that he would send Spirit back to be with us until Jesus comes back. He will take us all home to live with Father God, Spirit, and Jesus in heaven." Timmy sat quietly thinking about this new thought.

After a few moments, Faith asked, "Miss Lucy, would you like to wash up after that lovely tea Bailey made for us?"

"I surely would," Valentine said.

When Valentine came back out, Bailey was waiting for her. "Mama asks if you would please excuse her. Momma was getting tired, and the doctor told her to rest every afternoon. I begged her to go lie down. I told her you would understand. You do, don't you?"

"Of course I understand. You tell your dear mama I will visit tomorrow if you think that's okay. Please tell her to excuse me. I have to run. That way we'll be even. Do you think that sounds good?"

Bailey smiled a big smile. "Thank you for understanding." She walked Valentine out to the gate. "Would you come again for lunch? I really enjoyed serving a party. That's what I want to do when I get older. I want to be a chef."

"Yes, I will. I am pleased to accept your invitation to come to lunch."

Valentine turned at the corner, waved, then went on toward the main part of town. She found a small grocery store in the middle of town. Going in she bought a few things that would last her awhile on her travels. After paying for the items, Valentine continued down the street. She wanted to walk through town and then circle around back to the barn where she had left her supplies.

Valentine was almost to the end of town when she saw a church sign that read, "Welcome to Hoyt Seventh Day Adventist Church."

As Valentine started to walk by, she saw the front door open and a young man come out carrying a box. The man headed to an old pickup truck parked next to where she was now standing. When the he came closer, Valentine smiled, saying, "Your name wouldn't happen to be Joseph, would it?"

He looked questioningly at her, "Why, yes, it is. Do I know you from somewhere?"

"No, nothing like that," she said. "I just happened to have spent the past couple of hours sitting on your front porch, visiting with Faith and the children. I must say you have a lovely family. You must be very proud."

The young man's face broke into a huge grin. "I am very proud of my family!"

But then his face took on a sober look and he asked, "Everything is okay at home, isn't it? I've been so busy here. I keep telling Pastor Fred I can't be spending so much time away from home, with Faith so near her due date, and, well, I miss them. Pastor Fred keeps telling me just one more night here and we'll be done. I keep saying okay one more night. I told them positively this must be the last night this week and I can only work one night next week. Once the baby comes, I'll be a stay-at-home dad, every evening, to help Faith."

He looked back at the church. "We just have one more load of these videos to take to one last church in our area. Next week, at each of these churches, we start this new program, to introduce the youth to these videos. We'll explain to them the videos have really cool Bible stories that are written in their own youthful language."

When he paused, Valentine asked, "Joseph, have you watched the videos yourself? Do you like them, understand them, did these videos help you?"

"Well, I started to watch one. I had to go do something else at the time and never did get back to them. I'm sure they're very good stories. They are put out by the youth branch of the Catholic Church. Father Damien says they did wonders for the youth in the last city he came from."

"I see," Valentine said. "Well, Joseph, I have found, in my long life as Miss Lucy Pope, that prayer always helps me to find what God wants me to do. Don't you find that prayer gives you peace when you're struggling over any problem?"

Joseph smiled sheepishly. "You know, I've been spending so much time working for God I haven't had much time to talk to God. Lately I've been thinking about this very thing. I feel so distant from God these past few weeks. I've been neglecting Him, and I feel as if there's a gray cloud over my head all the time. In fact, just the other day I was feeling really bad. I was really missing my family. I looked up and saw Faith walking up the street. I was so delighted to see her, but instead of telling her how I felt and taking her home in the truck, I got mad at her and made her walk all the way back home. I felt so bad for what I said and did that I have gone home extra late every night and left the house early every morning this week so I would not have to see her. I just don't know what to say about the way I acted."

There was an uncomfortable pause in the conversation then Valentine said, "Joseph, would you like for me to pray for you and your family, that God will help you to work this hard thing out between you and Faith?"

Joseph looked up and down the street and asked, "Could you pray right now? I feel if I don't get help soon things will never be the same again, in my home or with my Heavenly Father."

Joseph had no idea how right he was.

Valentine replied, "I would be very glad to pray for you." So right there on the street in front of the church, standing beside Joseph's old truck, they bowed their heads and she prayed.

"Father God, we thank you for all the blessings you've given us, the ones we know about and the ones we don't. Please bring healing to Joseph's and Faith's relationship and family. Bring him back to daily talks with you, his Heavenly Father. Help him depend on Your Son, Jesus, who died for all of us, and to ask Spirit to live inside of his heart. We ask you for your help. However, we want only your wishes be done for us. Help us to see when it's our own will and not your will, Father God. Thank you, your friends, Joseph and Lucy."

Valentine smiled up at Joseph. "It's all in your Father's hands now. You can stop worrying and finish what you must here. However, then you must hurry home to your lovely wife and family."

Valentine and Joseph said good-bye. When she got to the corner, she turned and waved. Joseph was standing as she had left him, deep in thought. Absentmindedly he raised his hand to wave. Valentine realized she would not be continuing her trip right away.

By the time Valentine got to the barn, the sun was just setting. Her things were as she had left them. She soon got out of the Lucy Pope disguise and set to work getting things ready for night. One of her purchase at the store was some beef jerky. That was her supper with a bottle of water.

When it became too dark to see, Valentine got into her sleeping roll. After praying for guidance and understanding for the task God had set before her, she said good night and tried to go to sleep. Her thoughts kept going over the things she had learned from Joseph. She was not sure what to do with the knowledge of all those videos and a new church, the Seventh Day Adventist Church that appeared to be infected.

After squirming for a few minutes and letting her mind become more worried, she finally opened her heart again to her Father God. This time her prayer brought her peace so she could sleep.

In the middle of the night, Valentine woke with a start. She thought she had heard someone speak, but no one was there. She rolled over and went back to sleep. She woke again a bit later convinced she had heard somebody say something. Valentine put on her boots, grabbed her flashlight, and looked around—still there was no one.

She was just getting ready to take off her boots again and get back into bed when she heard a voice say, "Go to Faith's house!"

This time she understood the voice was in her head; it was a command from God. Without hesitating, she took her flashlight and ran out of the barn, headed to Faith's house as fast as she could.

Valentine was approaching the gate of Faith's house when she heard footsteps running toward her from town. In a minute she could make out the slight form of Bailey running as fast as she could back to the house. Valentine wondered where she could have been in the middle of the night.

They reached the gate at the same time and Valentine asked, "Bailey, what's wrong?"

Bailey stood gasping. She looked up bewildered at Valentine, "Oh, you scared me. Who are you?" Valentine had forgotten she was not dressed like Lucy. Saying the first thing she could think of, "My name is Valentine. I'm Lucy's daughter. She sent me to see how Faith is doing. Mom said she couldn't sleep and believed Faith needed help. Was she right, Bailey? Is your Mom in trouble?"

Bailey's tears were streaming down her face. "Momma said she had gone into labor and for me to run and get Dad."

Valentine hastily said, "Let's go see how your momma is."

As they entered the house, Bailey told Valentine that when she got to the church it was dark; no one was around.

"My dad's truck wasn't there, or any other cars either. So I ran back home, praying all the way for God to send someone to help us. And then there you were. Wow. He really does answer prayers, doesn't He! What did you say your name was?"

"Valentine, my name is Valentine, just like the holiday." She smiled at Bailey as they climbed the steps to the house.

"Momma's room is over here, Valentine."

As Bailey opened the bedroom door, Valentine could see Faith, her eyes were closed, and she was rocking a little. Just then a low groan was heard from the bed. Faith clutched her lower stomach and bit her lip—holding in a scream—a tear ran down each cheek.

Valentine went to the bed and bent down to take Faith's hand. "Faith, I'm here to help. My name is Valentine. I'm Lucy's daughter."

Faith opened her eyes and asked, "Where is Joey?"

"Momma, I ran all the way to the church, but Dad wasn't there. No one else was either. What are we going to do?"

Valentine said, "Call an ambulance, Bailey."

"The phones are out," Faith replied. "They do that a lot around here, and we don't have a cell phone. We can't afford one."

Valentine thought for a minute and said, "Faith, let's pray. Let's pray to God to help us and to send your husband home."

Bailey said, "Yes, Momma, let's pray."

Bailey and Valentine each took one of Faith's hands as they bowed their heads. First Valentine prayed for help and safety for Faith and the baby then Bailey's sweet voice softly prayed.

"Dear Jesus, we love you and thank you for our new baby. Please help Momma to be safe and get to the hospital so we can see our baby soon. Please make everything be okay. Thank you, Jesus, amen."

Valentine opened her eyes. After taking a deep breath, she started to ask a lot of questions. She surprised herself because she did not even know she knew to ask such questions. During those questions, Faith started having another contraction.

Valentine turned to Bailey and asked, "Do you have a hot pad? That could help your momma feel a little better."

Valentine timed the contraction. As it continued, she placed her hands on Faith's stomach. She could feel the hardness of the muscles as the contraction continued. When her stomach started to soften, Faith relaxed some.

"I started feeling my back aching at supper, but I just didn't think about it until I felt the first contraction about an hour ago. That's when I sent Bailey to the church to get my husband. We don't have a hospital here in this little town. We have to go thirty miles over to the next county to the hospital."

Valentine said, "Well, I guess we'll just leave everything up to Jesus and believe in His care for you and the baby. I timed the contractions and they are about five minutes apart. How long did it take to have your other children, how many hours?"

Faith thought for a moment and said, "It was about seven hours for Bailey. However, with the twins, my labor was five hours."

"Did you have any trouble with either of your deliveries, Faith?"

Just then, another contraction began, so Valentine rubbed Faith's back. Bailey came back into the room with a hot pad, plugged it in, and turned it on. When the contraction ended, Valentine asked Faith if her water had broken yet.

Faith answered, "No, not yet."

"Well, let's get you out of those clothes and into something comfortable. Bailey, where are your momma's nightgowns? Could you get one that's soft and kind of big? We'll help her get more comfortable."

After they made Faith comfortable, and another contraction had finished, Valentine told Faith to close her eyes and rest while she wasn't having a contraction. She put the hot pad against her back and a pillow to support her.

She asked Bailey to get a pencil and paper and write down the things they would need. "Let's see, where to start? We need a piece of plastic and an old sheet, some warm towels, a good pair of scissors, some olive oil, and some string."

Just then a small voice said, "I have some string in my box. Would you like for me to get it, Bailey?"

Bailey and Valentine turned to see the two little boys standing in the doorway. Timmy was holding an old sock monkey, and Tommy was holding his pillow. They were both wearing their footy pajamas and looked a little scared as Faith began to moan again.

Bailey answered, "Yes, Timmy, go find some clean string. You go with him, Tommy."

By the time the boys were back with the string, the latest contraction had ended and Faith was resting again.

Timmy brought the string up to Valentine and asked, "Who are you?"

Bailey answered for her, "This is Miss Lucy's daughter, Valentine. She's here to help Momma."

Tommy asked, as a tear started to roll down his cheek, "Is Momma sick, Bailey?"

Faith called out from the bed, "Tommy, Timmy, come here." The boys went to stand by their momma.

Faith began, "Boys, our new baby is coming tonight. Momma has to work hard to bring our new baby home. I need you both to do whatever Miss Valentine and Bailey tell you to do so we can soon hold our new baby. Okay, boys?"

The boys turned away from the bed with big smiles on their faces. Timmy asked, "Valentine, can we really help? What should we do first?"

Valentine told them that they must first have very clean hands to work around a new baby. They ran to the bathroom to wash their hands just as another contraction started. Both Bailey and Valentine went to help Faith. Between contractions, they got things ready for the baby. Valentine asked the boys to get some clean towels and put them in the dryer to keep them warm for when the baby came.

Sometimes, it seemed like hours, then it seemed like minutes as the contractions came closer together. The boys got ice from the freezer and put it in a bowl. Valentine put water in the bowl to keep Faith's face cooled off. The boys took turns watching the towels and watching the bowl of ice and wiping off their momma's face.

After a really hard contraction, Faith said, "My water just broke."

Bailey took the boys out to the kitchen, closing the door. She talked to the boys while Valentine changed the wet towel under Faith and checked to see if she could see anything.

Valentine said, "Faith, I need to check inside of you to see if the head is first. Do you understand?"

Faith had been resting with her eyes closed but told her to do anything she needed to.

When Valentine let the children in, Faith was resting again with another contraction just over. Timmy and Tommy returned to bathing Faith's face and held her hands during each contraction.

Valentine wondered how she knew what to check for and what to do. Either God is showing me what to do or I was a nurse in my former life—or both.

Finally, when Valentine checked Faith, she could see the baby's head crowning. She turned to the boys and said, "You boys need to stay out by the dryer, ready to bring the warm towels in. This might be a little scary because your momma might cry some, but in just a little while, we'll have a new baby."

The boys said they would do as they were told. Bailey got them a snack and some milk to keep them occupied until the birth was over. She made Valentine and herself a snack and they ate while waiting.

The boys were sitting at the table when they heard their momma cry out again and then everything went quiet. All of a sudden they heard a baby cry. They heard Bailey say, "Oh, it's a girl!"

In the bedroom Valentine tied the cord in two places with the cotton string they had boiled in water then cut the cord between the two knots. She laid the baby next to her momma, skin to skin, and helped the baby begin to nurse. Somehow she knew this would help both mama and baby. Then Bailey called out to the boys to bring in the warm towels.

When the boys came into the bedroom, there was a new baby lying next to their momma, and everything seemed okay. They went to their momma and kissed her, and looked at the new baby. Then they both yawned huge yawns.

"Go on to bed now, boys," Bailey told them. Without any arguing, they trudged out of the room to bed. When Bailey went into check on them a little later, they were both sound asleep; both had smiles on their sweet young faces. When she told Valentine, she complimented both for behaving as very good, helpful young men, when it was very much needed.

Valentine continued to monitor Faith that everything was going well. Just as they were wrapping the baby in a new warm towel and laying her back beside Faith, the front door opened and in walked Joseph.

He came into the bedroom with a startled look on his face and asked, "What's going on?" Before he could say anything else, he saw his wife and his new baby. He ran to the bed and dropped down to his knees. Tears started to run down his face. "What have I done, what have I done?"

Faith reached out and placed her hand on his head.

"We love you, Joey. Everything is going to be all right now."

That was all Valentine and Bailey heard because they shut the door on the parents of the new beautiful baby girl. Faith and Joseph needed time to be together.

Valentine stayed with the boys while Joseph took Faith, the baby, and Bailey to the hospital. She soon was fast asleep on the sofa.

Valentine didn't know anything until the boys came to her and asked, "Where is our new baby?"

Valentine rubbed her eyes and yawned. "Your daddy and Bailey took Momma and your new baby sister to the hospital to make sure they are both okay. He'll be back as soon as he can. Are you boys hungry? How about pancakes?"

The boys both yelled, "Yes, yummy."

Valentine stayed helping until Faith was back from the hospital and feeling well enough to take care of herself and her family. Joseph stayed close to his family for as long as he could. His boss had told him to take a week off with pay, to take care of his family. Joseph was only too glad to. He took a note to the church; it said he could no longer help after work or anytime because he must take care of his own family, like he should have been doing all along.

Before Valentine left, she told Joseph, Faith, and Bailey her story, what she had seen along the way. She wanted them to be prepared for the coming trouble. The night Valentine left, Joseph told her that he and Faith had decided to leave the area just as soon as the baby was strong enough to travel. They would go to family in the North. He told her he did not like the way the new Seventh Day Adventist pastor, Pastor Fred, was working so closely with the new priest. He didn't like the things they were doing to the church or the way they were acting toward him since he had stopped working for the cause, as they both called it.

Valentine asked him where he was thinking of going. He said he had family in the northern part of Idaho and they would head that way as soon as possible, before the winter snows started. He said he wasn't even telling his boss.

"I have no words to thank you, Valentine, for being here for Faith and all of us. I know we'll see you again, maybe not on this earth, but for sure in heaven. By the way, we've named the baby Valentine Faith."

With eyes full of tears, Valentine hugged both Joseph and Faith. She had kissed the boys good-bye before they went to bed. Now she gave Bailey a big hug and kiss, with a few more tears mixed in. Then she went and bent over baby Valentine, kissing her sweet cheek. She said a prayer for God to bless the baby and keep her safe. She turned, putting her backpack on, and headed out the door. She turned at the gate to wave to her new family, part of her family of God.

Valentine had good weather to travel in as she continued across the northeastern part of Colorado. She stayed on the back roads and, for the most part, saw very little traffic. If she heard a car coming, she would get out of sight. She knew the fewer people who saw a woman walking alone, the better.

One afternoon Valentine was sitting behind a cluster of trees reading her Gospel of John and resting, when she heard a car coming. She checked to see if she was completely concealed and then continued to read. However, she soon realized the vehicle had stopped. Someone was trying to get the vehicle started again, but it kept stalling. Valentine could hear the radio playing and a male announcer talking about the weather—something about the warmest fall weather they had seen for a decade. Then she heard a song start. The words floated to her on the breeze.

> Weak and wounded sinner, lost and left to die, O raise your head for Love is passin' by. Come to Jesus, come to Jesus, come to Jesus and live!
>
> Now your burden's lifted and carried far away, and precious blood has washed away the stain. So sing to Jesus, sing to Jesus, sing to Jesus and live!
>
> Like a new born baby, don't be afraid to crawl, and remember when you walk, sometimes we fall. So fall on Jesus, fall on Jesus, fall on Jesus and live!
>
> And sometimes the way is lonely and steep and filled with pain. If your sky is dark and pours the rain, then cry to Jesus, cry to Jesus, cry to Jesus and live!
>
> O and when the love spills over and music fills the night, and when you can't contain your joy inside, dance for Jesus, dance for Jesus, dance for Jesus and live!
>
> And with your final heartbeat, kiss the world goodbye, then go in peace, and laugh on Glory side. And fly to Jesus, fly to Jesus, fly to Jesus and live!
>
> Fly to Jesus, fly to Jesus, fly to Jesus and live!

As the song ended, Valentine heard the announcer say it was a song from Chris Rice called Come to Jesus. Valentine carefully looked around the tree. She could see an old truck stopped in the middle of the gravel road. Inside the truck was a young man with long hair and a beard. Valentine could see his head was bent and his shoulders were shaking; however, not a sound was coming from the truck. She could no longer even hear the radio.

Then Valentine heard a voice that was broken and empty, choking out the words, "How can I come to Jesus when I've done so many hurtful and horrible things?"

Valentine was suddenly up and walking toward the truck. While she was walking, she was praying.

"Please help me, Spirit. Help me to bring this young man to Jesus. He needs Jesus and he needs you, Spirit, in his heart. So please help me. Thank you."

Valentine had stopped and was standing beside the truck window as she silently said, "Amen."

She carefully put her hand into the open truck window and placed it onto the young man's arm. Softly Valentine said, "Jesus will forgive you no matter what you've done."

The man looked up, with unbelieving eyes, and asked, "Where did you come from?"

Valentine said, "I heard your call. I believe Jesus sent me to help you."

The young man sat shaking his head with tears coursing down his face. He finally said, "I asked Him to send someone, but I really didn't think He heard me because of what I've done."

"Why don't you tell me what's troubling you?" Valentine asked.

He replied, "I don't see how it will help, but I'm willing to try. You want to sit in the truck or what?"

Valentine thought a second then said, "Why don't you sit with me over there, where I was before I heard you coming down the road?"

He put out his hand to Valentine and said, "My name is Jay. Are you an angel or what?"

Valentine smiled. "No, I'm not an angel, far from it. But not long ago I was searching for someone. I didn't even know it was Jesus. I just knew there was someone out there helping me. I wanted to find out who it was and say thank you."

Jay got out of the truck, leaving it where it had stopped. They walked over to where her things were behind the trees and sat down.

Valentine started out by asking, "Jay, do you mind if I ask Jesus and Spirit to help us, help you?"

Jay shrugged his shoulders and said, "Sure. Do whatever."

So she made a simple plea to Jesus and Spirit to help Jay find the friendship she had found in them and Father.

Then Valentine said, "Please tell me what's hurting you so."

"Well, let me just say before I start my story that when I looked up, the sun was behind you. All I saw was your silhouette. I thought you really were an angel. I couldn't believe that just because I asked God to help me, He really would. I was raised by my grandma and grandpa. They taught me to believe in heaven and God and Jesus and everything, but lately I've gotten into a group of guys who don't believe any of this. They have put the Bible down a lot, and I didn't want to be made fun of, so I never said anything.

"These guys like to play games that are all about hunting people like cops and robbers—stuff like that. They want me to spend all my time with them. It's funny, but when I'm with them and I'm playing these games, I can't stop thinking bad thoughts. Then I want to do the bad things I've thought of, things I would never had done before. "I've stopped going to church with my grandma, and I haven't read my Bible in a year. Now I was on my way to meet the guys. I've stolen grandma's truck and all the money she had for food this month. And while I was doing this crazy stuff, all I could feel was hate for her and everything she stands for. I left her crying and pleading with me not to go. I just can't believe I did this. Something terrible had me in its clutches. What's strange is when I'm away from these guys and their games I start to think differently about everything. Anyway, my truck stalled, and that song came on the radio. You don't know how the words cut me deep, straight to my heart. 'Come to Jesus.' Did you hear that song, Valentine?"

Valentine smiled, "I did hear it. I've never heard that song before. The words hit me too. I have recently gone through a lot of what that song talks about. When it came to the part about dancing with Jesus, I realized I've been feeling like I've been dancing with Jesus for days now. I was in awe when the song finished. That's when I heard you. Before I knew what I was doing, I was up, standing beside your truck, touching your arm.

"Do you know what, Jay? I was almost going to start back on my walk fifteen minutes ago, but I heard a voice in my heart say, 'Stay here and read about me for a little longer. Wait upon your God.' Those are the exact words I heard. I am beginning to see what God can do for those who love Him and want to do His bidding. So after hearing those words, I sat and continued to read like He said. That is when I heard that song and your cry for help. Jay, God has given you a second chance to walk with Him and take His son Jesus for your Savior. He wants you to let Spirit come into your life and make you like Jesus. Do you want to accept God's offer and turn away from this thing that's trying to take over your life?"

After a long, quiet pause, Jay answered, "It's hard to believe that the God of the universe has taken the time to come to me, a young gone-bad guy, headed straight to the devil, to give me a second chance. But I can see this is what has happened. I can only do one thing."

He looked into Valentine's eyes, saying, "I must follow God. I just must."

"I guess now, Jay, you can dance with Jesus too. Let us pray right now and ask Jesus to come into your life."

Jay bowed his head. With tears streaming down his face, he gave his life to Jesus. He asked Him to forgive him, to send His Holy Spirit to come and live in his heart.

Valentine prayed and thanked God for letting her be a part of His work in bringing young Jay back to His loving arms. She asked for help to know what to do about what Jay had done and how to make it right.

When they looked up, there was a beautiful sunset. So beautiful they both sat, holding their breath, watching as the sun slowly set in a glorious array of colors. The two watched until the sky was almost dark. When it was over, they both let out a sigh.

"So," Valentine said, "let's go see what God wants us to do." They stood and Jay helped carry Valentine's backpack to the truck. He turned the key and the truck stared without a hitch. Looking over at Valentine, Jay said, "God is good!" then he turned the truck around heading in the direction that Valentine had been heading—west.

Valentine was worried as they drove toward Jay's grandma's home. She had been thinking that if Jay and his grandma stayed at their home, those people would be right back at Jay, and maybe hurt him or his grandma. She thought they needed to go someplace safe for a while.

"Jay," Valentine said.

"Hmm?" Jay replied.

His mind was dancing with Jesus; his heart was at peace for the first time in a year. He shook his head and came back to earth.

"Did you say something, Valentine?"

"Yes, I did. I was wondering if these guys you've been hanging with know where you and your grandma live."

"Umm, well, yes, they do. They were waiting for me at the corner of our road to make sure everything went well, but we were separated when we heard sirens. Then my truck stalled, and you know the rest."

"Jay, you need to go someplace safe for a while."

"Safe?" Jay questioned. "What are you talking about? Why would they bother me just because I'm not going to hang out with them or play their games anymore?"

Valentine explained, "Jay, I'm going to tell you a story. It may sound so outlandish, that had you not gone through some of this already, you would not believe me. However, with God in your heart, I believe He will open your understanding. No matter, you must hear this, for your protection."

Valentine told Jay her story. She ended it with her experience at the café with the young man and the Netter drink.

"Hey, I've heard about that drink! The guys were going to bring some of it to the meeting tonight!" Jay exclaimed.

"I believe that if you had drunk that drink tonight you would never have gotten away from it. God loves you very much. He needs you to work for Him to tell more people about the danger. I am beginning to wonder if this whole thing doesn't have more to it than just video games. It seems to me it will take a long time to cover the whole world with video games—and not all people are into that kind of thing."

Jay let out a long low whistle. "Wow, that's some story, but I believe you. Last week a young man on a motorcycle came to our game room. He was looking for a woman. Now that I think about it, the description is you, Valentine."

"Did this young man tell you this, Jay?"

"No, I heard the conversation by accident. I was in a bathroom stall, and the men who were talking about it never looked to see if anyone was in there before they started to talk. I don't know why, but I was kind of scared to say I had heard any of it. So I waited until everyone was long gone before I left the bathroom. I never said anything to anyone. I had forgotten it until just now."

"I heard something else that didn't make any sense," Jay continued, "until now that is. This guy, J. R.—I don't know his real name—told them to stay off cell phones, iPods, or any kind of electric device from now on. He told them to only use landlines. He went on to say that the plan would be in full swing starting the beginning of December, but that it would be safer to start now, to use landlines."

Valentine asked, "How many were in the bathroom talking?"

"I'm not sure. I recognized two guys. They are kind of the unspoken leaders of the group I was hanging with. One is Morty and the other is Lucas. J. R. also told them they would be getting their vaccinations soon, to keep them immune from the plan. I thought it was all some kind of joke. Nothing made any sense then, but now, it's beginning to really come together."

Valentine sat thinking for a while. She then asked if these guys said what the vaccination was or how it was given.

"No," Jay said. "Well, wait a minute. J. R. did say it would do something to their hand. Let me think. What did he say? Oh yeah, he said it would make a black mark on the right hand, but not to worry because it was just a small side effect. This all sounds so crazy. After tonight, nothing will sound crazy to me again. God came looking for me! He caused me to be separated from my crowd, stalled the truck, and played the song I needed to hear, to make me stop and listen to Him. He did all that to bring me back to my senses!"

Jay and Valentine sat in companionably silence for the rest of the ride. Jay was just pulling onto the road where he lived when he broke the silence, "I wonder if Grandma has called the police yet. If so, will I go to prison?"

From a distance, the farmhouse shone out, as a beacon to a weary traveler. Every light was on, from the attic to the basement and from the front door to the back porch. Jay looked a bit worried. Nevertheless, he pulled into the drive and stopped outside the kitchen door. He quickly opened the truck door, but even before he had it all the way extended, his grandma was at his side hugging him, crying. Her words stumbled over each other in an attempt to tell all.

"You've come back! Come in and eat. I've been cooking for hours. Ever since peace came into my heart, right before sunset. I knew it meant God had saved my boy."

"But Grandma, how did you know?"

"Well, when the peace came into my heart, I heard a voice seem to say, 'Your boy and his friend will be hungry, so cook something to eat. You must be ready to leave soon.'"

Jay gave his grandma a big hug, and together they stood outside the back door and cried. He repeated over and over, "I'm so sorry, please forgive me."

His grandma smiled up at her boy through tears of joy, saying, "All was forgiven before you left the house this afternoon. I wasn't crying because of me. I was crying because of you. Because of my fear that you would be lost forever from Jesus and from me. As soon as you left, I knelt down in the kitchen and started praying for you."

Then Jay turned to Valentine, "Grandma, this is the angel God sent when you prayed for me. This is Valentine—we have a story to tell you. But I think we do need to leave here and stay away until it's safe to come back home."

Because Jay's grandma had already packed her things and Jay's, there wasn't much to do. Grandma had a supper ready and food for later waiting on the kitchen table, along with hot coffee in a thermos.

Jay shook his head in amazement. "God is good. What else can I say?"

They quickly ate and were heading west away from Grandma's house and from the group of guys who had wanted to gain control of Jay's life.

Valentine asked, "Jay, do you have any idea where you can go to be safe? I don't think this thing is going to blow over anytime soon."

Grandma answered Valentine's question. "I've been thinking about where to go also. We'll need to go north. That's where I think God is directing me. Have you ever heard of Lemhi County, Idaho, Jay?"

Jay thought a minute and replied, "I think Grandpa used to tell me a story about Lemhi County, being the place where he first met you and asked you to marry him. Is that right, Grandma?"

Grandma smiled and nodded her head.

"You're very right. I still own my parents' home place. A woman who was my best friend and next-door neighbor has been taking care of the place for the past few years. My uncle, Leland, lived there until he died, and then we rented the ranch land to my friend's grandson and family. The house is still standing and in good livable use for us when we need it—and now seems to be when we need it. I had a letter from my friend last week when she sent me the rent money for the year. I had the money in my Bible for emergencies."

Again Jay said, "God is good!"

They drove until they came to a small town where Jay stopped for gas and a restroom visit. When they were all back in the truck, the three looked at the road atlas and decided to head north to Highway 14. There they would turn west again. The route would keep them away from most of the big cities. Valentine indicated she could stay with them until she felt it was time to head out on her own or until they turned north again.

Jay and Valentine took turns driving through the night. They stopped at a campground to eat breakfast and stretch their legs. Jay got out his Bible. Carefully he opened the pages and then got tears in his eyes at the inscription on the front page

> To Jay, on his 10th birthday,
> From Grandpa and Grandma
> May you always keep this near and dear to your heart
> Until we meet again in heaven.

Grandma laid her hand on Jay's. "I miss him too. Now that we're both on the right road, we'll be seeing him when Jesus comes to take us home."

They had a short Bible reading and prayer then started driving toward the Rockies.

Steamboat Springs Colorado was where Valentine felt the urge to go her own way. While looking at the map, she felt compelled to head to a town called Clark. The closer she got, the stronger the feeling became. Valentine said her good-byes at a crossroads just north of Steamboat Springs and headed north.

It was late morning when Valentine left Jay and Grandma. They wanted to take her to where she was going, but she told them she needed to walk this road alone. They thanked her for all she had done.

"Not good-bye—see you soon," she told them.

Valentine walked until noon. Seeing a small old road heading west, she took it. She had not liked all the traffic on the larger road. Since she had turned onto this small road, she had not seen anyone. The forests were beautiful there, and she was glad to be out in nature again.

It was late afternoon when Valentine felt the first snowflake on her cheek. There had been no old building to take shelter in, to get out of the cold and snow. She stopped in the middle of the road and started to pray. "Father God, I felt you leading me to go this way. Now it's getting colder, the snow is beginning to fall, and night is coming on. I need to find a safe place to spend the night. Please show me your way and help me to remain strong and not let the enemy get me down. Thank you for your love and guidance, Amen."

She continued to move down the road as the snow got thicker, as fog settled down around her. She was wondering what to do next when she felt a warm breeze flowing past her from the left. She started to move in that direction and up an incline. Soon she felt a stone wall in front of her. She moved her hands around and felt an indent in the wall with warm air coming out of it. The indent was big enough to crawl into and out of the snow. She got her wool blankets and tarp out, and rolled up in them. Laying her head on the backpack, she prayed again. This time to say thanks for a place to get out of the storm and a warm comforting breeze on her back. She was asleep before she could say amen.

20

Joy in the Morning

Valentine woke to the feel of warm air on her back and a cold breeze blowing on her face. She also heard a munching sound very near her right ear. Opening one eye, she was startled to see a big snout very close to her face. Teeth were munching on grass. She could see the snow had stopped and that it was not thick at this spot—probably due to the warm air coming from the rock behind her. She waited until the munching thing moved on then she crawled out of her sleeping place.

Looking around, Valentine could see she had left the road the night before. She was now on a hillside. The warm air was coming from a small cave with a crack in the back wall. There was a larger boulder in front of her. She could see cows all around her munching on the grass exposed from the warm air. Valentine stood up and stretched her arms and legs. She had slept very well but was a bit stiff from not having much room to move. When she stepped around the boulder, she could see a valley with more cows. At the far end, she could see buildings with smoke coming from one of them.

Valentine decided to head down there to scout the place out. She stayed close to the edge of the wooded area along the hillside. After about thirty minutes, she was close enough to the buildings to see that the building with the smoke coming from the chimney was a large log cabin. Removing her backpack, she squatted down to watch. She wanted to make sure she felt safe enough to go to the cabin door. While she was watching, she heard a sound behind her. The sound was loud in the quiet snow-covered woods. The noise registered to Valentine's brain like a gun being cocked.

A strong male voice gruffly said, "Don't move."

Valentine did as she was instructed; she didn't move a muscle. She could hear footsteps coming closer.

The voice said, "Stand up and start walking to those buildings over there."

As Valentine stood up, something poked her in the back, something hard. She started walking without hesitation. The whole thing seemed like a cowboy movie. She had never had a gun pointed at her, that she could remember anyway—it was not exciting. She walked until she came to the first building.

The voice said, "Open the door and go in."

Valentine started to turn around. The voice said, "Don't turn around or do anything until I tell you."

So far, she had not said a word. However, this whole thing was getting a bit bizarre.

"Look, I'm sorry I trespassed on your place. If you will just point me toward the road, I'll be out of your way and not bother you again."

The man stammered, "You're a-a woman! They are sending women now to try to push me off my land. I can't believe it."

"Yes, I'm a woman, but I've not been sent by anyone. I got lost in the snow last night, and I slept in a rock crevice with warm air coming out of it. I was awakened by some cows, which were definitely friendlier than you've been."

The man said, "Likely story! I can check that out in a few minutes. So why don't you go to that small room to your right and have a seat. I'll be back as soon as I've checked you out."

When Valentine stepped into the room, the man shut the door and locked it. *That was certainly different from what I had hoped for. All I had wanted was a little coffee and a place to freshen up. Then I would have been on my way.* She sat down on the bench beside the door and got out the Gospel of John. She decided she was in God's hands. Whatever happened next was His doing. Valentine stopped worrying and started to read where she had left off the morning before, at chapter four, verse fourteen: "But whosoever drinketh of the water that I shall give him shall never thirst; but the water that I shall give him shall be in him a well of water springing up into everlasting life."

Later on she read in John 3:16, "For God so loved the world that He gave His only begotten Son, that whosoever believeth in Him should not perish, but have everlasting life."

Valentine closed her eyes after reading that. She prayed for all the friends she had made along her strange journey: the Sanchezes, Mary from the bookstore, and Sara the waitress. She prayed for Caleb, Esther, Whitney, Rose, Uncle Billy, and Aunt Emma, for their safety through the coming months until the plan could be stopped. Her thoughts then went to Faith, Joseph, Bailey, Timmy, Tommy, and last but not least the new baby, Valentine. Her heart went out to the new baby who had been born in such difficult times. However, she knew God would take care of that new life just as He was taking care of herself, a woman, lost and alone. *I didn't even know that I needed You, Father God, for anything.* She continued her prayer with Jay and his grandma. Her prayer ended with a request: "Please help this man who seems to be in some kind of trouble. If he doesn't know you, help me to be a help to bring him into your kingdom."

Valentine's eyes were still closed when she heard the man say, "You fall asleep or what?"

Looking up, she smiled in the direction of the voice. She could not see well enough to make out his face with the light coming into the door behind him.

He said, "I found where you slept. That still doesn't show me you're not working for the company that is trying to buy me out—or kill me."

"Well," Valentine said, "I can't help you there. All I know is that I am who I said I was—just traveling through. I have no desire to do harm to anyone. Until you figure me out, do you think you could let me use your bathroom and have a drink of water at least?"

Valentine smiled again at the vague image in the doorway. She turned to put her book back where it belonged and sat waiting expectedly.

After some deliberation, the man said, "Okay, you can come into the house and use the bathroom. Just remember I've still got my rifle on you, so don't make any quick moves. The last guy snooping around had his own rifle and took a shot at me, so I'm not taking any chances."

She slowly got up. Picking up her backpack, she moved toward the door. The man moved out of the way, standing behind her, as she moved out into the sunlight. Valentine did not look around. She went where the man directed her to go. When they got close to the cabin, he told her to go around back. Valentine followed the porches around to the back.

The man said, "The bathroom is inside to the right."

She went where he indicated, shutting the door behind her.

"Don't bother to lock it. I'm not coming in unless you try something funny."

After using the restroom, she then washed her face and hands. She got her brush out and brushed her hair, braiding it, and wrapped her bandanna around her head. Valentine slowly opened the door. Finally she came face-to-face with her captor.

Looking into his eyes, she could see no evil—only deep sadness and bone weary.

He gave her a quick head-to-toe, declaring, "Well, you don't look like one of them, but that may be a new scheme of theirs, to put me off."

Using his rifle, he motioned her to go into the kitchen in front of him and to sit down at the table. He got two cups out of a cupboard and poured some of the blackest coffee Valentine had ever seen. He poured in sugar enough to make cookies with. From a glass pitcher out of the old refrigerator he poured something thick and white into each cup. Setting one cup in front of Valentine, he then sat down with his own cup and placed the rifle over his knee.

"So, what's your story?"

Valentine took a sip of her coffee—with a surprised look—and said, "This is good!"

The man said nothing, just looked at her, with a look that said his patience was running short.

Valentine made a quick decision to tell the man the truth—as much as she could anyway. "I'm being hunted by people who want to learn some things, and then I believe they will kill me."

That was all she said, no more, no less. Sitting back in her chair, she quietly drank her coffee.

The man sat quiet for what seemed like hours to Valentine. However, it was really only a few minutes. Then they both heard a sound, a whisper really.

"Abraham, is that you?"

He looked up, startled. Turning to Valentine, he said, "Don't go anywhere, because if you do, I will find you."

Standing up, taking his rifle, he went into the room where the sound had come from. Valentine didn't know what to think. Nevertheless, she felt this was where she was supposed to be. So she sat and enjoyed her coffee until the man came back. He had a bewildered look on his face she could not begin to read.

"My wife, Joy, would like to meet you. She doesn't know what's going on, so just visit with her for a minute then tell her you need to be on your way. Do you understand?"

"Not completely, but I will do what you've asked," Valentine said.

Setting her coffee down, she followed Abraham. They went into a room that had once been the living room but was now a sick room. A woman was lying in a hospital bed in the center where the warm air from the fireplace would reach her best. The woman in the bed was slender with long brown hair. By the looks of her hair, it had not been brushed or braided in a while.

The woman put out her hand, saying, "Hello, my name is Joy. It's so nice to have company. We don't have many people out here on the ranch. I'm so sorry I can't get up. I seem to be having trouble walking this morning. Please pull up a chair and tell me all about yourself."

Valentine was enchanted by the lovely lady in the bed. Pulling up the chair that was sitting nearby, she said, "My name is Valentine. I was just traveling through, and your husband, Abraham, was kind enough to invite me in to have a cup of coffee before I travel on down the road. You have a lovely home. You must enjoy it a lot, especially the beautiful view out front."

"Oh yes," Joy said. "Abraham and I enjoy sitting out on the front porch, of an evening, watching the sun set. Don't we, Abraham?"

Abraham was standing close. He smiled a sad smile at his wife and took her hand. At that moment, something happened that shocked Valentine so much she jumped up and moved away from the bed.

Just as Abraham touched his wife's hand, Joy screamed, "Don't touch me! Who are you? Get out of my room! I don't allow strange men in my room! Get out now!"

Abraham quickly turned and left the room. Valentine was bewildered, trying to figure out what to do next.

However, before she could think, Joy said in a perfectly calm voice, "Dear, what did you say your name was? Could you brush my hair for me? I just can't seem to get it right today." Indicating the brush on the table, Joy sat up in bed as though nothing had happened. She looked expectedly at Valentine for her to brush her hair.

Not knowing what else to do, Valentine unwound the braid and started to brush carefully. As she brushed, Joy talked about all kinds of things; none of them really going together. It was just a jumble of words and sentences. As Valentine finished re-braiding Joy's hair, her eyes closed. Valentine helped Joy lie down. She sat with Joy and hummed a song until the woman in the bed fell asleep, an innocent sweet smile lingering on her face.

Valentine got up quietly and went back into the kitchen to find Abraham. She found him frying bacon and eggs while sipping his coffee. He appeared to be in very deep thought. He did not realize she had come into the kitchen until he turned around to set the plates on the table.

He jumped a little, saying gruffly, "Sit down and eat." Valentine sat where he indicated. They ate in complete silence.

Abraham finally looked up, "Joy has Alzheimer's. She's had it for six years now. This morning, when she called out my name, it was the first time she has said my name for at least a year. Then she talked as if she knew me and could remember our life together, before she got sick. I knew it wouldn't last long, but I shouldn't have tried to touch her. I knew better."

Valentine replied, "I am very sorry. I didn't mean to cause trouble."

Abraham looked her squarely in the eyes, "If you remember, I brought you, by gunpoint, into the house."

Valentine smiled, "I must say I don't ever remember being held at gunpoint before, but there are a lot of things I don't remember about my past, so I may be wrong about that. The people who are chasing me might have held me at gunpoint, and I would not remember."

"So let me get this straight," Abraham asked. "You think you're being chased by someone, but you can't remember who?"

She laughed a little, "I kind of know who some of them are, but I can't remember why they want me. I do know they are not good people and have killed at least once to try and stop me. I've been walking since Baltimore, with some rides here and there. I figure I've been on the run for about a month now, give or take a few days."

"That's some story. Still, I do believe you. At least, I believe that you believe this story. I'm good at discerning if someone is trying to lie to me, and I feel you are being completely honest. Where are you headed now?"

"I'm not sure, although I'll be happily out of your way, as soon as you say the word. Could you please take your rifle out of my midsection?"

"Oh," Abraham said. "I'm sorry, I forgot."

He picked his rifle up off the kitchen table and hung it over the door on some hooks.

Turning he said, "You're free to leave any time you're ready. Sorry for the mix-up. I've been having trouble with this big company that wants the ranch. They've tried every kind of trick. When I saw you moving along the tree line, I thought you were a man, one of them, and you were sneaking up on me again. I can hardly leave the house to check the cattle. I don't want to leave Joy alone."

He stopped talking and sat looking at his empty plate.

"Abraham, that's your name, isn't it?"

"That's what Joy has always called me, when she remembers me anyway, but she's the only one who ever called me that. Most people call me Abe. I would prefer you call me Abe, if you don't mind."

She sat thoughtful for a minute, saying a silent prayer.

"Abe, I would like to help you. I need to tell you that since the hospital in Baltimore, I can't remember anything about my past. It's not just what these people want to know, it's any and all of my past life before waking up in that hospital room. I think I could have some kind of nursing training by things I seem to know when I need to. I would not presume to think that I could nurse someone who is critical, but I could help you. I could feed Joy, bathe her, things like that. If you think I could be of any help."

Abe had an astonished look on his face when he said, "You would help me after I treated you like a criminal, at gunpoint no less? Why would you do that?"

"Well, I've been following this path west. At first I thought it was just to get away from the people hunting me, then I met a family who introduced me to God, Jesus, and Holy Spirit. They told me the story of why sin came into the world and the universe and how God loves each of us and wants to help us. I learned that the mysterious presence that had been helping me out of the city and had taken care of me all along the way was God. I learned what Jesus did for me by dying on the cross. From then on I have been following where God leads me, and I believe He has led me here to help you and Joy. I know that was a very long explanation, but I needed to give you some of my background so you would understand where I'm coming from."

She finished with a sigh and looked to see if Abe thought she was crazy. However, he was looking off into space, in a world of his own. Valentine stayed quiet until he came back around.

He said, "I used to believe that stuff, but I stopped believing when God let Joy get sick. Even when we prayed and prayed, she only got worse. Now I just can't talk to God anymore. He could have made her well, but now it's too late. If I never talk to Him again, it'll be too soon."

He looked stubbornly at Valentine, "If you can live with the way I am, and not talk to me about your faith, I would be very grateful for your help, as long as you can stay."

Abe and Valentine discussed the particulars; it was decided she should sleep in the room adjoining Joy's room so she could hear Joy better. Abe told her he slept most nights in a chair beside Joy's bed, but he was beginning to really feel the lack of sleep. He decided he would sleep upstairs in his own bed from now on.

Abe put on his heavy coat and boots and headed out to check the cattle. Valentine cooked soup to feed Joy when she woke up.

Valentine put her things in her new room. She was just finished making up the sofa bed when she heard movement in the next room. She found Joy looking out the window humming the song Valentine had been humming before Joy went to sleep. Valentine sang the words of the song.

"Turn your eyes upon Jesus; look full in His wonderful face." Joy looked up at Valentine, and even though she didn't say anything, she smiled and kept on humming as Valentine sang. After Valentine straightened Joy's bed, she went into the kitchen and got a bowl of soup. She continued to sing as she fed Joy. Joy seemed to relax and eat better with the music. Joy had almost finished eating the soup when Valentine heard the back door open. Hearing footsteps coming down the hall, she looked up just as she heard a jubilant voice saying, "How is my best girl today?"

The voice sounded like Abe's, but something was different. Valentine looked at a person that could have been Abe if Abe could have grown a long beard and let his hair grow about a foot just since morning.

The man stopped when he saw Valentine.

"Who are you? I'm sorry, I mean where did you come from? I mean… Oh, I don't know what I mean."

He walked across the room, holding out his hand, "Hi, my name is Gordon. I'm Abe's twin brother. I didn't get your name."

Just as he finished talking, Abe came up behind him. With a chuckle he said, "This is an intruder who has decided to stay and help with Joy. Valentine, meet Gordon."

Valentine smiled and shook the huge hand still stretched out to her. Then she went back to feeding Joy. When she was finished, she got Joy settled on her side to go back to sleep. The men had gone into the kitchen and dished up some soup. Abe got three cups and filled them with steaming hot coffee.

The story of how Abe and Valentine met had Gordon laughing until tears ran down his face.

Abe and Valentine spoke at the same time, "It wasn't that funny." Then they began to laugh too.

It's good to see Abe laughing, thought Gordon. *And this is a beautiful woman! I wonder what her story is and why she was way out here in the middle of nowhere. We sometimes have hikers stop in to get a drink of water or directions in the summertime but this is November, not the first of June.*

Abe explained to Valentine that Gordon lived over in the next valley and ran his cattle there.

She asked, "So, Gordon, has anyone ever mistaken you for Grizzly Adams?"

He smiled, "Well, maybe once. This is a good look to keep people thinking I'm a bit crazy. It keeps most people from venturing onto my place, even when I'm not there."

"I can see it might make some people think twice before they bothered you," she laughed.

The talk then turned to a storm that was predicted.

"It should hit here about daylight, if the forecaster is right," Gordon said. "I'd best get home and get things snug before it gets dark. Thanks for lunch. See you, Abe. And it was nice meeting you, Valentine."

As quick as he came, Gordon was out the door. Abe cleaned up the kitchen while Valentine checked on Joy. She was awake, restless, and crying out, so Valentine got out her *Gospel of John* and began to read from where she had stopped reading that morning. Immediately Joy started to relax. She lay quietly and listened to the words. When she finally went back to sleep, Valentine looked up to find Abe standing at the door. She didn't know how long he had been there or what he thought of her reading from the Bible, but he didn't command her to stop, and Joy surely did benefit from the reading.

Valentine got up and went to put her book away. As she left, Abe went into his wife's room. He sat down beside Joy and quietly watched her sleeping. Valentine put on her coat heading outside to walk around the outbuildings. As she walked, she pondered how Abe must feel to sit beside his wife of thirty years, with her not knowing him. It must be devastating she thought.

When she went back into the kitchen, Abe was making supper and coffee was brewing on the stove. He looked to be in deep thought. Not wanting to interrupt, she went and sat down in her room. The chair was really comfortable; she quickly fell asleep.

The storm started about three in the morning. Valentine knew this because she was up helping Joy .She watched as the first flake settle on the front porch railing. By morning the storm had worked into a blizzard. It was four days before they saw the sky again. Abe and Valentine got into a routine of cooking, caring for Joy, and cleaning. Mostly Valentine took care of Joy because Joy seemed to get upset whenever she saw Abe in the room.

At noon on the fourth day, there came the sound of someone stomping the snow off their boots. In a moment, Gordon walked in. Under his arm was a package that he put on the table.

"I thought you might like venison steaks for supper."

It seemed to Valentine that the kitchen got a little brighter when Gordon walked in. Supper was a much livelier meal than the last few Abe and she had eaten together. Looking at the two brothers, it was hard to believe they were twins. But then again, there were times when they would say the same thing at the same time and sound just alike.

After supper Abe mentioned he would like to sit with Joy, so Valentine and Gordon cleaned up the kitchen. The two talked of anything and everything. It was not long before Valentine was telling Gordon of her newfound faith in God. Gordon told her he had given his life to Jesus when he was ten years old and had not turned back since.

"I had been studying with some friends of mine until I had to leave them," Valentine explained. "Now I have only the Gospel of John. Don't get me wrong, I love that part of the Bible, but I wish I could finish studying in Daniel." She told Gordon she planned to get a complete Bible as soon as she could, but as of yet, she had not found one. She also told him the one she had been studying with was an NIV Bible.

"Have you read from that kind of Bible, Gordon?"

"Well, I believe I have, but the Bible I have been studying and reading from is the Clear Word Bible, written by a man named Jack J. Blanco. A friend sent it to me on my last birthday. It's what the name implies, clear words."

"I would love to see it sometime. Could you bring your Bible the next time you come?" Valentine asked.

"You can bet on it." And so the plan was made. For as long as there was good weather, Gordon would come and study at the kitchen table with Valentine.

Valentine found she really liked reading the Clear Word Bible. She also found she understood a lot more of what she read. It was not long before Abe was bringing his rifle to clean or some piece of leather to mend, and sat at the table while Gordon and Valentine studied. He never said anything, but it seemed to both of them that he was listening. Valentine prayed as she worked around the house, for Abe's heart to be softened, to hear the Holy Spirit speak to him. She prayed also that Joy could be comfortable and at peace.

No one knows what someone, sick like Joy, might understand. However, Valentine thought Joy always responded in a quiet and calming way when she read to her from the Bible.

Thanksgiving was coming. Gordon said he had shot a wild turkey for Thanksgiving dinner. He would cook the turkey if Abe and Valentine would do up all the fixings. Valentine helped where she could, but she still did not know very much about cooking. So Valentine set the dining room table and made it look as nice as she could. Abe showed her where the good linen and china were and said he would be glad for her to use them.

All was ready when Gordon came with the turkey. The pan was wrapped in a heavy quilt and still hot from the oven, ready to carve. Even Joy seemed to know it was a holiday. All through dinner, while she lay in her bed in the next room, she hummed one song after another.

When dinner was over, Abe talked Gordon into getting out his fiddle and playing a few tunes. Most of the songs Valentine did not know, but Abe sang along with Gordon and the fiddle. They both had good voices, and the room filled with music. Valentine sat back and enjoyed every song. It was very late by the time they had sung every song they knew. Abe persuaded Gordon to stay the night because the temperature was dropping fast.

"It's just too cold to be walking home tonight," Abe said.

"Can't agree with you more, brother. I left my place with that very thing in mind."

While the men checked on the barn and animals, Valentine made one more check on Joy. Joy was sound asleep.

The music must have helped everyone sleep well because they all slept late the next morning. After breakfast Gordon went home—life, in the snug cabin, went back to the routine it had been before the holiday.

Abe gave Valentine a book he had bought on Alzheimer's disease. It covered everything from signs and symptoms to the progression of the disease. She read it from cover to cover and felt she understood a lot more on how to care for Joy as she got worse. The thought of Joy's disease getting worse saddened Valentine. Even though she knew this was not the real Joy, the Joy Abe knew, Valentine had come to love Joy as a sister. It would hurt to see her digress.

Abe repeatedly thanked Valentine for staying and helping him. Abe said he didn't know what he would have done without Valentine. He spent time each night reading to Joy. However, he soon learned that whenever he tried to read anything but the Bible she would grow more and more restless. So he read only the Bible.

One night, near Christmas, Valentine was awakened by Joy. It sounded like she was saying something. Valentine got up and stepped quickly to Joy's bedside. Leaning down, she heard Joy say, "Valentine, would you go get Abraham for me?"

Valentine was so stunned she almost tripped over the lamp table next to the bed. Quickly regaining her balance, she ran upstairs. Opening Abe's door, she called, "Abe!"

"What's wrong?" Abe asked, coming awake instantly.

"Nothing is really wrong, Abe. Joy is calling for you."

Valentine walked down the stairs behind Abe. After he went into Joy's room, she shut the door behind him. Going around to her room, she shut the adjourning door and went back to bed. Before going to sleep, Valentine thanked God for this blessing and prayed for Abe's heart to be drawn to Jesus.

When Abe went into Joy's room, he heard her words clearly, "Abraham, I've missed you. Please come lie beside me for a while."

Abe couldn't believe his ears. This was his Joy—she was talking to him! He carefully lay down beside his wife.

"Abraham," she continued, "I've just had a dream. It was such a lovely dream. I saw Jesus. He was standing at the gates of heaven and his arms were opened wide. His welcoming smile was so beautiful. When He spoke, his voice was rich with gladness, 'Joy it's almost time to go get my family on earth.' But then he had a sad look come upon His face as He spoke, 'Is our Abraham ready to meet me, Joy?' I watched as a tear slipped down His face. That's when I woke up and called to Valentine to go get you. She is such a nice friend. Thank her for me would you?"

The tears were running freely down Abraham's face, but all he could say was, "I love you, Joy, and I've missed you so much."

Joy turned her head to look earnestly into his eyes. She cradled his face with her opened hand as she spoke, "Please go to Jesus. He loves you and misses you. Please go to Him soon. I'm so tired, Abraham. Hold my hand for just a while until I go to sleep. I'll see you in the morning, Abraham."

Abe took her hand gently and touched it to his lips. It was then her hand slowly went limp. He heard her last breath slip from her and she was gone. He cried softly for a long time while he held her. Then he slipped to the side of the bed. Bowing his head, he poured his heart out to Jesus. Abe asked Him to forgive his selfish ways and take him back into His family. He asked Jesus to send the Holy Spirit to live in his life again. He prayed to his Father God to forgive him in Jesus's name.

Abe stayed on his knees, beside Joy's bed, until a faint light began showing through the window. He then gently got her ready; he bathed her and washed her hair. Then he quietly climbed the stairs to get the dress she had been wearing when they first met. She had kept it all these years because he loved to see her wearing it. Now he would always remember her wearing his favorite dress. He also brought down the quilt she had made for him. When he had dressed her, he laid the quilt over her. But he could not cover her face, not yet anyway.

He was just slipping out of the room and closing the door when Valentine opened her door. It only took one look at Abe's face for her to know; her tears slipped unhindered down her face. Valentine could say no words; she put her hand on his arm and gently squeezed in an attempt to say how sorry she was. She knew there were no words she could say to this grieving husband—her heart was breaking too.

They went to the kitchen together and started doing things, normal things that seemed to help just by the routine-ness of them. The coffee was just perking when the back door opened— Gordon walked in.

He took one look at their faces and he knew, "Oh no. I didn't tell her yesterday that she was my best girl."

The two brothers walked arm-in-arm to Joy's room to say their good-byes.

Gordon returned to the kitchen, saying, "Valentine, Abe wondered if you would come sing that song Joy loved for you to sing. He said it really was her favorite song."

Gordon reached out his hand to Valentine, she took it, and they walked hand in hand into Joy's room. Even through her tears, she was able to sing Joy's song.

"O soul are you weary and troubled? No light in the darkness you see? There's light for a look at the Savior, and life more abundant and free! Turn your eyes upon Jesus; look full in his wonderful face and the things of earth will grow strangely dim in the light of His glory and grace."

Gordon helped Abe bring in the beautiful casket Abe had built for his wife. He had carved her name on the top and had sanded it to a smooth shine. They gently laid Joy on the pillows already in the box, and Abe put her quilt over her. Gordon and Valentine left the room and closed the door as Abraham said good-bye to his wife, the Joy of his life, and then closed the lid. He had fixed the box to be closed and sealed without nails, so when he opened the door again, the casket was ready to be carried out to the waiting sleigh drawn by Abe's two riding horses. Gordon told Valentine that Joy and Abe had ridden on these horses daily until she was unable to ride. He also told her Abe had made a place ready for Joy up on the hill in the family cemetery. She would be buried beside their baby boy who had died at birth.

Valentine wondered how they could bury her without any one of authority examining her; however, she didn't want to say anything. Gordon had brought his sleigh, so he and Valentine rode to the cemetery behind Abe and the casket. When they got to the place where Joy would be buried, Valentine understood. Abe had built a beautiful stone crypt. Inside was a stone box that the casket fit perfectly into. Abe and Gordon placed a heavy wooden lid over the stone box. The lid had Joy's full name carved deeply into the top. Abe had placed a window facing east so the light now shone on the name.

Valentine cherished the beautiful and simple service. Gordon had brought his Bible and read the twenty-third Psalm. Valentine asked if she could sing a song about the Christian Journey. Abe replied, "Please do."

Valentine had written down the words to the song. She pulled the paper out of her pocket and began to sing.

Weak and wounded sinner,
Lost and left to die;
O raise your head for Love is passin' by.
Come to Jesus, come to Jesus, come to Jesus and live!
Now your burden's lifted and carried far away,
And precious blood has washed away the stain.
So sing to Jesus, sing to Jesus, sing to Jesus and live!
Like a new born baby, don't be afraid to crawl
And remember when you walk, sometimes we fall.
So fall on Jesus, fall on Jesus, fall on Jesus and live!
And sometimes the way is lonely and steep and filled
with pain
If your sky is dark and pours the rain.
Then cry to Jesus, cry to Jesus, cry to Jesus and live!
O and when the love spills over and music fills the night,
And when you can't contain your joy in side,
Dance for Jesus, Dance for Jesus, Dance for Jesus and
live!
And with your final heartbeat, kiss the world goodbye,
Then go in peace, and laugh on Glory side.
And fly to Jesus, fly to Jesus, fly to Jesus and live!
…Fly to Jesus, fly to Jesus, fly to Jesus…and LIVE!

As the last words of the song faded away, Gordon and Valentine left the crypt. They walked out of the cemetery, leaving Abe alone for a while.

On the way down the hill, Gordon asked, "Valentine, what are your plans now?"

"I, um, I don't know." She faltered, turning her head to gaze over the snow-covered valley as she pondered the question, "I'll wait for God to lead me as He has done all along. I must tell you both the rest of my story. It's important that I tell you before I have to travel on. Besides, I can't leave until the snow is gone. Can I?"

Valentine turned her head back and smiled into Gordon's eyes; he smiled back. An unspoken change began between them. Neither, if asked, would have admitted there was a change; however, something special was growing.

Later that day, Abe cleaned one of the upstairs rooms for Valentine. She moved her things up to the lovely guest room. She could see Joy's simple touches around the room—touches that made it very homey.

Over the next month, Gordon continued to visit, when the weather permitted, to study with Valentine. Now that Abe had given his life back to God, he brought his Bible to study with them. One evening Abe brought an extra Bible to the table and handed it to Valentine. She looked up with a questioning glance.

"From Joy and me. You need the complete Bible to study, and I want to see her Bible helping someone."

Valentine was very touched by the beautiful gesture. "Thank you so much, Abe. And it is an NIV Bible as well." The smile on Valentine's face was all the thanks Abe wanted.

That night Valentine told the brothers her story—all of it.

Gordon said, "You know, Valentine, I am convinced God brought you here to help Joy and Abe. If I believe He led you here, I must also believe He has shown you this evil plan and the work He has for you to do for Him. I can't do anything else but believe what you're saying is all true."

Abe said he had been thinking the same thing. They talked about what might be happening in the outside world, speculating on the changes and control of the masses.

Abe often spent time by himself. He was missing Joy more than he would have ever thought. Even when she did not know him, he had been able to spend time with her, but now he felt lost and empty. He realized he needed time to grieve.

One night in early spring, Valentine woke up with a dream so fresh in her mind that she knew it was from God. She got up and wrote down everything she could remember about the dream. In the morning Valentine told Abe what she had dreamt. She described seeing a town and heard the words, "Go home," so clearly that the words were what had wakened her. She asked him to pray for her to understand what God wanted her to do and how to go about doing it.

When Gordon arrived that evening, they all talked about the dream and prayed. They decided to sleep on it that night and Gordon would come early the next day. Maybe by then they would know what to do.

That night the dream came again. However, this time the dream did not come to Valentine; it came to Gordon. Gordon learned the name of the place where God wanted Valentine to go: Columbia.

The next morning, Gordon came to the cabin with a big grin on his face. "I know where you are to go, Valentine, and I know who is to go with you. Last night, in my dream, I saw the name Columbia as plain as day. I also know that God wants me to go with you, and protect you, Valentine."

Abe got out his road atlas and looked in Maryland, since that is where Valentine started from, for a town called Columbia. He found a Columbia, Maryland, as well as a Columbia, in South Carolina, Tennessee, and Missouri. So there were four states to check out, to try to find which one God wanted Valentine and Gordon to go to.

Gordon said, "Valentine, I know God wants me to take you wherever you need to go. I can't let you go by yourself. God has sent you to us not just to help us but for us to help you. I've been thinking about how we can do this and keep you hidden. Abe, if you wouldn't mind, since no one knows that Joy died, Valentine could dress as Joy and I could be you. We could travel safely as Abe and Joy and no one would know the difference."

There was silence in the room while Abe thought. Abe was beginning to see how God had worked in his life to bring him back to Jesus. He could see that they all three needed to help as many people as would listen to the Holy's Spirit's voice, before it was too late. So Abe agreed to the plan. They talked and got things together to make the trip. They wanted to be ready when God told them to go.

One evening Gordon was reading the description of Valentine's dream that she had written in her notebook.

Suddenly he said, "Hey, Valentine, you described the town as of an old town with a parade of mules or horses. Is that right?"

Valentine nodded her head and asked, "Is that important?"

Gordon answered, "Well, I heard of an event on the radio last night, called Mule Day in Columbia, Tennessee. The commercial said Mule Day is every April. Do you think your home could be in Tennessee?"

Valentine thought about it, repeating Columbia, Tennessee, a few times to see if it rang any bells in her memory, still she drew a blank.

Gordon suggested, "What would it hurt if we traveled there to see if that's where God wants you to go? This is March 4, so we have a month to get ready and travel across the country."

The three prayed about the trip and decided it was worth a try. Abe packed a suitcase with Joy's things. He started to grow his hair and beard so he could stay on the ranch and pretend to be Gordon, while Gordon and Valentine went to Tennessee pretending to be Abe and Joy. Valentine was very close to the same height and coloring of Joy. However, her hair was red and Joy's had been brown. Abe found a wig that Joy had worn for fun sometimes or when she didn't want to fix her hair at all. It was short and looked really nice on Valentine.

When Valentine dressed up in the wig and Joy's clothes, Abe had to turn away and wipe a tear from his eye. Gordon and Valentine started calling each other by their assumed names so they would be use to them, but tried to keep things light so Abe would not feel the pain of loss so much.

The day that they were to leave, Gordon shaved off his beard. Abe cut Gordon's hair to resemble his own. The change was startling to Valentine. The two men standing side by side were identical.

The truck was packed with things they would use to camp along the way. Everything was ready when they sat down at the kitchen table to make any last-minute plans. Not knowing what the world would be like because of "The Plan," they decided to travel nights and stay out of sight during the days. They marked the maps where Abe and Gordon had found places to stop and camp along the way. With everything ready early in the afternoon, Gordon and Valentine laid down to rest.

Before supper Valentine walked to Joy's grave. A bench had been placed near the door. Here she sat and took in the panorama. As she gazed below her, she talked with her Heavenly Father. She prayed for safety and that God's plan for their lives would be fulfilled.

After supper, Gordon and Valentine said good-bye to Abe. Valentine gave Abe a big hug. "God be with you and keep you until we meet again." She wiped a tear off of her cheek. Saying good-bye again was hard. She had said good-bye to so many on this journey. And she had spent most of her time on this wonderful ranch with no worries about anybody after her—or at least no one finding her. She had been given time to rest, study, and pray.

Gordon gave his brother a bear hug. "We'll be back as soon as we can, God willing."

Abe saluted his brother. Gordon opened the door for Valentine and then let his dog, Lelo, into the backseat of the extended cab.

Shutting his door, he started the truck, pulled out of the yard, and headed down the lane to the main road.

They had planned the start of their trip so they could drive through Steamboat Springs while it was still light so people who knew them would see that they were traveling. Abe had called the pastor of their small church to ask for prayers. He also called the post office and had them send his and Joy's mail to Gordon's box while they were gone. He told the postman, a friend of the couple's, that he and Joy were traveling to Tennessee to go to the Vanderbilt Hospital for Joy's health.

Valentine sat next to Gordon in the truck seat just as Joy would have done. When they got to town, they had to stop at the first traffic light they came to.

Gordon said, "Oh boy, this is providential. Don't look to the right. Just turn your head as if you're listening to me." Then he smiled at someone and waved. When the light changed, he took off as soon as he could. Then he explained.

"We were sitting next to the biggest busybody in town. Mrs. Tworog goes to the church Abe and Joy went to before Joy got sick. She will go and tell everyone she knows, and plenty whom she doesn't know, that she saw us leaving for Tennessee."

Valentine asked, "Do you think we fooled her, Gordon?"

"I think so. She was waving and mouthing the words, 'Have a safe trip.'" Gordon turned the radio on as he headed the truck east out of town.

It was soon dark. Valentine had tried to sleep that afternoon, but she had been too anxious. Now that they were on their way and darkness had settled all around them, her eyes started to feel very heavy. She tried to stay awake, but soon her eyes closed and her quiet breathing told Gordon that Valentine was fast asleep.

21

It Is Time to Get Tough

On the first of March, the Father was sitting at his desk at the Vatican thinking about his agenda for the day. Things had been moving amazingly fast these past few months, since the plan was in full swing.

As predicted, ninety-five percent of the people of the world were starting to come under their control. With the new Netters drink and the sugar substitute in almost every other drink, the treatment was working very well. He had a call in to Fakah, formerly second-in-command under Sonny, for an update on that area.

He was still baffled about Sonny's defection and his disappearance with all his immediate family. Thinking back, Sonny had shown no signs of a change of heart or mind for wanting out of the plan. When they had searched his home, a letter was found addressed to "Father."

> My friend, I know this will come as a shock. Nevertheless, I have become a Christian. I very firmly believe that Jesus is the Son of Allah, the God of our fathers, Abraham, Isaac, and Jacob. I have prayed to Allah and believe this plan to control the minds of people is wrong. To protect my family, I have decided to take them away, else I would have come and talked with you myself.
>
> I am praying for you to have a change of heart and begin to believe in Jesus as the son of God or Allah, as I believe they are one and the same. I also believe the

only beings who should have control over a man's heart is Allah, Jesus, and the Holy Spirit. I have been reading the Bible—the New Testament—all about Jesus and his love for each of us that includes the whole world. His story is so beautiful I cannot understand how you lost your faith in Him. As I said before, I am praying that you, my friend, will have a change of heart and turn to Jesus.

As always, your friend, Abdul-Rashid, servant of the rightly guided one (no longer "Sonny").

As Father reread the letter, he again felt baffled and somewhat saddened. He would continue to have his people look for Abdul-Rashid and his family. The former Sonny could become a very big problem if he started to talk and spread the news of the Plan. However, Father did not what to harm Abdul or his family—at least not until they had been given a chance to recant this newfound faith. It was a faith Father felt was outdated, designed for weak and uneducated people, not for people like himself and Abdul-Rashid.

The Father had decided years ago that the Bible was just a book of fables. It had been written to keep the masses in line by causing them to fear hell when they died.

I can still remember as if it were yesterday, he thought to himself. *When Mother got sick, I had done everything I had been taught. I prayed and prayed to the saints to heal her. When she died, I went to the church altar and cried out to Saint Raphael Archangel for healing. I then called out to God, "Why did you not heal her? She was a beautiful, God-fearing woman!"*

That was the first time he had met Father Adrian Damascus. His mind wandered back in time to when he was young. He had been on fire for God, a young man named Sebastian Berard. He wondered where that young man had gone. In introspection, Father could tell there was nothing left of that young man. Now he was a man for himself and himself only.

Then his mind again retuned to the altar. With the pain of losing his mother as new and raw as if it had happened yesterday. He remembered Father Adrian finding him there. Father Adrian had helped him through his pain, and they soon became friends. He thought of how Adrian had told him that the story of the Bible was for the weak masses, that there was really no God. He believed the church was a way to have power over the people. Adrian had also told him that there were others in the church, though not many, who believed as he did.

At first he had enjoyed Adrian's friendship even though he did not believe what he was saying. But the more Adrian talked, the closer they became, and his defenses began to crumble. His first real break away from his Catholic vows was when he met and fell in love with a young nun named Sister Patricia. He fell so much in love with her that he was thinking of leaving the priesthood and asking her to marry him. But Adrian told him he would be losing his career in the church.

So, with Adrian's encouragement, he tried to get her to break her vows and have a relationship with him. Unbeknownst to him, Adrian had become infatuated with the beautiful Patricia. One day, when Adrian was alone with her, he forced himself on her. Patricia did not know what to do when she discovered she was pregnant with a child—a child as the result of having been raped by Adrian. Who would believe a young nun against someone like Father Adrian Damascus? she had wondered at the time.

So she came to young Father Sebastian, the man who loved her. He had set up for an abortion. From then on, Patricia and he became lovers. Understandably, she was irrevocable chanced. She became more like Adrian. She lived her life as she pleased, careful not to let it interfere with her job as a nun. She began to have ambitions to rise in the church just as Adrian did. Together they planned how they could help each other.

Adrian died the year before the Twin Towers were destroyed. It was then Sister Patricia finally told Sebastian who had raped her. When Father Sebastian met "Sonny" and "Ghost" in Greece, the plan began to come together. With these four united, with their combined resources and knowledge, they moved forward.

But now "Sonny" had dropped out of sight. Luckily his second-in-command, Fakah, was very good at taking over. He was getting things done in the Middle East.

Father shook his head and realized it was time to get back to work. He had a list of areas in the United States where resistance was the strongest. He wondered how the resistance could have become so spirited. Last fall, all resistance seemed to have shriveled up and died. However, after a quiet winter, the resistance seemed to be growing in leaps and bounds. He looked over the names of the places where the trouble was: Baltimore and Gaither, Maryland; Atwood, Kansas; Independence, Texas; Steamboat Springs, Colorado; Columbia, Tennessee; and New York City. He then saw the new list even included California. How did this thing get all the way out to California?

He wondered what the places had in common—and were there more pockets of resistance they did not know about? He did not believe the resistance could ever get large enough to stop their plan. However, he was determined to keep the control in his own hands. They would have to make examples of some of these people and then the resistance would die. People, for the most part, did not like to lose their money, their homes, families, or their lives. Get tough with some of them, in a public way, and all this nonsense would stop. He would make a three-way call to Ghost and Patty to get a counter attack started.

The Father got his cell phone out of the locked drawer and made the call. It was time to get tough.

That nurse surely couldn't be the cause of these hot spots. No one had seen or heard about her in months. But just in case, he opened her dossier he had received from "Ghost" just yesterday. He knew Patty still believed she was out there somewhere, but he wasn't so sure. Maybe she was and maybe she wasn't. If he was a betting man, he would bet she had died soon after her escape from her wounds. Wounds incurred during their interrogation of her, down in the hidden rooms under the Baltimore Basilica. But Patty just could not let go; she was too close to the situation. It galled her to think someone had really gotten away from her clutches.

Well, he needed Patty to concentrate on those hot spots that were causing so much trouble. Maybe the nurse would show up in one of those spots.

22

New Friends

Valentine awoke to the sounds of the tires on the pavement. Her head was on something firm but comfortable. She could hear someone softly singing with the radio. It took her only a second to remember she was traveling with Gordon. They were heading to what she hoped was her home and her family.

It was still dark out, but the clock in the dash proclaimed the time to be 5AM. The sky should be starting to turn pink soon.

Valentine sat up and stretched saying, "Sorry, I didn't mean to use you as a pillow."

Gordon turned his head and smiled at her.

"You can use me as a pillow anytime, Val—I mean, Joy. I guess I need to really work at calling you by your assumed name. I would hate to get us into hot water."

"How far to the campsite, Abe?"

She smiled and shook her head.

"When I'm just looking at you, it's not hard to call you Abe, but hearing your voice could cause me to flub up on the name."

"My voice, Val—Joy? What do you mean by that, Joy?"

"Well, you sound like Abe sometimes, but mostly Abe has been so serious and you're always so cheerful. I sure can get mixed up. I'm hoping Abe can take this time alone to really say good-bye to Joy and get to know his Heavenly Father better. Did he tell you anything about his last few minutes with Joy, Gordon, I mean, Abe?" Valentine sighed, shaking her head in exasperation.

"No, but he said he wants to tell us both someday, maybe when we get back. I mean if you come back. Do you know what you might do after we get to Columbia, Valentine?"

Valentine thought for a minute and then answered, "I'm not at all sure, but I do know God will show us what we should do next. He has led me so carefully this far. When I find myself becoming worried about the future, I just remember how He has led in the past. That's when I start thanking Him. I wish all people would hear His voice, turn, and follow Him. I sometimes think how sad we humans must make Him by refusing to believe in Him or ignoring Him when He speaks to us."

They both sat quietly for a while listening to a CD of Abe and Joy's they both had come to love: an old gospel CD of Alan Jackson's.

The original plan had been to drive straight east. However, because of the forecast of a coming snowstorm, the brothers had rerouted their trip south on Highway 9. When Gordon thought it was safe, they would head northeast. *I wish we could stop to see Caleb, Esther, and the girls, but apparently we are being led in a different direction*, Valentine thought.

Soon they were nearing the cabin that was just past Breckenridge, Colorado, near the Hoosier Pass, their planned layover during the daylight hours. That way they would keep out of view of any police. Even traveling as Joy and Abe, they could run into other trouble they knew nothing about.

When they reached the cabin, Valentine took Lelo for a walk. The dog had been getting restless for the last hour of the trip, but Gordon hadn't wanted to stop before they were safely at the cabin.

Gordon and Abe had camped and hiked in this wilderness area many times with their parents and as adults. Gordon knew where there was a small cabin open to the public, that anyone could use as long as it was empty; and providing they left it clean and neat when they left. He gave Valentine a rough lay of the land, and off she went with Lelo while Gordon started a fire to cook something to eat. They had decided they would take turns sleeping while the other kept watch for any signs of trouble.

When Valentine got back to the cabin, Gordon had coffee started and was getting out other food to cook. Valentine got out the sleeping bags and made a pallet on the floor. Since she had slept for most of the night, Gordon would get to sleep first. Before they ate, they thanked God for their safe trip and the warm dry place to sleep. Gordon got out his Clear Word Bible and read the twenty-third Psalm. Before he barely finished eating, his eyes were closing. He stood, picked up his plate, and shook his head to rouse himself.

Valentine urged him, saying, "Please, Gordon, go lie down before you fall down. I will clean up the dishes." She reached her hand out for his plate and gestured to the pallet on the floor. "If you don't mind, I would like to read your Bible while you sleep."

Valentine was glad of the time by herself because she had wanted time to read this version of the Bible. She decided to start with Matthew. She read through the story of Jesus's birth and childhood. Reading it brought back memories of her time with the Sanchezes, and Manuel's voice as he told her the story for the first time. She realized the story became more beautiful each time she heard it. *I wonder if I had known any of this before I lost my memory. More importantly, did I believe it?*

Valentine went on to read where Jesus became a man and began His ministry. This part reminded her of her own book, the *Gospel of John*. She read about Jesus's baptism and His teachings to His disciples and all the people. She realized Jesus was not accepted by the church leaders. They had wanted to stop Him from telling everyone about His Father God's love for them. He told them they did not have to do all those rituals to have His love. God loves you now and forever. She read where He healed everyone who came to Him and believed: blind, crippled, sick, and the hopelessly lost in sin.

While Valentine read, Gordon slept. The fire burned softly— Lelo slept by her side. She came to a part in Matthew, chapter twenty-four, where Jesus talked about the end-time and the signs that would show His people He would soon be coming to get them. In verse nine Jesus told His disciples that His people would be persecuted and killed because they believed in Him. Valentine was fascinated in what she was reading all about the time of the end of the world. She was deeply engrossed in what she was reading when all of a sudden Lelo, growling deeply in his throat, jumped up and charged the cabin door.

Gordon bounded to his feet, groggy from a deep sleep, and asked, "What's going on?"

Valentine stood up from where she had been reading, trembling. She shook her head in response. Lelo was at the door still barking, so Gordon went quickly to the door to open it and let his dog out. Lelo went tearing around the corner of the cabin, headed to the creek. She stopped at the water's edge looking up into a tree. The tree was a large evergreen with a lot of low-hanging branches.

When Gordon walked up to the base, he said, "You can come down now, whoever you are. We won't hurt you, nor will my dog."

After a moment or two, the branches halfway up the tree moved. Slowly, whoever was up in the tree started climbing down. Lelo was no longer barking or growling. Nevertheless, she was alert to the sounds of the movements coming down the tree. Gordon moved back as a knapsack fell from the tree at his feet. A small booted foot was next seen and then more of the blue-jean clad leg and finally a young, agile person jumped down to the ground. The mysterious person was dressed in hiking clothes with a cap pulled down over the ears. It took a moment for Gordon and Valentine to realize the person was a young woman. She was very slender with light hair and greenish-blue eyes that sparkled and laughed as she returned their appraisal. The three continued looking each other up and down for a few more seconds then Gordon broke the silence.

"Where did you come from, and how did you get here? You look half-starved. Would you like something to eat?"

The girl chuckled, answering in a conspiratorial voice, "I'm running from the law, I came down the creek, and yes, I'd love something to eat. I haven't eaten in a day and a half."

Gordon did not hesitate. He picked up the knapsack, turned, and went toward the cabin. Valentine followed, and the girl, with Lelo behind her, came along last. In the cabin Gordon stirred up the fire. Valentine got the coffee ready. The girl came in and sat down where Valentine had been reading. Soon she picked up the Bible and started reading in Matthew where the page was open.

Her eyes got big with wonder. "This is a Bible! Do you read it every day? Are you part of the Five-Percenters?"

Valentine was startled, "What is a Five-Percenter?"

The girl became quiet; her face turned pale. She stood up and began edging toward the door.

Valentine said, "Honey, don't be afraid, we won't hurt you. Why did you get scared? We're not the law, and we're not going to turn you in."

Valentine continued to talk to her as if she were talking to a scared child.

"My name is Valentine, oh, ah, um, but you can call me Joy, and this is Abe."

The girl looked at her very strangely saying, "You said, Valentine. Do you know anyone named Lucy Pope?"

Valentine paused for a second, saying a quick prayer to her Father God. She opened her mouth to ask how she could possibly know that name.

But what came out of her mouth was, "Yes, I know Lucy Pope, and I know Jeb Bodiene also."

Valentine was startled at the words that had tumbled out of her mouth. She remained silent, waiting to see the girl's reaction.

A big smile came to the girl's face. With a sigh of relief, she started to speak very fast—something about her friends in the woods and someone's ankle being hurt.

Gordon exclaimed, "Wait a minute, slow down, and start over please."

The girl laughed, beginning again, "My name is Emmalyne, and my friends, Nicole and Annika, are waiting in the woods about half a mile back. Nicole fell and twisted her ankle. She can't walk without it hurting a lot. I came to get the food that was left hidden here in the cabin. We were going to try to make camp out in the woods again tonight."

When Gordon heard this, he didn't waste a minute.

"Emmalyne, show me where your friends are. We don't have much time. A storm is heading this way. You and your friends cannot stay outside tonight. You will get lost in the snow and freeze to death."

He turned to Valentine, "You need to stay here and cook something hot to eat—maybe soup. We'll talk when we get back."

Turning back to Emmalyne, he said, "Let's go."

Emmalyne did not need to be told twice. She followed him to the door; they were gone in seconds.

Valentine sat down for a moment to pray for the safety of the girls and Gordon. She thought about the others as she worked quickly to start the soup.

"What can this mean?" she spoke out loud to Lelo who was watching her with intelligent eyes. "How could this girl in the Colorado woods know anything about Lucy Pope and Jeb Bodiene?"

Her mind went back to the term Emmalyne had used 'The Five-Percenters." What could that mean, and where had she heard that term before?

As the soup cooked, Valentine got out her notebook from her backpack to reread what she had written last fall. Over the winter she had read it once or twice, but some of the facts were fading.

After she told Abe and Gordon about what had happened to her, she also told them about her notebook. They had all read it to try to understand more about the plan to control people's minds. As she reread about her escape from the hospital, she marveled again at how close she had come to being caught many times— how that unseen hand had pushed her into the thrift shop. *Where would I be without that thrift shop? When I get to Tennessee I will try to put together enough money to send to the thrift shop, and tell them how they had unknowingly helped me.* She did not see how it would hurt to write a letter. She turned back to the notebook and started reading about the phone call she had overheard when she had first heard about the plan. She read the one-sided conversation she had heard between the Sister and whoever she had been talking to.

Then she found the part she was looking for and began to read. The Sister had asked,

"What are Einstein's estimates after the last test group went through the treatment? ... Ninety-five percent, wow, that is excellent! What about the other five percent? Have you found out what is keeping the treatment from working on them?"

Valentine knew what was protecting them, reading—especially reading the Bible.

"What a good name for our cause!" she said to Lelo.

She got up, stretched, and went to the fireplace to stir the soup. She was just turning around when Lelo jumped up and started to wag her tail. Valentine heard what Lelo had already heard. Gordon was singing and the girls with him. In no time the door opened and Gordon came through it carrying a teenage girl with a strained look on her face. The girl was still trying to sing through her pain. Behind them came Emmalyne and another girl carrying the knapsacks.

Valentine said, "Gordon, please bring her over here to this chair and let me look at her foot."

He did as instructed and carefully lowered the injured girl to the chair. Valentine moved a second chair under the injured foot. Unwrapping the scarf bound around her ankle, Valentine examined the injury carefully.

Valentine turned to Emmalyne and asked, "Could you run outside for me? Back by the creek bank I saw un-melted snow. Could you fill this scarf with clean snow and bring it back please?"

Valentine asked the girl, Nicole, to move her toes. Then she checked for pulses and carefully moved the ankle. The movement caused some pain and the girl moaned a little; however, she did not cry out. When Emmalyne brought back the scarf, Valentine carefully placed the foot and ankle into the snow. She covered the top of the foot with a towel and then snow and tied the scarf ends loosely around it.

Valentine told Nicole, "I don't think your ankle is broken. It's not displaced, anyway, and you seem to have good feeling and good pulses. But I'm sure you will need to stay off it for a few days until it heals. Where were you girls going when you fell in the woods?"

Nicole looked at Annika. They both gave Emmalyne questioning looks as though asking, what do we say now?

Emmalyne said, "I'd like to ask one question first, before I explain what we're doing. How did you know who Lucy and Jeb are if you're not a five-percenter? And is your name Joy or Valentine?"

The other two girls spoke out at the same time, "Valentine?! You don't mean she is *the* Valentine?"

Gordon interrupted to say dinner was ready. He placed three bowls on the table for the girls, set a small pan down for Valentine, and the soup pan down in front of himself.

"Let's pray, shall we?"

Without waiting, he prayed, "God in Heaven, thank you for this good soup you've helped us make. We thank you for keeping these girls safe and for bringing us together to help each other.

Lead us as you have in the past, help us to be patient, and wait for you. We pray in Jesus's name, Amen."

The girls were hungry enough to let their questions wait until they had eaten their soup; it disappeared quickly.

The girls in unison said, "Boy that was good!"

They turned their heads toward Valentine, saying, "Well?"

Gordon and Valentine looked at each other and burst out laughing, which started the girls laughing. Lelo even joined the fun barking and howling at the same time. When finally the laughter died down, Valentine was ready to talk.

"My name is Valentine. However, I've gone by the name Lucy Pope and Jeb Bodiene. And somewhere I have a real name I don't remember, but I believe Father God is now leading me to learn it."

The three girls' mouths had dropped open, and for a minute they just stared at Valentine. Then they sat back in stunned silence.

At last Emmalyne whispered, "So you really are her! The Valentine, the woman God has been leading, to spread the warning about this evil plan that is spreading over to our world like a disease."

Valentine took her turn to ask, "But how do you know about me? I don't understand."

Annika answered, "Everyone knows about you! You're our hero. Your stories have given us all hope. We tell them at our resistance meetings, to help us be brave."

"But how could you have heard of me? I'm sure I've never met any of you, and I've never even been to this part of the country until today."

Emmalyne spoke up, "Everyone knows about you. Your story has spread like wildfire. To us, you're like Moses of old. You were sent to bring us out of the bondage of sin and to bring us all closer to God!"

Valentine sat with tears in her eyes and shook her head.

Nicole said, "Tell us about how you got out of the hospital. That's one of our favorite stories!"

But Gordon broke in just then, saying, "Valentine, girls, we need to talk about our plans. We can't leave you three here, and we also need to know more about what dangers are out there. Valentine has been living at my brother's and sister-in-law's home all winter, and we have not had much news about what's going on in the rest of the country and the world."

Emmalyne said, "Annika, I think you can tell it best. You've been in closer contact with Father Frances than we have with you being Catholic and he being the Sister's driver."

"What?" Valentine exclaimed. "You know the Sister?"

"No, we know her driver, Father Frances. He has been helping our youth resistance ever since he came to Colorado. Everywhere he goes he's been getting together kids who have been reading their Bibles and who believe in God. He's been helping us keep away from those who look for the five-percenters. Those who want to take us to prison."

Gordon and Valentine looked at each other in stunned disbelief.

Valentine said quietly, "I guess the world is a different place than the one I disappeared from last fall. I just can't believe it happened so fast. You know, before all this started, people were basically good but lived for themselves and didn't worry about the future. Something I read in Matthew just this morning reminds me of how most people were. Hand me the Bible, Nicole, would you please?"

Valentine scanned the chapter in Matthew until she found what she was looking for.

She turned to Gordon and asked, "Would you read it for me?"

So Gordon read Matthew 24:37. "Just as the world was in Noah's day, that's how it will be immediately before I come back. All that people thought about in those days was eating, drinking, getting married and living it up. They did this right up to the very day that Noah and his family went into the ark. They didn't think what Noah had been preaching would happen until the flood hit. By then it was too late. That's how it will be in the time of the end. Very few will really believe what my people will tell them. Most people will go about their duties with little thought about the future. Those who believe and those who don't will work together; one will be ready and one won't." Everyone was quiet for a moment pondering the words of Jesus.

Gordon said, "That was how things were last fall. Because people weren't keeping close to God, they have been caught in a trap of this evil plan. Because their minds are weak, they will probably not be able to escape."

Emmalyne spoke up, "These people are not just caught in a trap. The plan is using them to hunt down God's true people."

Annika continued, "People who turn in any resistance fighters get rewards of money and even new homes. The government will take the five-percenter homes and give them to the people who turned them in. I heard that on the news just last week. It's a new incentive for people to turn in their own families and friends. The idea is to scare the resistance. To scare them into not telling others of the plan's dangerous objective—to control people's minds, and rule the whole world."

Valentine said, "You were saying that Father Frances has been helping you young people. Please tell us more about that."

Annika looked at her friends, "Where should I start? To begin with, each night all kids between the ages of ten and sixteen were to go to the churches and sit though pep rallies. There were videos that the kids were shown. The first night I went I came in with my video game, appearing to play, but I didn't use it except when someone was really watching me. Farther Frances must have noticed that my game wasn't on. He came over to me and said, in a fierce voice, 'Young woman, come with me.' He led me to a set of steps up to the bell tower. I was really scared, but after he closed the door to the stairs, he turned and whispered softly, 'You were not using your video game. I need to know why.' I said, 'Do you know Lucy Pope?' He came back with, 'Yes, I know Lucy Pope, and I know Jeb Bodiene also.'"

Seeing Valentine's astonishment, Emmalyne explained, "Yes, Valentine, that's just exactly what you said. This is our way of knowing if you're one of us. How did you know to say those words if you've never been told any of this before?"

Valentine smiled, her face softly glowing, "I guess the Spirit told me to say it because I was about to say something very different. I guess it would have scared you off, Emmalyne. I believe God wanted us to be here to help you girls. Anyway, finish your story, Annika."

So Annika continued.

"Several nights ago, Father Frances told us, the next night we were not to get off the bus at the church and to wear warm clothes to hike in under our uniforms, including heavy hiking boots. He went around to all the churches and gathered all his five-percenters onto the bus."

"But didn't the other leaders notice when your bus left with kids getting on instead of off?" Gordon asked.

Nicole spoke up. "He had us walk backward but appear to be going forward. He said most people would never notice. Then when we got into the bus, we kept moving to the very back and got down on our hands and knees to make it look as if the bus was empty."

Gordon exclaimed in a tone of admiration, "How very clever."

Emmalyne added, "Yep, he told us he had seen that in a very old movie and had always wanted to try it."

"So," Valentine asked, "when you all left the churches, how many kids did you have, and what did he do with all of you?"

Annika continued on with her story.

"Father Frances had found ten cabins throughout the woods. He put food in each of those cabins over several weeks so when things got too hot for us he could get us out. There were several kids dropped at each cabin. We were the last to be dropped off at our cabin. When he saw a roadblock ahead, he told us to get out and to take the path through the woods. He had given us a map before we started so we would know where we were in the woods, and how to leave when it was safe."

"Wow," Gordon said. "I'm surprised we didn't get stopped by a roadblock also. I wonder how often they have these roadblocks at night."

Emmalyne answered, "Father Frances said this week they were to be every other night. They should not have been out the other night. He said they're set up to catch the five-percenters trying to leave the city."

Nicole spoke up with a catch in her throat as if she was trying not to cry.

"I hope my parents and little sisters got away. The schedule they have for the roadblocks will be all wrong. We were going to meet on our way out of town, but they never came."

Gordon turned to Emmalyne and Annika and asked about their parents. "Are they safe, and are you to meet up with them anywhere?" Emmalyne explained that she lived with her granny, and Granny wanted her to go and be safe.

"I hated to leave her, but she said she couldn't travel and that she would be safe. She said the New Law does not trouble themselves about a sick old woman."

Valentine asked, "Could we pick her up somehow, Emmalyne?"

"No," Emmalyne answered, "Granny is on dialysis. She does it at home, and there is no way for her to go far from home because she must do the treatments three times a day."

Annika answered next, shaking her head as well, "No, my parents are in Hawaii. I was here last fall to go to a Young Woman's Retreat with Emmalyne when all of this started. I couldn't get back home. My parents called and told me to stay with Emmalyne and Granny. They would try to get me home or they would come over here. Dad is in the Air Force."

The room was quiet for a few minutes with the only sound coming from the crackling of the fire.

"Well, then," Gordon said, "it would seem that you girls need to come with us. We need a plan of action. First off, let me introduce you to Joy, and I'm Abe Peck. You must try to think of us only as Joy and Abe. We assumed my brother and his wife's names. We borrowed their names to try to get Valentine to her home. Do any of you girls know how badly the back roads are with snow and if they're watched?"

Annika replied saying, "Father Frances said we should tell Nicole's parents to take only back roads because right now they are not being watched at all because of the snow. I'm sure that will change in the spring and summer, but for now, the back roads are our best bet."

"Then let's get busy and get ready to leave at nightfall."

"But what about my parents?" Nicole cried out. "I don't want to leave them. They won't know where to find me. What am I going to do?"

Emmalyne and Annika went over to where Nicole was sitting with her foot up and gave their friend a hug.

Emmalyne brightened, saying, "We'll leave one of those encrypted notes like we talked about. You remember, Annika, we make the sign with a five and a percent but we put the percent sign on top and the five under it."

"How did it look?" Valentine asked.

"Do you have a piece of paper?"

Valentine got out her notebook and turned to an empty page. Emmalyne drew a percent sign sideways so it looked like eyes. Then she made a number five under the sign to look like a mouth. It was a funny-looking thing, and they all laughed when she was done. Still, unless a viewer knew what to look for, no one would see the five and percent in the face.

Annika said, "So how do we make this? What should we add to it to tell Nicole's parents she is safe and where we've gone?"

Valentine answered, "To start, how about some sticks and rocks outside by the back door?"

Gordon nodded in agreement, "You girls go see what you can find. Joy and I will see what else needs to be done before we leave."

Emmalyne and Annika jumped up and, blowing kisses at Nicole, ran out to find the things to make the sign.

Valentine said, "You know, Gordon, when I was traveling with Manuel and his family, I hid under a box made to look like several cardboard boxes. Maybe we could fix something up like that in the back of your truck. It's a good thing you have a topper on your truck. What do you think?"

Gordon thought for a minute and then said, "I was trying to decide if it would be safe to let them sit up front with us, but I guess it could be easily checked out that Abe and Joy don't have any kids. I have some pieces of plywood I keep in the back of the truck under our gear. Let me go see what I can do. Be back in a jiffy."

Valentine checked on Nicole's ankle. The snow had melted into a puddle under the table. Removing the scarf and towel, she could see the swelling had gone down.

"We'll put that back on in a while. We can't keep ice on your skin all the time."

"Oh good," Nicole said, "my foot was getting really cold. Do you believe God will keep us safe, Val—I mean, Joy?"

"Nicole, there is nothing I believe more. Our God will send his guardians to watch over us. Whatever is in store for us, he will be there with us. If I can, while we travel, I will tell you some of my story. Let's read the twenty-third Psalm. That always helps me when I'm worried. Do you know, Nicole, that someone spoke those words to me while I was hiding in Manuel's truck? These words were so helpful I stopped being terrified and went off to sleep. I dreamed a beautiful dream about what I think heaven must be like."

Valentine opened the Bible and read the twenty-third Psalm. As she read, Nicole said the words with her, for she knew them by heart. There were tears in both of their eyes when they finished.

Valentine gave Nicole a big hug, saying, "I feel as if I've known you forever. I guess we have always been sisters in our Father's family!"

Nicole read out loud as Valentine cleaned up the dishes and packed everything to be ready to leave. The fire was softly crackling. The room had a peace that was so real Nicole felt like she could reach out and touch it. As she sat there and read, she realized she had no more fears about the future or for her parents. God had sent the Holy Spirit to give her peace.

Everyone came back in at the same time.

Gordon said, "Come see what I've done so far. Maybe you can give me other ideas."

Even Nicole came along because Gordon picked her up and carried her out to the truck. Everyone looked in the truck, but all they could see were camping gear and a tarp folded in the back. Gordon sat Nicole on the tailgate. He climbed in, moving the tarp and a board. Under the board was a hole.

"You two girls climb in and see what you think. Nicole, you can get in when we are ready to leave." Emmalyne and Annika crawled in the hole carefully, wiggling in under the boards.

"See girls," he said, "you can sit up or lie down when no one is around, but when we see there might be trouble, you need to lie down and pull the board over you. The tarp will move with the board and look as if it was just thrown up there. Do you think there will be enough room for all three?"

Valentine was smiling and said, "However did you do this? It looks great. I'm very impressed."

Gordon said, "I think God led me to leave these boards in here, because I was about to take them out. Then I thought they would be weight for us if we got into snow, so I left them."

He next showed them that, if need be, when the tailgate was open, the girls could scoot out the end by moving a few items of the camping gear. Plus, for the most part, that would be the way Nicole made her way in and out until her ankle healed.

After that they went to look at the message left by the girls at the back door. It was quite cleverly done. If someone knew what to look for, the number five and a percent sign could be seen clearly. Leading from the sign were rocks, seemingly haphazardly placed, but going around the corner. When they followed the rocks, Emmalyne moved the last rock to reveal a hole they had dug. It was just big enough for a note. When the rock was over the hole, it was completely covered and no dirt appeared to have been tampered with.

"Now," Annika told Nicole, "all you need to do is write a note. We'll find a small plastic bag and we'll be ready to go."

Valentine asked if Nicole's parents knew about the five-percent sign. Nicole answered by explaining that her little sisters knew to look for the sign wherever they were. They had been playing a game to see who could find the most signs. Nicole's youngest sister was the all-time champion at the game. Nicole was sure her sisters would find the sign and the note. She went on to say that her parents knew about the sign, but until lately, they had not really believed it would get this bad.

Everyone washed up and got ready to leave. Emmalyne got the supplies Father Frances had left for them. When all was inspected, and the fire was completely out, Gordon closed the door. They all stood beside the tailgate around Nicole and prayed to God to guide them and help them stay close to Him in times of trouble. They all said amen together, and the girls scooted up into their hole. The back part with the tarp was left open so the girls could sit up and talk to Valentine through the sliding window between the truck and topper.

Because Valentine had promised to tell the girls her story from the beginning she sat in the backseat while Lelo sat in the front. The girls were eager to hear Valentine's amazing stories.

As Gordon put the truck into gear, Valentine started her story by saying, "The first thing I remember was an eerie black/gray craven. Next came the pain in my head. I couldn't even open my eyes because my head hurt so badly and I didn't have the energy to move a muscle."

23

Rahab's House

Valentine smiled in her sleep. She was dreaming again of heaven. The lion and the lamb were resting together by a beautiful river. She walked up to the lion. He was a magnificent male lion with a golden mane encircling his kingly head. Intelligent eyes gazed at her. Valentine slowly and carefully reached out her hand and placed it on his head. The fur was warm and soft; a feeling flowed through her fingertips and up her arm like a blessing. As she stood motionlessly, she could feel a soft breeze moving her hair and heard it rustling the leaves over her head. The sweet scent of fruit ripening on the tree overpowered her senses.

As Valentine stood quietly, she began to hear singing. The song was so beautiful it nearly took her breath away. The words seemed to flow through her entire being. Valentine was swept away with a great longing to be singing the song; however, she could not. She looked anxiously around her to see where the music was coming from. Her eyes caught movement on her left. A solitary man, clothed in white with a golden sash around his chest, walked across an enormous plane. His arms were outstretched. Valentine's eyes were riveted to his hands; she could see the red ugly scars on his palms. These were the only things that marred the beautiful scene. Valentine was irresistibly drawn to him. Every fiber in her being wanted to walk into His arms. For she knew this was Jesus, He was love, unfathomable love. He was home and Christmas morning. He was the arms of a mother to a small child when hurt. Jesus was everything your heart ever desired. Only now did she fully understand her need of Him. She could not tear her eyes away from His beautiful face. Nevertheless, from the corner of her eye, she saw movement. Valentine soon perceived a multitude of people walking toward Jesus. They were singing the song she had first heard. She tried to move, to walk toward Jesus as the others were; however, she could not. Tears started to run down her face, and a great sadness came over her. Just as Valentine was beginning to lose all hope, she felt a presence surround her. She heard a voice calling her name, "Valentine." The voice was so soothing she immediately felt a peace flow over her. She did not try to see who was speaking to her because she could not take her eyes away from Jesus.

The voice continued, "Don't despair, Valentine. Jesus is coming to get you soon. Keep strong for Him for just a little while longer. Soon you will see him coming in the clouds. You must watch the sky to the east for a small black cloud. This will be Jesus and His angels."

Then the soothing voice changed, and with a tone of warning, the voice explained, "Beware of the false christ who will try to deceive all people. Don't go see him or look at him, for he is the devil, the fallen angel Lucifer. He will cause many, many people to believe a lie and follow him."

The voice changed back to the soothing tone, "Just a little while longer, dear girl. Be strong for a little while longer."

Those words were still ringing in Valentine's thoughts when she awoke. She looked around somewhat bewildered. Where was Jesus? Where is the lion and the lamb, she wondered. Then she realized, *I am still in the woods in Colorado.* She looked around and saw she was in the backseat of Gordon's truck. She felt darkness settle over her. She quickly closed her eyes. Valentine wanted to see Jesus again, see heaven again; she was beginning to panic. Then softly, as if on a breeze, she heard those words, "Just a little while longer, my friend. Be strong for a little while longer."

"Dear Heavenly Father, thank you for this beautiful message of love and warning. Please help me to be strong for you. Help me to help your people. Thank you for the friends you have sent to help me—most especially my good friend, Gordon. Be with these three girls and help them to stay strong in whatever you need them to do. Thank you for Your Son Jesus, for His life here on earth. How He showed us of your love and how we're to live. Thank you, Jesus, for your death on the cross to pay for my sins. Keep us today in the palm of your hand, Amen."

Sitting up, Valentine looked around. The truck was parked in a thick stand of trees. Out the side window to the right were only trees and more trees. However, when she turned to look left, she could see Gordon standing by a fire. The three girls were squatted close to it warming their hands and laughing. It was a happy scene, helping Valentine begin to feel more cheerful. She opened the truck door and took a short walk into the woods.

Walking up to the fire, Valentine smiled at everyone, "Good morning."

Gordon turned at Valentine's greeting then exclaimed, "Your face is glowing!"

"Why, thank you, Abe, that's a nice thing to say to a lady in the morning."

"No," Gordon continued. "I mean your face is really glowing like the sun is shining, from within you."

The girls stood up and looked at her. Their eyes got big, and Emmalyne agreed, "He's right, Val—I, I mean, Joy, your face is glowing. Something is different about you this morning."

In a breathless voice, Valentine explained, "I've been dreaming of heaven. I saw Jesus. He was so beautiful I couldn't take my eyes away from Him."

Gordon said, "Sit down, Joy, tell us. The dream must be important because you look as if you have truly been to heaven."

Valentine sat down, telling them everything from the beginning. When she finished, the others sat in complete silence, their thoughts on the pictures Valentine had described.

Emmalyne broke the silence by saying, "I feel now as if I've been to heaven, Valentine. I have never heard anything so real about heaven before. I could see everything you described, as if I was watching a movie. Thank you for telling us. I shall never waver or doubt again."

Annika had tears on her cheeks when she looked into Valentine's eyes. She spoke in hushed tones, "Thank you, Valentine."

Nicole sat staring into the fire. She finally began to speak, "I don't think I really truly believed until this moment. I wanted to believe. I did what I needed to do to stay away from the mind controllers, but I think I felt it was more like a game. If I read my Bible every day, it would be enough. But I never really gave my heart to Jesus or believed that He and God could love me. I've not always been a nice girl. I've hurt people. I've told stories about other girls in school—to get them in trouble. I even lied to my parents whenever I thought I could. Just now, Valentine, when you were describing Jesus, I felt like He was saying, 'Come to me, Nicole, believe me when I tell you that I love you and will save you from your sins no matter what you've done.'"

Nicole's look encompassed everyone then she settled her eyes on Annika. "Please forgive me. I talked about you and tried to get you in trouble. I was jealous of yours and Emmalyne's friendship. Will you forgive me, Annika?"

Annika jumped up and sat down beside Nicole. She put her arm around the stricken girl. "I love you, Nicole, and I forgive you. It's forgotten, and as Jesus said, it's thrown to the bottom of the sea, never to be thought of again."

Nicole looked up at Valentine and Gordon. "I want to be baptized. Can you baptize me, Gordon? Please."

Gordon looked at Valentine and then back to Nicole. "I don't see why not. We'll look for some water—a river not too full of spring runoff or a spring—and we'll have an old-fashioned baptism, with singing and dinner on the grounds."

Valentine was quiet for a moment. "You know, guys, I've not been baptized either."

Looking at Nicole, Valentine asked, with longing in her voice, "Can I be baptized with you, Nicole?"

Nicole's face broke into a bright smile, "I could think of nothing nicer than to share my baptism with you, Valentine!"

"This is a safe place to spend the day," Gordon said. "We're far off any blacktop roads, and the trees are so thick here that our smoke won't give our position away. There is a small stream behind that big rock. Why don't we make breakfast? After everything is cleaned up and put away, we'll go for a walk. Maybe we can find a stream big enough for a baptism. What do you all say about that?"

Everyone agreed it was a good plan. Soon all were busy making a good breakfast.

After eating, Gordon got out his Bible. They prayed and sang a few songs. He read more of Matthew, starting in chapter 24 and continued until Jesus finished the warning to His friends and the world. When he had finished reading, they all said the twenty-third Psalm as their closing prayer: "The Lord is my Shepherd..."

While the others were cleaning up, Valentine checked Nicole's ankle. Nicole had been walking on it carefully and said, "It really doesn't hurt, Valentine." When Valentine took off the wrappings, she could see the swelling was almost gone. When she moved it to examine it, Nicole explained that movement did not even hurt.

Valentine exclaimed, "This is a miracle, because I'm sure it should have taken longer than a day to heal."

"Maybe I was supposed to hurt my ankle," Nicole said, "so we could meet and start traveling together. What do you think, Valentine?"

"I think many things we consider bad or trouble are God's way of teaching us and leading us. We don't always realize it, possibly, not until long afterward, because most of the time we humans see only one little picture—not the whole book God is trying to show us."

After their talk, Valentine and Nicole helped the others clean the camp area.

When they were finished, Nicole said, "Why are we putting everything back in the truck before we go for our walk? We'll just have to get it out again to make lunch."

Valentine answered her, "We must always be ready to go quickly, or hide, if need be. You never know who is coming. I learned this while I was traveling last fall—it's a good habit to get into."

Nicole nodded her head thoughtfully, "I see what you mean. I guess I was in a hurry to find a nice place for a baptism. Well, what are you all standing around for? Let's get everything ready." They all laughed and, in a happy, friendly way, worked together to put everything away.

It was a beautiful day for a hike. Gordon found walking sticks for Nicole to protect her healing ankle. They each took their own backpack with snacks and water in them. With Lelo on a leash, they started up the path along the creek to see where it would lead. They hiked about an hour. While they walked, they talked about what Valentine had seen in her dream. They also talked about what they had learned from the Bible reading that morning, how it went along with Valentine's dream. Sometimes they walked along in silence with deep thoughts about everything that was happening.

It was during one of those quiet times that Gordon stepped between two big boulders and stopped in his tracks. Everyone else squeezed in around him. They also stopped to gaze at the scene before them. Down a little incline was a beautiful mountain lake.

Nicole was first to exclaim, "How beautiful! But there is just one thing wrong with this scene: the water is frozen hard as a rock."

Gordon smiled, "I guess I wasn't thinking about the time of year. If it was a few months later in the season, the lake would be thawed. Even though it will still be very cold, you could have been baptized. I guess God wants you ladies to wait a little longer." They decided it was time to eat their snacks and take a rest then head back to the truck.

"No matter where I get baptized, I'll remember this lake as part of the journey," Nicole mused.

They hated to leave, but the wind was picking up and the temperature was beginning to drop. So packing up the trash and water bottles, they headed back to the truck. When they got to the campsite, it was time to get back on the road. The storm, which had been forecasted before Gordon and Valentine left the ranch, was now imminent. If possible they wanted to stay far ahead of it. Gordon checked the fire to be sure it was completely out and the girls got back into their places in the truck.

Lelo hopped into the front seat and faced forward looking as if she knew where they were going and she was going to be the copilot. Valentine made her move to the backseat, but Lelo didn't like it very much. She hopped to the backseat; however, she continued to sit up on her haunches, facing front, with a disdained look on her face. The girls and Valentine were laughing at Lelo when Gordon opened the truck door and got in.

"What's so funny?"

Emmalyne explained as she tried to control her snickering. "Lelo looks like she wants to be a human being. The way she's sitting we could put a wig on her and no one would guess she's a dog."

Gordon reached back and petted his faithful dog's head, "It's okay, old girl. They don't know how many trips we have been on together where you were my only companion and a really good copilot."

"Everybody ready?"

Gordon bowed his head asking God to send His guardian angels to keep them safe and guide them in the way they needed to go.

Gordon drove for about half an hour before they got close to Highway 9 again. He did not want to travel any principal highways for fear of running into roadblocks. But each time he tried a smaller road, which he thought would be safer, the road would be blocked with rocks or downed trees. His plan had been to stay close to Highway 9 as long as it headed south and then find another secondary road to continue their trip. But when he had crossed Highway 24, the road they were traveling on was also blocked—this time with large cement roadblocks. The roadblock was at a place in the road with a rock wall straight up on the left, and on the right a drop-off straight down hundreds of feet.

As he was turning the truck around, he said, "It would seem we're being herded toward Colorado Springs by either God or something else."

As they headed back toward Highway 24, Valentine said, "Let's pray, girls, that God will keep us safe going through this big city."

So for a while all was quiet in the truck as the prayers of five trusting people went heavenward to God. After a while Valentine started to sing the song she loved best: O soul' are you weary and troubled?

The girls joined in at the chorus and sang the rest of the song with Valentine.

Emmalyne said, "You know, those words just took on new meaning to me. We need to be telling a world that is dying, about Jesus, before it's too late."

Valentine said, "Looking back, I can see that God has been leading in every step of my journey. I started in Baltimore then I met the Sanchez family where I first heard about His son Jesus. I soon realized God wanted me to spread not only the word about this terrible plan of control, but more importantly, about Jesus's love for everyone. I just had no idea my story would spread so far and so fast. God's Holy Spirit is doing His work, taking the message and spreading it to everyone who is open to His voice."

When Gordon reached Highway 24, he slowed to check for debris, or if there were any roadblocks in sight with police officers. It looked safe for the moment, so he turned on Highway 24 and headed toward Colorado Springs. The road was empty.

Gordon asked the girls, "Where are all the people who would normally be on these roads?"

Emmalyne was the one to answer him. "People have been told to stay in the cities. Most everyone is under control and do as they are told to do. Messages run on the TV all the time about what to do and what not to do. We, the five-percenters, stopped watching TV last winter around Christmas time when we started to feel strange each time we turned it on. We still have one in the house in case anyone comes to visit or spy on us. We had to be careful of our friends and teachers because we were never sure who was a five-percenter or who wasn't. I'm glad we're out of our city, but I do miss Granny, and I hope you will all pray for her. Her faith is strong, but she has been sick for a long time."

Gordon said, "Boy, have things changed—and in a very short time! Tell me, Emmalyne, what are the cities like at night? I'm worried about going through Colorado Springs and being stopped by the police."

"Well, I don't know about Colorado Springs, but back in our city, everyone had to be off the streets by 8:00 p.m. or they would be questioned and possibly taken to jail. One family we know who are five-percenters were trying to get home from a meeting and got stopped. No one has heard from them since. My friend, Celeste, lived next door to them and she said a moving van came. Men moved everything out of their home and put up a for-sale sign in the yard. The sign stayed for three days and then someone else moved in."

"How very strange," Gordon said, as Valentine shook her head in bewilderment.

With no other vehicles to compete with, driving was no problem. They soon came to a small town called Woodland Park. Gordon took as many small roads around the town as he could to keep away from the center. By the time they came close to Colorado Springs, it was dark. With not another living soul to be seen, it seemed downright creepy.

Gordon told the girls to get into the hiding place and keep really quiet. With the girls safely hidden, and more camping gear over the hiding place, they were ready for the city. They had just driven under an overpass, and were passing the off ramp, when a police car came down the ramp. Gordon kept driving as if there was nothing wrong. But as he was about to pass the next corner, he felt a very strong urge to turn left.

Valentine was looking into the side mirror to see if the police car was going to follow. "Oh good, the police car didn't turn."

Gordon looked concerned. "I feel as if we're sitting ducks out here being the only vehicle on the streets except for the police. But maybe we're all right since that car didn't follow us."

"I think you spoke too soon, Gordon," Valentine said. "I just saw car lights turn onto the street behind us."

They both said a silent prayer as Gordon continued to drive. When he came to a red light, instead of waiting for the light to turn green, he turned to the right and continued down that street.

Valentine was watching for the lights of the car behind them. She nearly shouted, "It's turned in behind us again!"

To keep from getting caught at the next light, Gordon turned again, but this time he turned left onto a smaller street.

After a few seconds, he said, "I don't like the looks of this part of town. It's beginning to look really shabby, don't you think, Valentine?"

Gordon had no sooner finished speaking when a woman stepped out in front of the truck. Gordon slammed on the brakes and swerved to miss hitting her. Before they knew what was happening, she was at Valentine's window. Valentine rolled it down quickly.

The woman said, "You must trust me or you will be caught by that police officer behind you. Go one block up and turn left then turn left again. Halfway down that block you will see an old gas station with the big door open. Back into that opening, quickly turn off your lights and close the big door. It looks old, but it will close quickly and quietly. I will come for you when it's safe. Don't move or make a sound. Go now, hurry! I think I see lights. I will come for you! Go!"

Gordon didn't hesitate. He did as he was told. Finding the gas station just as she said, he backed up into the opening and turned off the lights. Quickly he got out and ran to close the garage door. Gordon stood to one side of the window. Within a minute a car drove slowly by. Down the street, it turned around and drove by again.

Valentine had quietly opened the window between the truck and topper and whispered to the girls, "We're safe for now, but be very quiet and pray."

It seemed like an eternity before they heard a small door on the side of the gas station open and shut.

A quiet voice said, "I told the police you turned the other way and they needed to hurry to catch your truck."

Valentine got into the backseat with Lelo, and the woman climbed into the passenger's side. Gordon got back into the truck and turned to the woman. With the streetlight shining into a window, Gordon quickly took in the woman's appearance. Her eyes were outlined in black, her lips were blood red, and her hair was short, black, and spiked. She wore a very short black leather skirt. Her long slender legs were covered in fishnet hose with thigh-high, high-heeled boots. Gordon knew in a glance she was a "lady of the night," which made him all the more astonished that she had helped them.

He said, "Thank you, but you don't know us from Adam. Why are you helping us?"

As her face broke into a big smile, she said, "Because I'm a five-percenter too."

Gordon and Valentine were stunned. How is it that this woman, who appeared to be a prostitute, would know anything about five-percenters?

The woman went on to say, "Last night I had a dream. The same dream I've been having for a week now. At first I could only remember part of it, but this morning, when I woke up, I remembered the whole dream. I realized God had a special job for me to do for Him. I was so happy I didn't hesitate. I got everything ready to help you when you came down the street. I saw in my dream this very truck and I saw your face, Valentine, through the window."

Valentine could not believe her ears. "You even know my name? I just can't believe it! Thank you, God, for hearing our prayers and answering them before we even knew what to ask for."

The woman said, "My name is Rahab. Well, that's my street name. My real name is Rhonda, but the guy who got me started in the business said Rahab was a woman in the Bible who was a prostitute. At the time I thought it was funny, so I took the name. Since then I've read the story of how Rahab saved two men of God by hiding them in her house and then helping them escape from the authorities of the city. Does this story sound familiar to you guys?"

Gordon and Valentine shook their heads in wonder.

Gordon said, "Since you've helped us this far, did God show you a plan to get us out of here without getting caught by the authorities in this city?"

Rahab said, "Yes, He did. What's so amazing is that he has been getting me ready to help you for more than a year now. Since we need to stay here for a while longer, why don't you help the girls out of their hiding places and let them hear my story too."

"You even know about the girls hiding in the back of our truck? This is wild! I can hardly believe it," Valentine exclaimed.

While Gordon was helping the girls out of their hiding places, Rahab spoke to Valentine, "You should not be so surprised. From what I've heard about your own story, God has shown you many times He is leading you."

"So you know my story too?"

Just then Nicole popped her head into the truck door. "I told you, Valentine. Everyone knows your story."

When everyone was settled into the seats of the truck, Rahab began her story.

"I ran away from home when I was sixteen. I wanted to see the world. I didn't want to be hampered by my parents' rules. I wanted to have some fun. So I stole some money from my mom's desk drawer and, with my boyfriend, left town on a Greyhound bus. We headed west toward California. We didn't have a good plan. We just wanted to get into the movies or something—whatever we could find. We were just looking for adventure.

I had taken a lot of money from my mom, and when my boyfriend saw how much I had, he decided he could have more fun without me. He beat me up and stole my money. We were headed for California, but I made it only as far as Colorado Springs.

I woke up, from my beating, in an old shabby apartment. A man was standing over me wiping the blood off my face. His name was Tony. He told me he would help me get into the business and I could stay in his apartment when I wasn't working, but I couldn't stay there for free. I told him thanks but no thanks. I wasn't going to be a prostitute. He just laughed and said, 'Okay, honey. You'll see.'

"So off I go looking for a place to work and somewhere to live. I looked and looked for work. No one wanted a high school dropout with no training at all unless you count being a spoiled rich kid. I didn't want to go home and face my parents, so I just kept looking. One night I was hiding in an alley. Some guys found me, beat me up, and did some other stuff to me. I guess I fainted because the next time I woke up, there was Tony standing over me wiping my face again. This time I was starving and was coughing my head off and running a fever.

"Tony took care of me until I was better. He said, 'Well, are you ready?' I knew what he meant. I was tired of living on the street being hungry and dirty all the time. By that time what he described didn't sound that horrible. It was better than getting beat up every night. So I went to work for Tony. I ate well, dressed well, and thought I was doing okay. But one day I came back to the apartment and Tony said, 'I'm sorry, honey, but I've found a new girl. You're going to have to go live somewhere else.' I was back on my own and wandering the streets.

"One very cold day, I came around the corner and ran into this place. All I wanted was to get warm, but what I found was a very dear friend named David. He was very old then but healthy and fit. He worked on cars during the day, and at night he went home to his cabin up in the woods. He took me there that first night and told me to go take a bath upstairs in the room on the right. He said I'd find some clean clothes in the dresser drawers. I could throw my clothes in the trash. When I came downstairs I was a different girl. I felt cleaner on the outside and even somehow a little bit on the inside too. David was sitting at his table reading a book.

"When I sat down, he asked, 'You hungry?' Of course. I was starving. After eating I fell asleep almost immediately, in a room all to myself, with clean sheets on the bed. I slept for eighteen hours. David had gone to work and come back and was making supper when I woke up.

"I lived with David for three years. I worked in his shop and learned to fix cars almost as well as he could. Every night before we ate, he would read aloud from his Bible. At first I pretended like I was paying attention, but one day I heard about a man named Jesus, how He had befriended a prostitute. That was when I started to really listen to the stories David was reading.

"Slowly the Holy Spirit changed my heart until one night, after tossing and turning for three hours, not able to sleep, I climbed out of bed. I had been thinking about how Jesus had died for my sins. Then I knelt down beside my bed and cried out, 'Are You really there? Jesus? Do you really love me, a sinning prostitute?' It was then I started to feel a peace come over me. I felt as if His arms were around me. I gave my heart to Him that very moment. When I got back into bed, I slept like a baby.

"The next morning at the breakfast table, David said, 'You gave your life to Him, didn't you?' I guess I looked up at him with a quizzical look on my face because he said, 'Your face looks like you've been with Jesus.' From then on I studied with him every night. I just couldn't get enough of the Bible."

There was a pause in the story as Rahab sat thinking.

Annika asked, "Where is David now? Is he waiting for you at his cabin?"

"No," Rahab sadly replied, "David went to sleep in Jesus this winter. He is waiting for Jesus to blow His trumpet and wake him from his sleep. Then he'll go to be with Jesus in heaven with all of God's people. When he died this last winter, his nephew inherited the cabin—I inherited this gas station."

Nicole said, "It sounds like you got the bad end of the stick."

"No, Nicole, because David knew something I didn't know. He already knew last summer that God was going to use me. I had no idea, until I started having these dreams. That is when I realized he had been fixing things for me. When he died, the last thing he said to me was, 'I'll see you in the morning, child. I'll see you in the morning.' He never used my name. He always called me 'child.'"

Valentine said, "That's a beautiful story of how you came to Jesus. You know we are two women Jesus drew to Him when we had no idea we even needed Him. What love! What amazing love!"

After a moment or two, Rahab said, "Are you ready to get on the road?"

Gordon said, "Are you sure it's safe now?"

"Not in your truck, Gordon, but we'll be very safe in my vehicle, trust me."

"I do," Gordon said. "I really do!"

Rahab reached up and switched off the overhead light so they could open the truck doors without the light coming on. Then she quickly got out. Gordon exited the driver's side and met her in the back of the truck. Rahab opened a door in the back of the building then took one step and opened a different door. She stepped up one step and motioned Gordon to follow her. Once inside, she turned a very small light on.

When Gordon's eyes adjusted, he let out a small whistle—what he saw astounded him. They were standing inside a bus. It had been fixed up for living quarters in the back, and up front was a driver's seat with the steering wheel.

"Does this thing really go?"

"Yes, it goes, like hot grease in a frying pan. Last summer David and I drove it to this alley, and he did a complete tune up. He checked all the tires and lubed everything to be ready to go when I needed it. He said if something should happen to him, his nephew would get the old home place, but he was leaving the gas station to me along with this bus. He said I might need to take a journey sometime. I said, 'A journey?' He said, 'You never know when you need to be a Rahab to someone.' That was the only time he ever used that name, and I puzzled over what he had said, but he never said anymore about it. She's stocked with food, water, and gas, so we're ready to go right after you store your stuff under the bus in the storage bins."

Gordon shook his head, "Okay, let's get going. The sooner we're out of this city, the better."

They all worked together. Soon the truck was empty. Gordon removed the license plates and every scrap of paper from the truck so their identities would not be easily discovered. He then pulled an old tarp over the truck.

At midnight Rahab took Gordon through a different door around behind the station. They soon came to a set of iron gates. When he looked through the gates and down the alley, neither he nor anyone else could guess that a bus was parked there. David and Rahab had cleverly disguised the entire thing so it looked like a bunch of boxes were stacked there. Rahab unlocked the gates, and together they swing them wide open. All they had to do was move a few boxes from the front and drive the bus out.

When all was ready, they stood inside the bus while everyone bowed their heads—first Gordon then Rahab prayed; each of the others followed. They thanked God for their safety. They asked for His protection and guidance for the coming trip.

After the prayers, Rahab climbed into the driver's seat. Everyone else found a place on the floor in the back of the bus. Rahab shifted into first gear and the bus slowly began to move. They could hear boxes falling quietly as the bus moved.

When the bus came to the corner, Rahab stopped to look for any vehicle lights. Seeing none, she pulled out onto the city street, only then did she turn on the headlights. No one spoke as the bus moved from one street to the next. Rahab had the route memorized for the best way to leave the city without being seen.

They had not gone far out of the inner city when Rahab said, "I see the lights of the roadblock. We're probably okay though. I have taken this bus out every night for a week. They checked me the first night, but after that, they didn't bother to stop me. I dressed as I'm dressed now and they think I'm going to Fort Carson, the army base down the road a few miles."

She slowed and waited her turn to go through the roadblock.

Suddenly she spoke up, "I don't know what's happening, but there is extra activity going on tonight. Keep very still and pray!"

When it was their turn to be checked, the officer on duty loudly commanded the guard, "I don't care if it's just a prostitute and if you've checked her every night for the last year. Every vehicle will be checked inside and out—do you hear me, private?"

Everyone in the bus could hear the officer. Valentine remembered going through another roadblock and hearing the twenty-third Psalm being softly spoken in her ear. She spoke very softly, barely breathing the words.

"The Lord is my Shepherd; I shall not want."

That's all she said; nevertheless, it helped the others—they began to say the words to themselves. Each of them felt a peace come over them, and they did not fear anymore. Rahab had been saying her own prayers as she heard the officer's words. Just as one of the soldiers was reaching for the bus's door, a different officer came up. This officer was head and shoulders above the others. Rahab remembered later how he carried himself with supreme authority. He stepped up to the soldier and spoke quietly; the soldier immediately turned and walked away.

The officer came around to the driver's side window and said, "Go in peace."

Rahab did not wait to see if she had heard right. She put the bus in gear and moved ahead. When she looked in her rearview mirror, she could no longer see the officer who had let them go through. All she saw was the loud officer telling another soldier to check the trunk of the next car.

Rahab drove for a few miles then turned off onto a smaller road and stopped the bus behind a barn.

She turned around and looked at the others in the bus. "That was an angel! Can you believe it? That was my guardian angel! I thought we were goners for a moment, but then He came and all was well."

Rahab turned to Gordon. "I've slept all day today so I could drive. You must be very tired. Why don't you get some sleep? I'll wake you when I need a break? How does that sound?"

He agreed and found a place to lie down for a while. Soon the others heard soft music playing on the sound system in the bus. The soft music and the moving of the bus lulled all of them asleep.

The big bus went on through the night passing three more roadblocks. Each time the same thing happened. The tall officer would come and say something to the soldiers then he would pass the bus through. The eastern sky was starting to lighten when Rahab pulled onto a dirt road.

While the others continued to sleep, Rahab slipped into the little bathroom to wash her face and change out of her disguise. She pulled on jeans and a sweatshirt that read Go Red Sox. She removed her wig and brushed out her long blond hair before braiding it into two long braids. When she had finished, she looked very much a young girl, not much older than the three girls sleeping close by. She left the bathroom and found a place to rest. She closed her eyes and thanked Jesus for sending her a guardian angel to help them through the roadblocks. Before she could say amen, she was asleep.

24

Go in Peace

The morning sun was shining on Valentine's face when she woke. Looking around she saw she was the first up. Looking at her sleeping friends, she noticed someone she had not seen before. Lying on one of the couches was a young lady Valentine knew must be Rahab. However, she would never have recognized this peacefully sleeping girl as the woman dressed for business, standing in the street last night.

Stretching, Valentine stepped around Lelo who opened her eyes and wagged her tail. Valentine moved to the front window of the bus. She was surprised to see a desert landscape and not mountains. *We must have really traveled during the night,* Valentine thought.

Finding Joy's Bible, she sat down in the driver's seat, and after talking to God, she opened the Bible and let it fall open where it would. She noted the book was 1 Kings in the seventeenth chapter. This was where she began to read. She read for nearly an hour before she heard movement behind her. Gordon was sitting up and rubbing the sleep out of his eyes. Their eyes met and a slow smile spread across his face.

He whispered, "Good morning!"

She whispered back, "Good morning!"

Gordon looked out the window. He also looked surprised when he saw the desert terrain.

"I wonder where we are," he whispered to Valentine.

From behind them, they heard Rahab's voice say, "We're somewhere past Amarillo, Texas." Gordon and Valentine turned and saw the girl was awake and sitting up.

Gordon stared at the young woman sitting on the couch. "I know you must be Rahab, but I would never have recognized you as being the woman who helped us last night."

Rahab chuckled and quietly moved to the front of the bus to stand beside Valentine and Gordon.

"I thought," said Gordon, "that you were going to wake me when you became tired. What happened to change your mind?"

"Well," Rahab answered, "I saw the gas gauge was getting pretty low. When I pulled over and stopped, you didn't move, so I knew you were still very tired. I decided it would not hurt to stop for a while and let us all rest. There is a gas station a mile back. We can go back there after we eat. I have about two thousand dollars saved. That should be a good start on the gas for our trip."

Gordon replied, "I have about five hundred dollars. That should get this bus to Tennessee, and then we'll see from there."

The girls were beginning to move around in the back where they had slept on a built-in bed. After each person took a turn in the little bathroom, they made breakfast.

Gordon said, "There are just enough eggs and bacon for one more breakfast after this one. We had better find a place to buy some fresh food as well as gas."

Before eating, Rahab read from her Bible, and they all said a prayer of thanksgiving to God for His safekeeping during the night.

While the others were cleaning up, Emmalyne and Rahab took Lelo for a walk. The sun was warm and felt good on their backs as they walked and talked. Emmalyne talked to Rahab about her granny and her worries about her disease. Rahab said she would put her on her prayer list. Rahab said she had been praying for her parents and little brother.

"I have not heard from them since I left home. I sent my parents a letter, told them I was sorry and asked if I could come home. That was not long after I moved in with David, but the letter came back marked, 'unaccepted return to sender.' I guess they couldn't forgive me for what I'd done."

Emmalyne put her arm around Rahab. "I'll pray for your family, Rahab. We'll be praying pals together."

Rahab smiled, "How old are you, Emmalyne?"

"I'm eighteen. Why do you ask?"

"It just seems strange that we're close to the same age, but sometimes I feel like I'm fifty years old and you look closer to fourteen."

Emmalyne laughed. "The bane of my existence! I've always looked years younger than my age. The first day of school I was sent to the principal's office because the teacher thought I was too young to go to school. She sent me to the office to find my parents. She figured I lost my mom or dad while bringing an older sibling to school. I kept telling her I was old enough, but she didn't listen. I can still remember her face when the principal came back with me to the classroom. I didn't say I told you so, but I wanted to."

Rahab was laughing when the story was done. "You're funny, Emmalyne. I'm glad we're together on this trip."

"I do have a serious side," Emmalyne solemnly began. "When I was eleven, I contracted a condition called Guillain-Barr'e. I basically had to learn to walk again. I believe the experience also caused some depression, which I am now dealing with. The wonderful thing is God was with me every step of the way. I could sometimes feel His arms holding me tightly. You know, Rahab, laughter on the outside can sometimes cover sadness on the inside." Rahab took Emmalyne's hand and squeezed it conveying her support without saying a word.

By the time the girls got back to the bus, everything was cleaned and put away. It was close to ten o'clock in the morning before they started out again. Gordon took the driver's seat and everyone else found a comfortable place.

Gordon followed Rahab's directions back to the gas station. He pulled into the station and pulled up beside the pump.

"It would be best if not all of us go in," he said. "Let me go in and pay for the gas. While I'm pumping gas, Valentine, you can go in and look around for some food to buy. How does that sound?" Everyone agreed. Gordon opened the bus door and headed into the station.

He walked up to the counter and said, "Good morning. I'd like to get some gas."

The man behind the counter said, "Sure, just put your finger on the scanner." At Gordon's blank look, he added, "You're registered, aren't you?"

"Registered?" Gordon asked. "What do you mean?"

The store clerk said, "You must be from Mars or something if you don't know what registered means."

"I do live on a ranch up in the mountains and haven't been out this winter. Can you tell me what being registered means?"

"Well, sure buddy. Last week Congress passed a new law that will stop all crime by having everyone use their fingerprints as ID. This is how you'll do any transactions, any buying or selling, working and getting any kind of license. Everything will be controlled by your fingerprints, even your bank account. Cash money is not used anymore."

"But how will I get gas for my bus?" Gordon asked.

"That's easy," said the clerk. "You just need to go to the next town or city, and go to the city clerk's offices. They'll get you and anyone with you registered. Then you can buy whatever you want. But I can't sell you anything until you get registered. Everyone has a week to go get registered. After that you'll be considered a criminal and arrested.

"But you'll be fine. Just get back on I-27 and go to Lubbock. It's the next big city. Follow the signs to register and you'll have no trouble."

Gordon thanked the clerk and went back to the bus.

Valentine was about to go into the store when Gordon said, "Better get back into the bus. I have some news."

Valentine turned and went back up the step into the bus. Gordon climbed in and told Rahab to drive back down the road to where they were parked earlier. "We need to talk."

Everyone was quiet until Rahab pulled to a stop where they had been before and turned off the bus.

She turned and asked, "What's the trouble, Gordon?"

After Gordon finished telling what had happened, everyone was stunned to silence. Then everyone started talking at once.

Finally Gordon said, "Quiet down. One at a time—you first, Emmalyne."

"I was saying that I had heard about that law, but no one thought it would pass and I had forgotten all about it."

Gordon turned to Rahab and asked, "Have you heard anything about this?"

Rahab shook her head.

"No, after David died and I moved into the bus, I didn't hear much news. I didn't want the possibility of being under control, so I didn't use any electronic devices at all."

"What are we going to do?" Nicole asked.

She looked scared. They all did.

Annika quietly said, "I know the one thing we can always do when we're worried. Let's pray about it."

Everyone held hands while taking turns telling God about what was happening and asking for guidance to know what to do next.

When they finished, Rahab looked up and said, "I feel much better! We do have some fuel left in the tank, so let's get going and see how far we can go. We'll let God lead us the rest of the way."

"Good thinking, Rahab," Valentine said. "Let's hit the road. As they say here in Texas, daylight's a-burning."

Gordon, Rahab, and Valentine looked at the map and decided to head for Rahab's hometown. She very much wanted to see her parents. She was hoping they would believe and come with them. Valentine asked Rahab where her parents lived.

"It's a town just west of Austin called Fredericksburg."

She showed them on the map where it was. They checked the map to see how to best get there without going through any big cities.

The atmosphere was much lighter after the prayer. As they traveled along, they sang and talked and got to know each other better while Gordon and Rahab took turns driving.

Valentine said, "I'm not too sure about driving a big bus like this. I'll take turns being copilot with Lelo."

The girls were just glad to be out of the cramped hiding place. They talked and played a game of road alphabet. After they tired of that game, Emmalyne started reading to them from Revelation. There was a lot of what she read that they didn't understand. Gordon tried to explain as best he could. He had read and studied Revelation, but it had been a few years back, and he was a little rusty on the subject. He explained that part of what they were reading might be based in time periods of the past but there were other parts that sounded more like something that had not yet happened. They decided to read the whole book through once then they would reread it and make notes of any questions they had.

Reading and studying helped make the time go by quickly. Everyone forgot about the gas. Before any of them realized it, the sun was getting low in the afternoon sky and they were beginning to feel hungry. Gordon had been driving for a while. He had been seeing signs for a state park ahead. Soon he was pulling into a park that looked like no one had been there for some time. The park store and ranger's office were boarded up tight, and the place had a neglected look to it.

Gordon parked the bus behind one of the bathrooms out of sight. Everyone got out and looked around. Valentine found the bathroom was not locked.

When she came out, she called to the others, "You won't believe this, but there is hot water and a shower in this bathroom!"

Everyone made the camp ready. After the fire was started and wood gathered, they each took a hot shower. Gordon, Emmalyne, and Annika cooked. Rahab, Nicole, and Valentine washed clothes in the sink and hung them on bushes to dry. Valentine started to laugh to herself and Rahab wanted to know what was funny.

"Hanging these clothes reminded me of something that happened to me on my trip west."

"Tell us!"

They were walking back to the fire. By then Emmalyne asked, "Tell us what?"

"Valentine is going to tell us a story about her trip last fall when she came west."

Gordon broke into the conversation, saying, "Maybe Valentine will tell us after we eat because supper's ready. Anyone hungry?"

When supper was finished, Valentine was reminded of her promise to tell them a story. She got her notebook out and started turning the pages until she found what she was looking for.

"I want to read it for you, because I wrote it all down and it will help me to remember."

She started to read: "Day three, after the hospital room: The soft crisp breeze woke me as it blew dry leaves around my head. I listened to the sounds around me and tried to remember where I was. I could hear birds talking to each other overhead and the sounds of something scampering above me. I also heard a sound like water rippling in a brook. 'That would be too good to be true,'

I said to myself, 'to have some kind of clean water close by where I'm sleeping.'"

She read about her den under the trees and then about falling into the water and taking a bath in the cold water. She continued on about how God had led her to see the fishing line and how standing there for those few minutes saved her from being seen by the plane flying over.

"I think that's enough story for one night, but I did want you to see that even before I knew anything about my Heavenly Father, He was taking care of me. I've thought a lot about this, and I'm sure I would have gotten caught if I had been walking out through the trees and not hidden in the safe place He found for me."

Rahab looked at Valentine from across the fire. "That's a really neat story, and I would love to hear more stories, any time you want to tell them!"

Before going to bed, they sang a few songs and stood around the fire, finishing the evening with a prayer. They let the fire die mostly out, and Gordon covered the coals with dirt. They all went inside the bus to sleep. They had left one of the windows down and the night sounds drifted in. They could hear the wind in the trees and small animals scampering through the dry leaves; soon those quiet sounds lulled them all to sleep.

Valentine awoke with a start in the middle of the night. She had heard something outside the bus. The noise did not sound at all like a little animal. She listened for a while longer. However, she did not hear the sound again. She knew Gordon was sleeping close to the bus's only door and he would not let anything get to them. As she was falling back to sleep, she remembered the officer who had let them through the roadblocks. She remembered him telling them to go in peace. Smiling to herself, she drifted back to sleep.

25

Against the Tide

Valentine woke to the smell of smoke from a campfire drifting in through the open window and the sounds of the girls' voices and their laughter. She smiled to herself thinking of how nice it was to have friends along on this trip. She thought about the night before about reading part of her story. She thought of her trip west—a trip that had opened her eyes to a loving God and Father. Valentine knew if she had to do it over again she would not change one moment. She sat up and stretched. Deciding not to worry about her disguise, Valentine got out her old jeans, flannel shirt, and red bandanna. She took everything to the bathroom and again enjoyed a hot shower. After the shower, she combed out her long hair and braided it into one long braid down her back. She tied the bandanna around her head like a headband. Taking a long look into the mirror, she tried to remember who she might have been before all this started. Seeing only the new person she had become, she turned away from the mirror.

Suddenly she had a flash of memory. She saw a woman dressed as a military nurse bending over a patient giving the man a drink. Before the memory faded, the woman turned and smiled at a man wearing a black shirt with a white collar. Valentine knew that woman. The memory, for she was sure that's what it was, was gone in a flash. But while it lasted, she caught a glimpse into her own face.

"I am a nurse for sure! I remember!" she said out loud. She had experienced so few memories since the hospital room that each one was special. Valentine was deep in thought as she walked out of the bathroom and headed toward the camp fire. With these new thoughts racing around in her head, she was not paying attention to her surroundings. Nevertheless, even with her mind preoccupied, she suddenly realized she heard running feet behind her. Before she could turn around to see who or what was running up behind her, a force knocked into to her. Two arms grabbed Valentine from behind.

With her heart pounding and her mind racing, she knew she had been caught by the police. She began to panic. Valentine tried to turn her head around to see who had grabbed her, but all she could see was the top of a head with dark curls all over it.

Then Valentine heard a sweet, young voice saying, "Valentine, Valentine! You've come back, you've come back!"

Just then she saw beside her two young men. They walked up with big smiles and tears streaming unhindered down their faces.

"Samuel, Juan, and Manny, how did you…where did you? I mean, where are your parents? Where did you come from?"

Valentine was so shaken she couldn't finish a thought. She looked down into Manny's beautiful smiling face and her knees grew weak.

"I've got to sit down. Come over to the fire, guys, and meet my friends."

After catching her breath, she introduced her new friends to the Sanchez brothers.

Valentine then turned to Samuel and asked again, "Where are your parents?"

The happiness faded from each of the boy's eyes; their smiles disappeared. It was Juan who answered. "They're in jail. They have been in jail for almost a month now."

It was very quiet around the campfire for a few moments as the reality sunk in of what Juan had just told them. Then Samuel finished the story.

"It was getting dark and the three of us were walking home from our youth resistance meeting. I was in front. I was just about to step into our side yard when bright lights came on, all at once, and from all around the house. A loud voice through a police speaker said, 'Come out, all of you in the house, or we'll send the dogs in after you.' I could hear vicious barking and then the voice came again, saying, 'You have till the count of five. One...two...' Then we saw the front door open and Papa walked out onto the porch, Mama was just behind him. Dad started to say something, but I never heard what it was because the police stormed the house and knocked him down. They handcuffed him. One guy grabbed Mama and dragged her into the yard. Manny cried out and tried to run to them, but I clamped my hand over his mouth and we hit the ground and lay very still. I wanted to run to them too, but Papa and I had already talked about this. He had told me, 'Son, if anything happens to Mama and me, you must take the other boys and go into the woods. Go where we stash the camping gear and wait.' He made me promise not to try to follow them and to keep the three of us safe. We've been moving around a lot and eating what we could find—which isn't much."

Gordon broke into the story, "We're just about to start to cook breakfast. Why don't you boys put your backpacks down and go wash up. Then we'll all eat. What do you say?"

None of the boys said a word. They just smiled and threw down their packs, racing each other to the bathroom. Valentine sat in stunned silence thinking about her friends, Manuel and Maria, in prison. She said a quiet prayer to God that He would keep them safe and comfort them until they could get out of that horrible place and back with their three sons.

Breakfast did not take long to prepare—bacon, eggs, toast, and hot coffee. Emmalyne helped Gordon put everything out.

Suddenly Emmalyne turned to Gordon and said, "Didn't you say yesterday, Gordon, that there was only enough breakfast food for one more meal? Look, we have enough eggs and bacon for today and tomorrow, even with three more to feed!"

Valentine was standing near the campfire drinking her coffee and heard what Emmalyne said. It started her thinking. She got Gordon's Bible out and turned to where she had been reading yesterday, before anyone had gotten up. It was just an interesting story yesterday. However, with the development of the new law, and the way their food supply was just enough today, the story had a whole new meaning for them.

After breakfast Valentine said, "There is something I want to read. I think it will give all of us new hope and a stronger faith. Let me read to you the story I read yesterday."

Valentine turned again to 1 Kings, chapter 17. The story was about a prophet named Elijah. God had sent him to an evil king named Ahab. Elijah was to tell the king that because of his and the people's evil ways, there would be no rain for three years. To protect Elijah, God sent him out to the wilderness to live by a brook where God fed him by sending ravens with food for him. While he stayed there, the brook never ran dry, so he also had plenty of water to drink.

After a while God sent him to stay with a widow woman and her son; these two were not even Israelites. Nevertheless, they believed in the One True God of heaven. Every day she would use her oil and flour to cook with. Every day she would use all she had. However, each morning she would get her oil jar and flour bin, and there would always be enough to make food for the three of them for that day.

"This story is working today just as it worked back in Elijah's day," Valentine said. "God has provided us with enough food for today, even when our numbers have increased, and we didn't run out of fuel yesterday. Did anyone remember we were very low on fuel in the morning, still we drove all day and didn't run out?"

With reverence and awe in their hearts, they bowed their heads. Valentine prayed, "Thank you, Father God, for your loving care for each of us. We ask for your guidance today. We thank You, Father, for bringing the boys safely here. Please help Manuel and Maria to be strong for you in jail and send your guardian angels to comfort them, Amen."

After breakfast the group talked about the plan for the day. Samuel told how he was in touch with his parents through a guard at the jail, a five-percenter. He explained how the guard put himself in danger every day helping people escape from jail and also getting them started to safety.

Valentine interrupted Samuel by saying, "Why don't your parents get out that way, Samuel?"

He explained, "Papa believes they are in prison to help others keep up their faith and hope. He knows we can fend for ourselves and we'll be ok until they can get out and find us. We were going to stay here until Mama and Papa got out, but I heard from George, the guard, that there is to be a search tonight of this park and the surrounding woods. We were planning on leaving early this morning, but last night Manny said he heard singing, and I thought I saw light from a fire over here somewhere. So I left the other two and went exploring."

He laughed then and continued, "I ran right into the end of your bus. It was so dark last night I never saw a thing until, *bam*, I collided with your bus."

"So it was you that I heard in the night," Valentine asked excitedly.

Laughingly Samuel turned to Gordon and said, "I don't know how you did it, but there wasn't one red spark from your fire when I came looking. That's why when I turned the corner around this bathroom I ran smack into the bus. I couldn't see a thing."

During all the talk, Manny slipped his hand into Valentine and softly murmured, "I dreamed about you last night. I dreamed you were coming for us. When I woke up this morning, I told the guys, but they said it was just a dream—I was dreaming because I heard the music. I heard your favorite song, Valentine, the one we taught you to sing. Were you singing 'Turn Your Eyes upon Jesus' last night?"

Valentine felt such love in her heart for this little boy she could hardly speak. When she did speak, there was a catch in her voice.

"Yes, Manny, we were singing my favorite song. You can ask the others. I sing it every night. They are most likely getting tired of it by now, but I feel compelled to sing that song before I go to sleep, just as we did the night you taught it to me, the first time I heard the name of Jesus."

Manny and Valentine were content to sit together and listen to the others make plans; they were happy just being together again. Valentine realized he must be missing his mama a lot and maybe she could ease a little of the loneliness for him.

Gordon, Samuel, and Rahab talked together about the best way to get in touch with Rahab's parents. "We need to find out which side they are on. People will have to make a choice between the two sides. There is no longer any fence to sit on. There is God's way or the devil's way," Rahab spoke with strong conviction in her voice.

Samuel said, "Before we leave, we must write to our parents and tell them where we're going. Where are we going, Gordon?"

Gordon answered, "First we're heading to Columbia, Tennessee, and then we're headed back to my ranch in Colorado. We think we'll be safe on my ranch, for a while anyway. Can you get a message to your parents and give them my address without anyone else seeing it?"

Juan spoke up, "I write all the messages to Mama and Papa. We have come up with a code using the Bible and a number system so they can read the message inside the Bible verses."

"Aren't you afraid someone else can figure out the code?" Emmalyne asked.

Turning beet red, Juan stammered a little when he said, "The, ah, the other guards don't want to read any parts of the Bible, so the only time one of our letters was intercepted the officer threw it into the toilet and flushed it without taking a second look. George said he was standing close by when it happened. The officer threw it away so fast as if it burned his hand."

"Good," replied Gordon. "That settles it then, Juan. You go write a letter and put this address into it. Tell them we hope to be there within two or three weeks."

As Juan turned to go, Emmalyne asked, "Juan, will you show me how to write in code?"

"Sure," he stammered, "come on. Let's go to the bus and use the table." As they moved to the bus, Juan explained how they used Bible verses they knew by heart, since they lost their Bibles. Soon all the others could see of them were two heads bent over the letter Juan was writing. When they were finished, Juan and Emmalyne walk to the ranger's station and hid the message in the prearranged spot.

After removing all signs of being in the park, they boarded the bus. They started with a prayer for their safety and that the fuel would last. Then, with just a little fear and trembling, Gordon turned the key. The engine started and ran beautifully.

Samuel knew of a back road out of the park, so with Gordon driving and Samuel directing, they exited the park onto a very old and unused road.

The girls showed the Sanchez brothers the Book of Revelation where they had been studying. As they drove along, they talked about what Revelation told about the end of time. They compared the Clear Word Bible with the King James Bible, and the NIV version. In chapter thirteen, a huge beast caused the world to worship it. Verse four showed that by worshiping this beast the people were worshiping a dragon or Satan. They read in verse eight that everyone on earth would worship this beast, all those whose name had not been written in the Book of Life as belonging to the Lamb. Through their studies, they realized the Lamb was Jesus.

They continued to read until they got to verse seventeen, which said, "After this no one could buy or sell anything unless they could prove their loyalty to the huge beast."

Rahab asked, "Does this remind you guys about yesterday at the gas station? Gordon said the man at the station wouldn't sell him any gas because he wasn't registered with the government. Now that is something to think about!"

They continued to travel and read together trying to understand everything they were reading.

Gordon asked, "Could this plan to control the minds of the people of the world be what's written about in Revelation? Or at least part of it? You know the devil is trying to get as many people away from God as he can before Jesus comes back. When Jesus comes back, He will put an end to the devil and to evil."

As everyone thought about this, Juan spoke up and said, "It's so good to be reading the Bible and studying with people who love God and Jesus. We have been missing this so much."

"Yes," agreed Samuel. "This is a blessing. You just don't know how we have missed hearing the word of God."

"Where are your Bibles?" Valentine asked.

"We didn't dare to take them with us when we went to our meeting, for fear of being caught with them," Samuel explained.

Juan finished by saying, "You'll be put in jail, no questions asked, if you have a Bible on you when stopped by the police."

After this everyone was quiet for a minute and thought about what the boys had said. Emmalyne added, "This sounds like a story my granny told me about the Second World War and the Nazis' control in Germany. They didn't want anyone to read God's Word then either. What's our world coming to?"

"It sounds to me like it's coming to an end," Rahab spoke quietly.

"Well, if that's what's going on, we need to tell everyone we can about Jesus and His love for them," Valentine declared. "To anyone who will listen, that is. A lot of people are already so deep under the devil's control that they don't think for themselves anymore. I was just realizing that almost everyone I came into contact with on my journey out west was someone who needed me—or I needed them. Everyone listened to what God needed them to hear, to get ready for this time of trouble. Like God had gotten them ready to hear what He had me tell them. Do you see what I'm saying?" Valentine looked around at everyone in the bus. They all started nodding their heads in understanding.

"So what you're saying, Valentine, is we were sent to meet you in the woods," Annika speculated. "And if we meet anyone else on our trip—God has prepared them to hear our message too—He is wanting us to help them too!"

"I think so," Valentine continued. "We don't know how much time there is left, to help people. We want to save as many for God as will listen."

Manny had been asleep on a couch and was just waking up. He sat up and looked around, turning to glance out the bus window. He quickly took a second look.

Jerking his head back, he shouted, "Stop the bus. Miguel is out there! I saw him hiding. We have to stop the bus!"

Gordon put on the brakes and everyone went to the window to look.

Samuel asked, "Who did you see, Manny?"

"Our cousin, Miguel, and he needs our help. I just know it!"

Samuel said, "Juan, let's go see. If it's Miguel, he might run if he sees someone he doesn't know."

Samuel and Juan walked toward the area Manny had pointed out. While everyone watched, the brothers stood just inside the tree line talking to someone. They bent down and helped someone to stand. Placing their arms under his, they helped him stumble to the bus door.

As soon as they got in, Samuel said, "Gordon, start driving now. There are police in those woods coming this way."

Gordon ran to the driver's seat and drove as fast as safely possible on the old road. After the young man slumped into a seat, Manny threw his arms around the Miguel's waist.

"I knew it was you! I saw your special walking stick and part of your arm when you fell. I'm so glad I woke up when I did!"

"You were sleeping so soundly," Valentine remarked. "What woke you up?"

Manny thought for a minute and said, "I was dreaming of police chasing me, I was running really hard. I guess I scared myself enough to wake up."

Miguel spoke for the first time.

"I don't think it was an accident you were dreaming that dream, or that you just woke up by yourself. I had been praying to God to help me. I could hear dogs barking and voices now and then. I knew they were getting closer. I prayed that if I was captured I would be strong for Him, and would be a blessing to others. But if it wasn't my time to be caught, could He please send some help? Then I heard the bus coming. I tried to stand and hobble out to see who was in the bus. I felt like it was the answer to my prayer—but then I fell—I saw the bus passing me by. I was trying not to be disappointed. I closed my eyes and started to pray for strength."

"Just then I heard footsteps and a voice I would know anywhere say, 'Miguel, we're here to help you.' I couldn't believe my eyes! Then we heard the dogs really close. That was when we decided to talk later."

Miguel looked around at everyone and asked, "Where did all of you come from?"

Samuel asked, "First tell us why you're way out here hiding and what happened to your foot."

Miguel answered, "I was looking for you guys to tell you to get out of the park and these woods. In my hurry, I caught my foot on a root and fell down a little hill."

Nicole broke into the conversation, saying, "Just like me! If I hadn't stumbled and fallen, we would never have run into Valentine when we did. Maybe your fall was no accident either."

Miguel looked up and smiled a beautiful smile at Nicole. "You might be right. Did you say Valentine? Not the Valentine you guys met on your trip last fall, is it?"

The boys nodded. Nicole turned and pulled Valentine next to her, putting her arm around her waist, and said, "Let me introduce you to Valentine. We're going to get baptized together—as soon as we can find a safe place."

Miguel pulled himself up on his good leg. After making a slight bow, he said, "It's a great pleasure to meet you, Valentine. I have heard so much about you and your discovery of this plan."

Then he turned to Nicole and asked, "But what's your name, and who are all the others?"

Samuel stepped forward. "Let me introduce you to our group."

It was decided to follow the travel plans that Gordon, Samuel, and Rahab had mapped out earlier. God was definitely leading them, for He had led them to Miguel.

When they came to a bigger, more well-traveled road, they stopped and asked God to protect them and help to take them to Rahab's parents—if it was God's will. Gordon and Rahab took turns driving while the others spent time studying more of Revelation. Miguel got his Bible out of his backpack and joined right into the study.

They traveled on through the day, staying away from towns and cities. Several times they were stopped at roadblocks, and each time an officer came and bid them, "Go in peace." The first time this happened, the young men now traveling with them were stunned and excited to see the hand of God protecting them.

Manny said, "Let's look up every verse we can find about God protecting His people. What do you think, Valentine?"

She smiled at Manny. "That's a wonderful idea, and I think I have a really good one to start with. I read it way back last fall when I was staying in a friend's house. Turn your Bibles to Psalm 91. Will you read for us, Manny?"

Manny read from Gordon's Clear Word Bible.

"He who comes to the secret place of the Most High will find rest in the shadow of the Almighty. I will say of the Lord,

He is my refuge and fortress, my God, the One I can trust. He will deliver you from Satan's trap and from the deadly disease of sin. He will cover you with His feathers and hide you with His wings. His truth will defend and protect you. Don't be afraid of the enemy who attacks at night nor of his arrows that fly by day. Don't be afraid of sickness that spreads at night nor of the plague that strikes during the day. A thousand may fall beside you and ten thousand die around you, but if the Lord decrees, death won't come near you. This is because you've made the Lord your defender and the Most High your refuge."

Manny paused then and Miguel said, "That's heavy, man. It reminds me of something I read in Revelation."

Miguel picked up his Bible, turning the pages to the last book, to Revelation.

"It's somewhere in chapter thirteen, I think."

Everyone turned back to Revelation. Miguel found what he was looking for and began to read, "Verse ten, the last part. 'God will take justice into His own hands and will deliver His people.'"

Everyone was quiet for a while reading, until Emmalyne broke the silence by saying, "Listen to this, in verse twelve. 'This large animal began to admire the beast and to control the consciences of the people just as the beast had done. So the animal used its power to make everyone in the world worship the beast just as the beast had done.' Don't you see, whoever is after Valentine wants to control the minds and consciences of the people of the world. The things that are happening today were prophesied in the book of Revelation—two thousand years ago. Even though this group today is using electronic devices to do the controlling, it is still the same thing. People are allowing their minds to be controlled because they have not gotten ready. Granny said the only way to get ready is to be close to God and Jesus, and by allowing the Holy Spirit to live in their hearts. If it had not been for Granny teaching about Jesus, when I was a little girl, I would be right there, with everyone else, being controlled by these people. I would be blindly following as most of the people of this world are doing."

Nicole said, "We must study deeper so we'll know who this beast is and not fall into its trap even yet."

Miguel said, "Samuel, last night, before I started out to find you, something happened to me that opened my eyes to the dangers all around us. Over the past few days the police and youth groups that are under their control have been putting up posters all over town. The posters are advertising for a great meeting. The meeting is with Jesus and the new Pope Constantine II. It's to be held out in the desert, so there is room for thousands of people to see Jesus and His miracles. I had seen the posters and was drawn to them. I had decided as soon as I found you guys I would get you to go with me, and we would travel to this meeting to see Jesus. I don't know why, but it was as if I had been hypnotized just looking at the poster.

"Last night, as I was getting ready to leave the house to go into the park to find you, I was packing my Bible in my backpack. I tripped and dropped the Bible on the floor and it opened to Matthew, chapter twenty-four. It was as if a light was shining on these words in verse twenty-six: 'If they say to you, we saw Jesus in the desert.' I sat right down and read the whole chapter, along with chapters twenty-five and twenty-six. I had been ready to go blindly to that meeting in the desert without asking for God's guidance and care. I was almost caught in a trap—I would have led you guys into the same trap. The Holy Spirit had to literally knock the Bible out of my hands and point His finger at Jesus's message of caution, before I would wake up from my blindness to see His light. What I read in Matthew was about the time of the end and what Jesus explained to his disciples on what to expect and to watch for. I read something that really shocked me, in chapter twenty-four, verse twenty-four. Jesus talks about a false christ and false prophets, who will do miracles that if it were possible would convince the righteous that the false person is the real Jesus. There will be people who say they saw Jesus on earth in the desert, or in a secret meeting place, but Jesus said not to believe them because His Second Coming will be so awesome that everyone in the world will see him at the same time. As I read this, I realized what I had almost done and I fell on my knees by my bed. I prayed and thanked God that He had shown me the danger I was about to get myself into."

"Miguel," Gordon asked, "where is this meeting to be held at?"

"Just north of Austin, outside of a town called Temple. Why do you ask?"

"Because I don't know if any of you have noticed, but traffic is becoming thicker with car after car and bus after bus of people heading east. Most of them are passing us like we're standing still. I'm glad we're almost to Fredericksburg and can get out of this rat race."

They carefully pulled back the window curtains and peeped outside. Just as Gordon had said, the road was packed with traffic.

Gordon said, "I don't know where they've all come from, but all at once they are passing me. I'm going to try to ease out of the flow and get onto a smaller back road before we get caught in a jam we can't get out of."

Gordon tried to move to the outer lane, but no one would let him through.

Valentine said, "Let's pray for help. I feel we're being drowned in a pool of possessed people."

Everyone except Gordon knelt down in a circle. Holding hands they began to pray. After each one prayed, they stayed in a circle and began to sing. They started with the song "'Tis So Sweet to Trust in Jesus." Soon Miguel pulled out his harmonica and began to play while the others sang. They stood and sang louder and louder with everything they had. As they sang, the lane to the right began to thin out a bit. Soon, up ahead, Gordon saw a road turning to the right. Just as he was coming up to the road, a car to his right stopped. All the cars behind it ran into the car that had stopped unexpectedly. With this break in the flow, Gordon quickly turned the bus off the highway.

Valentine began to sing her favorite song, "Turn Your Eyes upon Jesus," and quietly, as in a prayer, they all sang.

When you're all alone or afraid, or in need of help, turn your eyes upon Jesus—all will be well.

Rahab guided Gordon to drive the bus into a parking lot behind some abandoned warehouses about a mile out of her hometown. He stopped between two of the biggest building.

"It will be dark in couple of hours. I think it will be safe then, to go find my house," Rahab said. "I've been thinking, and I think only three of us should go. Gordon, because you're the only other one who can drive this bus, I think you should stay here. I was hoping that you, Valentine, would go with me along with one of the guys. Samuel, would you go too?"

Samuel nodded his head.

Turning to Juan, he said, "Juan, take care of Manny should anything prevent us from getting back, okay? I know God is with us all, but that doesn't mean we know what His plan is for us."

Rahab said, "I think I'll just take a short nap before it's time to go. How about you, Valentine? Don't you think a rest would do you good before we go off into the night?"

Valentine yawned, saying, "I think you might be right. I am just a bit tired after all the excitement today."

Soon everyone except Miguel was asleep on the beds, the floor, or the chairs. The quiet was soothing to Miguel's nerves. He had, had a wild day, but he could not think about sleeping. He wanted to pray and give God his thanks for saving him and to ask him to bring his family through safely. He sat in the driver's seat and watched as the sun set. The colors of the sunset were beautiful and it reminded him that God was still in control of the world and of nature. Before he knew it, his eyes were drooping and he too was soon sound asleep.

26

The Beginning of the End

Someone was shaking Valentine's shoulder and saying, "Valentine, Valentine! It's time to wake up."

Valentine opened her eyes and saw Rahab standing over her. Behind Rahab, through the front window of the bus, Valentine could see it had become very dark outside.

She yawned and stretched, saying, "Boy, did I sleep well. How about you, Rahab?"

Rahab smiled apprehensively and shook her head. "No, I guess I'm too excited and kind of scared. I'm not sure how my parents will receive me. With all that's happened in the world, I don't know what I'll find at my home."

Valentine gave her new friend a hug. "Let's cross that bridge when we get there. Father God has led us here, and we can feel safe in leaving the rest up to Him."

Rahab, Samuel, and Valentine were soon walking toward Fredericksburg to find Rahab's parents' home. They walked through dark tree-lined streets with many beautiful old homes. They stayed close to the trees in case a police car came near. It took about forty minutes to get to the house.

Coming up behind the house, they stopped to check the place out. Rahab's family home sat on a little hill with a few trees in the backyard. A long paved drive wound its way from the main road.

Samuel said, "Why don't you let me go up and ring the doorbell, Rahab? I'll get the feel of the place, so to speak, and try to see if they're five-percenters or not. I'll tell them you want to see them. If things go bad and I don't come back, you two run back to the bus and I'll catch up with you as soon as I can. If it looks safe, I'll come get you."

Without wasting any more time, Samuel ran across the yard and rang the bell at the back door. There was a small light somewhere deep in the house. However, when he rang the bell, it had a hollow sound, as if it bounced off the walls in empty rooms. He slowly tried the door knob. When it turned in his hand he silently slipped into the dark house. He crept silently from room to room, finding nothing except empty rooms and naked floors. The light he had seen was a small light over the stove in the kitchen.

He walked back out to Rahab and told her what he had found.

With a voice full of sadness and regret, she answered, "I've got to go in there and take one last look. Is it okay if we take a few minutes?"

"Of course we will all go in," Valentine said. "We can't just leave here without you going in, Rahab."

At the back door Rahab paused to take a deep breath then she opened the door. As she walked from room to room of her old home, empty now of any memories she had grown up with, she began to feel as empty as the room she was standing in. She stopped in the living room remembering the last time she had been here. Her mom and she had had a big argument, and she had run out the front door. The last thing she had said to her mom was, "I hate you! I hope I never see you again as long as I live."

The tears started falling and her shoulders started shaking with the grief of it all. Then, in the depth of her sorrow, she heard something behind her. It sounded to her like the intake of someone's breath. Rahab slowly turned. Standing in the doorway was her mom. She could see her clearly by the light of the moon shining through the naked window. Without a second thought or hesitation, she was in her mom's arms crying.

Her mom was crying also, saying over and over again, "My little girl, my dear little girl, you've come back. I didn't think I'd ever see you again."

They stood, for what seemed like an eternity, holding each other—with sheer wonder of the impossible.

Samuel interrupted, "There is a car going by on the road. You two should get out of the window."

Rahab's mom said, "Come with me." Holding firmly to Rahab's hand, she turned and led the way downstairs to the basement. At a first glance they could see the entire basement was empty, except for a mattress thrown on the floor in a dark corner. Lying on the mattress was a very old-looking man.

After a moment Rahab said, "Daddy, is that you?" She ran to the mattress and dropped to her knees grasping for the outstretched hands held out to her. "Daddy, what's wrong? Are you sick?"

When her dad spoke, his voice was weak but clear. "Not sick, baby girl, just really tired and I must say very shocked. Your mom and I had talked about trying to find you, but we didn't know where to look. Even though we have been praying God would bring you back to us, we were beginning to think it wasn't in His plan. But now here you are."

"Did you say you've been praying?" Rahab exclaimed in amazement and wonder. "Does this mean you're Christians and five-percenters too?" She turned to her mom and looked questioningly into her eyes.

Her mom smiled through her tears, "Yes, we're Christians and five-percenters. Your brother helped us find Jesus."

Rahab looked around for her little brother.

"Where is Johnny, anyway? Isn't he here with you?"

Rahab's mom dropped down beside her husband. Her voice dropped to nearly a whisper, "Johnny fell asleep in Jesus last fall, after a long and painful battle with cancer."

Rahab's whole frame shuddered. She covered her face with her hands, crying out, "No, oh no, not my beautiful little brother."

Rahab's mom and dad reached out to her where she had collapsed. Putting their arms around her, they rocked her as if she was a small child—until her terrible sorrow subsided a little.

Her mom explained, "Johnny met a beautiful Christian man in the hospital who told him the story of Jesus and showed him Jesus's love for him. Johnny tried to talk to us about his new friend, Jesus, but we didn't want to hear any of it. We wanted to find a cure for his cancer. We were so busy looking for this doctor or that treatment we didn't have time to be with our own dear boy. Finally one night, when I had lost all hope, Johnny begged me to listen to him. He said, 'Mom, I'm not going to live very much longer. I so much want you and Dad to know what peace and hope I have found in Jesus. I know that someday, when He comes to take us all home to heaven, we will be together again. All you have to do is believe in Him.' He pleaded with me, 'Please, Mom, listen to my friend, Daniel. He will tell you all about Jesus.'"

Later that same night, Johnny told Daddy and me he had something to confess. He told us he had carried a secret, locked in his heart, for more than two years. Even though it hurt him to tell us this, he needed to before he died. He told us one day, about six months after you left, he came home and found a letter from you in the mailbox. He told me that he liked the attention he had been getting since you were gone. He liked the peace and quiet, and he didn't want you to come back. So he wrote, 'unaccepted' and 'return to sender' on the letter and sent it back. He said the next day he felt very bad about what he had done, but it was too late. He had not thought to look at the return address or even the town where it was mailed from, so he couldn't even find you if he wanted to. He said he didn't want us to be mad at him, so he never told anyone. He just let it fester inside him. I really think the guilt was partly what made him sick."

Rahab looked quietly down at her hands. Finally she whispered, "I guess I am ultimately to blame, for leaving in the first place. I was so selfish back then. I always wanted to have my own way. I'm so sorry, Mom and Daddy. Please forgive me."

It was very quiet in the room. You could feel Rahab holding her breath, until her mom said, "You were forgiven long ago, dear. All we wanted was for you to come home so we could tell you all about Jesus. Had you not left, and Johnny not gotten sick, he would never have met Daniel, and none of us would know Jesus right now. Doesn't God work in a wonderful way? He has brought you back to us and led you to be a believer also. I just can't believe it. Johnny believed. He told me, 'Jesus will take care of her, Mom. I just know it.'" Rahab kissed each of her parents. "Now, Mom and Dad, I want you to come with us. We have a bus, and we're going somewhere safe with my friends."

Rahab turned to her friends. "Valentine, Samuel, I want you to meet my parents, John and Lee Cunningham."

Everyone said hello. Rehab asked, "Is there anything keeping you from coming with us now?"

Her parents looked at each other. Lee said, "We're waiting for Daniel to come tonight to bring us food and to check on us. He should be here really soon."

Just then, off in the distant, they heard a siren. By the sound of it, it was quickly getting louder.

Samuel said, "I think we need to get out of here and head for the woods behind the house. We can wait for your friend there. Can both of you walk about a mile or so, without getting too tired?"

Lee said they could. Taking only a few minutes to get their things together, and attempting to make the place look deserted, they left out the basement door. They were just closing the trap door when they heard footsteps. Looking up, they saw a lone man running toward them.

As he ran up, he said, "John, Lee, we must leave! The police are coming."

When he looked at the others, John said, "They're friends, and they have a safe place to go. Come go with us."

Lee and Valentine started for the trees at the back of the house. Rahab and Daniel took hold of John's arms and helped him to hurry across the uneven ground. Samuel brought up the rear. They did not talk as they walked. Instead they used all their senses to escape to safety.

It took them longer to get back to the bus than on the trip in. When they finally arrived, they all dropped on the seats of the bus breathing heavily, trying to catch their breaths.

Rahab said, "Daniel, we haven't met. My name is Rahab, better known to my family as Rhonda. These are my friends: Gordon, Miguel, Annika, Nicole, Emmalyne, Samuel, Juan, and Manny, last but not least, Valentine. We're headed to Tennessee and then on to Colorado to Gordon's ranch."

Samuel turned to Daniel and asked, "Do you think we're safe here, or should we leave now?

"I think we should stay until after midnight." Daniel answered. "Most of the town's people go to bed early, as they are instructed; however, the police or the New Law, as they are called now, patrol the streets till well after eleven. After that they attend meetings at the town hall. I have spent many long hours in the heat vents near these meetings and have learned a lot.

Gordon whistled, "That must be a dangerous pastime, Daniel. Maybe it is time to leave your clandestine work behind you. Is there any reason you must stay behind? Would you like to come with us?"

Daniel shook his head and said, "No, there is no reason for me to stay. In fact, I was on my way to get John and Lee to come with me because it wasn't safe for them at their house anymore. Rahab, if you and your friends had come a few minutes later, you would not have found your parents at all, just police swarming the house. I had a tip from a buddy of mine—he also knows where the best heat vents are—he told me that the police knew John and Lee were hiding in their old home and were coming to get them. The police want to get their hands on your parents because they have been outspoken in their work to bring people to the real Jesus. They are on the most-wanted list in this area. I even heard that Sister Patricia was to be at the jail tonight to interrogate them herself. She brings fear to anyone she comes in contact with, that is, anyone who can talk about it afterward. Mostly we never again hear from the people she interrogates."

In a strange voice Valentine said, "I can vouch for that. I was in the same room with her more than once. Just hearing her voice and smelling her strange scent infected me with an extreme fear, one I've never quite gotten over." Everyone turned to Valentine.

Samuel asked, "Is this *the* Sister you talked about, the one who's after you?"

"I'm sure it is. I acquired her name when I was in Kansas. She was everywhere getting this plan started and looking for me. I wonder if she is still after me."

Daniel replied, "If you're the Valentine who started the resistance, she is very much after you. She would like nothing better than to kill you herself. They believe they will have ninety-five percent of the world's people under their control by this summer. After the meetings this new Pope Constantine II and his fake Jesus are conducting, most of the population will do anything they are told, right up to murder. At these meetings, this fake 'Jesus' does 'miracles.' He tells people the Bible is not his Holy Word and the five-percenters are not his followers. He is inciting people to turn in the five-percenters by telling the people that we are going to cause God to bring a terrible time of trouble onto the world. They have big rewards out for anyone who will turn in any five-percenter. People will turn us in out of fear or greed."

Everyone was quiet for a moment thinking about what Daniel had said.

Gordon took a deep breath and said, "I got a good sleep earlier, so I'll take the first watch while the rest of you get some sleep. Then when the time is right, I'll start on our way to Tennessee." Everyone agreed it was a good plan and they settled down to rest.

Daniel and Gordon sat in front and talked about their faith in Jesus and the changing world they found themselves in. They talked into the night. Before he went to sleep, Daniel said he could drive the bus if Gordon needed a break later in the night. Then he went to find a corner to sleep in. The bus was becoming full with God's people. However, no one seemed to mind the cramped space. They were glad to be safe for now and to be with other people who believed in God, Jesus, and the Spirit.

Rahab had put her parents in the bed in the back so they could rest and regain their strength—especially her dad. She was worried about his health. He didn't seem at all well to her. She decided to try to get him to eat some beef broth when he woke up; maybe that would help him feel better. Making her bed next to her parents on the floor by their bed, she started her evening time with God by thanking Him for bringing her back together with her parents again. She thanked Him for sending Daniel to bring her family to Jesus. She liked Daniel. He had a quiet strength that drew her to him. She would like to talk to him more and maybe ask him about her brother, Johnny. She said amen and was soon fast asleep.

Later in the night Daniel came to the front and told Gordon he thought it was safe to leave. He also asked if it would be okay for him to drive for a while because he knew the lay of the land and he would know the back streets to escape town safely.

"Thanks, Daniel," Gordon said as he smothered a yawn, "I think I was wrong about needing more sleep. We're headed to Columbia, Tennessee, as we said before, so the best and safest way to get there is fine by me."

Gordon laid down in the spot Daniel had vacated, while Daniel started up the bus. Saying a silent prayer, Daniel steered the bus out onto the road. Heading east, skirting around Austin, he headed toward Louisiana. He had lived in Texas all his life and knew all the small country roads to get him from one place to another without ever coming close to a big city.

As Daniel drove along, he thought about the day, how he had prayed that very morning asking God what He wanted him to do. Daniel had left his home, not sure where he was going to sleep that night. He was told that a raid was planned for his home. The law was hoping to capture him and put him in jail. He had packed what he could carry and destroyed any evidence that might get someone else in trouble. He had left out the back door, headed away from the only home he had ever known. He stopped by the family graveyard on his way out to say his good-byes to his parents and grandparents. He knew that they were all believers and he would see them when Jesus came to take His children home.

Daniel had gone to visit a friend who was also leaving the area. Before they said good-bye, his friend had told him that the police were also going to search John and Lee's house that night to try again to catch them. He had been on his way to their house when he heard police sirens and knew he didn't have much time. He had thanked God when he saw them coming out the basement door, ready to leave. Thinking about all of this made him realize just how God had been working constantly in all their lives. He started to hum quietly to himself some of the songs he had learned as a child. "Amazing Grace" was the first one to come to his mind. He had surely seen God's grace working.

As he was finishing humming the song, he heard a sound in the back. Glancing back, he saw Rahab making her way to the front. She came and sat down beside him.

"Tell me about my little brother before he died," she requested.

Daniel started out by saying, "He had a beautiful childlike faith in Jesus, Rahab. He loved to roll down the halls in his wheelchair and tell anyone who would listen about the love of Jesus. I'll tell you, most of them did listen to him, and I know he brought many closer to Jesus. He talked to me about you too. He was so sorry for what he did with your letter. Did you hear about that?"

She nodded her head; she couldn't speak, for the lump in her throat was threading to choke her.

Daniel continued, "We prayed to God and asked Him to forgive him for what he did. He prayed for you each and every day, that you too would meet Jesus. I know he had peace in his heart about you when he died. He said he would see you in heaven. He just knew it. Why do you go by Rahab when your name is Rhonda?"

"That's the story of my meeting Jesus," Rahab answered.

As they drove on through the quiet night, she told him her story. She didn't know how he would take the part about her being a prostitute, but she told the story just how it happened leaving nothing out. When she finished, all was quiet.

Then as they watched the sun rise in front of them, he spoke, "That was a beautiful story. I'm so glad you told me. I'll call you Rahab if that's what you want."

Rahab spoke in a hushed voice as she watched the colors change in the sky. "I go by Rahab because this name reminds me always of what Jesus did for me when He carried my sins to the cross. I never, never want to hurt Him again. Also, Rahab is the name I feel God gave me. He wanted me to know He had a work for me to do, just like the Rahab in the Bible. He was getting me ready to help Gordon and Valentine and the girls when they needed help. You know Rahab in the Bible was an ancestor of Jesus. Isn't that cool?"

They sat in companionable silence for a while and enjoyed the beauty of the spring morning. It wasn't long before Emmalyne woke up, stretched, and came to the front to sit on the floor between them.

She smiled up at them, "Good morning! Wow, isn't this a beautiful morning?"

She asked where they were. Daniel told her they had just passed the Texas-Louisiana State line.

"Do either of you know why we're headed to Tennessee?" Daniel asked Emmalyne and Rahab.

Emmalyne was the one to answer. "From what I understand, Valentine thinks her family might live there, and God, through a dream, is leading her to go there. She's not sure about anything else. She said she'll know when we get there."

"Did I hear my name being thrown about up here?" Valentine asked with a laugh as she walked to the front of the bus.

"Daniel was wondering why we're going to Tennessee. I told him you're looking for your family. Isn't that right, Valentine?"

She nodded her head. "That's about all I know."

Soon everyone was up. They all were hungry and wondering about a park or someplace to cook breakfast.

Daniel said, "There's a national park just up the road. I'm taking a smaller road to get there."

Within twenty minutes they were turning into the park. As at other parks, it looked abandoned with no one in sight. Daniel parked behind the restrooms. They piled out and stretched and checked the bathrooms for unlocked doors and water. This time they had cold water but no hot water. Still, they could use the toilets and wash up. Gordon and Valentine had a cook fire going while the younger ones went to find more dry wood.

Breakfast had a festive atmosphere to it. Rahab and her parents were reunited, also being together with believers in Jesus showed joy in each face.

As they made breakfast, they saw they had enough food for all of the group once again. Before eating, they sang a song and Miguel read a verse from his Bible. They thanked God for His guidance and for the food. Soon they were all eating silently but with enthusiasm.

John said, "This is good coffee. We haven't had any for a long time—or a hot meal for that matter."

After everyone cleaned up and walked around a bit, they got back on the road heading to Columbia.

They were stopped by roadblocks two times that day. As always, their guardian angel was there to send them on their way. Daniel, John, and Lee were surprised and excited when they realized what had happened.

Lee quoted Psalm 34, verse seven, "The angel of the Lord encampeth round about them that fear Him, and delivereth them."

They pulled into Columbia, Tennessee, late that night. They found the town full of people, campers, and horse trailers. Gordon explained it was Mule Day weekend and that the weekend festivities was how they had realized Columbia, Tennessee, was where they needed to go in the first place.

Signs directed them to park in the Walmart parking lot because that was the only place left to park. It was a record year for the Mule Day festival. It seemed the government wanted things to look like nothing had changed. They had encouraged Mule Day to go on as scheduled.

It was late when they had arrived in town; they decided to sleep until daylight. In the morning they would head out to find why God had led Valentine to this town. Gordon took the first watch. Everyone else said good night. Soon the bus was quiet.

27

In the Fullness of Time

A fine mist was falling as Gordon watched the first gray lights creep over the eastern horizon.

Valentine was also awake, so Gordon said softly, "I'm going to walk to the store and see if I can get some information on the Mule Day activities today. Then we can make our plans."

As Gordon disappeared into the fog, Valentine opened her Bible and prayed to God for guidance.

"Please help us to know what we're looking for. Keep us safe and help us to witness to those who are still able to decide for themselves. Thank you, dear Father, for your love and for Jesus's sacrifices so that we can live forever, and one day see Him coming in the eastern sky as my dream showed me. Amen."

She turned to the first verse of Psalm 91 and read, "He who comes to the secret place of the Most High will find rest in the shadow of the Almighty."

She continued to read and draw strength from the words of David. She was deep in her reading when Gordon returned. His returning woke the rest of those on the bus. The misty rain had stopped and the sun was peeping through in places. They all wanted to know what he had found and what the plan for the day was.

Gordon said, "I found an event flyer for Mule Day, with the time of everything and what's happening. The best time to get lost in town is during the parade that starts later this morning."

Valentine was looking at the flyer to see if anything sparked her memory. On the back was a full-page AD for one of the meetings with the Pope and the false "Jesus" to be held in the parking lot of the mall. It was to be that evening at six. The advertisement said the overflow would be set up at Walmart. Valentine realized if they stayed where they were they would be able see the "miracles" that the fake "Jesus" would perform.

Valentine told the others. Everyone started to talk at once, asking what they were going to do, where they would go, and how they would hide if spotted.

Gordon spoke above the noise and said, "Quiet, everyone! There are other people parked around us. We don't want anyone hearing us. Let's think this thing through."

Valentine quietly spoke, "I think I need to be at the parade this morning. I feel God will tell us what else we need to do. First thing, I think we should have a prayer together. We need to ask for God to send the angels to come go with us, to lead us, and keep us safe." Quietly they crowded around each other. Valentine started the prayer, each person continuing on, until Gordon finished.

Gordon picked up the flyer again pointing out that there was a map in it.

"I think we need to look for a safe place to park closer to the town square—someplace where we could have a quick departure if need be. Whatever we do, we need to get out of this parking lot. There is only one way in and one way out. I, for one, am feeling a bit trapped."

After a closer inspection of the map, they saw a hill with no buildings. It was within walking distance to the center of town and the parade route. Gordon started the engine; it purred quietly with the gas gauge still pointing to three-fourths empty. Next he started quietly singing "Our God Is an Awesome God," with everyone else in the bus following his lead.

Daniel watched the map, directing as Gordon drove. When they left the parking lot, they came to the red light on James Campbell Boulevard. When they tried to turn right, they were told they must take a detour. The traffic cop stated the road was closed in preparation for the big event.

The detour led them around several buildings and into a parking lot above the street, where they could see the preparations in full swing. A large platform was being constructed in the road above the mall. From where they were, they could see open areas for people to see the platform as far as the Walmart parking lot.

Valentine said, "I don't want to be anywhere close to this place tonight. Seeing the prophesies that Jesus spoke of in Matthew chapter twenty-four, coming true before our very eyes is awesome but terrifying at the same time. This is a reminder that Jesus, the real Jesus, is coming soon." All in the bus were quiet and somber at the thought of the end of the world and the beginning of a life with God, Jesus, and God's Holy Spirit.

Gordon weaved the bus around town, turning right up a hill. On top of the hill, behind some trees, they found a parking place.

The streets had been relatively empty when they started. However, by the time they reached their destination, traffic was getting very thick. There were trucks pulling animal trailers and wagons being pulled by mules all heading toward the center of town.

People appeared to be normal at first glance. With only one exception, everyone had some kind of device they were listening to. Gordon and Valentine decided they needed to be wearing headsets to look like everyone else. Juan and Samuel said they could wear their iPod and headsets. They made sure they each had ID with them with the names of Abe and Joy Peck. Valentine decided to use her walking stick to make herself look feeble. Everyone else would wait in the bus and stay out of sight.

Before leaving, they again formed a circle and prayed that God would guide Gordon and Valentine and keep them safe.

Gordon pulled Daniel aside and said, "If we don't get back by midnight, you must take the bus and head west, to my ranch in Colorado. Just follow the map. Rahab will show you where we have marked the route to take."

Without another word, they started down the road to the center of town with Valentine holding onto Gordon's arm and using her cane. Her old lady purse hung on her arm, the same one she had gotten from the thrift shop. Now that they were headed down into Columbia, Valentine was beginning to feel uneasy. Fear crept up her spine, not for herself, for Gordon. *What if he was captured because of me?*

She could feel panic starting. All the fears of the Sister and being in a dark room threatened to overcome her.

She cried out silently, "Help me, Jesus."

Just then Valentine glanced down at the purse. Memories flooded her mind of the night she had been in the thrift shop. How very long ago that seemed to her and what a different person she had become. A feeling of beautiful peace came over her as she remembered how God had led her and kept her safe, even before she knew Him. Valentine realized in a blink of an eye all the fear was gone. God is watching over us; He always has been. Nothing will happen to Gordon and me today without God's plan.

Valentine looked up at Gordon's face. Worry lines were deepening on his forehead, his eyes were grim, and his lips were set in a firm determined line.

A brilliant smile spread over her face. "God just sent me a message! He is with us today and not to worry. Gordon, I was panicking. I was worrying that something would happen to you and it would be my fault. I was almost ready to turn back when God reminded me of all the ways He has protected me in the past. A beautiful feeling of peace came over me. I know we'll be safe wherever God leads us."

Gordon shook his head saying, "I was thinking the very same thing, only I wasn't worried about me, only about you. I was thinking how those people would treat you if they caught you, and panic was rising up in me also. I would be devastated if anything happened to you, Valentine."

He stopped walking and turned to look into her eyes.

"You know I'm in love with you, don't you?"

Seeing surprise and something like wonder in Valentine's eyes, he hurried on.

"If it wasn't for this crazy world we live in, and these fearful times, I would ask you to marry me."

Valentine stood gazing up into Gordon's cherished face. "I think I started falling in love with you from the minute I first saw you. Do you remember when you were calling out to Joy? You made Joy smile then, and you have been making me smile ever since. Gordon, if I knew about my past and family, I'd say forget the crazy times. I would cherish every minute we were married together here on this earth."

They were both quiet for a minute smiling at each other, with their newly proclaimed love.

Gordon took Valentine's hand. "Let's get going and find out about your past."

They headed on down the hill, this time with no fears or worries to mar the beautiful spring morning. Soon they found themselves walking down a residential street. Majestic old oak trees lined the sidewalks. Behind the walks were well cared-for eighteenth-century homes. As they continued on, they began to mix with other people heading to town. They ceased to talk to one another and focused on appearing like everyone else.

Following the crowd they turned on a side road that led to a larger street. People were lining the roadside of the parade route; still there was some traffic passing.

When Gordon and Valentine reached the larger street, they turned east, following the map toward the courthouse. Going was slow with so many people crowded onto the sidewalk. After walking three or four blocks, they finally saw the courthouse with the big clock in the tower. Just then the bells began to chime the time; twelve times the bells rang.

We have twelve hours to find what we're looking for and be back at the bus, Gordon thought.

They stopped for the red light a block from the courthouse. Soon the light turned green, and the crowd hurriedly started to push Valentine and Gordon along. That is when Valentine saw the car. It was big, and black, with tinted windows on the side.

With her hand still in Gordon's, she tried to step back, but the people were so packed she could only go forward. Gordon immediately felt something wrong. Glancing at Valentine, he followed her eyes. The black car loomed in front of him like a dragon. He could see through the front windows. Behind the wheel was a man dressed in black wearing a white clerical collar. Their eyes met. Gordon saw concern in the other man's face. Then another face came into view from the backseat. Gordon perceived only the raw hatred on the face of the woman. The hatred was directed straight at Valentine. He muttered under his breath, "So this is the Sister."

We're trapped, Gordon thought, *like rats in a box.*

For one second, Valentine and the Sister's eyes locked. Valentine whispered, "The Sister. That is the Sister, and she recognized me! Did you see her, Gordon?"

Gordon nodded his head, "We need to get out of this crowd. There will be police storming this area in minutes. But where can we go?"

Immediately, two people came up beside them—a teenage boy and girl.

The boy said, "If you want to stay alive, you must come with us, now!"

28

Lost without a Clue

The new pope, Pope Constantine II, sat in the luxurious bedroom of the recently vacated home of a very popular country music star and his family. The estate, just outside of Franklin Tennessee, was beautiful, a fitting place for a pope to stay while visiting this area. He thought to himself, *What a beautiful room this is. I am surprised to find such graceful accommodations in this seemingly small town in Tennessee. Too bad the previous owners could not be made to see the light and give up their silly notions. They will soon find out that their so-called beliefs are empty promises from an old book of fairy tales, the Bible.*

It had surprised him how much resistance was found in the country music business. He would have thought that being famous music artists would have turned their head. For some it had, but there were many of these musicians that really read their Bibles. They could not be controlled in any way by the treatment. The owner of this place, to mention only one, had been strong in the resistance. He and his family had been allowed to carry on their so-called work for a time—until it suited his plan to have them publicly arrested and placed in one of the labor camps. The pope made sure they had to do very hard labor; not only the man, but his lovely wife and children. A few weeks of that kind of work and unpleasant living conditions, and they would be ready to come back to their beautiful home. He would make sure they recanted, to the world, this silly idea about reading their Bibles. He would make them deny the rumors that there was a real and different Jesus. They would bow down to his Jesus on national television. *Yes, I will let them sweat it out in the camp a few weeks.*

It still puzzled the pope where this Jesus Being came from. He wondered about these miracles and how he did them. To reach him, the pope just had to place an AD on the Internet, where and when he was needed, and Jesus showed up as if from nowhere. Anyway, if I can get one of those big shot music singers to publicly tell the world he or she was wrong, it would go a long way in bringing around many other musicians and their fans.

The pope was enjoying the peace of the moment. He could feel his eyes getting heavy just as his cell phone rang. This was the cell phone he kept just for his Patty, as he called Sister Patricia. He reached out his hand on the second ring and said, "Yes dear, what can I do for you?"

Sister Patricia's voice was very agitated when she said, "Sebastian, I mean Your Excellency, I saw her right here in Columbia. On the street right in front of me, and then, as if she was never even there, she vanished. I can't believe that she was right in front of me and now she has disappeared again!" The sister stopped to take a breath.

Sebastian Berard, the newly appointed pope, said, "Calm down, Patty. Have you called the police in the area?"

"Yes, yes, I called them immediately. They are now combing the crowds throughout the town looking for her and the man that she was with."

"I'm sure," Sebastian replied in a soft reassuring voice, "that she will be found soon. Then you can interrogate her to your heart's content. Besides, you know she is of no danger to us anymore. If she had known anything, she would have told long ago, when her information might have been investigated. However, now that almost everyone is under our control, she is no threat to us. You are still mad only because she got away from you, my dear. Patty, why don't you forget about this woman for a while. Come on up to 'The Farm' and spend the afternoon with me. You need to relax, you need to be at your best tonight for then cameras. You know this meeting is being broadcasted around the world. You must show your serene and holy personage for the masses, when I introduce you to the world as my, soon to be, God-given holy wife. You know, Patty, this idea of mine to say that I've had a vision from God Himself was brilliant. I will tell the world how God told me I must take a wife, a wife to help me lead the world into a new beautiful time of peace. Just think, we can have a great public wedding. Jesus, God's own Son, can marry us. We will rule this planet! Come to me, my dear. Forget this woman and let me help you relax. You know I know just what makes you feel your very best!"

The other end of the line was quiet for only a second. Then the purring voice of Sister Patricia said, "Maybe you are right. When they find her, we can display her at the meeting tonight. We will let our Jesus heal her of her wayward ideas. She will help us conquer the rest of this resistance around the world. Yes, I think I will have my driver bring me to your new little farm, as you call that place." Sebastian could hear the sound of a window being lowered and Patty telling Father Frances to take her to his address. Then she rolled the window up again, returning to the phone.

"Tell me, Sebastian, are we ready to set up the Ghost into his role of being president of the United States of America?"

"Yes," Sebastian answered, "he is to be voted the Speaker of the House tonight, and then when the next terrorists attack kills both the president and the vice president, the Ghost will step into his new place of leadership—under our control, that is."

"When does that all happen?" Sister Patricia asked.

"It will be soon. I am letting Fakah, our new Sonny, take care of all the details. I don't want to know anything about his plans. I trust him completely. He will do everything we need and will place the blame on the ISIS. They want to take the credit for being the ones to bring down the infidels, the great United

States of America. Fakah says it will honor his cause to do this great thing."

It was quiet for a minute, then Sister Patricia said, "I am almost to your place, so I will say good-bye."

As Sister Patricia sat back into the seat, she relaxed and let her mind wonder a bit. She was thinking of Sebastian and the first time she had seen him, how he seemed to be so very close to God, way back when she still believed there was a God of the universe, a God who had created all things. She thought of herself back then. She had just taken her vows to be a nun; she was such an impressionable girl. Her heart gave a little tug for that young woman she once was, for her belief that Jesus was her friend, that He would always keep her safe. Had she lost something real, or was it all a sham as Sebastian and Father Adrian had lead her to believe? It had not been hard to change her beliefs as she lay on a table in that dirty room, as she felt the life of her child die within her. She knew she was a murderer, that God would never forgive her. She remembered feeling the deadness of her own heart. She also remembered the decision she had made, that from that day forward, she would do whatever she wanted to do in this life, because she was going to hell in the next one. She shook her head. *What brought on all these old memories? There is no hell. All these people who believe in a heaven and hell, they will be the ones to be surprised and disappointed, not me. Won't they?*

The car was turning into the long drive to the Farm where Sebastian was waiting for her. She could see him coming out of the front door to greet her. She emptied her head of all these silly thoughts, putting on a smile for her lover. She was not the lost one. She knew right where she was and what she was doing.

29

Found

Gordon did not say a word; he simply nodded his consent. The two youth steered them down to the next corner and across the street. Continuing straight on, they passed the first store. Turning right again they walked into an alley between the buildings. The alley had been fixed up with a water fountain in the center of the walk. Skirting the water fountain to the right and before they reached the end of the alley, the boy turned toward the back wall of a brick building. Placing his hand on a brick, he pushed. With what seemed to be no resistance at all, the brick moved inward. As it moved, the wall opened and steps going down came into view.

The girl hurriedly started down the stairs. As she did, she said, "Come on, we gotta hurry!"

Valentine entered the stairs behind the girl and asked, "What is this place?"

The girl answered, "This was part of the underground railroad during the Civil War."

After everyone was inside the stairwell, the boy pushed the same brick. Just as quickly as the hole had opened, it was gone again. All that could be seen was a solid brick wall.

The girl, still in front, said, "Come this way."

Valentine felt a sudden overwhelming déjà vu. "I've been in this place before," she whispered aloud. She felt very safe in the dark stairway. She somehow had not been surprised when that brick wall had moved. When they reached the bottom of the stairs, they turned left into a small passageway. Ahead, Valentine could see a thin strip of light coming from under a door. When they reached the door, the girl opened it and they entered a large well-lit room. In the center of the room was a table with a man and woman sitting with their backs to the door.

All Valentine saw was that the man was dressed in black; she began to tremble. As he slowly turned, Valentine could see a white clerical collar. However, as he continued to turn, she could see more of his face. She saw it was not the same priest she had been running from. This man's face was very familiar. Then the woman turned. The old lady's hand started to shake. The cup she was holding hit the floor with a crash, dark liquid stained the floor. Her face turned ashen; she whispered a name.

"Bonnie Ruth! We thought you were dead! We, we...went to your funeral. The speech faltered. "How, how can this be possible?"

It was at that moment Valentine's memory came flooding back to her. She walked slowly toward the lady who was still standing, but noticeably beginning to sway. She gave the lady a gentle hug and helped her to sit back down. "Auntie Alexis, is it really you?"

Turning, Valentine studied the two teenagers. "Victoria, Eli, I know you! You're my niece and nephew. Darcy's kids, but where is my sister Darcy?"

Everyone was talking, crying, and laughing all at the same time. The priest, who had been standing nearby watching, cautioned, "We need to be quiet and to let Bonnie talk."

When the man said that, Valentine turned and really looked at the priest.

"I know you too. You're my friend, Father Anthony, Tony!"

With tears running down his face, he softly said, "I never thought I'd see you again. All is not lost. There is still time."

Valentine looked at him questioningly, "Time for what, Tony?"

"There is still time to bring you to Jesus."

Valentine looked strangely into his eyes and then she remembered. *I never believed in God and had called the Bible a fairy tale.* The memories of her father came flooding into her mind. *He prayed for me, pleaded with me, and finally, in his hospital bed, he cried for me, but nothing could change my hard heart.* Valentine stood transfixed remembering. She stood beside her father's bed holding his hand. She remembered his last words to her. In a voice so weak, she could hardly hear him.

"Please, Bonnie Ruth, just once, say a prayer and ask God to change your heart. Will you do that for me?"

He then used his pet name for her, "Please, baby girl."

His eyes were pleading. Her heart was breaking. She could not bear to look into his eyes anymore. She slipped her hand out of his and turned away from the bed. Valentine walked out of the room to smoke a cigarette, thinking it would calm her nerves. She remembered thinking, "I just need a moment then I could face him again. Then I might know what to say to ease his mind." She had been away from his room for only ten minutes. As she neared her father's room, she could hear crying.

She heard her sister, Darcy, cry out, "Dad, don't leave me! Please, Dad, don't leave me!"

Valentine heard her mother's calm voice trying to soothe her sister. She knew her father was gone. She had not been able to ease his sorrow or answer his question. Valentine remembered turning and stumbled out of the hospital. Her sorrow was almost too much to bear. She knew at any moment her heart would break into a thousand pieces and she would die.

Valentine remembered all this in a flash of only a few seconds. Suddenly she knew why God had taken her memory. She remembered the evening before she had been scheduled to meet the reporter, Clark Cartee, to go to a Catholic Church, the Baltimore Basilica. They were going there to search for more information about this treatment plan, looking for the identity of the people in charge, to discover how the treatment worked and what it would do to the minds of humans. Valentine had fallen asleep waiting for midnight. While she slept, she had dreamed she was back in her dad's hospital room; she could again see his pleading eyes. When she woke with a start, she was sweating and shaking all over. Valentine had sat on the side of the bed and spoke, "Dad's God, if you're really out there, and if you even can, do whatever it takes to change me so I can see my dad again."

Valentine remembered sitting on the bed for a moment or two, feeling nothing, no change at all. She shook her head and stood up to go into the night, not knowing she had just given God permission to do whatever was in His power, to bring her to Him.

Valentine looked up into her longtime friend's eyes. The friend who, with her father, had tried to bring her to Jesus.

She said, "God has already brought me to Jesus, and I gave my life to Him."

Through tears of joy, Valentine looked around at family and friends. "I have a story to tell you. Just remembering it all causes my heart to overflow with love for my Father God, my Savior Jesus, and my friend Spirit. What an awesome God!"

30

The Incredible Journey of Love

Valentine had finished her story. Everyone sat spellbound throughout her entire journey. They continued to sit quietly thinking about all she had been through, and all that God had done for her.

She turned to her aunt and said, "Auntie Alexis, I've been down here in these rooms before, haven't I?"

"Yes, dear," her aunt answered. "I brought you down here when you were only seven years old, just as my granny brought me down here when I was a child. Our ancestors were Christians. They believed all God's children were equal. No one should be a slave to another. They were very big in the Underground Railroad, helping many families relocate to safety in the North. I remember, like it was yesterday, when my granny brought me down here. I never forgot that day. However, I never knew if you remembered our secret day. After that your family moved away, you grew up, and then you died."

Her voice caught, as a tear ran down her cheek. There was a pause before she could continue on. "When things got too hot for us out in the real world, I showed the twins, Eli and Victoria, how to get in here. We've been spending a lot of time down here for the past few weeks."

Aunt Alexis looked into Valentine's face and added, "But you didn't die. Now I understand the words I heard this morning: 'Your chariot awaits.' My prayers have been answered about the twins. I didn't know how to get them reunited with their parents.

I have been praying for help, that God would send His angels to carry them away. Now He has." She was smiling with tears streaming down her old wrinkled face.

Gordon spoke for the first time, "Eli, how did you know to help us? I take it you didn't recognize Valentine as your aunt."

Before Eli could answer him, Victoria asked Gordon a question. "Gordon, why do you call her by her last name, Valentine? Don't you know her name is Bonnie Ruth?"

Gordon looked puzzled. "Do you mean to tell me her real last name is Valentine?"

Turning to Valentine, he said, "You picked it without even knowing the name was your own last name!"

Valentine replied, "I remember when I chose the name it felt right, but I never guessed for a second that it was a memory. Valentine is my maiden name, Gordon—I've never been married. I never found a man I wanted to spend my life with."

Gordon looked into her eyes, smiling. "Now, that's a nice surprise." Gordon winked and she blushed, causing her face to be as red as her hair. Gordon's warm strong hand slipped around Valentine's hand as he again turned to Eli. "I'm still wondering how you knew to help us."

"Victoria and I were coming back from taking a message to my friend, Tristan. I spotted the black car. Everyone knows to watch out for a big black car with tinted windows, and to stay as far away from it as possible. I had just noticed it and was trying to get Victoria's attention when I saw a face come out from the darkness of the car. The face looked daggers at a woman walking by. God must have helped me because I didn't know it was my own Auntie Bonnie Ruth. I only knew that what I saw was pure hatred toward this woman, and she must need our help. I got Victoria's attention, then we grabbed your arms, and, well, you know the rest."

Eli turned to Valentine. In a hesitating voice, he spoke, "I never told anyone, not even my own twin, but I cried myself to sleep the night of your funeral. You were always so much fun when you came to visit. I felt like you took the time to listen to me, and understand me, and you were my friend. I've learned a lot this winter. Before your funeral, I didn't even know if I believed in God anymore. I was getting out of control. I ran around with some guys who were a bad lot, kind of a gang. I know my family was worried about me. After I came back from the funeral, that all changed. That evening I was sitting on my bed trying not to cry. I had locked the door. I didn't want to see anyone, not even Victoria. I threw myself back on the bed. My bed hit the wall, and the bookshelf fell on my head.

I remember Mom coming to my door, saying, 'Are you okay in there, Eli?' I grumbled at her and told her I was fine. But guess what book hit me?"

Victoria was smiling when she answered, "I know! It was your Bible! Because I was in my room that very minute praying for you. I knew you were going out that night with those guys. I was afraid for you. I heard the bookcase fall. Still, I just kept on praying. You never went out with the guys that night or any night after that—something started changing in you."

Eli smiled at his twin sister, saying, "So that's what happened. You were praying for me." He gave his sister the thumbs-up and continued.

"I remember reading in the paper that my gang had gotten into a gun fight with the other gang in town. The guys that didn't die that night were sent to prison. You saved my life, little sis."

"Ha," she came back at him, "don't be calling me little sis! I'm three minutes older than you. Just because you're two feet taller than me doesn't give you the right…"

She nudged him in the ribs and he pulled her hair. They both started laughing at each other.

"Well, that was quite a story," Gordon said. "I want to thank you both for keeping us out of the clutches of that woman. You most likely saved our lives. I also saw the hatred in her face. I had never seen the Sister before today. Nevertheless, I knew who she was the instant I saw her. They really want to get their hands on you, Valentine—I'm sorry, but I can't call you anything except Valentine."

Valentine shook her head. "Don't change, Gordon. Now that I remember my life as Bonnie Ruth, I still don't feel like anyone else except Valentine. I guess Bonnie Ruth means a different time and a very different person for me. I know my family will call me Bonnie Ruth, and that's all right, but I guess I'll always think of myself as Valentine from now on. I feel like it is the name God gave me."

Tony walked over to a box at the end of the table. From it he pulled out a package that he handed to Valentine. "This is what got you and me into espionage in the first place. You remember when I came up to visit you from Atlanta. I showed you this package. I told you the story of how I had met Father Frances and Father John Luke at the conference in Quebec." Valentine nodded her head in assent. Tony went on, "When I came home from that conference, I found this package in my suitcase under the lining. After reading it through twice and praying about it I thought of you, B. R., I mean Valentine. I knew you would be the best person to put on the trail of these people. With the fact that you were retired military and a traveling nurse, you could travel anywhere. It never entered my mind that someone would kill you—I mean, try to kill you. I felt so terrible when I found out what had happened.

"At the funeral I met your family: your sister, Darcy, and her husband, Jack. I showed them this information and we made plans to help as many people as we could, since we believed we had lost you, that you had died before giving your life to Jesus. I gave them this information and told them the story of how I had gotten you to go and investigate. Your family and I determined to work together. They have been working here in middle Tennessee and I in Atlanta."

Valentine asked again, "Where is my sister? I want to see her and let her know how Jesus has changed my life."

Aunt Alexis said, "They left for Idaho last month. The kids stayed to ride with friends. A big snowstorm hit and they have had no way to leave."

"Well," Gordon said, "your chariot awaits. We just need to get back to the bus before midnight. I think, if there are no objections, we should be going. Is there any reason Aunt Alexis and Tony can't come with us also?"

"It's funny you should ask, Gordon," Tony said. "We were just talking, before you came, about how we've done as much as we can in Columbia and Atlanta. Not to mention this new law to be registered or we can't buy or sell. We decided it was definitely time to unite with Darcy and Jack in the mountains of Idaho."

"I for one would be honored to travel with you on your bus," Aunt Alexis said. "We just need to get a few things together and remove any signs of our being here in this room."

Gordon asked Aunt Alexis, "When do you think it will be safe to leave? I'm sure the police are still looking for us out in the streets."

Aunt Alexis smiled. "Does a fox have a den without an escape route, just in case the bear is digging out his front door?"

She was laughing as she walked around the room checking for anything left behind. When the room was checked and rechecked, Aunt Alexis turned to the others in the room.

"Let's thank our Heavenly Father for bringing our Bonnie back. And ask Him to keep us safe and guide us, and that His will be done."

The room became quiet as they stood in a circle and Aunt Alexis prayed. Her voice was shaky with emotion with all that had happened within the past few hours, but her words were strong in her faith of her Father's care. When she was done, they all repeated Jesus's prayer together.

"Our Father, which art in Heaven, Hallowed be Thy name...." When the last words of the prayer died away, each of those in the room felt the presence of the Holy Spirit around them. They had a hard time breaking the bonds of that circle of prayer, but time was of the essence.

So, with hesitation and a hushed voice, Gordon said, "Let's go."

They turned and followed Aunt Alexis. They walked through a tunnel that was completely bricked with large beams every few feet, for strength. Gordon was amazed the tunnel had withstood time and was still safe to walk through. While they were walking, he asked Aunt Alexis who had built all of this.

"The story goes that my great-great-grandfather Albert Worth Valentine, who was a Christian man, owned the store building we were in. He built these tunnels. He had inherited a plantation with many slaves. Even as a boy, he believed slavery was wrong. He vowed when he was older he would do something about it, if he could. He wasn't the oldest heir. His brother had first inherited the plantation. Albert took his inheritance and bought the ground the store is on and built the building himself. That was how he was able to make a secret room under the basement floor of his store.

"He also built a beautiful home up on the hill above the courthouse. When his brother died, leaving no heirs or even a wife, Albert inherited the plantation and about a hundred slaves. Still believing slavery was wrong, and not wanting to own another human being, he devised a plan to help all the slaves live free in the North."

Taking a pause from the story, Aunt Alexis said, "I need to save my breath. I'll finish the story later."

They soon came to a split in the tunnel, and Aunt Alexis sent Eli on up the tunnel to the left, to scout out the opening.

He came back quickly. "It's not safe to leave yet. There are police all though the woods and the backyards of this street."

"I guess we'll need to wait awhile," Aunt Alexis said. "Let's go into the house and wait. It is a more pleasant place than these damp tunnels."

That said, she turned and walked up the other tunnel to the right. At the end of this tunnel was a set of stairs. To Valentine, the stairs seemed to go on forever. While climbing, she again felt as if she had been in this place before.

When they reached the top, they were standing in the attic of a very old home. The room was furnished in a way to allow a family to live comfortably for a time. There was a double bed and two sets of bunk beds—one on each outer wall. There was a round table in the center of the room with six chairs placed around the table.

Valentine noticed there were no windows in the room and asked "What is this place?"

Aunt Alexis did not answer right away. Panting with exertion, she took a moment, at the top of the steps, to catch her breath. "Boy, I'm winded. I used to run up those stairs when I was a kid, and even later when I was twenty-five—I guess I've finally gotten old." She went to the table and sat down with a deep sigh. "I'll tell you all about it in a second. Everyone, come sit down. Victoria, would you start the coffee? I think I could use some. How about the rest of you, would you like something to drink while we wait for nightfall?"

Victoria opened a cabinet on the middle wall and withdrew an electric coffee pot to start the coffee.

When the group had all settled around the table, and after everyone had gotten their coffee, Gordon asked, "Aunt Alexis, would you finish your story and also tell us about this room? I'm fascinated by all of this."

"I would be delighted to do so," she said. "I've never been able to tell many people. You see, we needed to keep the tunnels and these rooms a secret, in case a time came when we might need them again—that time is now." There was an ominous quiet in the room as these words sunk into each person sitting around the table. Aunt Alexis continued, "It is our family heirloom—the Secret of the Rooms. This room housed one or two families while they were waiting for safe passage to the North. There is a room just like this one on the other side of the house. You can get to it by crawling along the eves. However, this room has the only stairs to the tunnels. My great-great-grandfather started using his most trusted slaves, who were all Christians. They dug and built the tunnels between his store and this house. No one back then suspected a thing, because, in all outward appearances, Albert Valentine was a very outspoken, pro-slavery advocate. His family had always owned slaves and they were very active in politics. They encouraged the passing of laws to keep their slaves. They were also in favor of succeeding from the North, if need be, to keep things status quo. Albert kept up this pretense so he could do his work without suspicion. He married a beautiful woman named Mary Kathleen who believed in the same things he did. Together they worked to free as many slave families as they could. Black families came here from all over the South and lived for a few days or even a month waiting for safe passage.

After the war was over, there were five families who stayed with Albert and Mary. Together they worked the plantation, sold the produce in his store, and made everyone a good living. Before he died, he and his son, Albert Worth Jr., agreed that the plantation would be split five ways. They deeded one-fifth to the head of each of those five families. Albert Worth Jr. inherited the store and this house."

"Jr.'s son was my grandfather, and his wife was my granny, who showed me the secret rooms. She had a way of making everything so exciting. On the night that she took me to the underground rooms, she had a special tea party ready for the two of us. We walked up the tunnel and climbed those stairs, into this room. She had made up these beds and fixed the room just as it would have been in those long years gone by. We stayed up late into the night pretending. We also slept here that night and many nights after that. I wanted to do the same for you, Valentine, but I only got to show it to you once before your family moved away."

While everyone had been listening to Aunt Alexis's story, Eli had been going from one wall to the other. He interrupted Aunt Alexis suddenly. "I've been looking through the watch holes, and I just saw Mike drive slowly by in his police car."

Gordon got up and said, "Police car?"

"Yes," Eli answered. "Mike is one of us. He stays on the police force to help keep us informed about ordered searches by the New Law. I just saw him drive slowly by. Now he has stopped and is walking toward the back entrance to the tunnel. I think I should go talk with him. He only gets out of his police car if he has information. Gordon, why don't you and Tony come with me? Maybe you girls could help Aunt Alexis get our things together just in case we need to move in a hurry." He then turned and headed for the stairs; the men followed.

When they were gone, Aunt Alexis said, "I guess we need to go into the main part of the house to pack some clothes and my Bible. We have been sleeping in the house at night, without any lights. We stayed up here or in the room under the store during the day, just in case the house is searched again. Victoria, why don't you lead and we'll follow you to the main house."

Victoria turned and headed down the stairs. She didn't go far before she stopped and began to pull a cable on the wall. As she pulled, the wall slowly started to move sideways. When the opening was big enough to step through, she stopped pulling and stood aside for Aunt Alexis to go first. Then Valentine followed, stepping into a delightfully old-fashioned room. She saw at once it was a lovely bedroom still looking as it must have when Albert first built the house back in the middle 1800s. When Valentine turned, she saw the secret door was located near a beautiful oak fireplace mantel. Between the mantel and opening was a beautiful picture of Jesus carrying a lamb snuggled safely around His neck.

Victoria touched the side of the picture—it snapped open on hinges. Behind the picture was an opening in the wall with a cable just like the one near the staircase. Victoria pulled this cable and the door moved quietly and smoothly back in place. Valentine looked at the wall but could not find anything to hint that there was an opening there.

"Wow, I sure wish we had not moved so far away from here when I was a kid. What a neat place to play."

Victoria was smiling. "I know what you mean. I've loved opening and closing that door ever since Aunt Alexis showed it to us."

While Victoria and Valentine were looking at the secret wall, Aunt Alexis was putting a few clothes into a very old suitcase.

Placing her Bible on top, she snapped it shut and said, "Let's go get yours and Eli's things, Victoria, so we'll be ready when the men come back."

Across the hallway was another bedroom. Victoria quickly put a few things in her backpack and said she was ready. In Eli's room, Eli had his backpack ready to go and placed under the bed.

Victoria said, "He is always ready, just in case we need to go quickly."

They took their things and went back into Aunt Alexis's room. This time Valentine opened the picture and pulled the cable. Aunt Alexis stopped before going through the door and looked around.

"I moved into this room when I was twelve years old, and I have never lived anywhere else. My children were born here, my beloved husband, Peter, died here. All the memories of a lifetime right here in this room. Nevertheless, I am happy to walk out and never look back. I know Jesus is coming soon. The home He has waiting for me will be far beyond anything I could ever imagine. You know, maybe He has made a house with a secret door in it just for me."

She was smiling as she turned around, pulling the cable, to close the secret door for the last time.

Just then Gordon came to the foot of the stairs and said, "You girls ready? We need to go. I'll tell you all about what Mike had to say later."

When they reached the bottom of the stairs, Gordon took Aunt Alexis's suitcase from Victoria. They turned and headed up the left tunnel again. When they reached the end, where Eli and Tony stood, Eli explained what his friend had told him.

"Mike wanted to know if I knew whose bus was parked up on the hill because he had seen it and so had another officer. The other officer isn't a five-percenter. When he tried to call in the alert, the radio wouldn't work, so he left Mike here to continue to patrol the area. The other officer returned to headquarters to see what the sergeant knows about the bus, and if they should search it. We need to get up there and move the bus now or we'll all be caught. Mike said he would try to hold off the other officers as long as he could, but we really need to leave now."

Aunt Alexis exclaimed, "Let's go. I am ready for my new adventure."

Eli turned and leaped up the steps, two by two. Turning a wheel on the wall, the ground above his head began to open. Eli motioned for Gordon to take a look. After a few seconds, Gordon signaled to Eli to send everyone else up. Eli came last. He turned another wheel above ground that closed the opening, leaving only an empty fishpond. Then he turned a spigot on. Quickly the pond started to fill with water. It took only a minute to fill the bottom of the pool. Eli turned off the water and headed up a path into the woods. He must have known just where he was going because he led them to the bus within only a few minutes.

Gordon whispered, "Everyone stay here. I'll go up to the bus to check out the situation."

He moved quietly up to the darkened bus. Before he got to the door, he saw a shadowy form moving toward him from the woods on the other side of the bus. He stopped and waited to see who it was. If it was the police, he would run away from where the others waited, to conceal their whereabouts. He was ready to run when he heard his name quietly being called; Daniel's face came out of the darkness.

Gordon sighed in relief. "Where is everyone, Daniel?"

"They are all waiting in the woods. We saw a police car slowly drive by, just before dark. We got concerned we might get cornered in the bus. We didn't want to leave you guys. Gordon, where is Valentine? Is she okay?"

"Yes, she's fine, and we have a few more to add to our group. Let's not waste any time. We need to load everyone on the bus and leave here now!"

With that said, they hurried back to the two groups waiting in the darkness of the woods. Just as they were all out in the open, before they could board the bus, they saw car lights coming their way.

"Keep moving, everyone." Gordon called out. "Don't stop. If the car gets here before we're all on, then continue to board while I go see what this is."

The car kept coming then pulled right in front of the bus with the lights pointing at the group entering the bus.

Eli was standing next to Gordon and said, "That's a police car, but I can't tell if it's Mike or not."

Both front doors of the police car opened, and two officers climbed out. Both raised their arms, as they leveled shotguns at the group.

One of the officers said loudly, "Stop right where you are. Tell those other people already in the bus to get out."

Gordon had only a second to think before he spoke in a strong confident voice, "Help us, Father!" Then he said calmly, "I think we had better do as they said. Everyone come out, and while you're walking, pray!"

Gordon stepped in front of the others exiting the bus speaking loudly, "What can we do for you officers?"

A rough-sounding voice said, "Don't worry, you will be told what to do soon enough. Just step away from the bus. Don't move and don't speak."

The second officer said, "I want all of you to put your hands up. Get into a line so we can see you. We're looking for only one person. If we find her, the rest of you can go free."

The officer described the woman. Of course, it was a description of Valentine. No one spoke, however. Everyone in that line was praying for God's help.

Gordon heard one of the officers ask the other one, "What are we waiting for, Jimmy?"

The second guy replied, "I was told to hold these people until some nun in a black limousine arrives."

They stood with hands up, waiting, for what seemed like hours. Their arms were beginning to sag when they heard a car coming up the hill, in the direction of town. They could see headlights slowly moving. Soon a long car pulled up and stopped with its headlights pointing at the officers. Gordon tried to see if it was black; he felt sure it was.

Then the doors opened. A tall man dressed in a priest robe stepped out of the car. The priest walked over to the police officers. As he stepped into the light, Tony, Emmalyne, Nicole, and Annika all spoke as if one voice.

"Father Frances!"

Everyone stared at the man as he stood talking to the policemen. Rahab looked closely at the man they called Father Frances; she wondered where she had seen him before. Then it dawned on her: this was her guardian angel! This was the officer who had told them to go in peace. She was staring into his face. He glanced at her smiling face and nodded his head ever so slightly. The nod told Rahab, yes, but this is our secret."

The priest turned back to the two police officers, continuing to speak. The two listened intently, turned on their heels, put their shotguns back in the trunk, and drove away in the squad car.

When they were gone, the backseat of the black car opened and Mike stepped out.

He walked over to Eli. "I got help! Did I do good or what?"

The three girls ran to the tall man, calling out his name again. They nearly knocked him down trying to hug him all at the same time. Tony was shaking the man's hand as Valentine walked up to the group. She smiled up into the tall man's face. "How can we ever thank you?"

Tony said, "Father Frances, may I present Valentine."

Father Frances said, "It is a pleasure to meet you. We have never met officially, but I have seen you twice. Once in a dark cell, deep under the church in Baltimore, the second time was a few days later when I saw you under the overpass. I guess you could say, in a sense, I'm your guardian angel. It was I who carried you to the hospital emergency room, where I left you on a stretcher."

Valentine stood there speechless with tears running down her face. She finally choked out, "Words escape me. I just don't know what to say except, thank you. Such inadequate words."

Father Frances gently squeezed her hand. "It was an honor to help you. I knew God was using you to do great things for Him. I was so glad I could help. Now I hate to cut our time together short, but you must hurry and get out of Columbia. I must go back to my job ferrying around the Sister."

"Yes," Gordon said. "We must go. Everyone onto the bus." He turned, saying, "I must shake your hand, Father Frances, before I go and say thank you for everything you've done for Valentine— and now all of us. Be careful with that job of yours. If you're ever found out, your boss won't be very lenient toward you."

Father Frances smiled confidently, "Thank you for your concern, but don't you worry about me. I'll be fine. Just worry about getting your precious cargo to safety."

Father Frances turned. Seeing Mike, he said, "Mike, you need to go with them and get them out of the city. You really should think about getting yourself and your family out of here also. Your work here is done. It is time for you to think of your own family."

Mike said, "Thank you, friend. I'll think strongly about what you've advised. I hope to see you again sometime. Maybe you will need to get away to safety soon also."

With all the good-byes said, everyone loaded into the bus. Father Frances walked back to the big black car and drove away, down the hill, out of sight.

Mike stood beside Gordon to direct him on the best route out of the city. As they headed out, they could see the lights of the meeting place bright in the night sky. The lights seemed eerie to Valentine as she watched out the window. It was as if the devil's angels were all around the place causing the big spotlights to move and sway, looking like strange ghostly dancers in the sky. She turned her eyes away. Bowing her head, she thanked God for all He had done for her. Not only for that day, but for loving her enough to take her on an incredible journey. A journey that was not over yet.

Valentine thought of her dear earthly father. She now realized she would see him again, very soon. She could tell him it was his prayers, and his last request, that had saved her eternal life.

Valentine fell asleep dreaming of the last day on earth. She saw a small group of people standing spellbound, watching the eastern sky. Their eyes bright with the tear of joy as they watched Jesus coming on a cloud of angels. In her dream, she saw her own sweet daddy's face as he comprehended that his little wayward girl had indeed come home to Jesus.

Note from the author: I have alluded to things in the Bible. However, never take my word, your parents' word, your spouse's, or even the pastor's word about God's message to you. Read the Bible for yourself, ask the Holy Spirit to help you as you read, and you will find your way, Dealia.

CPSIA information can be obtained
at www.ICGtesting.com
Printed in the USA
FFOW01n0602280916
28028FF

9 781683 330882